Redeem Me

Redeem Me

ELIZA FREED

New York Boston

Copyright © 2015 by Eliza Freed

Excerpt from *Forgive Me* © 2014 by Eliza Freed

Excerpt from *Save Me* © 2015 by Eliza Freed

Cover design by Elizabeth Turner

Cover photos from Shutterstock

Cover copyright © 2014 by Hachette Book Group

Forever Yours

Hachette Book Group

1290 Avenue of the Americas

New York, NY 10104

Hachettebookgroup.com

Twitter.com/foreverromance

First ebook and print on demand edition: February 2015

Forever Yours is an imprint of Grand Central Publishing.

The Forever Yours name and logo are trademarks of Hachette Book Group, Inc.

The publisher is not responsible for websites (or their content) that are not owned by the publisher.

The Hachette Speakers Bureau provides a wide range of authors for speaking events. To find out more, go to www.hachettespeakersbureau.com or call (866) 376-6591.

ISBN 978-1-4555-8357-7 (ebook edition)

ISBN 978-1-4555-8358-4 (print on demand edition)

*To my brother, who's given me a guided tour
of the high road.*

Acknowledgments

Thank you to Megha Parekh and Marissa Sangiacomo for ushering this series into the world. I would be lost without you.

Thank you to the Kern and Waddington Families for allowing me to tag along on the corn harvest and ask a million questions.

Thank you to the farmers of Salem County and the world. You amaze me.

Redeem Me

Prologue

Would you like to get out of here?" he asks as he leans into me. His skin is hot on my own and a chill travels through my entire body. I look around the room and make eye contact with my aunt Diane. She looks as if she could burst into tears at the sight of me. It's a look I've seen repeated over and over again today. From the grave sites to the luncheon—pity pulling everyone's face into a grotesque glower.

I look up and our eyes are almost at the same level. Jason stands in front of me, broad and solid, his eyes asking me a thousand questions. "I would love to," I answer to each of them. "I have to tell Sean I'm leaving." Not because it's the right thing to do but because he's all I have left, and I'm trying not to add to his misery.

I stay still, leaning back on my mother's countertop, and never release Jason's eyes. I've seen them my whole life and right now I want to crawl inside of them and never come out. He doesn't smile; he doesn't say any of the useless words the others have tried to soothe me with. He only sees right through me. I take a deep breath and turn to find my brother.

Sean's talking to some firemen, still trying to digest the known details of the accident. I overhear them saying how awful that crossroad is. The land is flat and barren there and that somehow adds to the number of accidents. People drive right through the stop sign, not expecting it. Another fireman chimes in, the drugs and alcohol in the truck driver's system didn't help either. The company's words of apology and concern over how damning it is to Speed Demon Delivery's reputation churn in my stomach. The firemen pat Sean on the shoulder as they all decide my father being killed instantly was some kind of a blessing.

I have to get out of here.

"Shame about your mother, but at least she didn't suffer long either," one says, and I want to be angry, but instead I smile with all the emotion of a piece of plywood. As I approach, the firemen disperse, escaping the inevitable discomfort of figuring out what to say to me.

"Sean, I'm going for a ride with Jason Leer." It occurs to me that leaving my parents' funeral with a classmate, for lack of a better term, may not be appropriate. The look in Jason's eyes told me everything I need to know today. *Run.*

Sean looks straight at Jason without smiling. "Good. Get out of here before these people try to adopt us. They're all so supportive it's depressing."

I nod and move toward the door, where Jason is waiting for me. My heart beats faster as I acknowledge the rescue operation. In just a few steps I will not be in this horrible luncheon anymore. I'll be with Jason Leer somewhere. I don't care where. A new purpose is coursing through me—to escape the living. I wave to Margo on my way out, sure she'll pass word to the others that I've deserted without providing an explanation; I have none to give her.

Cars are lined up in makeshift rows, covering the entire bulging hill that is my parents' front yard, and it's quite a walk to Jason's relic of a blue truck. We're halfway there when he grabs my hand. It's so small in his, so fragile. Jason opens the door for me and it lets out a loud, sharp groan, a battle cry for our retreat.

I take one last look back toward the house before attempting to climb in the truck. The dress I bought yesterday, to wear as I buried my mother and father, is a fitted black sheath and I can't spread my legs far enough to step up. Without a word, he lifts me and I wrap my arms around his neck, hiding my face behind his ear. I shamelessly inhale the kiwi smell of shampoo mixed with cigarette smoke. The combination, or something else, makes me run my fingers through his hair. Jason places me on the seat and slowly moves away from me, never breaking his focus. His gaze steals the breath from my mouth and I'm thankful when he shuts my door and walks around the truck to the driver's side.

There's a cooler on the seat between us. He takes out a beer, opens it, and hands it to me. *Does no one care about driving sober?* Thanks to a delivery guy whacked out on alcohol and pain pills, I don't care anymore either. He opens one for himself and starts the truck without speaking. It answers with a roar and begins to vibrate under me. The beer is ice cold and I hold it in both hands to try to combat the heat I feel from Jason touching me, but it has little effect.

The familiar fields are foreign as he drives a few miles down the road and turns right onto Stoners Lane. The entire world is different now. The lane ends where the trees open up to a circular gravel area about a half-acre wide. It backs up to a few acres of fields, and the entire clearing is surrounded by woods. Stoners Lane was always a place to go when there was no place else. Day or night you could come back here and not be seen from the road; the enclave's only drawback is the single entry and exit. When the troopers would come to break up parties, it was impossible to get out unless you crawled through a soybean field.

He stops the truck and silences the engine; we're alone. I take a long drink of my beer and look out the window at the clouds rolling past. They barrel in from the west and roll to the east and begin to darken on the edges; the rain will arrive before the day is over. My grandmother's words pour into my head: *Happy is the dead the rain rains upon.*

Today is different from my grandmother's funeral. We were so alike, two comrades laughing through life, but when she became ill, watching her die silenced the laughter. By the end I wanted her to go. I would sit by her bed in the middle of the night and pray she died. She shouldn't have been alive without being able to laugh.

Today, though, today there is no sadness, and there is no prayer. Just two dead eyes watching the world with only a void to process the information. I don't care. I don't care about the service. I don't care about the luncheon. I don't care about the rain. I'll never again care about another thing in this life. *God, let it be a short one.*

Jason gets out of the truck and opens my door. He lifts me out and stands me up, my back to the truck. The air smells of the coming rain; it's just short of a mist. It's probably already raining over the river.

"I'm sorry this is happening to you, Annie." My middle name from his lips feels right today. My mother "tried it out" for a year as my name and switched back to Charlotte. It always stuck with the Leers and now that my mother is gone, it conjures up all the times I teased her I'd be in therapy by age thirty because you can't just change a kid's name.

His consuming stare is burning holes into me. He leans toward me, placing each hand on the truck by my head for support. My breathing quickens and I can think of nothing else but the chill I feel standing this close to him. There's something in me that knows I should speak, but instead I arch my back, my breasts endeavoring to touch him for themselves. He bends his arms and comes closer to me and I sigh and raise my lips to his. Jason kisses me hard, holding nothing back.

I retaliate and force my head farther in his direction, moving my body away from the truck. He slams me into the door and the pain in the back of my head is welcome. I wrap my fingers in his hair and pull him to me, but he resists and peers into my eyes and I could scream from the hunger I see in his. My open palms rest on the hot, stiff fabric of his shirt. They move to his buttons as I concentrate to undo them. With each one I struggle to breathe. My physical needs are suffocating my emotions, drowning them to the point I no longer covet my lost life.

The urge to rip it off his body is making me angry. I'm desperate to have him. The buttons are the last obstacle to touching his skin, and something in me knows he's what I need more than anything else still walking this earth. I breathe deeply as I push his shirt over his shoulders, knowing I should regain some control but deciding there's no such thing.

Freed, his chest heaves as he inhales and I feel the wetness between my legs. In a single, frenzied push, his shirt comes completely off and I stop to admire the strength of his forearms. Arms that wrestle steer, and rope cattle, and ride bulls. Impatient with my exploration, he pulls his undershirt over his head and my hands are on his chest before his arms come back down. I lean forward to take his nipple in my mouth and I lick it. The wind whips up around us, and the birds circle above, and I bite it hard. I am lost with no idea how to get home.

With a finger under my chin, he pulls my face up to his and kisses me gently, sweetly, again slowing me down, and I want to punch him for it. His hard-on rests between my legs and my hips thrust toward it. He pulls back and spins me around to put both my hands flat on the truck door. He lifts my hair and kisses the back of my neck and my knees buckle. Jason catches me and wraps his arm around my waist and spreads my legs with his ankle.

My head falls onto his shoulder and I look up to the horrible sky. The clouds race from one side of the clearing to the other as he breathes in my ear. His hand reaches between my legs and trails up the inside of my thigh, dragging higher and higher until he moves my underwear to the side and teases me with the tips of his fingers. I close my eyes, abandoning the sky.

"Annie," he says as he slips his finger into me, and I moan with only the birds to hear me. Jason unzips my dress and pulls it down to my waist, leaving my arms hooked in the fabric and still at my sides. He spins me around hard and stares at my bare breasts. My skin confines me as my chest heaves. Jason stares at me for an eternity and I reach out to pull him down to me but my arms are trapped.

He smiles, a tiny devilish smile, and picks me up and carries me to the back of the truck. Jason tosses me down and my head lightly bounces off the pickup bed. The pain is exquisite and I arch my back, raising my breasts to the darkening sky. He forces my skirt up to my waist and rips off my panties.

With one arm he yanks me to the edge of the truck and I want him in me. I say his name with as much sound as I can create without air in my lungs, and he unzips his jeans. He spreads my legs wide and my skin burns where his hands are. I want to reach out and touch his chest, but I still can't move my arms. Holding my thighs, he drives into me hard and my back scrapes on the bed of the truck. He pauses, still breathing heavy, and waits for me to say something, but I can't speak. My tongue is only good for touching now. I part my lips and breathe to regain some control.

"Again," I demand, and brace myself. He drives into me again, and again I feel alive. Jason starts a rhythm I can barely tolerate. I'm arching my back and matching his thrusts, my body trying to protect itself and lose itself at the same time. I can see the clouds blackening the clearing. His hands are on the tops of my thighs and he pulls me toward him, maximizing each movement. I want to touch his chest, his face, and try to move my arms, but he slows and puts my arms back at my sides.

I won't move again.

He cannot slow down again or I'll lose my grasp on the world and float up to the clouds. The dark, dismal clouds. He places one hand on my thigh and the other around my neck.

He picks up his pace and I cannot hold on to myself. The clouds advance and I feel him one last time before I crumble around him, arching, moaning, and shivering as he continues his rhythm that is breaking me.

"Jason," I whisper, and he surrenders, letting go of my neck and falling on top of me.

And I cry.

At first only a few errant tears, but it evolves into deep sobs I can't control. He pulls my dress onto my shoulders and lifts me into his lap. Jason is silent as he holds me close, willing the pieces of me back together. I quiet the deluge and concentrate on his bare chest touching my face.

"Happy is the dead the rain rains upon," he says as he rocks me back and forth. The rain comes hard from the start and he carries me to the passenger side, placing me on the seat.

It's the most I've felt in three days.

~ 1 ~

Beyond Recognition

August 14, Two Years Later

The pain in my head won't stop. It's a hammer pounding the sides of my skull, gutting my existence. I wrap my arms around my head, holding it tightly, trying to thwart the pain. The room is completely black, but the hammering doesn't mind the darkness.

I rock back and forth, repeating, "Please, God, just make the pain stop. I'll do anything if you just make it stop."

Like a hammer that breaketh the rock in pieces...

Thanks be to God.

~ 2 ~

A Slow Death

The roar of the plane about to hit my house wakes me. I roll onto my side, annoyed the sun has risen again. It's unfortunate the plane won't actually hit the house. The pilot will pull up just before impact and descend again on the other side. It's deafening. I've heard it my whole life and know it won't crash. It always reminds me of what World War II bombings must have sounded like. If only this crop duster would drop a bomb on my house.

The windows are open; the temperature dipped into the low seventies last night. The breeze is still present this morning and the sheers covering my windows billow out on one side of the room and are sucked in on the other. I close my eyes and roll onto my stomach as the attack continues. Fertilizer, pesticides, fungicides…whatever it is…I should go out there and open my mouth. Drink it in. It's better than opening my eyes. My stomach churns. It's either a response to utter despair or the mere concept of another day beginning. When will the daybreak finally break?

The house phone rings. It must be 8:00 a.m. Every morning his calls begin at eight. As usual, I don't pick up, but the machine does.

"Annie." My middle name on his lips cuts through me and I begin to cry again. "Please pick up the phone." His voice is low, tormented. "I love you." I run to the bathroom and make it to the toilet just in time to throw up, a little bit getting into my hair. I can still hear his voice, but I can't make out the words. My back aches as I try to stand and catch a glimpse of myself in the mirror. My reflection is horrifying—bloodshot eyes, mangy hair, and dry, cracked lips. I look like I have a serious drug problem. I shrug at the fresh idea and go to my parents' room to search their medicine cabinet for any kind of painkiller. As I enter the hall, I hear, "Not knowing where you are is killing me. I need you. I need to talk to you. I need you here, Annie. Or there. Anywhere, please pick up."

"Fuck you, Jason Leer!" I yell at an outdated answering machine.

No pills here. How difficult would it be to establish a drug connection? Apparently lots of people are hooked on drugs. I can probably get an addiction up and running in a few days. If I'm not going to kill myself, I'm going to need something to cope. This house is like walking around in an old photo, except my parents have been missing from the picture for the past two years.

I turn each bottle in my hand and read their names and birthdates on the prescriptions. Kathryn O'Brien...Jack O'Brien. *Where are the Percocet, Mom? Didn't you guys ever have any pain?* I've always blamed the delivery truck driver for their deaths, but everything's different now. I completely understand the desire to be out of my mind on something. Now I assume the driver discovered that his reason for living had sex with someone else, and he only knew about it because there was a baby on the way. For the first time in two years, I feel some empathy for him.

I head back to my bedroom and stare at the bed Jason spent every night in last summer. It's still at least six inches lower on the top left corner from the time we broke the frame…yet another source of agony. I walk over to the headboard and untie the scarf he gave me last Christmas. It's never been worn except that first night when he tied my wrists to the bedpost with it. A dull ache in my pelvic bone subsides and I put the scarf in the pile on the floor with my semiformal dress, my Oklahoma sweatshirt, and some pictures of Jason and me.

I walk to the garage and get a screwdriver. The headboard detaches more easily than I thought it would. I put it next to my mattress with the other things that need to be destroyed.

"I hate you, Jason Leer."

This is my new daily affirmation. I should be looking in the mirror when I say it, but after that first glimpse, I can't stand the sight of me.

I fall back on my bed and switch on my laptop; the homepage announces it'll be sunny today with a big, happy sun. *Yippee!* It's August 21, officially seven days since I heard the outstanding news—Jason had sex with Stephanie Harding and now she's having his baby—and I'm still not recovering as well as my brother would like.

I shut the laptop and toss it across my bed. This is not a life. I slide off the side of the bed and wander back to the mirror in the bathroom, this time wanting to masochistically bask in the effects of loving Jason Leer.

"What? I look awesome," I say sarcastically as I wince at my reflection. This is what safety looks like.

I am gross. My emerald-green eyes have been replaced by blood-drenched circles surrounded by black shadows. My hair, once long and lustrous, is a matted web atop my head. I think there's a hair tie in there, but I'm no longer sure. There's barely a trace of its former bright, blond color. Angry, selfish, and gross. No wonder he cheated on me with Stephanie. Oh yeah, and depressed. Angry, selfish, gross, and depressed. Wretched in general.

My pep talk is interrupted by a knock at the door. In keeping with my new system of communication, I ignore it completely. Whoever the hell it is can continue to lead their life without interrupting my progress through the stages of grief. I yawn and my lip cracks and starts to bleed.

I return to my computer and google "signs of dehydration." *This is fun.* Much better than moving all my things to Oklahoma to be with the man I love.

Loved.

Hate.

Want to set on fire.

I have one more week off from work for the move. A move from a city I love and an office I love. Six months it took. Six months of working insane hours with impeccable results to sell my boss on the idea of me telecommuting from Oklahoma. Now I'll have the pleasure of explaining why I'm still in New Jersey. First I'll have to figure it out myself because when I can complete a thought, it's usually, *What the hell am I doing in my hometown? Our hometown. Mine, Jason's, and that whore*

Stephanie, who's carrying his baby. I think I'll just quit my job and focus full-time on sleeping.

The knocking stops and I head back to bed, exhausted by Day Seven of my new life.

* * *

"Hey, it's your brother." Sean comes in the same way he's come in the last eight days, without me answering the door. He follows the sunlight into my room. Yet another beautiful day. "I heard you've been starting fires," he says as if this is normal. "Camping out?"

"How did you hear that?" I sneer.

"By living in Salem County, that's how. What are you burning?"

"Old clothes." I don't bother to even lift my head off the pillow. From this vantage point, he looks much taller than his six-foot-one-inch height. Sean goes silent and I assume he gets the nature of the fire.

"Do you have any other old clothes to burn?"

"Am I breaking some sort of ordinance or something?" I mock.

"Actually, yes. The state of New Jersey is under a water-emergency restriction because of the drought. You can't go around starting fires. You'll burn the whole town down."

I resist the urge to roll my eyes because, even though I couldn't care less how many towns burn down, I do care about Sean. He's already lost his parents; he doesn't need a bitch for a sister as well. I sit up in bed and my beautiful appearance registers on his face.

"Man, you look rotten."

"Rotten or rot*ting*?" I enunciate the last syllable. "Because I think I'm both."

"Come out to the kitchen and eat. Michelle sent soup. She's worried sick about you."

I lower my eyes to my blanket in guilt.

"I wish she wasn't. I wish neither of you were," I say, rather than *I'm sorry*, because I'm a selfish beast. I follow Sean's bear-like self to the kitchen. His usual lighthearted expression has been replaced with one of debilitating concern.

"Eat," he says as if he's not leaving until I do.

The soup's still warm and it burns the crack in my lip. The pain feels good. Maybe I'll start hiring some of those people who will come to your house in leather and beat you.

"Look," he starts, wringing his hands, "I have no idea how this feels, but I'm starting to grasp that it's beyond shitty." I nod just to help him out. "You've got to start showing some signs of...recovery."

I keep eating silently.

"I've started researching facilities to send you to if you can't turn this around. I don't know what else to do. You won't talk to anyone; you won't take care of yourself." Sean runs his hand through his blond hair and I become distracted, eyeing the mange that used to be my hair—it used to be the same color as his.

Angry, selfish, gross, depressed, and crazy. It's a new low. I like it.

Sean leaves. I promise to shower every day and head back to bed as I hear the phone ringing.

~ 3 ~

The Specialists Are Called In

The doorbell rings and I ignore it. I'm not receiving any visitors today. Or tomorrow. Or the next day.

I think I can make out two people talking but refuse to take my head off the pillow to utilize both ears. I hear the key in the door. Most people would be alarmed, but I still don't care, because Jason fucked Stephanie and now she's pregnant and because I'm not receiving any visitors today.

"Charlotte?" one voice yells, and its familiarity causes my eyes to flood with tears.

It's impossible. It is absolutely not possible.

A second voice bellows, "Charlotte Anne O'Brien!"

I sit up too quickly and get a head rush. "Margo? Jenn? What are you doing here?"

They bound into my room and stop at the sight of me. They are repulsed.

"That bad?" I ask, already reading the answer in their eyes.

Yes, I am gross. My two best friends, the girls whose backpacks hung on the hooks next to mine in pre-K when I was suddenly covered in chicken pox marks, the teenagers who watched me throw up spaghetti in the back of the bus during our senior trip to Disney, the women who held my hand at my parents' funeral, *now* think I'm gross.

"Geez, Charlotte. I knew it was bad, but you look like hell! What have you been doing?"

Embarrassed, I meekly say, "Resting. How did you guys get here?"

"Sean called," Margo says quietly. "He's scared to death. He flew us in last night."

"Sean flew you in? From Hawaii and Colorado?" I ask, not quite believing her.

Understanding, Margo answers, "Yes. It's that bad, Charlotte. Have you talked to him?"

I know she doesn't mean Sean.

"Just long enough to beg him to stop calling me. I can't talk to him. I can't even say his name..." I trail off in a whisper. Margo hugs me as Jenn surveys my room. She yanks my closet door open and throws my overnight bag onto my bed. Methodically, she begins opening my drawers and pulling out clothes.

"What are you doing?"

"I'm packing your bag," Jenn says. "It's Labor Day weekend and we're going to the shore."

"No," I answer to everything. No shore, no restaurants, no bars, no fun, no people, no living.

My protest is met with her complete disregard. "Get in the shower and shave everything. You're turning into a woolly mammoth."

"Is this your version of a pep talk?" I ask, and swallow hard.

The thought of moving is terrifying. *I can't live without him.*

Margo senses I'm getting upset and tries to mediate. "Look, you've been cooped up in here for two weeks and I'll bet you don't feel any better than you did the night you came home from Oklahoma. It might be good to go to the shore for the weekend." She is tiny and merciful and somehow her confetti-blue eyes start to make sense.

We both know there's no point in arguing with Jenn. I resign myself to a weekend at the shore and trudge into the bathroom. Jenn yells, "Brush your teeth," and I dive into self-loathing a little deeper. In all the times we've been together, they've never had to take care of me like this. Not even when my parents died. I close the door to the sound of Margo reminding her to be gentle and that they're here because Sean was afraid he was going to have to lock me up in the cuckoo pen.

"I can totally hear you guys!" I yell.

"Good! It'll keep us from having to repeat ourselves, you freakin' loon," Jenn barks.

I hear Margo sarcastically whisper, "Much better," and I can't help smiling because they're here, and besides Sean, they are the closest thing to home I have left. I wish it was for a better reason.

* * *

Teeth brushed, body shaved, bag packed. Besides the obvious mental instability, I look like a new woman. Margo opens the back door of the Volvo and I slide onto the hump spot in the back of my own car. I am a dead body they're driving around. Jenn's behind the wheel. She's my height, so the seat's already in the perfect position. Her long curly hair's been highlighted by the Hawaiian sun and floats like an overgrown lion's mane around her face. I open my bag to see what she selected for me and find an extra bathing suit, sundress, miniskirt, tank top, two thongs, and a hoodie. There's also a bag of Cool Ranch Doritos, a pack of Parliament Lights, my birth control pills, and a bottle of Jack. *Aw, just like Mom used to pack.* I roll my eyes and rest my head on the seat back.

* * *

As we approach the causeway to Sea Isle City, the smell of the back bay fills my head and I feel at ease. No...I feel peace. It's been so long I almost didn't recognize it. Oh, how peace is underrated. I slide to the door and lower the window and ride across the bay with my head hanging out like a golden retriever's. The salt air invades every cell of my body with tranquility. Maybe they're right. Maybe the shore will restore me.

Irreparable, I think as I wipe away a lone tear falling down my face. I didn't even know I was crying.

"Where are we staying?" I ask, remembering that Jenn's aunt has a shore house. Maybe I'll buy a book to read and take my mind off things. I tilt my head from one shoulder to the other, stretching out my neck. It's been weeks since I've moved.

"I'm working on that," Jenn says, and I freeze. My car crawls through the streets as she examines each house.

Oh God, no. I can only guess what this means. I begin to calculate a protest when we pull up to a house with tons of cars in front of it and three full trash cans of recyclables on the curb. There are several shirtless guys leaning on the porch railing of the second floor.

"We're home," Jenn says as she puts the car in park.

"Do we even know these people?" I am forlorn, already weak from life, and not interested in meeting new people.

"Well, we're not going to with that attitude," Jenn says as if I'm ridiculous. "Margo, turn off your phone," she adds, pulling her scheme together.

"Give me a pen." Jenn makes the "gimme" hand motion into the backseat.

"No," I say, already knowing my fate is sealed.

"Give. Me. A. Pen." Her eyes bore into me.

"I can't. The only one I have I'm going to jam into my eye." I speak the last few words slowly, without resignation.

"Can I please use it first before you make a mess of it?"

I take a deep breath and hand her the pen.

Margo looks at me like I'm silly to argue. "You know what they say: if you can't get out of it, get into it."

"Nobody says that!" I spout. "Seriously! I don't know where you heard it, but nobody fucking says that."

"Get out of the car," Jenn orders as she writes down the house and street address along with the name Bob.

"Get in the shower, brush your teeth, give me a pen, get out of the car. So freaking pushy. Where's the Aloha spirit?"

Jenn calms and turns to face me. "I'm sorry." Her blue eyes sparkle against her tanned skin. "I expected you to *not* let him kill you. I'm taking my anger at him out on you."

Her gaze morphs into pity and I realize she's only doing all this because she loves me. "Now get out of the car and try to be nice. You need to get out," she reasons.

"Really? Because I'm pretty sure I need to lie in bed and

cry myself to sleep. I have a routine, you know? It's important to have some stability in times of tragedy," I say with all the conviction of a girl who spent her college afternoons watching *Oprah* as therapy.

Jenn gets out of the car and Margo opens my door so we can follow her. As I step out, Jenn asks a guy on the porch if Bob's here. *You know, nonexistent Bob.*

"No Bob here," Amazing Abs replies. A couple of the guys yell into the house asking if anyone knows a Bob. Jenn shyly explains to the shirtless man that she's supposed to meet up with Bob, her coworker whom she's not dating and has no interest in dating, at this address so we can all go to the Carousel for Happy Hour.

"We're going to the Carousel. Grab a beer and we'll walk over together," he offers.

Jenn's anxious and says she'd better call him. She makes a point of leaving a message on his cell that she thinks we're at the wrong address and to call her back as soon as he gets this. She makes eye contact with me and sheepishly cracks open her beer.

And here we go.

As Jenn entertains the troops, Margo pulls me aside to assure me that if I want to go home—or in this case back to these strangers' house—at any time, she'll go with me but makes me promise to try to have a good time. My mother always said that although the three of us were nothing but a worry, we always had a good time. God I miss her. She also always said a rather sweet version of "suck it up," so I'll give that a try for tonight.

As we're having our private conversation in the far corner of Amazing Abs' deck, beers are delivered by another shirtless guy. This one seems a little buzzed already, or perhaps his sober personality is a little annoying. It's hard to decipher halfway into Happy Hour.

Margo rushes off to use the bathroom as he opens my beer for me and says, "I'm Mike."

Great, now I'm alone and have to communicate.

"I'm mourning," I say without smiling.

"Well, good morning!" His enthusiasm reminds me that we're at the shore on Labor Day weekend and all the fish in the sea are down here. It's going to be a long night, so I take a long swig of my beer.

* * *

I unsuccessfully try to lose Mike most of the night. Even in this crowded bar it's impossible. Eventually I discover he works for a collection agency, so that at least explains his tenacity. I introduce him to any girl I can get the name of, but by now he's pretty sloppy and most seem uninterested. He's actually growing on me. He's twenty-six and living in his hometown, Warminster, Pennsylvania. He's moved out of his parents' house but shamelessly admits he still goes there for laundry and most meals. While he's not the independent man most girls seek, it endears him to me a little. I still miss my parents beyond comprehension. Mike tells me about his ex-girlfriend, who, in my opinion, he still loves. I'm actually starting to feel bad for him when—

"You look just like her, you know?" he says.

How the hell would I know that?

"I do?" I ask, repulsed, as Mike pulls out a picture of him and her at some type of formal. *Why, God? Why?*

"Do you want to get out of here?" he asks, slurring slightly.

Oh, what to say? *Yes, but not with you.* Or perhaps, *No, I'm not leaving this bar until I'm sure you've passed out at home.* I can tell he's going to turn into a weepy fool by the end of the night.

I've got nothing for you, Mike.

"Okay, I'm just going to lay it out for you. I'm not interested in hearing about your ex-girlfriend, in starting a relationship, or in seeing you after this weekend. If you want to go back and have sex, we can, but I'm going to need your best effort because I'm kind of in a bad place myself lately."

Mike is stunned, then bewildered, then almost frightened. It's becoming difficult to predict my own actions, let alone Warminster Mike's. Either way, I'm losing my patience with him, this bar, and this night. If having sex with him is going to end it, then that's the plan.

"Wow, Morning." I consider interrupting him and telling him my name is Charlotte, but why bother. "That's hot."

Funny, because in my head it was the exact opposite of hot. He takes my hand and starts to lead me out of the bar. I pass Margo as Jenn grabs my arm.

"Charlotte," she says, and looks at Mike holding my hand. "Where are you guys going?"

I lean into Jenn's ear. "Don't worry. I'm not going to murder him. I'm just tired and want to go to sleep."

"Does he know that?" she asks, surveying his sloppy posture.

* * *

I help Mike negotiate the stairs into the house and am relieved to find he has his own room with a queen-size bed. There's an air mattress on the floor, but no overnight bag near it.

Noticing me staring at it, Mike says, "That's another guy's bed. He's not coming down this weekend."

"Oh." I watch Mike stumble onto his bed. I climb in, too, and give him a short kiss on the lips. When I pull away, he's smiling, but his eyes are still closed. Mike appears to be on his last leg.

"I'll be right back," I whisper.

He gently grabs my arm. "Where are you going?"

"I'm just getting a glass of water. Would you like one?"

"Oh yes. Thanks, Morning. You're a sweetheart."

Wrong again, Mike.

The house is empty. I turn on the radio and begin inventorying the kitchen. The refrigerator's packed and there are bags of food on the counter no one even bothered to put away. There are two coolers stationed under the double windows in the dining room. One has Miller and Corona Light in it, and the other has Blue Moon and Harp. I help myself to a Harp. It's 2:30 a.m. and the rest of the house will be home soon.

I slip onto the quiet balcony and inhale the ocean air. The almost-full moon drags my eyes up to appreciate it. It's been twenty days since I've noticed the sky, my world consumed by darkness. I'm disgusted; the sky has betrayed me, too. My glare retreats to the end of the block and I see Jenn and Ray kissing. I can't seem to turn my head and just give in to staring at them.

God, I hate you, Jason Leer. That could be us right now. I hope your kid is born with three heads.

A tear runs down my cheek and I wipe it away with my free hand, willing myself to move toward the door.

I am so going to hell.

I stealth back into the house and up to Mike's room. I curl

up in his absent roommate's bed and cry myself to sleep as silently as possible.

* * *

He yanks my wrist away and my body remembers how Jason Leer touches me. He is rough and it triggers something deep inside me that is slowly erupting, escaping my control. He kisses the tips of each of my fingers as I watch and swallow to keep from drowning. The last one he takes between his teeth and bites it until I should cry out, but the pain is too perfect to stop him. I can't take my eyes off his lips.

He releases my finger and pulls me to his chest. I breathe in the scent of him, compiling the pieces of me dismantled by his eyes. Jason runs his fingers through my hair. His movements are slow and calculated. He's thinking and I'm terrified of what he'll do. What I'll do. He fists his hands in my hair and pulls it, tilting my face to the ceiling as he grazes my neck with his lips. I close my eyes and hear a tiny moan exhaled from my own lips.

"Come back, Annie." His voice is harsh in my ear.

My God, what will we do?

* * *

I open my eyes and listen to the sound of Mike snoring. The streetlight shines on the ceiling. This room, and the inside of my head, and everything I've ever known, is foreign. My God, what will we do?

~ 4 ~

A Faint Pulse

I wake up to the morning sun and my mouth feels like I sucked on a wool sweater all night. My tongue has obviously been licking up dirt because it hurts to even try to swallow. I make my way to the bathroom and trip over my duffel bag outside the bedroom door. I brush my teeth, wash my face with the liquid hand soap, and since no one else is awake, jump into the shower for a quick rinse.

I dry off and marvel at the healing power of a shower. Of water in general. I find a bikini in my bag and put it on. A little loose, but functional. I should have eaten more yesterday. *Must eat.* I go back to Mike's—and now my—room to store my bag. The blow-up mattress is still pristine. It whispers my name and I only had about five hours of sleep. I lie back down. This time I drift off peacefully.

* * *

The seagulls are squawking, sounding some type of bird alarm. Someone must have dropped a sandwich right outside my window. I wish I were deaf.

I wish I were dead.

I roll off the air mattress at the sound of a light tapping on the door. Margo's eyes peer into the doorway as she opens it a slit.

"It's all right," I whisper. "I'm coming out." She closes the door softly and I grab my beach towel out of my bag. Mike is still snoring, completely oblivious to the world around him. Jealousy fills me.

"What happened last night?" Margo asks as soon as I reach the living room.

"Nothing..." Nothing's ever going to happen again. Consider me empty.

"Charlotte, it's going to be okay."

I watch Margo watching me, and the vision is too familiar. "I feel like you've said that before."

"I'll keep saying it as long as you need to hear it." The corners of her lips turn up, a smile trying to penetrate my ugly reality. Jenn opens the screen door and walks in balancing coffee and bagels on a tiny cardboard drink holder.

"Did I miss something?" she asks, surveying Margo and me.

"Unfortunately, you're all caught up," I say, and take the bagels off the top of the tray.

We head to the beach and eat the bagels. *Must eat.* The rest of "our house" joins us and we play on the beach like children. Mike's accepted his empty bed as a silent declaration of my disinterest and settles into a day of friendship on the beach. There's Frisbee, football, and of course paddleball, which quickly becomes a tournament. Half of us spend most of the afternoon in the ocean. We swim out past the breakers and float over the incoming sets of waves and listen to them crash on the shore. It's an absolutely perfect day with a bunch of people I hope to never see again.

* * *

By dinner my cheeks are pink, I'm hungry, and I think I even smiled once today. I trip on an uneven sidewalk seam as we head into a crab house on the back bay. Jenn and Margo catch me. I can't even walk right. I thought some of our housemates were going to come with us. It's like they've completely forgotten they don't know us. They finally relented when pizzas were delivered and we promised to meet them at the Ocean Drive later. The house has been fine, but it's nice to be just the three of us. We climb onto the benches of a picnic table near the water and order beers and crabs. That's all we need. And each other.

"Are you coming back to Hawaii with me?" Jenn asks, as if the answer is obviously yes.

"Or Colorado with me?" Margo chimes in as our first round's delivered.

"Yes…no…I don't know. I just want to be home with my parents." They both watch me apologetically, not knowing what to say. "Sad, I know."

"Charlotte, you don't deserve this," Jenn says, and looks like she might punch someone. "What the hell was that whore Stephanie doing in Oklahoma anyway?"

"She goes to school there." I hammer a crab. "She transferred in our junior year." Again, I beat the crab. "She's looked me in the eye a hundred times and every time Jason was holding my hand." I pound the crab so hard a large piece flies off the table, and I take a sip of my beer. "I can't even think about it. It makes me sick."

Jenn and Margo seem a little frightened.

"Are you going to keep your job in New York?" Margo asks, her voice thick with sadness.

"Yes." I take a sip of my beer and my eyes wander to the water lapping on the boards beside us. "I have to go up there next week and meet with my boss. I have to tell him how the fairy tale ends." I pause as the thought of it makes my stomach cramp. "How long are you guys home?"

"I'm leaving Wednesday," Margo offers.

"Next Sunday for me," says Jenn.

"I still can't believe you're here. I love you guys."

"Aah, get this girl another," Jenn says to break the emotional moment.

We eat more crabs than I think possible and Margo tells us all the Salem County gossip. I'm thankful to hear someone else is doing something worth talking about.

"Do people know I'm home?"

"Not yet, from what I can tell. I'll keep you posted. I'm monitoring the situation closely. Oh, and Nick Sinclair's called me a few times asking about you," Margo says, and orders us another round.

"Noble, huh?" I ask sadly, and hammer a crab leg. If things had been different, Noble would be with us this weekend. He loves the shore as much as I do.

"Still calling him Noble?" Margo interrupts my thoughts.

I've never called him anything but Noble. "That's his name."

"But no one else on the planet calls him that but you. I

thought maybe when you guys went to Rutgers together you'd concede," Margo says.

"I teased him with it for the first half of our lives, and now it just fits him. He'll always be Noble to me," I say, and the memory of a strange conversation with him in August haunts me. "I think he knew about Stephanie before I did."

I drop my hammer on the table, disgusted. Noble was always the one to pick me up, to help me out. He's one of my best friends. How could he have known?

"He definitely seems to know the shit hit the fan," Margo adds.

He betrayed me, too…

Jason, the sky, the air, the entire fucking world, including Noble Sinclair.

* * *

The Ocean Drive is just short of mobbed. Is there anyone *not* at the shore this weekend? Within a half hour, the rest of the house joins us and I relax, able to blend into the anonymity of the crowd. The group blocks guys from hitting on me and is large enough that I don't have to interact beyond simple conversations. They're a diverse bunch from what I can gather, having invested only about six sentences in them. Each housemate was brought on board by a friend, or a friend of a friend, who had an extra share in their shore house. When I can, I lean back on the bar and attempt to smile. I quietly observe everyone around me who has apparently never lost a thing in their lives. They absently leave me alone, not realizing they've lost me.

Jason blares in my head, begging me to stay with him, to

not leave him. What did he think I would do? Did he really believe I would ever be able to forgive him? The music, the crowd, none of it's enough to drown him out. Not even his death would rid me of him. He's locked in my head. *One foot in front of the other*, I think, and realize I've stopped smiling. I put the crazy grin back on my face and inhale deeply.

I need to go back to work. Something else to think about, something to engage some other part of me. I force a sip of my beer down my throat. *I'm going to need about twenty-six more of these.* I peel the corner of the label off the bottle. The anticipation of the coming week and the thought of talking to my boss sours my mood. This is the problem with living; you have to actually *live* your life. All of it, even the shitty parts.

I go to the bathroom and the strategic mission of maneuvering through the crowd takes my mind off Jason. There is, of course, a line and I lean up against the wall as I take a deep breath. *I can do this. I can have a fun night.* Sloppy, Too Loud, and Whiny finish in front of me and stumble out the bathroom door.

When I come out, I decide to get a beer at the nearest bar rather than fight my way back to the group. I order a Miller Lite as Clint East walks up beside me.

"Clint!" I wrap my arms around him. "It's so good to see you." I mean it, too. I'm actually glad to see him. I never thought I'd be happy to see someone from Salem County again, but Clint's been pure fun since kindergarten.

"Charlotte, what are you doing here?" he asks, as high as a kite.

"Hanging." *Surviving. Kind of.* "Margo and Jenn are here," I say, and a huge smile anchors my face. I take it in. All of it.

Clint has never been anything but a playmate and seeing him here takes me back to a time before now.

"No way. Where at?"

"They're up by the door," I say, pointing toward the front bar.

"Hey, Charlotte, I'm sorry about everything that happened."

Clint's so kind I can't even be upset with him, but his words slap me back to reality. *Everything that happened.*

"It's okay. Really. I'm going to be okay." Not really, but we'll go with that. I'm not going to be okay. *Okay* is a goal for ten years from now—that is, if I'm cursed to live that long.

"Hey, I have to go. I'm working this girl over there and she's getting mad. I have my own construction business now." He hands me his card: CLINT EAST CONSTRUCTION—I'LL MAKE YOUR DAY.

"Clint, it's fantastic," I say, still looking at the card and wishing I could run away with Clint. Just run away from all of this and smoke pot, and go to the shore for the weekend, and not be what I am right now.

"I know! It took me over a year to come up with it." Clint kisses me on the cheek. His sweet smile warms me and I can't help giving him a big hug before he rushes over to his now obviously irate new friend.

I take my time and wander back to the front bar. I can let this go. At least for tonight I can let it go. On my way, a guy grabs my arm and insists I answer a few questions for him and his friends. *Doesn't anyone care about originality anymore?* I'm in such a good mood from seeing Clint that I actually consider letting him throw his line until he pulls me close and drapes his heavy, sweaty arm around my shoulders. I duck under his arm and out of his drunken reach.

I think I'm done here. I tell Margo I'm leaving, that I'm going home to bed. But when I get back to the house, I change into my bathing suit and walk to the deserted beach. The full moon won't let me go to sleep. It hovers over the sea, spreading a faint light onto the sand, and I know I shouldn't go in alone. But that's what I am now...alone.

I drop my towel and dart into the water. I hurdle over the breakers and dive into the last wave before it breaks. The water crashing behind me drowns out my thoughts and leaves peace in its wake. When I surface, I swim deeper and float on my back. My toes and nose pointed to the glorious moon above me.

It's Labor Day weekend and I'm at the Jersey Shore. There was a time in my life when this was exactly where I was supposed to be. A burgeoning wave lifts me up and over it just before breaking. I swim farther out and return to my back. I return to the moon.

I'm supposed to be in still water. Stillwater, Oklahoma, with...I close my eyes and remember the look on his face right before the wretched words came out of his mouth.

"I fucking hate you, Jason Leer."

I roll over and swim toward the coast. A wave catches me and I ride it to shallow water. *How could he?* I scrape the wet sand beneath the water through my fingers and listen as the waves come in around me. The ocean pulls me back out as Jason begging me to stay screams through my mind. Even the ocean can't erase him. Not without erasing me, too...

~ 5 ~

Morning, Mourning

The morning light beams through the window, heating my face and reminding me of hell. I roll over in Mike's absent roommate's bed and reach for my phone. I silence it and send a text to Margo and Jenn.

Can we please go home now?

My phone vibrates twice. From Margo I get:

WHY? R U OK? I THINK WE SHOULD STAY.

And from Jenn:

NO

Seriously, it's time to go.
Exchange the info, say your
goodbyes, and get your crap.
I'll be at the car in 10 minutes.
I've been a very good girl—now
reward me.

* * *

Margo and Jenn close the car doors without a word and we head west toward Salem County. We stop at Wawa on the Route 40 circle and pick up subs to take to Sean and Michelle's. They're renting on North Main Street until their dream house is completed sometime next spring. It's the perfect location, just three blocks from Sean's physical therapy practice. I think Margo and Jenn are anxious to show off my improvements. We eat on their back deck and tell Michelle and Sean all—well, almost all—the stories from the weekend.

"It's just good to see you eat," Sean says, probably relaxing for the first time since he brought me home from Oklahoma. Michelle gets up from the table and runs inside. I look at Sean, concerned.

"She thinks she might have the stomach flu."

"That's terrible." I watch her run toward the bathroom and feel bad for her. I wonder if the stomach flu is going around. I had it once a few years ago and it was awful. The memory of the disgusting virus comes back to me. *Poor Michelle*. I take a moment to acknowledge the long-departed feeling of concern. A genuine emotion about someone…other than pity for myself, hatred for Jason and Stephanie, or contempt for their baby. The baby part is the worst. The rest I could swallow; the baby and my feelings toward it are killing me. It's a one-way ticket to the hot spot way down south.

* * *

The key turns in the door and I enter my parents' house alone. Instead of craving the solitude, I feel it today. The windows are open but it's still, the ocean breeze not reaching this far west, the absence of the waves' melody depressing me. One bird squawks to the world, probably talking to itself, and Mr. Heitter is out plowing the back field.

I miss the shore. It was an effective diversion. It let my mind slip into the memories of how it felt to go there before my parents died. How it felt to do anything before their deaths and before…I take a deep breath and push the thought from my mind.

It's steamy out, but I don't turn on the air-conditioning because there is none. The Jersey humidity is far worse than the eighty-nine-degree temperature. Sean offered to install a window air-conditioning unit for me, but it'll be cold in a few weeks, possibly much cooler than this in just a few days. I start the water for a cool bath and unpack my bag. Most of the clothes are still clean. We left the whiskey at the house as a thank-you and the Parliaments are still unopened, thank goodness. I'm looking for a drug habit, something clean like prescriptions, not cigarettes.

I find Clint's card and pin it up on the bulletin board at the kitchen desk. If I'm going to stay here, some updating will be in order. It's my house, after all. I can do whatever I want with it. I jam another pin into the opposite corner of the card and laugh at how Jason thought it was a crazy idea to buy Sean out of this house. I still wanted a place to call home. Jason said we were never planning on coming home.

Oh, Jason…a liar, a cheater, and an idiot.

The past few weeks' mail is piled on the counter next to a shoebox-size package from Violet, one of my favorite college roommates. Violet has a way of making everywhere she goes feel like home. She's traditional in an uncommon way.

I throw out the two letters addressed in Jason's handwriting and rip open the box to find a small stuffed doll with jeans, a button-down, short black hair, and cowboy boots Violet has drawn on with a marker. The doll has a large hat pin sticking out of his stomach. There's a card in the box that reads:

When all else fails,
Try voodoo.
Love you more than anything,
Violet

It's completely disturbing and brings a smile to my face as I remove the pin and place it in the groin. I pull it out and shove it in the doll's heart. I stare at it for a moment, still not satisfied. I pull it out and stick it back to the groin again. "I'm going to need another pin." I leave the doll on the table and walk to the bathroom.

I throw my clothes on the floor and ease into the tub, still sore from last night. My aching body adjusts to the feel of the cold water as I hear the phone ring. I'm not getting it. Margo's voice fills the air:

"Hey, Charlotte, heads-up. My cousin just told me her friend saw you in the Ocean Drive. Her friend is Janice Harding, as in Stephanie Harding's sister."

This town should be its own news media outlet. Margo, who now lives in Colorado but is visiting New Jersey, just heard that someone saw me ninety miles away *out in public* and might tell someone fifteen hundred miles away about it. It's not even two o'clock the next day. I couldn't care less what they say. Let Stephanie Harding know that this show is going to go on. It's going to be an R-rated memoir of a defeated, downtrodden statistician who used drugs to numb the pain—I hope—but it's going to go on.

I sink deeper in the tub and try to figure out what I'm doing to keep myself busy the next few hours. Maybe clean the house. Some exhaustion will help me sleep, too. I close my eyes and let the cool water cover me like a blanket over my aching body.

My eyes pop open; there's no peace here.

Impatient with my convoluted relaxation, I wrap myself in a towel. The phone rings again and I almost pick it up without looking, assuming it's Margo, but the Oklahoma number catches my eye and I drop it like a burning ember.

"I know I'm not supposed to call you." His voice is rough and barely in control. "I'm sorry. For calling…and everything else." There's a pause and I close my eyes and listen to his breath on the machine. "Stephanie told me you were in Sea Isle this weekend and…" He chokes up a little. Her name from his lips rips me in half. My body trembles as I shake my head. "And…I just wanted to tell you we're going to be together again soon. Don't be with anyone else. Don't meet anyone. Please, Annie."

Un-fucking-believable. The chick he cheated on me with tells him I'm out having fun and he has the nerve to call and ask me to stop? It's like he can't breathe without pissing me off.

"I promise I won't call again," he starts as I pick up the answering machine and hurl it against the wall, smashing it into a million jagged pieces of plastic. I wish he'd been here to aim at. I take a deep breath and snort it out my nose. He's a bigger ass than I realized. I storm back to the kitchen and tear open the silverware drawer. I yank out a fork and in one swoop of my arm spear it into the heart of the voodoo doll. I take a deep breath.

There.
That's better.

* * *

We decide to eat in Delaware to avoid seeing people we know. Margo, Jenn, and I drive from my house to the Delaware Memorial Bridge, passing one field after the other, lined up like dominoes fitted end to end. It is, as my mother always said, God's country.

We find street parking and a table close to the windows, and I wish they'd just move home and drive me to dinner forever.

"How was work today?" Jenn asks as our drinks are delivered. "Did you ask them about a possible bereavement leave?"

It's not an implausible idea. Mom's dead, Dad's dead, relationship's dead, I wish Jason was dead…I feel dead. Okay, half dead.

"It was fine. It was actually good to have something to think about. I told Bruce I'd come up and meet with him on Thursday. He seemed happy to wait to bombard me with work. He did sound shocked I'm still on the East Coast."

"What are you going to do? Are you going back to New York City?"

"I don't know. I've only been with the company seven months, and four of those were an internship. I've been working my ass off to convince them to try a virtual work arrangement, but I just don't care that much anymore. I'm not sure I can put the same effort into it."

Margo, who's still finishing her degree, and Jenn, who is currently waitressing and learning how to surf, both nod in agreement.

"I don't know why, but I want to stay in Salem County," I say, and as soon as it's out of my mouth, I know it's the truth. I need something. Something to keep me alive, and it's not in

New York and it's not in New Brunswick. If it's anywhere in this world, it's in this tiny, barren county I call home.

"God help you, Charlotte. You need to get out of Salem County," Jenn says, and looks at me like this is common knowledge. "You need to make a new home. One without all these memories. You should come to Hawaii. You'll never be this unattached again."

"Unattached" is a gentle word for *completely alone*. I guess not completely since I have Sean and Michelle, and these two fools with me, but it feels completely alone and will only get worse next week when they're gone. I'll be in a weakened state. If it can get any weaker.

"Where else can you be within twenty miles of an international airport and a rodeo?" I ask, sounding like the Salem County Bureau of Tourism.

"Who cares?" Jenn says.

"True. I'm not planning on ever going to the rodeo again."

"What are you going to do?" Margo asks.

Do about what? I can't let my mind consider what she might be talking about.

"Do you guys remember my parents' funeral?" They nod. No one ever knows what to say when your parents die. "When I told you Jason was taking me for a drive?"

"Yes. It was bizarre," Margo says.

"We had sex that day. And pretty much every day we've been together for the last two years. I think there's something wrong with me." I sigh, slightly grasping the depth of how fucked up I am.

"I think I use sex to work through grief. Or worse, I use it to not work through grief."

Their faces display their confusion.

"I can't even talk to him. The sound of his voice makes me physically ill. Is that normal mourning?" I ask, and they both just stare at me, still not knowing what to say. "I think I'm in such bad shape now because instead of just losing Jason, I'm dealing with the loss of my parents, too. Jason and I ran from our grief. We avoided everything with each other." *I want him here now. I want to lie down with him and forget any of this happened.* I shake my head and look at my menu. And when the tears fill my eyes, I squeeze them shut. I lay down my menu and Margo takes my hand.

"Think about yourself right now," Margo says. "I want you to go to church next Sunday. My mom said she'd take you if you want."

"That's nice of her." I haven't been to church in forever. "I'll try to go. I should go. I think I'm going to hell."

Jenn and Margo stay silent, neither one looking to go there. I miss my mom.

We eat. Well, they mostly eat. Nothing tastes anymore. There are no smells. No cool breezes. No music I care to hear. No reason to exist. They drop me off and I curl up in my parents' bed trying to escape the memories of Jason in mine. After hours of staring at the ceiling, I succumb to the horror I now call sleep.

* * *

Gravel spits at the undercarriage as he pulls the truck to the shoulder and turns off the ignition. We'll make love here. Along the side of this road, at least an hour west of Stillwater. My nipples harden as the chill dances between them, and my breath deepens. The anticipation of him pulling me on top of him throbs between my legs. Jason grabs my hand and to my surprise, pulls me out of the truck.

"What are you doing?" I ask, almost laughing. He leads me at least thirty feet away from the road and then faces me. With his arms around my waist, I lean up on my toes to kiss him. Jason's usual hunger is replaced by a gentleness that's foreign in his body.

"Look up, Annie," he says, but I can't take my eyes off him. I lean back and try to concentrate on his words. "Look up."

I let my head fall back and attempt to take it in. The black sky is teeming with stars. Millions of them, millions more than I've ever seen in my life. I step away from Jason. My gaze straight up, I amble in a circle, unable to fit the whole scene into one vision, one picture in my mind.

"My God, it's raining stars here," I say, wonder consuming me. "Jason, it's incredible."

"If you come to Oklahoma, you can see this every night," he says, and I stop three feet from him and let the conniving tone of his words sink in.

"Is that why you brought me here? To convince me to come back?" He's so beautiful in the dim moonlight. A wall of muscle beneath his cowboy hat.

"Whenever you're…upset," he says, seeking the right words. He's distraught. "You search the sky for something. Something that settles you. I thought you should see an Oklahoma sky." His eyes hold me with the same grip he has on my soul. I can't look away any more than I can comprehend staying away.

"But I want you to stay, Annie. I want you to never go back to New Jersey without me." The silence waits. It waits for me to relent, to say the words that will keep us together forever. A chill runs through me and a star shoots across the sky, stealing me from him.

This incredible sky.

I abandon it and drop my head, and then he's upon me. Threading both hands in my hair and clenching them, pulling my hair down and my face toward the sky.

"Forgive me." His words describe some perfect scenario I can't accept. Perfect died in a car crash eight weeks ago and now shreds of hope, mixed with reminders of pain, propel me forward.

"I can't do that," I say, barely above a whisper, and his chest heaves with frustration. He forces me to look at him and then releases my hair. I wait for his anger, but there's none. I lean into Jason and kiss him. It's hunger and desperation and a thousand things other than good-bye. He lifts me and I wrap my legs around his waist, never letting my tongue leave his mouth. I could crush him with my need.

"You can do anything, Annie." The heavy night air flows across my breasts and Jason wills me to believe his words. "You forget how strong you are. You can do this..." I watch him, wanting to let go of everything that's not him. I take one last look at the star-drenched sky.

* * *

I wake up sobbing. I can't do anything.

~ 6 ~

Re-Fucking Connecting

Margo leaves and I can barely breathe; a weight slowly crushes my chest. Her departure came before I fully realized she was here. When the three of us are together, it's as if not one minute's passed since our last gathering. Our world together is on a different plane from the rest of our days. They're family and an incredible distraction.

The cargo train on the tracks next to us catches my eye as a yawn engulfs my face. I can feel myself succumbing to the warmth of sleep.

"Charlotte, how can you be tired? We just got up," Jenn asks, barely looking up from her magazine.

"I don't actually sleep anymore. When I do, I either dream of having sex with Jason or killing him," I say.

Jenn nods. "I dream of killing him, too."

"Plus, riding the train relaxes me. I've always loved it."

The windows go dark as the train enters the tunnel. We're right on time for our 8:14 a.m. arrival in Manhattan.

"It'll be good to see Julia. I haven't seen her since Homecoming last year," Jenn says. "What fun that was." *Homecoming was a year ago?* It was a lifetime ago. My mind wanders to all the weekends Jenn came to visit at Rutgers. Julia and my other roommates loved her as much as I do.

"I know. Julia's been great about taking care of the condo. She's handled everything since we bought it."

"It makes the most sense for you to move to New York City. You already own half of an apartment. What are you going to do with it?" Jenn asks, focusing on the obvious.

I sigh, sick of the obvious. "Julia and I bought it because the market was in shambles and the rates were low, and I had a lot of money from the settlement. We always planned to either sell it high or she'll buy me out. I just had the majority of the down payment since I'm rich now that my parents are dead." I shake my head and close my eyes. *Life makes no sense—why should I?* "You know, tremendous wealth as a consolation for being orphaned," I say, and Jenn says nothing. I really don't know why my friends hang out with me. They deserve better. "How about you drop me off at the office and I'll give you the key to the apartment?" I offer as a plan. "I don't know how long I'm going to be, but I'll keep in touch."

"Take your time. I want to go shopping and get my nails done," she says.

"How very New York," I add as my phone dings with a text. It's Margo.

NICK SINCLAIR LEFT ME A MESSAGE LAST NIGHT. HE WANTS TO KNOW IF YOU CAME BACK TO CO WITH ME.

I run my finger across the screen of my phone. Noble...he's

always had a way of consoling me. Maybe he didn't know before I went to Oklahoma. It's hard to remember a time with Noble when I wasn't laughing. I rest my head on the window as we pull into Penn Station. There's no laughing now. I text Margo back.

Just tell him no.

* * *

Robertson's Reports is a survey creation and interpretation company occupying ten floors of a midtown office building. I wish my parents had lived to see it. They would have been impressed. I take a deep breath and head to the elevator bank just as the door's opening. Fourteen of my closest friends and I file onto the elevator. There are several field offices throughout the country, but the offices we occupy on floors 48 through 57 of this building are the corporate headquarters. The elevator stops several times on the way up, providing more room with each stop. I take a few deep breaths as the door opens on 55 and I squeeze my way past the last four men in the elevator.

As I step out, comfort and familiarity sweep over me. Even though the study of statistics bores just about everyone else on the planet, I love it, and my boss, Bruce, and I did some great work here the past few months. The receptionist sees me and runs from the other side of the desk with her arms outstretched. She's taller than me and slightly plump in a provocative way. She knows it and wears curve-hugging dresses and pencil skirts with thick belts. She's irresistible to men and women and is an island in the sea of hard, skinny shells inhabiting the city. Her hair is long, as brown as dark chocolate and as big as the rest of her. She pulls me into a big hug and my head rests on her jiggling bosom.

"Charlotte!"

I pull away, an unplanned smile on my face.

"What are you doing here? I thought you'd be in Oklahoma or somewhere else that sounds like hell." She pulls me back and looks me up and down. "You look like absolute shit."

"I know. My plans changed. Hey, Renee, do you have a minute?" I ask, unsure of what I'm doing.

"Sure. Let me put the phone on send. No one calls this early anyway."

We move into the break room not far from the lobby and I shut the door.

"Listen, can you do me a favor?"

Renee's intrigued. "Anything, girlfriend. What's up?"

"When I got to Oklahoma, I found out Jason cheated on me in May and the girl's pregnant with his baby." I say this as if I am talking about someone I barely know. "We broke up and we're not speaking anymore." This is partially true, or at least sounds true.

"Oh no, Charlotte. What the fuck? That jerk-off!" Renee's dirty mouth is jarring no matter how much time I spend with her. She walks toward me to put me in the boob squeeze again. I hold up my hand to stop her.

"I'm okay. Actually, I'm close to okay, but I can't tell this story over and over again today. Can you spread it around and tell everyone not to talk to me about it?"

Renee looks completely confused. "Let me get this straight. Something ass-fuck horrible and embarrassing has happened to you and you want me to spread it around the office like common gossip?" she asks, starting to catch on.

"Do you mind?"

"It's brilliant! For you, I'll fucking do it. And I thought this week was going to be a total yawn."

"Thanks, Renee. I owe you. Oh, and I brought my friend, Jenn, from home up with me. Julia and I are taking her to Rise for Happy Hour if you want to join us."

"Aah, shit-talking tourists. Maybe I'll meet a rich business ass from out of town at the Ritz."

"Undoubtedly. How could they resist you?" I say as I think, *Not with that mouth*.

"True. Like moths to the motherfucking light. I almost feel bad for them most days." We walk back toward the lobby. "You call me or come up here if anyone bothers you. I'll bash their fucking heads in with my stapler."

I've missed NY.

I use my ID badge to open the door behind Renee and make my way to Bruce's office. I try to avoid the few people already at their desks until Renee's had a chance to speak with them. Bruce is sitting at his desk, facing his computer, which is off to the side. Something about his office, and him in it, makes me happy. It's good to be starting again.

He sees me and beams as he comes around the desk. "Hey!" He kisses me on the cheek and hugs me, and I pull away, a little out of practice with all the kissing. Bruce ignores my lack of enthusiasm and shuts the door. "Sit down." He motions to a chair in front of his desk and sits in the one next to it. I'd be more comfortable with him behind his desk the way he usually is, but I know he's trying to put me at ease.

"So, do you want to tell me why my luck's changed and you're back in the city?"

"Well," I begin with a huge sigh, "I'm no longer moving

to Oklahoma, and I have a great deal more time to devote to work."

"That's good news," Bruce says exaggeratedly. "Are you moving into the city?"

"No."

"North Jersey?" Bruce asks, surprised.

"Actually, I'd like to stay in South Jersey. I've been staying at my parents' house for a few weeks now and it feels right." Bruce's disappointment is apparent. "I was thinking I could come to the city a lot more than I'd intended to from Oklahoma. Maybe even once a week. That should make things a little easier." I'm rambling at this point. "And if we're working on time-critical materials, I could stay a few days. It'll give us a little more flexibility," I continue.

"It's okay." Bruce raises his hand to halt my nonsense. "I still can't believe I approved you working from Oklahoma. I'm glad you're going to be closer. We've submitted a proposal to Sure Auto Insurance and if they accept, we're going to be spending a lot of time in Saratoga Springs together."

"New York?" I ask.

"That's the one," Bruce answers with an excited grin. "We'll work it out as we go." His smile makes me uncomfortable. I glance back weakly.

* * *

The clock hits 5:30 and I'm running toward reception. Renee's ready to escape as well. She's providing directions to a man leaving our office and has traded her explicit language for her sweetest receptionist tongue. "That's right. You'll just need to go down three blocks and you'll see it on your right."

We walk to the apartment, catching up on her life the entire way, her X-rated vocabulary fully restored and illustrating every story.

"Thanks for giving me the awful-ass scoop. It made today fly by. I didn't realize you knew so many fucking people. They were stopping by all day," she says happily. "Oh, and Brody in accounting's going to ask you out. He asked me how long he should wait. I think he's been spanking off to your Facebook page for months."

My face twists in disgust. "Tell him at least a year or two."

"You know Bruce is going to try and fuck you."

I freeze in horror. "What?"

"Don't worry. He tries to fuck everyone eventually. You'd be insulted if he didn't."

"No. I would not be insulted." I keep walking, but I'm still completely disturbed. Even more so at the thought that Jason was right all along about Bruce wanting to do more than statistics with me.

* * *

By the time we get home, Julia and Jenn are already drinking a beer and rolling a joint. I drop my bags by the door and take off my shoes. Renee barrels in behind me and introduces herself to Jenn.

The apartment looks different. The refrigerator is blank except for a Chinese takeout magnet. The bulletin board hangs like new on the wall. I carry my shoes to my room. The shelves and the top of the dresser are empty and unfamiliar, and the only thing left is a picture of Julia, Noble, and me at the shore last summer. We're huddled together in a bar with enormous smiles covering our sun-kissed faces. I barely recognize myself.

"Are you sure you're okay?" Julia asks with concern gripping her face.

"I'm not sure I'm even alive," I blankly admit. I continue to survey my empty room.

"I hope you don't mind. I redecorated a little," Julia says.

I stare at the sterilized frame around my mirror. It used to hold a picture of Jason riding a bull on the left and a picture of us from my cousin's wedding on the right. All of it gone, with one swipe of Julia's little hand. I remember her complete intolerance for infidelity. It was the cause of her parents' ugly divorce, and even eight years later she still cannot forgive the indiscretion.

"No," I say, still eyeing the room. "It was thoughtful of you."

"I didn't throw anything away. I wanted to but didn't think it was my place. I boxed it all up and put it on the top shelf of the linen closet."

I glance numbly at Julia and take a long drag of the joint.

~ 7 ~

My Return to Hell

Jenn and I invite Clint over for dinner on Saturday night. I figure he already knows I'm home and I want to make sure he keeps it quiet. I also want him to do some work on my house. It's only a small part of me that's in desperate need of repairs. It is the only part I can subcontract out, though, so remodeling it is. We make homemade pizzas and a big salad. Clint shows up all smiles. He's either really high or thinks he's been invited to a threesome. Hopefully he won't be too disappointed. I give Clint a tour of the house and tell him some of the things I'd like to do, including turning Sean's old bedroom into a library, redoing the kitchen and the master bedroom, and all the baths. Clint has some great ideas for built-in bookcases in Sean's room and promises to start on an estimate tomorrow.

We eat on the back deck and talk about moving home as the sun sets crimson in the sky. Clint has the advantage of never having left Salem County, so he doesn't know any different. Jenn is never coming home, and I find myself here under duress. We smoke the joint Clint brought with him and I think, *Red sky at night, sailor's delight,* as the day disappears.

"You know, I was shocked when you and Leer first got together. It just seemed to come out of nowhere," Clint says. I stay still, not releasing the sky, not wanting to remember that day. "Do you still talk to him?" Clint is sweet, but I may have to kill him.

"No. I don't even talk about him." I smile at Clint to take the sting out of my words.

"Oh, sorry."

I don't bother to say it's fine, or no worries, because it's not fine and he should worry.

"Hey, do you want to go camping sometime? I'm thinking about getting a group together before it gets too cold." Clint attempts an easier subject.

"I could be convinced to go camping." Maybe a bear will eat me or a hunter will shoot me.

* * *

Clint's presence softens the blow of Jenn's departure, but I still throw myself on my bed and cry when I close the door behind them. Like Margo leaving on Wednesday, it's as if my lifeline's been pulled. They filled my days, my nights, and my heart, and now they'll be miles and time zones away while I return to hell.

"Hell is only getting to see you one weekend a month," Jason says as he sits up next to me. "Can't you do your senior year at Oklahoma?"

I roll over and straddle him, completely naked. Jason places his palms on the top of each of my thighs and stares at me, waiting for an answer. We sit eye to eye for a long, silent moment.

"Are you trying a Jedi mind trick on me?" I ask as he takes his thumb and strokes me.

"Your mind would not be my first point of offense."

With his thumb keeping a perfect rhythm, he pulls my face toward him and kisses me hard on the lips. He pulls back slightly and I try to catch my breath as his thumb, his incredible thumb, keeps going around and around. I don't look up and he kisses me again, separating my lips and forcing his tongue into me at the exact time his two fingers enter me, his thumb still stroking.

I'm throbbing and panting and completely his. He pulls his face away a few millimeters to tell me, "This could be every day," and kisses me again. My heartbeat quickens as he reaches his other hand up and pulls my nipple. The sweet pain triggers my release.

"I love you," he says. "Annie, I love you. Please pick up the phone."

I open my eyes, out of breath and sweating. I barely make out the remainder of his message on my new answering machine. I focus on breathing. Is it possible for a man to give me an orgasm without even being here? Without me being awake?

Will he always own me?

~ 8 ~

Give It to God

My mom's voice in my head should comfort me. "Get up and get something done. Don't just sit around and feel sorry for yourself. Yes, it's bad, but lots of people have it worse." But it doesn't.

She'd send me to church. I haven't been to church since the Christmas Eve before they died. My relationship with God was severed the instant the Speed Demon Delivery truck hit my parents' car. I open my closet door, searching for church clothes. If my parents were here, we'd all drive together and then go out to lunch. None of my clothes feel like church. Probably because I don't feel like church. I slip a red and white wrap dress over my head and pair it with nude heels. It's as good as it's going to get at this point. I pull my hair back in a low ponytail and throw on some lip gloss. I'm still too thin, my hallowed cheeks framed by harsh cheekbones, but thanks to my recent trip to the shore I have a healthy glow.

I choose the 10:30 traditional service since that's the one my mom always liked, and go in right before the service starts. I am one of only ten people under fifty in the sanctuary. *Even better.* I choose a pew three-quarters of the way back from the altar and take a seat. There's one other woman in the pew with me. She's alone and holding a Bible with a pretty embroidered cover. My mom always brought her own Bible. I try to appear peaceful as she looks over at me, but I said good-bye to peaceful a few years ago.

"Is that Charlotte O'Brien?" I hear from a few pews back.

"Good morning and welcome," Pastor Johnson begins.

I busy myself reading the church announcements and calendar before surveying the congregation for who I need to avoid after the service. Over my shoulder I see Butch Leer limping into a pew across the aisle and two rows back. He walks with a cane from a war injury. Which war I'm not sure, but it definitely adds to his miserable bastard exterior.

I'm finally starting to understand Butch's demeanor. I'm on a bit of a decline myself. In the two years Jason and I were together, I spent only four meals with Butch. Jason seemed just as happy without him. He told me that when his mother died it was as if his father died, too. He'd been "alone" an entire year before my parents' accident.

Butch labors to sit down and looks up at me. I stare at him for a minute, searching for some resemblance to Jason. There's none. Jason's beautiful like his mother was. Butch is tall, but completely gray and wobbly. His face is frozen in a scowl that could scare a coyote. I turn back toward the front of the church; Pastor Johnson gives me a small nod and I smile back. I mindlessly participate in the service until it comes time for our silent confessions. Because really, if not here, where?

Dear God, please forgive me. I have wished death on Jason, and Stephanie, and their baby. And on everyone who knew they were together in Oklahoma. I have considered different ways to physically injure or kill all of them. I hate every pregnant and every happy person.

I've questioned your existence.

I've thought of killing myself.

Oh yeah, and after all that, if he walked in right now I'd take him in the church bathroom and have sex with him, which I hate the most about myself. I think that's it for now.

"Hear the good news, believe it, bet your life on it, in Jesus Christ's name you are forgiven," Pastor Johnson absolves us. And we sing.

I don't feel any better. I feel disgusting. I want to leave, but nothing says town scandal like running out of church after confession. I'll save the dramatics for after I actually kill them. The offering plate is passed but I only have three dollars in my purse, so rather than embarrass myself, I pass and make a mental note to send a check. My father lectures me in my head. *"Don't drive around without any money in your pocket. What if you have an emergency?"*

The service ends and everyone files out, being received by Pastor Johnson at the front door. I stay in my seat with my head down, hoping to discourage any friendly neighbors and avoid the line waiting to speak with the pastor.

"Charlotte?" It's the pastor's wife, one of the nicest people I've ever met, and she sits down next to me.

"Hi, Mrs. Johnson." I haven't seen her in months, but she always reminds me of my mother. And this church reminds me of my mother. I start to cry. This church was her home.

"Oh, Charlotte, it's all right. Let God have it." She sits next to me and rubs my back as I try to regain my composure.

"I'm sorry." My voice is weak—one more thing I hate about myself.

"Oh, please, Charlotte. You have nothing to apologize for."

"Obviously you couldn't hear my silent confession."

Mrs. Johnson laughs, and I take a deep breath and actually do feel a little better.

"Do you want to talk? If not to me, maybe to Mark or one of the deacons? There's a lot of wisdom in the ten-thirty service."

I shake my head. "I want to go home, but maybe next time."

"Charlotte, promise me there'll be a next time."

"I promise. I'll come back next week. I kind of have to."

Mrs. Johnson raises her eyebrows in confusion.

"I stiffed you on the collections." I smile and leave Mrs. Johnson sitting in my pew.

My pew.

I give Pastor Johnson a little hug on my way out, and with a sympathetic posture he tells me how wonderful it is to see me. *Even Pastor Johnson's heard about Jason and Stephanie?* Why am I surprised? As I walk down the front steps of the church, I see Butch by his car. He's leaning over the hood and something's awkward about the scene. I run over to the car and he's grabbing his knee.

"Butch, are you okay?" I ask, taking him by the elbow to support him.

"I'm fine. Get off me!"

I jump back as his words roll around in my head, the sound of his voice disorienting me. His voice is Jason's. I never noticed before, but he sounds just like him.

"What are you staring at?"

I acclimate to the pain and shake my head to gather some thoughts. "Are you okay?" I ask again.

"Of course I'm okay. I was just resting." Butch starts to move and his right knee gives out, causing him to fall onto the other. "Goddamn it!"

Nice talk on the church lawn.

I bend down, grab Butch under his arm, and hoist him up. He brushes himself off but can barely walk. "I think you should go to the hospital."

"Have you lost your goddamned mind?"

"Just about, yes," I say, and not waiting for his response add, "Look, you can't drive. I'll take you home."

"The hell you will!" he says as I lead him to the passenger side of his car and wait for him to unlock the door. He stubbornly stands in front of it on one leg.

"Whenever you're ready, old man. I've got nothing but time."

My father would be furious at me for speaking disrespectfully to Butch. He always shook Butch's hand and shared a few kind words. He'd say, "Butch, like every veteran, deserves our respect. They've surely earned it."

Butch takes the keys out of his pocket and unlocks the car. I open the door and help steady him as he carefully falls into the car. He lifts his right leg up and carries it in without bending it. I walk around to the driver's side and get behind the wheel.

We silently drive out of town. I want to say something, but I'm cognitively paralyzed, and I don't want to hear his voice—Jason's voice. It's a straight shot out of town to the Sinclair farm, and for the first time I wonder how the Leers ended up here. I grin, thinking of the train tracks that sever the Sinclair lane. It always reminds me of the Polar Express. As we pull up, a train is approaching the lane.

"On a Sunday?" I say as I pull to the side to wait while the train passes.

"Yeah. They're testing something."

I wave like a child.

"First train you've ever seen?" Butch asks, salty as always.

"Something about a train makes me wave at the engineer." The train consists of four cars and is moving slow enough that I can see the engineer's face clearly as he waves back.

Butch and I return to our silence. The train passes, and I put the car in drive and head down the lane of the Sinclair farm. His house is a small, unpretentious white rancher on the left of the lane. I pull his colossal sedan onto the lawn and park as close to the tiny house as possible.

"Trying to hit the house?" he asks.

I ignore him and get out of the car to help him. Beyond Butch's house is a large pole barn, before the lane breaks into a circle with the Sinclairs' white farmhouse at the keystone. The L-shed, packing shed, and another large building are behind the farmhouse. *Is this all Noble's now?* The last time I talked to him was at the fair in August and he said his parents were leaving for Florida after Labor Day and he would be on his own with the farm. I shiver, remembering the way Noble hugged me that day. He knew about Stephanie.

By the time I get to Butch's side of the car, he has his door open and is swinging his legs out of the car, trying to get up without my help.

"Give me your house keys," I say, holding out my hand.

"I'm not giving you shit. Now get out of my way."

"You Leer boys really know how to treat a girl."

Butch stops trying to get out and looks at me apologetically. I smile to let Butch know I don't hate him, at least not yet. He drops the keys into my outstretched hand and stares out the car window. I try several keys in the lock, not wanting him to speak any more than necessary. The lock finally turns and I try the handle, but it's locked, too. Again, I start the key game. The second lock turns and I open the door, which leads into a shed area. It's hot and foul-smelling from lack of ventilation. I see the inside door and its three locks and want to give up, but I know that's probably what Butch expects.

"What the hell are you doing in there?" he yells, and I jump at the sound of Jason's voice.

"My nails," I yell back as I finally get the third lock. Making him angry has a certain appeal to me. "What exactly is in here that's so freaking valuable?"

With both doors open, I come back out and the fresh air soothes my mood. Butch is sitting in his car with his legs facing out, one hand on the dash, the other trying to find a point for leverage. The scene is too familiar to trying to help my grandmother in and out of cars. These low ones are the hardest. He tries three times to pull himself up, and I just watch because offering help is useless until he's desperate.

"Damn knee," Butch spews, and I think he's about ready. I close the door halfway and wrap my leg around it. I use both arms to support his right side. Butch pushes off the dash and once he's up, grabs the top of the door to steady himself. His relief on his face turns to appreciation and I just smile, not wanting to make a big deal of it. Between Butch's cane and me supporting his side by the arm, we're able to get inside, but it's not pretty.

I keep an eye on the floor, making sure nothing will threaten Butch's footing, and don't look up until I have him safely in a chair at the kitchen table. When I do, I'm in shock. The last time I was in this house was the day of Jason's mom's funeral. The luncheon was out back and I came in to use the bathroom. The house still spoke of her then, but now it screams of neglect. In the three years since she died, the house has become dark and decayed. There are stacks of carefully tied newspapers and magazines in every corner of the room. The windows are dirty and the dust-covered curtains block the sun. There are open jars on the counter, some with white mold forming atop the food, and dirty dishes in the sink. The house is too warm and stuffy, and it smells as if the windows haven't been open all summer. Papers, empty envelopes mostly, are strewn across the table with notes scrawled on them, and there are several empty cans holding pens and pencils. A dish with what looks like dried-on egg sits next to a half-empty cup of muddy coffee. When I try to lift it, I find it's stuck to the table.

"Leave it!" Butch barks as I pry it loose. I carry it to the sink, and a large black bug crawls across the peaks of the dirty dishes strewn in it. I'm not sure if it's the smell, the heat, or the sound of Jason's voice, but I feel dizzy and steady myself with the counter.

"What happened to her?" I ask.

"To who?" he yells, angry now.

"To Mrs. Leer. There's nothing left of her," I say as I turn around and motion toward the room.

"She's dead, goddammit." Butch's words house the years of loneliness and anger I'm embarking on. Is this what will come when I let go of numb?

I find a glass in the cupboard and wash it, fill it with water, and go to the freezer for ice. The freezer is empty except for some ice that's formed into a giant block.

"Oh, Butch," I whine as I place the glass down.

"Shut up," he snaps.

I sit down beside him. "You can't live like this." My voice is gentle. This man needs to be taken care of.

"No one cares how I live," he says, quieting down.

"Who's your doctor?"

"Grubb, why?" he grumbles.

"Because you need to see him about your leg."

I google Dr. Grubb in Salem County on my phone. The number comes up and I press call. I'm surprised when a familiar voice answers the phone.

"Yes, I'm calling on behalf of Butch Leer." I pause as Mrs. Dubois explains that Dr. Grubb's phone is forwarded to her on the weekends, but she has his appointment book. "Oh, hi, Mrs. Dubois." I intentionally leave out my name. "He's hurt his knee and needs to see Dr. Grubb." I look at Butch and notice his coloring's not good either. His skin's as gray as his hair. "He could use a general physical, too." Butch rolls his eyes and reminds me of Jason. I wish he were here right now. I wouldn't even try to kill him. "Yes, ten o'clock will work. Thanks. We'll see you then."

Butch scowls at the mention of both of us going.

"I'm coming back at nine-thirty tomorrow to get you. We'll go to Dr. Grubb's and to lunch. While we're out, a cleaning crew will be in here straightening up." He starts to simmer and I want to get out of here before he boils over.

"For the love of Christ, get out of here. Would you?"

"What are you going to eat for dinner?"

"I've been eating just fine for years without anybody's help."

I take a deep breath and let Butch maintain his control. He is a grown man, after all. He doesn't need me to feed him. I think.

"I'll be back tomorrow at nine-thirty. I'll lock up behind me and take the keys. That way you won't have to get up to let me in tomorrow."

He starts to sputter and stammer as I rush out the door and walk down the farm lane.

* * *

My head rests on Jason's stomach as we lie in the center of the field. He's caressing my arm, back and forth, as I watch the clouds float by. I hear a voice calling, "Annie, Annie."

I know it's Mrs. Leer because she and Jason were the only people who ever called me Annie. It was left over from the year Mrs. Leer was my Sunday school teacher and my mom was experimenting with the name. She decided against it, but it stuck with the Leers.

"Annie, Jesus loves you," she calls to me again, but I can't see her.

I sit up and she's standing right in front of me. Mrs. Leer looks as pretty as she did before the cancer. She has on a long denim skirt with a blue sweater that makes her eyes sparkle against her jet-black hair. She takes my hand and pulls me into a big hug. She smells of the same kiwi shampoo Jason always smells of and I inhale it deeply.

"Put on therefore, as the elect of God, holy and beloved, bowels of mercies, kindness, humbleness of mind, meekness, long suffering." Mrs. Leer quotes Scripture to no one in particular.

She holds me at arm's length. "Annie, promise me you'll always take care of my boys. Please promise me."

"I will. I promise."

I turn around, and Butch is standing next to Jason, who's

holding a baby in a blue outfit. Stephanie's standing on the other side of him.

"*Remember your promise,*" *Mrs. Leer says as she walks away.*

"*No! No! Please don't go. Come back,*" *I yell as I begin to cry.* "*I can't help them. Please!*"

I wake up sobbing, clutching my pillow. I want to call Jason. I want to tell him I dreamed of his mother. He'd want to know. He'd want to know I've dreamed of her. He'd want to know that someone else is missing her.

I roll onto my back and stare at the ceiling. The world moves forward. From the minute my loved ones left my parents' funeral, they slipped back into their lives, their obligations, their daily routines, their things to be excited about. But everything stopped for me. Jason would want to know that someone else still dreams of his mother.

~ 9 ~

Family Obligations

Can you help me with something tomorrow?" I ask Sean hesitantly.

"Sure, what?" The worry in his voice is obvious even through the cell phone.

"Can you meet me at Butch Leer's house at nine thirty? I'm having a cleaning crew out of Mullica Hill come to his house and overhaul it while I take him to the doctor's."

Silence.

"Sean?"

"Yeah, I'm here. You're taking Butch to the doctor's...and having his house cleaned?" Sean's tone reinforces the absurdity of the statements.

"Yes. Look, he's in a bad place and needs some help."

"Are you sure you're the best person to help him?" His voice is full of fear.

"Oh, I'm far from the best person, but I'm the only person," I admit, hoping to ease Sean's angst.

"All right. What time?"

"Nine thirty and thanks a lot. Oh, and one more thing. If you run into Noble, don't give him any information."

"That's right; I forgot Butch lives on the Sinclair farm. Why are you hiding from Nick Sinclair?"

"I'm not."

Sean doesn't ask any more questions. It's part of his charm.

* * *

In an effort to psych myself up for a day with Butch, I blare patriotic music through my car speakers on the drive to his house. I'm sure he'll be much sweeter today. I continue belting out the lyrics. My stomach flutters from nerves and I put the song on repeat.

The drought has worsened and dust from the Sinclair lane swirls around my car as I drive the length of it. Instead of picking up Butch, I want to drive right past his house and go into Noble's. Go in, pull a beer out of the refrigerator, and plop on his couch the same way he used to when he'd come to my house at Rutgers. But that was a thousand years ago, and Noble talks to Jason. If Jason can't find me, Noble will be the first person he reaches out to for help. He may not have liked our friendship, but he knew what Noble meant to me. *He knew everything.*

I again pull up close to the door so Butch won't have to walk far. The cleaning crew speaks Russian, which Butch will kill me for if he finds out, and they'll be here at ten. Thank God for Sean. I couldn't pull this off without him.

Sean's truck is already parked by the tree and he gets out as I park.

"Didn't want to wake the bear?" I ask, smiling.

"You know I think you might be insane," he says.

"I know. I'm a little concerned myself. Can you help me get him into the car?" This is completely insane and I should be committed, but it's refreshing to smile, to laugh with Sean. Even if it's for the benefit of the crustiest bastard in town, it's good to feel alive again, to have a purpose outside of self-loathing.

We walk up to the door and I again fumble through the keys to find the right one. Sean is shocked.

"You have keys to Butch Leer's house?"

"Just temporarily. He hurt his knee pretty bad yesterday, and I didn't want him to have to get up to let me in today."

Sean nods his head in exaggerated understanding. "Of course."

"Brace yourself," I say as I get the last lock on the inside shed door. I brace myself, too, as I turn away from Sean and walk into the house.

Butch is at the kitchen table, looking as gruff as he did yesterday. He has a shoebox in front of him and a different shirt on than when I left him. This one is a blue and red button-down; he's dressed up for the doctor.

"Butch, do you remember my brother Sean?"

Sean walks over and shakes his hand. "Hi, Butch."

"He's going to stay here with the cleaning crew and make sure they just clean."

Butch nods. This is going well.

"You ready to go?"

"Do I have a goddamned choice?"

I sigh at his nastiness and wonder how long it took to harden after sorrow abandoned him. "No, I'm afraid you don't."

Sean looks at me again, silently asking what the hell I'm doing, but I don't respond. "Sean, we're going to need your help to get Butch to the car."

Sean takes one side of Butch and we raise him to his feet. He's able to walk using his cane and leaning heavily on Sean as I open the doors in front of us.

"My box. Get my damn box," Butch barks, and I grab the box containing God knows what. Sean eases Butch into my Volvo. It's an SUV and higher than Butch's car. I hope it's easier to get out of. Sean closes the car door and walks me around to the driver's side.

"How the hell are you going to get him into the doctor's office alone?" Sean asks.

"I have Grandmom's wheelchair in the back."

"Good luck with that." Sean and I look back at Butch staring out the car window, his scowl firmly in place. "You, Charlotte, are going to have a very bad day."

"Just stay here and make sure they don't steal anything. Have them stack any papers neatly and help them figure out what's trash, recyclable, and so on. Here's cash for the balance." I hand Sean five hundred dollars. "I think it's going to be between three and four hundred, but I wanted to make sure you had enough."

"Geez! Maybe I should give up physical therapy and start cleaning houses."

"You haven't seen the whole place," I whisper.

* * *

Butch and I ride silently to Dr. Grubb's office. I park in the back and feel relief at the sight of a ramp rising up to the back door. I hop out of the Volvo as Butch tries to turn himself around and place his legs outside the car. I pull the wheelchair out of the back, open it, and wheel it up to him as if we've used it a hundred times.

"What the hell is that?" he yells at me.

"Why, it's a wheelchair, of course," I say, keeping the smile glued to my lips.

"You're out of your goddamned head if you think I'm getting in that thing."

"I am out of my goddamned head. Now get in the goddamned chair before you fall again and end up in some rehab facility with a hairless man named Rex giving you a bath every day," I say, and wait.

Butch's face turns from anger to disgust and finally to resignation. "How the hell do I get in it?" he asks, not hiding his frustration.

"We'll get you standing the same way we did last night; then you'll turn around and sit right into it."

Butch looks at me like that's the stupidest idea he's ever heard, so I know it's okay to move forward. I hook my leg around the door to steady it and hunch over to help support him under the arm. As he rises, he wobbles but uses the door to steady himself. When I'm sure he's stable, I move the door and pull the wheelchair over. This is exactly the way we used to transport my grandmother the last ten years before she died. Butch turns around and drops into the chair and I exhale, relieved. I bend down, open the foot flaps, and help him lift his left leg into it. His face contorts in pain. I hope the rehab facility was a threat rather than a prediction.

It's been a while since I've pushed a wheelchair and Butch is heavier than my grandmother was. I manage to only bang him into the railing and the doorway on the way into the doctor's office. He's mumbling the whole way and I catch, "stupid goddamned...no one asked you for any help...horseshit idea."

"Good afternoon, Butch," the receptionist says sweetly, not taking her eyes off me.

"Hello," I say as I wheel Butch over next to the couch in the waiting room and take a seat with a magazine to minus myself from the equation.

Dr. Grubb himself comes to the door. "Butch, you can come on back."

"Do you want me to come with you?" I ask, wheeling Butch toward the doctor.

He turns around in the chair to face me in disbelief. "Are you out of your chicken-shit head?"

"Yes," I say without any emotion, and push the chair through the doorway. "I'll be out here if you need anything," I say sweetly to Dr. Grubb.

While Butch is in the doctor's office, I text Sean.

How's it going?

Man, I had no idea Butch was in such bad shape.

Really bad?

It's good you took him to the doctor's. There's tons of stuff in his room he's mail-ordered to self-medicate different ailments.

Oh

Doesn't he have any other family?

I try to remember if Jason ever mentioned any other relatives. I know his aunt Rita was his mother's sister, but I never heard of anyone else. Aunt Rita lives in Pennsylvania some-where.

I don't think so

...is all I can respond.

"Charlotte, would you mind coming back for a moment?" Dr. Grubb asks.

I put away my phone and follow Dr. Grubb back to the ex-amination room. Butch is seated in the wheelchair. His sunny disposition is still intact.

"Butch has several prescriptions that need to be filled. Would you be able to pick them up if we call them in for him?"

"Yes, of course."

"I'd also like you to pick up a knee brace. Here." He hands me a piece of paper. "I've written the style down. You can try the drugstore, but you might have better luck online."

I read the paper, making sure I can decipher Dr. Grubb's writing.

"And finally, Butch is slightly malnourished. He's going to need to be much more deliberate about a balanced diet."

"Of course," I say as I try to digest all the information. Poor Butch.

* * *

My luck improves when an old friend agrees to help with Butch. Marie's more of an angel than an old friend. She and another woman split twelve-hour shifts sitting with my grand-mother when she came to my parents' house for hospice care. They helped bathe her and made sure she was comfortable. Now Marie will help Butch with some cooking and light cleaning. I think it'll be good for him to have some company, but I'd never mention that to Butch. It was hard enough getting him to accept Marie's help. I put whole milk and extralarge eggs in my shopping cart before moving down the aisle to the bread. Once Marie's been in there a few days, she'll be able to tell me what groceries Butch needs and what foods he likes to eat, but for now I'm just grabbing some staples.

I hit the fruit-and-vegetables aisle hard and add in some canned fruit and frozen vegetables. I need to check if Butch has a microwave. This would be easier if I could talk to Jason. I'm sure he knows the answers to all my questions. Does Jason know how Butch has been living? Does he care?

I stop in the bakery and select some sticky buns. One with nuts and one without. My grandmother used to love these. Butch is a lot younger, but he reminds me of her. When he's not killing me with Jason's voice. Thank God he never says a kind word. With that voice it might push me over the edge.

I take my time checking out and loading my car. If I time this right, I can avoid running into Noble at lunch. About a mile before I get to the Sinclair farm, I see a small group of men and machinery working in a field. I can't make out faces, but Noble's truck is there. I pull down the lane and park next to Marie's car. As I put my key in the final lock and open the door, I think I catch the sound of laughter winding down, but that's impossible.

Marie greets me with a maternal look and grabs a bag from around my wrist. Butch is seated at the kitchen table, and although he doesn't smile, he doesn't regard me with hatred either. An awkward silence falls over the room. Marie announces she's going to get the mail.

"So, how's it going?" I ask.

"How's it supposed to be going?" Butch says, but it lacks the usual nastiness. I resist the urge to close my eyes and take deep breaths at the sound of his voice.

It's Butch, not Jason.

"Do you like Marie? Is she helpful?" I try again.

"Yeah, she's helpful, but I don't need help."

I raise my hand to stop him. I'm not going to have, for the thousandth time, the conversation about how he was doing just fine before I brought him home from church.

"Well, you agreed Marie can come Monday, Wednesday, and Friday for a few weeks. At least until you're feeling better."

"I know. Who the hell is paying her?" His anger is returning.

"Let me worry about that for now."

Butch looks at me like he's going to kill me.

"I'm looking into using insurance to pay. I'll keep you posted," I say, and put the subject to rest for at least a few days. I finish unpacking the groceries and floret the watermelon. Marie would do it, but I'm not ready to leave Butch and we seem to do better with a task, rather than silence.

"Are you feeling any better?" Butch just looks at me. "I mean since you started taking the medicine Dr. Grubb prescribed."

"I guess I am," Butch says almost kindly, and I realize it's a great time to leave.

"Listen, do you think we can keep my visits just between us?"

Butch is confused.

"I'm not asking you to lie to anyone, I just...well, I just haven't told people where I'm living now and I'm...I'm just not ready to talk to everyone yet." My eyes roam around the room avoiding Butch. When I do look at him, he's almost sympathetic.

"Believe me, I'm not going around bragging about this."

"Okay," I say, and exhale. "I'll see you tomorrow."

"See you," Butch says as he swats his hand through the air.

Maybe someday I'll come see him without sighing when I leave. It's a feeling of surviving or escaping something.

I only lock the handle on the outside door since I've surrendered my keys to Marie. As I turn around, I hear a strangled chirp that is frantically repeated. I follow the sound to a bird huddled in the grass. It squawks and squawks its tortured little cry but never flies. The bird is plump with light blue feathers, and I consider for a moment she might be pregnant. I look the little bluebird right in the eye and it never flinches. I turn around to search for a nest and see a cat crouched in the bushes, ready to pounce. I look from the bird to the cat and walk to my car and leave.

* * *

The first day of fall is as sultry as July. Even though the sun's lost some of its intensity, my skin's hot and a bead of sweat slides down the side of my face as the truck pulls up to the side of the house and stops. A small blue feather catches my eye in the grass, and I push it aside. How long has it been since I've seen Noble? It feels like forever, and yet the time's not exactly flying by. It's been weeks.

He's at home, hopping out of his bright red pickup truck, wearing jeans and a T-shirt that outlines his well-worked body, muscles toned from working under the sun rather than in a gym. His sandy brown hair is a bit too long and falls out the sides of his hat. Even seeing only a few small pieces I can tell the sun's brightened it. It's as if I'm seeing him for the first time in years.

So much has happened. So many horrible things. Actually, just one horrible thing, but I'm a different person than I was in August, one not worth knowing. I use the back of my hand to wipe my brow.

"Well, if it isn't the hardest person to find in Salem County," he says as he clears the distance between us with long strides. Noble is tall, six-two. I know because I've heard him tell girl after potential girl at Rutgers over the past four years.

"Have you been looking for me?"

"Me and about a hundred other people. I even called Margo to get your new number, but she's hardcore. Said she couldn't share any information about you." He crouches down beside me, and I become aware I'm covered in dirt and most definitely have some on my face. "And then I pull into my own driveway and find you here, planting flowers. I would have guessed New York City." He flashes the most perfect smile. It moves from his lips straight up to his sky-blue eyes and it's suddenly even sunnier outside.

"Was there something you needed?" I ask, avoiding his smile.

"What do you mean?"

"Why were you trying to find me? Do you need something?" He plops down right in the mulch where I'm working as if we're settling in under a shady tree.

"I just wanted to make sure you're still alive." With that his smile fades. His eyes sadden and the clouds come back.

"Haven't hung myself yet," I answer, and force a smile. "I have some free time this afternoon, though, after I cross self-loathing and wallowing in humiliation off my to-do list." I return to planting the mums, but we both start laughing. I forgot how easy it is to laugh with Noble. How easy it is to laugh.

"Come to lunch with me?" he asks.

"No."

"Come on."

"No," I answer again, back to sharing no emotion.

"Charlotte, come on. Don't make me beg." Now he's lying flat on his back in the flower bed, his hat pulled low over his eyes. He makes me want to lie down with him and be happy the way he is.

"I can't go out to lunch with you. Look at me. I'm a complete mess."

"Who cares? It's not the prom. We'll go to the Wagon Wheel. No one'll even notice us." He exaggeratedly rolls his eyes, mimicking a thirteen-year-old girl. "Get over yourself."

I stare at him for a few seconds. I have no idea why, but I get up, walk to the spigot, and wash off my hands. The cool water soothes my sun-drenched skin. I'm pretty sure I'm going to be sunburned tomorrow. "You're seriously going to let me in your truck looking like this?"

His grin and eye roll call me absurd without him having to speak a word.

* * *

The little bell hanging in the doorway rings, announcing our arrival just like at the prom, and believe me, we're noticed. I'd almost swear Christine Mattos gasps at the sight of us. Is it our appearance, the sight of us together, or the mere fact that I'm in Salem County instead of anonymously living in a foreign country? I'm not sure. If Noble notices, he's giving no indication. We pick a table on the side of the small dining room and order sweet tea from our waitress. I pretend to read the menu as I contemplate the different escape scenarios. It won't be easy.

"Don't bother wasting your time trying to figure out how to get out of here. The worst is over." He leans in as he whispers, holding his menu up to shield us from the now rather quiet dining room. "Besides, you look like you haven't eaten in a month."

Noble flashes his sweet mug at the waitress and orders a BLT. I order the same since I haven't read one thing on the menu and don't want this lunch to last any longer than necessary.

"It's going to be number five," he says as if I know what he's talking about.

Embarrassingly, I do. The Wagon Wheel has a number light box above the kitchen door. When an order is ready, the number lights up and a bell rings. My entire life I've passed the time here by guessing which number will be next.

"Number three, without a doubt." Again we both smile.

"Why didn't you call me?" he asks as his face turns serious. "Maybe I could have helped."

"There's no way to help this. I love you too much to inflict me on you," I answer, and my face contorts into a sneer, angry at myself for becoming so unwantable.

I see her coming out of the corner of my eye, but not soon enough to brace myself. "Well, if it isn't Charlotte O'Brien! I had no idea you were back in town. Are you going to be here for a while? Moving home for good?"

I know Nadine from high school. Knew her sister better but had always liked them both.

"I don't have any definite plans yet. Just here for lunch today." I look at Noble and silently plead with him not to give me up.

"After everything that happened with Jason, you should be home, with people who love you and can support you."

The mention of his name makes me wince. I try to cover it but the look on Noble's face makes it clear he's seen it. Nadine keeps talking about coming home without skipping a beat. She trails off as she glares at the top of my head in horror. For a moment I actually think she's speechless, but she sits down, looks me straight in the eyes, and says, "Now, let's talk about your hair. *What* is going on? You do realize people can still *see* you?"

"Nadine, ease up." Noble looks at me with an unspoken apology. Perhaps now he will help me escape.

"What? It's my business to make sure people look good in this town, and, Charlotte, there's no better revenge than being hot. Did you hear I opened my own salon? Here's my card." She hands me a chartreuse business card with SALON NADINE scrolled across the center. "Call and I'll get you in. I'll do you myself so you don't have to worry about anyone asking a lot of questions."

"I don't kn—" I try to get out, but Nadine's standing up to leave.

"It was great seeing you. Call me later and we'll get you fixed up. Oh, and you need to eat something. You look like a cancer patient."

The bell rings and I look up to see the number five light up.

~ 10 ~

Forgiveness

Back in the saddle, trying this church thing again, I think as I look for my wallet to confirm I have some money for the collection. I finish blowing my hair dry and put on eye makeup and lip gloss. I'm determined to look nonsuicidal at church today. Nadine calling me a cancer patient, while difficult to hear, did have an impact on me. My parents would insist I dress my best at church. My mother thought I should dress my best every day, no matter where I am, but there was absolutely no excuse for not "putting your best foot forward in the house of the Lord." So here's me, putting my best foot forward. *God help me.*

I half listen to the church announcements as I read the bulletin. Butch comes in and, again, sits in a pew diagonally behind me. I show no sign of recognition. It may be in my head, but every person in the church is watching my reaction to his arrival. Pastor Johnson takes his place at the pulpit and asks us all to prepare ourselves for worship. The lady next to me sits quietly with her Bible in her lap, listening to the organ play. What's she doing to prepare herself? I figure it's probably like yoga and I try to breathe calmly as I look through my third eye. I'll bet I look weird sitting here with my eyes closed. I open them and look at the lady again. This time I'm annoyed.

Is it normal to feel this self-conscious in church? Shouldn't this be more natural? *Sweatin' like a whore in church* comes to mind and I smile a little. I'm pretty sure this isn't the preparation Pastor Johnson has in mind.

We pray together for the forgiveness of our sins and Pastor Johnson asks us to silently confess. Why do I keep coming here?

Dear God, please forgive me. As I mentioned before, I've wished death on Jason, and Stephanie, and their baby. That's actually not me repeating myself. I did it again this week. Every day this week. I hate them all. I think of ways to hurt them. I have detailed daydreams about him being caught in a fire, or trapped in a sinking ship, or crushed in a car accident, or shot during a bank robbery, or worse. I'm wretched. I've also spoken disrespectfully to Butch, who's not only my elder, but also a veteran. Although he totally deserves it. Oops, forgive me for that one, too. I think that's it.

Oh wait…I also saw a little bird minutes before it was murdered by a cat and did nothing to help it. I don't know why I didn't help it. It's haunted me ever since. Please forgive me, Lord, and I hope the little blue bird's enjoying his time with you.

"Hear the good news, believe it, bet your life on it, in Jesus Christ's name you are forgiven," Pastor Johnson absolves us. And we sing.

I take a deep breath and exhale. Pastor Johnson's sermon

focuses on forgiveness this week. Not exactly my favorite topic. If I forgive Jason and Stephanie, how will I defend myself for killing them? Sure, he has some excellent points. Forgiveness is a gift for myself more than for my fellow man. Holding on to animosity and anger allows the devil to have a place in my heart. And the most compelling: If God is to forgive me, I must be able to forgive those who trespass against me...*trespass or fuck some whore when they should be at Rutgers with me*...I look at my Bible as if I'm studying the Scripture.

Pastor Johnson asks, "Do you think it's God's will to use your tongue to curse others?"

I think I'm not quite where Pastor Johnson needs me to be. I'm okay with it, though. It'll give me something to confess next week. *God help me.*

* * *

A long week of early rises for 7:30 a.m. teleconferences with Bruce has left me craving my bed this morning. Which makes me wonder: If it's Saturday and it's 8:30 a.m., why is someone ringing my doorbell? I yank myself out of bed, and through the dining room curtain, I see Noble's truck in my driveway. The doorbell rings again and I stumble to the front door.

He's like sunshine penetrating the storm door. "You up?"

"No," I say.

Noble ignores my taunting. "I'm playing hooky today and I want you to come with me."

"Where are you going?" I ask, already knowing I'm going to say no.

"The shore."

The shore. There's not another destination on Earth I would consider.

"Come in while I grab a few things."

How is it he gets me to do these things? First the Wagon Wheel and now a shore outing. I pull a tote out of my closet and throw in a towel and underwear. I brush my teeth and slip on a bathing suit and dress. I search all over my house for sunscreen, as Noble patiently waits in my foyer. I know I had it Labor Day weekend.

"Do you have sunblock?" I ask.

"I have some SPF fifteen in the truck, but you might want something stronger."

I raise my eyebrows, questioning.

"We're going out on the water."

I pull my hands to my chest in a praying motion. "A boat?"

"Kind of. Don't expect too much."

"No problem," I say with signs of delight creeping across my face.

I climb into Noble's truck and find a brown bag with a chocolate glazed donut, my favorite, on the seat. "You remembered," I say, peering into the bag. It's a small gesture in the scheme of things, but it's Noble being noble the way he used to be...before everything happened.

"I've only been out to breakfast with you at least a hundred times," he says, lessening the significance.

* * *

It is a glorious morning. The most perfect blue sky, dotted with clouds you could spend the entire day identifying by shape. We ride east with the truck windows down and my elbow resting on the door.

"How's work?" he asks.

"Uh, it's okay," I answer, taking a huge bite of my donut and getting glaze on my chin.

"That good, huh?"

"Well, the job is good. But I'm going to Saratoga Springs with my boss next week and I think he might want to have sex with me."

Noble's face hardens. "Interesting. He might want to? Are you going to do it?"

"Probably. It's just about time for management to start allocating yearly bonuses," I manage, keeping a straight face until Noble starts laughing. The sound of it pulls me back to my house at Rutgers, and the back of his pickup truck in high school, and the eighth-grade dance, and our fourth-grade class trip to the Franklin Institute. It seeps into me and fills some of the emptiness I've been clinging to.

"Seriously, what're you going to do? Do you want me to come with you and pose as your boyfriend?"

"Not yet. I'm thinking about just telling him the truth," I say, settling down.

"Which is?"

"That I just ended a relationship and I'm not ready to start a new one." I sigh. "That I don't have sex with married men and that I'm in general not interested in him." I say all this as if it's a great plan and will obviously work.

"Okay, where are we going and what time do you need me at your house?" Noble offers again.

"What? It'll be fine." Of course it'll be fine. Bruce is my boss; that's it.

"You're going to tell your boss that he's ugly and an adulterer after he hits on you. It's not going to be fine," he says. Noble's analysis does make Bruce seem less of a boss and more of a jilted suitor.

"Oh. I'll keep working on Plan B." I study the sky. Noble always gives great advice. He took care of me. There's a cloud shaped like a sword next to one that resembles a flower.

Noble pulls into a parking spot on Fifty-Eighth Street in Ocean City. I run to the bathroom and when I come out, Noble's inflating a boat with a pump hooked to the truck's cigarette lighter. I'm elated at the sight of it. I stand still and acknowledge joy—she so rarely visits anymore—and run back to the truck.

"It's awesome," I say, and I can't hide my excitement.

Noble's pleased with himself. I grab my bag and we load our minuscule pile of belongings into the boat along with two empty milk gallons tied to ropes and paddles. We carry the boat out to the beach. I take off my dress and use Noble's sunblock. Noble helps me with my back without me asking him to and I return the favor.

I overpour the sunscreen and end up with a pool of white on his shoulders. I spread it all over his back and massage it in as Noble patiently waits. I work across each shoulder and down his biceps, losing myself to the contours of his arms. I've known him my entire life, but never touched him like this. I realize I've slowed and pick up the pace, forcing my eyes to the ocean in front of us. When the sunscreen's finally disappeared, I step back, a little unsure of what just happened.

The beach is deserted, except for a fisherman a block north. Most day-trippers are probably up by the boardwalk. There are only a few left; it'll be October next week.

"Put your valuables in here." He hands me a large Ziploc bag.

"Are you planning on sinking?" I ask, and Noble looks at me, amused, as I place my money, cell phone, and keys into the bag. We leave our towels and clothes on the beach and stuff the Ziploc bag into a compartment in our boat. We carry our boat out past the breakers, fighting to get it over the few large waves we encounter. Noble tells me to jump in. I do before it gets too deep and Noble gives us one final push out to sea before climbing in himself. The water is still warm. It's a dark gray, like steel against the flirty blue sky. We paddle a little farther out to make sure we won't catch a wave.

"Does this look like a good place to drop our anchors?" Noble asks.

"It's perfect," I say, tilting my face to the warm sun.

Noble fills a milk jug with salt water, caps it, and hands it to me to drop it on my side and tie it to the handle of the boat.

"Leave enough give in case a big wave comes," he says as he ties the other jug to his side. Noble and I are facing each other. I lie down and prop my ankles up on the edge of the boat behind him.

"What do you think we should name her?" he asks, and I can't think of a thing except how happy I feel in it.

"I can't think of anything. It's too beautiful out here."

A flock of geese honk as they fly by, heading south. They're probably trying to figure out what direction to go since it's still seventy-eight degrees here.

"I know what you mean," he says, and I shade my eyes to see him in the bright sunshine. Noble is looking at me in a way he never has before. More than just a friend.

"How about we call her *Mindless*?" I suggest, smiling at

Noble. He lies back, too; we're floating feet to head. I rest my head again and let the sun warm my face, and the sounds of the waves lapping against *Mindless* heal my mind. I'm glad I came.

"I've missed you, Noble," I say without opening my eyes.

"I figured you had. I mean, it's been obvious the way you keep calling me." His tone is curt, absent of his usual playfulness.

"Are you mad at me?" I ask, sitting up a little.

"Charlotte, I saw you almost every day for the last four years at Rutgers, and every day before that for our entire lives. Then something horrible happens to you and you change your phone number and refuse to answer your freaking door." He pauses and looks out to sea. "I was worried about you. Really worried." His tortured face confirms it.

I sit up completely now.

"I'm so sorry, Noble. I just didn't want to put you in the middle...and I don't want him to know I'm home. I couldn't ask you to lie." I feel myself getting hot and I hope I don't start crying. I splash myself with a handful of water from over the side of the boat.

"He knows you're home."

The water in my hand falls to my leg as I absently watch my fingers open. The horizon catches my eye and something about it reminds me to breathe. *He knows you're home.* Noble sits up, his eyes forcing mine to look at him, but he doesn't say a word. A thousand questions run in and out of my mind, but I never take my eyes off Noble, too afraid of what releasing him will allow me to do. He's disgusted by the situation. Probably because I'm such a coward for hiding from Jason.

"How do you know that?"

"He called me two weeks ago. He said Ralph Tighe saw you

in church. He wanted to know if I could keep an eye on you for him." He pauses and I try to remember if I saw Ralph Tighe. "I told him I'd love to, but you won't take my calls or see me." Noble turns away from me and looks at the horizon.

"Did he say anything else about church?" I don't want to keep talking about this with Noble, but I need to know if Jason knows I've seen Butch.

"Like what?" Noble asks, trying to figure out what I'm getting at.

"Nothing." I let it go and lie back down. "Noble." He turns from the horizon and looks down at me. "I'm sorry. You're one of my favorite people in the entire world. I shouldn't have cut you off. I was terrified. Can you forgive me?"

Noble looks as if he wants to ask me something else, but relents. "You are forgiven," he says, and he flashes me a smile that confirms it. "You know how you can make it up to me?"

"How?" I ask, thankful for a happier subject.

"Give me your new cell phone number so I don't have to keep knocking on your door to talk to you."

I consider the request. I've only given it to Sean, Margo, and Jenn from Salem County, and Violet, Sydney, and Julia from Rutgers. Noble's another step, a step toward a normal life again. "I'll give it to you on one condition." Noble eyes me. "You have to save it in your contacts under an alias." It's a ridiculous precaution, but Jason's been relentless in trying to get a hold of me, and I *can't* talk to him.

"An alias." He nods in agreement. "No problem. I'll save it under 'Mindless.'" We both laugh until the boat rocks. Everything's always so easy with Noble. This is what I need now. Easy…peace…Noble.

I lie back and remember Jason's and my only trip to the

shore. He wore cutoff jeans and I asked him before we left if he wanted swim trunks. He scoffed at the suggestion. As soon as we dropped our things on the beach, we headed right into the water. It was crowded and Jason was having trouble keeping his hands to himself. I suggested we sunbathe for a while, but his shorts were driving him crazy, and he kept touching me, which was driving me crazy in all the right ways. We ended up having sex in my mom's Camry back by the bay. Only Jason and I could screw up a day at the shore. We were home in time for a late lunch. We really are from two different worlds.

~ 11 ~

High-Minded

When Noble first asked if I was going to the Rutgers homecoming game, I said no.

I said no to Julia, to Violet, to Sydney, and three more times to Noble.

It wasn't until Noble "happened" to mention it to Sean that Sean convinced me to go. I know I'm exhausting him, probably Michelle, too. He's been so worried. He told me it might do me good to get out of Salem County, and I figured the least I could do is leave town and give him a break. Noble was kind enough to offer to drive, which will give me about ninety miles to bitch at him about bothering Sean.

I watch Noble hop out of a Jeep at exactly 7:30 a.m. properly attired in his alumni garb. Smiling, this boy is always smiling. Red Rutgers shirt, long camo cargo shorts, and a Phillies cap. He's more like a surfer than a farmer. His skin is sun-kissed from the harvest and his hair is wavy and perfectly too long.

His smile broadens as I come out the garage door. It's easy to understand the appeal of Noble.

"Where's your truck?" I ask, walking to the Jeep.

"I decided to bring the Jeep today."

"Good choice."

"It's going to be windy. Do you want the top on?"

"No!" I practically yell at him as I grab an old cowboy hat out of the garage. "I love Jeeps. My father had one for a while."

"I remember," he says, and it floors me how often I associate Noble with Rutgers and forget the lifetime I spent with him in Salem County before we went there. The passage of time continues to confound me.

"What's this?" I ask, picking up the brown bag before plopping onto the passenger seat. I open it and the aroma of bananas forces my eyes shut as I take a deep breath. "Mmm."

"Banana bread. My sister Jackie brought it over yesterday."

I unwrap the bread and hand a slice to Noble.

He shakes his head. "You eat it." The generosity in his words is hidden by the worry in his eyes. "You're fading away on me."

You have no idea, Noble.

He cranks the stereo and I close my eyes and rock my head to the music while I devour both slices of banana bread. By the time we get to the turnpike, my shoes are off and my feet are resting on the dash. The last of the warm October sun is already starting to beat down on us. I open my eyes and Noble's looking at me. A normal person would quickly look away but Noble just keeps watching me—smiling, of course.

"It's good to see you happy."

"Is that what this is? It's been so long." How long? August, September, October—three months. I remember I have sunscreen and get my bag. I diligently apply the lotion to my arms, legs, and face, even though it's mostly covered by my hat.

"Sunscreen?" I ask, holding it up as if I'm handing out samples at Costco.

"Uhhh, sure," he says, trying to figure out how to apply it and drive at the same time. He holds out his arm and I massage the lotion using both hands, being careful not to miss a spot. As I knead the lotion, I conjure up the images of him shirtless I've filed away from our Rutgers days. The only things better than his arms are his shoulders. I warm inside and look from his shoulders to his neck, to his eyes, which are again focused on me. No smile this time. The look on his face moves me, but I don't understand in what way. I drop my hands but not my eyes and try to steady my breathing.

"You should keep your eyes on the road," I manage.

"Would you mind putting some of that sunscreen on my thighs?"

I look at his long shorts; even seated they hang almost to his knees. I put the sunscreen back in my bag, ignoring my naughty Noble.

We travel the rest of the way listening to Noble's eclectic playlist, which includes some of my favorites, many of which I forgot even existed. And he's right, I'm happy. What other things have I forgotten? Surely I was happy before Jason. Before my parents left me. The mileposts pass quickly and I'm disappointed when we come to our exit. Today is different from my trips here the past two years. Returning to Rutgers every time since my parents died was heart-wrenching, another separation from Jason.

I wanted to finish for my parents' sake, but it was a complete barrier to being with him. He didn't go to school here, and categorically did not fit in here, so even when he did stay longer, the time was strained. He and his cowboy boots were as close to an alien as North Jersey had ever seen. I don't think any of my friends knew what to make of him.

This trip is easy with Noble. He belongs at Rutgers, probably more than I do.

"Where are you staying?" he asks, breaking my reverie.

The sound of his voice returns the smile to my face. "Julia and I are sharing a room at the Hyatt. You?"

"I'm crashing at Harry's. That's the benefit of having friends on the five- and six-year programs. What's your plan for today?" he asks, seemingly as a courtesy. The football field and all of the homecoming tailgate parties are in Piscataway, interspersed within thirteen color-coded parking lots, making the need for a plan essential and the odds of running into someone by chance impossible.

"Well, we're going to meet Violet at Olde Queens Tavern at nine." According to the clock in the Jeep, it's going to have to be a fast check-in.

Noble notices my time check and offers, "Why don't you run and check in and I'll drop you guys off at Queens on my way to Harry's? Where are you going after that?"

"Heading to the field. We hope to get over there by eleven. I think we're meeting other people in the Blue Lot. What's your deal?"

"Don't know. I'm going to Harry's and I'll probably have to wake those guys up. Eventually we'll make it to the field. We're going to try and meet up with Buzz, Bowl, and Hammer."

"Are they with Wheels, Donger, and Slu?" I laugh, remembering all the nicknames. I love those boys from Brigantine.

"Probably...and Rob and Tony...and the rest of the

Bartlett Street boys. If I don't see you again, call me when you get up in the morning."

"Perfect."

"Don't lose your cell phone," he warns.

"I'll try." Many cell phones will be lost this weekend. Cell phones, shoes, girlfriends, boyfriends, freedom, pride, etc. Rutgers Homecoming is not for the weak.

The front desk informs me Julia has already checked in and she's upstairs. I find her spraying her hair and toss my bag on the bed.

"Charlotte! How are you?" she asks. Julia knows I don't like a big hug-and-kiss hello and I love her for remembering. "Sorry about the king-size bed. They were out of doubles."

"I don't care if you don't. Noble's waiting downstairs to give us a ride to Queens."

"That's awesome! Let's go," she says, and starts walking out the door. I grab my phone, ID, money, and ChapStick, and put them in the pocket of my hoodie.

Julia gives Noble a big hug-and-kiss hello and I hop in the back of the Jeep to let Julia avoid the wind. I gaze at Noble in the rearview mirror. I wish he was staying with us; my favorite memories of Rutgers include him.

"Oh. Before I forget, take this." Julia pulls out a room key from her pocket. "Just in case we get separated."

"Oh God, please don't leave me," I say, and Noble looks at me, concerned. In my limited forethought about this weekend, I never included the possibility of being alone, or at least without Julia or Noble. I want Noble to turn around and take me back to the hotel.

"I won't, but you should have a key," Julia says, calming me.

"Can I have the one in the envelope with our room number

on it? I'll never remember it." I can only see Noble's eyes in the mirror but he is, yet again, laughing at me. Julia hands it over and I lean forward to slide it into my back pocket.

Violet is yelling our names before we even stop the car. Noble double-parks to get out and collect all his hugs and kisses. He charmed all of my friends our first weekend at Rutgers, and they've loved him ever since. Noble and his roommates would come over when the campus was quiet, and we'd start a party at our house. Julia was the only person brave enough to mention that the girls were disappointed when Jason came to visit because we didn't hang out with Noble as much.

Violet smothers me with a big hug and a bright red kiss on the cheek, which will probably be there all day. She also knows I hate hugs and kisses hello but forces both on me and I love her for it, too. It's as if she refuses to give up on me. Noble pulls away as we walk into Queens just as the line at the front door begins to form.

Beers, bagels, pictures, kisses—it all flows fast and we're hopping in Violet's boyfriend's SUV to get to the stadium. We park in the Purple Lot and begin unloading the coolers. On the way to the Blue Lot I run into Tom and Falvey, Shappy, Doug, Rob, and Sonal. I hadn't even realized I missed them but am elated at the sight of them. Julia's done a thorough job of spreading the word that Jason and I have broken up and that I don't want to talk about it because no one asks a thing about my love life. I picture her tiny self, walking five feet ahead of me threatening people, and her protection brings another smile to my face. Noble was right; I needed to come. I'll have to remember to tell him.

* * *

We make it into the stadium but never to our seats. Within minutes, Julia and Violet disappear into the crowd of ZTA sorority sisters

"Charlotte! I've been looking for you everywhere." Sydney walks up and forgets she's yelling at me as she appraises Noble's friend Rob, who's standing next to me. "Julia thought you went back to the car. I'm glad I found you before I went all the way out there."

I embrace Sydney out of habit and happily step back as she begins chatting with Rob. Sydney and I waitressed together while we were at Rutgers. She's never met a person she didn't like or had a conversation she wasn't interested in. Sydney has a network with everyone or will have one by the end of the day. She's definitely a connector.

"Charlotte, I'm so glad I found you," Sydney says, and literally pulls me back into the conversation.

"Why didn't you call me?" I ask. She's one of only seven people who have my cell phone number. She might as well use it.

"Charlotte, I did. I called like five times."

I check my phone and there are three texts and five missed calls. I linger over the screen, disappointed there are none from Noble. "I just saw Nick at the Rail. Farming agrees with him," she says, practically purring.

Rutgers scores and shoots the cannon, and about six of us head out to the Blue Lot. I text Julia and Violet to let them know I'm heading back to the parking lot and hope they're already there. As I exit the gate, Sydney jumps in front of me. "Hold up. What are we doing for our birthday next month? I was thinking a girls' trip is in order."

I stop walking, stunned. I'd forgotten my birthday, our birthday. Sydney and I were born on the same day. My mom gave me a childhood of birthdays as special as any national holiday. It was fitting that I found Sydney at Rutgers. She's the perfect person to carry on the celebrations. The last two years I would have been satisfied with just Jason, but Sydney will *always* make sure our "big day" is properly recognized.

"I don't know," I say, unable to even consider a celebration.

"We'll talk more next week. We have to get on it," she says, and hugs me.

* * *

Before I can sink too deeply into that thought, the sky opens up and unleashes a driving rain. We scatter and I don't even know where I'm running. I hear Rob and Julia yelling my name from a small brown hatchback, and I squeeze into the back with Julia. Rob and a guy I've met a few times but whose name I can't recollect are up front. The four of us are soaking wet. My cutoffs are sticking to me and I'm not sure if my shirt is see-through. I suspect it is since I notice Rob surveying my chest in the rearview mirror.

"Holy shit! It's really coming down," Rob says.

Most people are still running, trying to find shelter. Some have succumbed to the black sky and are dancing in the rain. I watch them splashing in the new puddles and twirling arm in arm until the rain drives harder and I can't decipher a thing outside the car.

"Hey, Charlotte, reach behind the seat and check if you see a towel."

I do and also find his overnight bag and a brush. Handing

him the towel, I raise the brush and ask him if he minds. From the Jeep, to a day at the field, to the soaking rain, I'm not sure if a brush will ever go through my hair again. I untie it and begin the torturous process.

"Wow, Charlotte, your hair has gotten long. Looks good," Rob says, and Julia raises her eyebrows, out of sight of the guys.

"Yo, Tony, light up."

Aah, Tony. That's right.

Tony pulls out a plastic bag and a one-hitter and takes a long hit. He hands it to Rob, who passes it to me as he turns on the radio and music fills the car.

"Oh yeah," Julia sings, and Rob turns the volume up and the music engulfs us. I nod my head as the drums hypnotize me and belt out the chorus.

"I am a great singer," I say, completely serious.

Julia laughs hysterically. The one-hitter is passed, and passed again, and the rain continues, and I'm still profoundly happy I came to Homecoming. I can't comprehend not being happy right now.

I tap the beat with my left foot and try to tap every other with my right. When I think I've mastered it, I bob my head in sync with my right foot. "I'm also a musical genius," I half yell, and Julia doubles over laughing. Something about this song forces you to move your entire body.

I try closing one eye at a time to check my single vision. It must be fine because the examination quickly loses my interest and I focus on watching the raindrops streak down my window. We quiet down and realize Rob's phone is ringing, which we all find hilarious. He turns the radio down and fumbles with the phone, finally getting it to his ear.

"Hello," he manages, half chuckling.

It makes me think we're the definition of chuckleheads and I laugh out loud.

"Oh hey, yeah, that's Charlotte. She, Julia, Tony, and I are stuck in my car in this downpour. Where are you guys?" Rob pauses and Tony offers him another hit. He takes it and I imagine the caller can easily discern his activity. "Oh shit, you never made it over. No worries. Seriously, man, there are a ton of people but most are headed back to the bars anyway." Another pause and Julia makes a funny face, and I think I might pee my pants I'm laughing so hard.

"I think I have to go to the bathroom," I whisper to Julia.

"I think I'm going to hook up with Tony," she whispers back. We both giggle. I should be high every day. This is awesome.

"All right. We'll meet you guys at Queens. I don't know how long it's going to take to get out of here."

Rob pulls his seat up so I can climb out into the rain, which has now steadied to a pour. As he's shutting the door, I hear him say, "That was Sinclair," and I make a run for the porta-potties. There's some brighter sky over the Raritan River. We have another hour until sunset but the temperature will drop fast this time of year. By the time I get back to the car, the rain's only a drizzle and they're again passing the one-hitter. What's one more...?

* * *

Queens is packed. Rob surveys the bar but can't find anyone. Sydney texts that she's partying at the Rail with some new friends. It's crowded and I can barely move. I'm grateful Rob has cornered me; he forms a jersey wall around me, preventing people from stepping on me.

"This crowd is killing my buzz," Rob yells to Julia and me. Tony is about five feet away, trapped in a serious conversation with some girl. "Let's get out of here." Rob goes to collect him, and Julia asks if I'm into Rob.

"He's okay in that 'nice but on steroids' kind of way." Julia knows exactly what I mean. "I'm not hooking up with him if that's what you're asking."

We peel ourselves out of the bar and walk toward Rob and Tony's house. More beers, more smoking, more music, more laughing. After thirteen hours, it's starting to hit me. By the looks of Rob, it has coldcocked him. He's dozing off and I try to figure out how to get back to the hotel. I can crash here, but Rob's asleep on the couch. If I get in his bed, he'll follow me for sure. I try to think straight and get lost in the music.

I close my eyes and don't bother to open them when the door opens. "Charlotte."

I turn my head to the side and see the most tormented face on Noble Sinclair I've ever seen. Noble should never look this way. He's my happy Noble, my happiness. I close my eyes again.

"Charlotte," he says, this time louder and in my ear. His breath is hot on my neck and I want him to lie down with me.

"Noble?" The music is deafening. "Oh, Noble, I'm so glad you're here." Noble makes everything better. I start to fall asleep again.

"Charlotte, let's get out of here."

The last thing I remember is Noble picking me up, and me wrapping my arms around his neck and resting my face on his shoulder. His wonderful shoulder.

* * *

My head hurts and I try to force out the pain with a hand pressing on each side. Jason is rubbing my back and saying, "I'm sorry. I never meant to hurt you. It just happened. We fell in love." I release my head from my hands and look up to see him. My beautiful Jason with his arm around Stephanie and they're holding a baby that is blue and lifeless. Stephanie is crying and I scream.

I wake up as every muscle in my body tenses. I inhale deeply and realize I'm draped over someone.

"Are you okay?" Noble asks as he raises his head.

"Oh, Noble. Thank goodness it's you." I close my eyes to keep from crying and rest my head back on his chest.

"Were you expecting Rob?"

"Rob? No." There's a dull ache near my hairline that throbs behind my eyes. I can't remember the end of my night.

"What time is it?" Noble sits up. He steadies me with his arm, still balancing me on top of him as he rises. "It's nine twenty."

I look down and realize I'm wearing the pajamas I brought.

"Did we—" I interrupt my own question, trying to compile the fragments that are floating around in my head.

"No." He's amused. "When I make love to you, you'll remember every minute of it," he adds more seriously.

How the hell is it that I wake up and start talking to Noble about making love? Seriously, is life not confusing enough? Noble's completely comfortable. He's naked, talking about sex. I never sit around naked and talk about sex with Julia.

I ignore his promise and stand up as the pain stabs behind my eyes.

"How did I get changed?"

"You did it. I offered to help, but you insisted on doing it yourself." *Oh, thank God.* "In front of me."

I turn purple as I reach up to touch my bare breast under my shirt. My hand darts down in search of my absent underwear beneath my shorts.

"And you were right, I love the mermaid tail. I can't believe you never showed me before," he says, and leans down to kiss my forehead as he heads to the bathroom. He's completely naked. My mouth is hanging open and I'm gasping for air. He's beautiful. Noble has slept in my bed dozens of times at Rutgers, but never naked. Just friends; we were best friends. Never…ever…naked. My heart races. I am such an idiot. I can just imagine me showing Noble my tattoo as if it's a greeting card my grandmom sent.

I jump as the sound of my ringing cell phone startles me.

"Hello," I say, still trying to see Noble in the bathroom.

"Charlotte, it's me." Julia's voice is raspy.

I finally stop trying to cop a look. "Hey, Julia."

"Where are you?" she whispers.

"What's wrong with your voice?" I ask.

"I don't know. Listen, have you talked to Violet?" She sounds so serious, I'm frightened.

"No, why? What happened? Is she all right?"

"She's engaged."

Ka-boom.

There it is—love, joy, and marriage.

"Charlotte, I'm sorry. Blake proposed last night on the steps of Kirkpatrick Chapel. She's probably going to announce it at breakfast and I wanted to give you a heads-up so—"

"So I don't make a scene or burst into tears, or is that the scene you're talking about?"

Noble walks out of the bathroom and dives onto the bed. I turn toward the window, seeking some privacy.

"Where is she?"

"They stayed at Blake's parents' last night but I think she's going to text everyone about breakfast at Le Peep."

"What do you think I should do?" I glance back and Noble is watching me intently.

"I don't know. I'm sure she's worried about you, but she's also on cloud nine. It won't be easy."

"Okay. Let me think about this." I go over to the bed and Nestea Plunge onto it. "Thanks for calling. Where are you?"

"We'll talk later." She dismisses me, and the subject of Tony.

"All right. Bye."

I press end and turn toward Naughty Noble. He's lying under the covers, leaning up on one elbow.

"What's up?" he asks as he slides me back to lie next to him.

"Violet and Blake got engaged last night." I absently play with my hair as I try to sort out my feelings.

"How do you feel about that?" he asks.

"I feel like everyone who hears Violet and Blake got engaged last night is going to ask how Charlotte's handling it. And that makes me crazy."

"Er," he says, and I look up at him, confused.

"Crazi*er*," he restates, enunciating for meaning.

I can't help but laugh at him. "Yes, of course. It makes me crazi*er*." Noble stays deadpan, which makes me laugh even harder.

"She's going to text us to go to breakfast and make the big announcement." I sigh.

"Good timing. I'm hungry."

"Well, this is mainly about when you're eating, so that's

good," I say as he absently plays with my hair. As if we're on a long bus ride to a faraway field trip in middle school. But he's still naked. I try not to let it affect me.

"It'll be hard, but not impossible," he says gently.

"I know. And fifteen years from now I don't want to think I ruined her day, but I just want to go home," I selfishly admit.

"I'll help you. In fact, if you want, I'll help you shower," he says with a corrupt grin.

For a second I forget about the wedding announcement.

My phone dings with a text from Violet:

CAN YOU GUYS DO BREAKFAST TODAY?
LE PEEP AT 10:30? WOULD LOVE TO
SEE YOU! :)

I hate the happy face, or is it happy faces? Oh wait, I remember, I hate myself. I show the phone to Noble and bite my lip, contemplating.

"Ask them to pick us up," he says.

It's a wise idea. Let her tell me first, away from the crowd.

"You're a genius," I say, and text back. I immediately receive:

WE'LL BE THERE IN TWENTY. LOVE YOU.

I take a deep breath and head to the shower. Noble grabs my wrist and pulls me back onto the bed. I look up at my admirable friend. "You can do this. You're a good friend."

"I was just thinking the same thing about you." I give him a tiny smile because he deserves it more than I do and head to the bathroom.

* * *

Jason and I had been to only one wedding together and it was one of my favorite nights with him. I loved when we dressed up, but Jason was always more comfortable in jeans. Unlike formals at Rutgers where Jason never fit in, the wedding was in South Jersey. It was my cousin Sandy's wedding and my family was enchanted by his rodeo and ranching stories. The reception was in the parish center across the street from the church. We left a little early, unable to keep our hands off each other, and I climbed on top of him in the parking lot. When we got home that night, Jason made me promise I'd marry him someday, that we'd be together forever.

I stop crying and sniff as I hear the bathroom door open.

"Hey, I was thinking maybe I could be clean for breakfast, too."

I turn the water off and reach out of the curtain for a towel. I wrap myself up and step out to Noble's waiting grin.

"I think we'd all appreciate that," I say as I slide past him, leaving him alone in the bathroom.

* * *

"Are you ready?" he asks as I finish brushing my hair. I pick up my hoodie and it has something red dried all over it. I scrape it.

"Candle wax?" I say as I examine it more closely.

"Here, wear this," Noble says as he throws me his hoodie. I put it on and zipper it to my neck. It's warm and comfortable, exactly like its owner.

"Now I'm ready." I take a deep breath and let it out.

Noble grabs my hand and we start to walk out of our hotel room. Holding his hand makes me uncomfortable. Jason wouldn't approve; Noble was always a sore subject. Even though I hate Jason, it's a line I'm not ready to cross. I pull it back.

"You know, it's okay for us to hold hands. We've done it a hundred times before." He pushes the elevator button.

"It feels different now," I protest.

"That's okay, too."

I raise my eyes and meet his gaze, but I can't deal with Noble possibilities knowing Violet is sitting in a car downstairs, engaged.

~ 12 ~

The Bash

Sydney is a laser beam fixed on November eleventh. She is not letting the idea of a celebration go, not letting me hide from our "special day." She's called almost every day since Homecoming with options, none of which were appealing. Our birthday falling on a Wednesday this year is absolutely no deterrent to her. She moves the celebration to Saturday night and includes the threat of a surprise party if I try to cancel. The pre-party is at Julia's and my apartment in New York City before meeting the usual suspects at a club downtown. I asked Noble if Julia invited him to make sure I showed up, but he reminded me he's celebrated Sydney's and my birthday the last four years. He called himself an honorary member of 108 Hamilton Street, our off-campus house at Rutgers.

Noble and I take the train since I've amassed enough Amtrak miles to go anywhere for free. Noble lets me board first and I select two seats together facing the same way the train's traveling. Noble and I each have a backpack and a parka, but we easily have enough room in our double. He puts the armrest up between us, making the seats seem even cozier.

"Are you excited about your birthday?" he asks.

"More like apprehensive. You know how these things end up. It's like a birthday celebration on crack since it's Sydney and me. Sydney alone would be enough."

He truly does know. Last year we almost got into a brawl when Sydney dismounted from her bar-top dance into the arms of a guy whose girlfriend was standing next to him. The girl was so unimpressed she dumped her drink on Sydney while she was still in his arms. It all went downhill from there. In Sydney's defense he did take his time putting her down.

"I'm sure everyone will be on their best behavior." Noble half laughs as he says it, knowing there's a slim chance. "I have something for you," he says.

"Ah, man. Seriously? Please tell me it's not a present."

"It is. It's a birthday present and you're going to graciously open it and thank me for it."

He pulls out a large, soft package from his backpack. It's wrapped in newspaper, the Sunday comics. I study him holding the present. How can Noble be so utterly adorable and still single?

"Open," he orders.

"Okay, okay." I unwrap the comics, and inside is a Rutgers hoodie matching my favorite one I ruined at Homecoming.

"I know candle wax is hard to get out," he offers.

"How do you know that?" I ask him accusingly. I hug the hoodie before dropping it in my lap to hug Noble. "I love it. Thank you." My lips brush his neck and I almost kiss him. He's kindhearted; surely my lips know that, too. I tilt my head to nuzzle in closer and remember it's Noble. And this can't happen.

I don't pull away and Noble says, "You're very welcome."

* * *

The party has already started when we arrive and the girls are clearly ready for a celebration. Noble and I stash our bags in my room and go out to the living room for a drink before we get ready. As we catch up with the crowd, Violet and Blake arrive and the guys decide to give us all some time alone and head to the bar early. Julia and I begin peppering Violet with questions about the upcoming engagement party and what she'll have us wear in the wedding. Sydney quickly bores of the entire topic.

"Charlotte, are you finally going to put Nick out of his misery and have sex with him?" Sydney asks. Only Sydney can ask questions like this, in her matter-of-fact way, and make it sound like an inquiry about the weather.

"No, I'm not. Why don't you have sex with him?" I retort.

"I'm going to if I can get him to take his eyes off you for a minute."

I smile, but my chest tightens at the thought of Sydney and Noble together. One night would be tolerable, but if they start dating I'll be lost. It's a mix of jealousy and need that makes me sick. I don't want Noble. He's only a replacement for Jason. But without Jason in the picture, things are suddenly complicated with Noble. I don't want to lose him. He'll start dating someone soon, though. I'm not going to keep him around with my sparkling personality, especially considering how sweet I've been the past few months. I put the whole notion aside. For all I know, Noble is already dating someone at home. They probably celebrated her birthday yesterday. It's not like I've asked him.

Eventually, the boys call Violet's cell, looking for us. We swallow the last of our drinks as we hurriedly finish getting ready. I change into the off-white, short sweater dress from my backpack but keep my cowboy boots on. The dress has a scoop neck and long sleeves and might be a tad boring if not for the fact that it's just this side of see-through. If Jason were here, this dress would surely not be. We hail a cab and pull up in front of the bar where a long line has already formed out front. Sydney tells security it's both our birthdays, and after checking our IDs, they send us to the front and tell the bouncer at the door not to charge us. Sydney explains our big day to the hostess, who takes us to the VIP section. So much for a low-key night. Violet texts Blake and the guys waste no time meeting us at our table. We order vodka, rum, and Jack Daniel's from the bottle service menu, and everyone is poured a double shot of vodka to officially begin the birthday celebration.

"To Sydney and Charlotte, two of the greatest friends a girl, or boy, could ask for. Happy birthday, ladies," Julia toasts us.

I throw the shot right over my shoulder and smile as the others finish theirs. It's going to be a long night; best not to start it with shots.

I mix my first drink and see Sydney and Noble talking. If they keep this up, I'm going to need a shot. Noble looks up and sees me staring. I smile, hoping it conveys permission. I've depended on him so much lately, but I don't want to get in the way of him being happy. And I love Sydney. Hopefully I still will after tonight.

I turn away and walk to the railing above the dance floor.

The DJ is playing a crazy mix of house music and hip-hop, and it's impossible to stand still. The dance floor is filling already even though it's barely eleven o'clock.

"Care to dance?"

I'm not even sure where he came from, but he looks good. I glance over his shoulder and see Sydney laughing at something Noble's said. He's charming the pants off her. According to Sydney, that won't take much effort. According to Noble, that's common.

"Sure," I say, and allow this guy to lead me onto the dance floor. He not only looks good, but he's also a decent dancer. Violet and Julia join us and they begin to house my new friend. I'll bet he had no idea we come as a threesome. They twirl him around and sandwich him. They are unruly but hilarious. I let Julia know I'm going for a refill and make my way upstairs again. Sydney and Noble are missing, so my timing is perfect. I mix a Jack and Coke, heavy on the Jack. I'm already tired of the hoopla. Violet's bachelorette party will be easier. She's much better equipped to be the center of attention. I pick up my purse and grab my phone. There are two texts on the screen.

IN CASE YOU ARE WONDERING, I
AM NOT INTERESTED IN HOOKING
UP WITH SYDNEY.

And then…

I WOULD APPRECIATE IT IF YOU
RETURNED THE FAVOR REGARDING YOUR
NEW FRIEND.

Relief flows through me. Why? He should be with Sydney, or someone else. What are we doing? I text back without thinking:

You should hook up with Sydney.

You are both aces with me.

I hope he argues with me. I disgust myself. Noble is one of my best friends. He's going to fall in love with someone. Someone else. Why is this all of a sudden a problem? This is what desperation and loneliness have done to me. I am selfish. I retreat to the dance floor. It's wall-to-wall people now; everyone is bumping and grinding together. The Jack is starting to sink in and I raise my hands above my head, moving to the hypnotic beat. As I'm shaking my rump, someone comes up behind me and puts a hand on each hip, moving in unison with me. I take my time turning around. I may as well enjoy it before I beat the poor guy off me.

When I do turn, Noble pulls me in close and moves his hands to my backside. Startled, I start to back up and he draws my arms to his neck, the entire time moving to the music. Noble's blue eyes entrance me as I let one hand drop to his chest, his broad, perfectly taut chest, and the other moves through his hair at the bottom of his head. The sensation of touching Noble is confusing me. The music dulls to a single throbbing drum and the lights pulse in harmony, and I twirl his hair around my fingers with the motion of a slow gear. My breathing slows and I'm not sure it hasn't stopped when he leans down and says, "Happy birthday, Charlotte," in my ear.

I tilt my head in response, my body telling Noble things I'll never say. I'm hot and confused and lost in his arms. There's no doubt in my mind that I want Noble right now. I pull back and the satisfaction on Noble's face tells me there's no doubt in his mind what I want either.

This cannot happen.

I pull away from him, searching for some distance. He lets me go, wisely sensing my determination. "I'm going to get another drink." I motion behind me toward our table.

"Okay," he says, but he still looks like he's won a silent debate.

I try to organize my thoughts as I make my way through the crowd. What am I doing with Noble? More important, what the hell is he doing with me? To me? We're going to have to have some kind of talk and I'm still emotionally drained from August. I've settled in nicely to my role as a selfish taker, but it's no fun doing it to Noble.

Sydney and Julia come back to the table and I sit down between them, insulating myself from any further male contact. They both proceed to crack me up telling me about work, dating in Manhattan, and their ideas for Violet's bachelorette party, my favorite of which is a trip where we all get tattoos. We double over laughing when we realize we took that trip last year on spring break.

Across the room I see Renee from my office talking to a guy in his late twenties. I get her attention with a little wave and she beelines it toward me.

"What the holy fuck are you doing here?"

Holy fuck...really? Is nothing sacred?

"I'm celebrating my birthday."

"Without Renee?" she asks, stomping her foot. "I'm more fucking fun than a mute hooker at the Super Bowl."

What does that even mean?

"I'm here with my college friends. One of my roommates and I have the same birthday. Come say hi. Julia's here."

"Oh, don't stress. I still fucking love you, you dumb whore. I'm charming this dumbass, though. I have to get back." Renee gives me a hug and my face is again engulfed in her signature boob sandwich.

The girls and I go dance some more, and I don't see Noble again for at least an hour. I start to think he's left, but he resurfaces at the other end of the bar. He's on his way toward me right as something hits me hard and I fly off the dance floor. I slide a few feet and stop dead, a piercing pain hitting the side of my head. I look up and I'm somehow under a high-top table on the side of the dance floor. The heavy wooden stool that I just hit my head on falls over and covers my legs. I grab my head and curl up in a ball. Two girls I don't know are standing above me saying something, but I can't hear them above the music. People are running and pushing, and my head feels like it's cut. I keep touching it, looking for blood. Sydney comes into focus above me. Noble is by my side, lifting me to my feet.

"Charlotte, are you okay?" He's searching my face as I glance from side to side, trying to absorb the chaos. Noble's pushed from behind as enormous bouncers try to tear guys off one another. My hands land on his chest, instinctively shielding myself, and he takes a step back but still holds me with his eyes.

Two bouncers are pulling someone out by the neck, dragging his feet behind him toward an emergency exit, and I swallow hard as the crowd disperses from their path. My head is still throbbing and in my peripheral vision I see people everywhere around Noble. I can hear them yelling and a sharp bang in the distance as more furniture is overturned, but I stay safely under Noble's gaze.

"I want to go home," I say without allowing thoughts to invade our isolation.

"Don't let go of my hand," Noble says in my good ear, and grabs my hand tightly in his. He leads us through the crowd, glancing back every few steps to check on me. When we get to the lobby of the club and can finally walk next to each other, Noble puts his arm around my waist and we walk out the front door. He hails a cab and we're on our way home. I grab my head; the pain is still there, as if a knife is stuck in the side of it.

"What happened?" I manage.

"Let me see your head." He leans forward and gently moves my hand. My fingers are stained red. We both see it, but Noble stays calm. "Can you take us to the nearest hospital?" he asks the driver.

The cabdriver looks at us in the rearview mirror and nods, satisfied I'm not going to die or expel anything in his car.

"I don't want to go to the hospital. I think the bleeding's stopped," I say, and add to the driver, "Norfolk and Delancey, please."

"Charlotte, you have a head injury. You're going to the hospital."

"Can we just go home first? We'll take a look at it in the light and if it's bad I'll go without any arguments. I promise!" I plead with him. "It's my birthday."

My phone dings but I have no idea where it is. Noble hands me my little gold bag. It's Julia:

WHERE ARE YOU GUYS? R U ALRIGHT?
BLAKE SAID HE SAW YOU GET WIPED OUT
WHEN THE FIGHT BROKE OUT.

I'm fine. Hit my head on something.
Noble is taking me home.

I'LL BET HE IS. WE'RE GOING TO
BERNARD'S ON 47TH IF YOU WANT
TO COME BY AFTER.

After what? I'm done for the night.

:)

When we get to the apartment, Noble leads me straight to the bathroom, where he says the light is better. He puts the toilet lid down and motions for me to sit on it. I do as I'm told, still on my best behavior to avoid the hospital. He tilts my head so my injured side is facing the light and begins to gently push the hair away from the cut. Based on the throbbing pain in my head, I hit the stool right behind my ear. I guess I'm lucky my ear wasn't torn off.

Since he's looking toward the back of my head, my view of him is all biceps and shoulders. *Yum.* He smells of the slightest bit of fresh cologne and deodorant. I close my eyes and take a deep breath to drink him in, no longer paying attention to his inspection.

"I don't know, Charlotte. It's hard to see. Your hair has blood in it and it's matted to your head," he says, sounding worried.

"You are incredibly gentle," I say with my eyes still closed. When I open them, he's gazing at me, puzzled. "What? You are. Gentle and patient."

"I can be patient, especially if it's something I really want," he says, and his eyes grow darker. His hands feel warm cupping my face and I know I shouldn't, but I can't stop looking into his eyes. They're filled with concern, or some other emotion between love and hate I haven't felt in a while. "Charlotte, we have to wet your hair so I can see what this cut looks like."

Anything to not go to the hospital. "Okay."

"It's going to hurt."

"Yes." *I'm into pain these days.*

Noble leads me out to the kitchen where the sink is bigger. He runs the water to a comfortable temperature and gives me the all-clear motion. I bend over, and with great care, he leads my head under the faucet. It's a slicing pain, like a giant paper cut every time the water runs along it. I close my eyes tightly and push my thumbnail into my finger to not move or cry.

"I'm almost done," he says. Noble sounds as if he's in pain, too. "Don't move for a minute. I'll be right back."

Noble gets his phone and tilts my head toward the light and takes a picture. He hands the phone to me. It shows a long red cut about two inches in length right at my hairline. It's still juicy but is not actively bleeding.

"See? It's fine," I say.

"It's not fine."

"The bleeding has stopped and heads bleed a lot." I'm feeling confident now. I straighten up and feel a little dizzy. I grab the counter so Noble won't see me falter. "Really. I feel fine."

"Fine like, I may fall over fine? Because I see you swaying," he says. "Let me see your eyes." Noble pulls me directly under the kitchen light and I open my eyes wide in exaggeration. He towers over me and looks down into my eyes, one hand on each side of my face. I warm all over under his stare and my breathing quickens. The sound of it is deafening. His face is only a few inches away. My eyes drop to his lips and without permission my body rises up and kisses them.

Delicately, lips touching lips, without asking a question or seeking an answer. I've abandoned all meaningful thought.

I open my eyes and search for answers from Noble. His eyes never leave mine.

My skin burns under my clothes. Hungry this time, I reach up and wrap my arms around his neck and kiss him hard. I force him back to the wall without my tongue ever leaving his mouth. I can't get enough, my starvation feasting on him. I'm pushing myself against him and pulling him down to me at the same time. I may devour him.

This will kill Jason.

You are a selfish bitch.

I step back, my fingers to my lips, which are still burning for his. I'm four feet away facing a stunned Noble and after everything that has happened tonight, now I'm on the verge of tears.

"I'm sorry," I manage.

"You should be," he says, "for stopping." He's trying to catch his breath, too, as if we've just had a brawl.

"I'm so sorry," I say, shaking my head. "Being with you feels like I'm cheating on you, on our friendship." I'm out of breath and not making any sense. "And him." That part I'm sure Noble gets because I detect some signs of anger. "Something is impossibly right, even though I know it's completely wrong."

Stop talking, Charlotte.

"It's clear you don't know a thing," Noble says, and walks out of the room. I lower my head and close my eyes, my fingers still touching my lips to keep them from registering the absence of his.

What have I done?

* * *

When I get to my room, Noble's lying in my bed under the covers. It's mortally dark and I wait a moment for my eyes to adjust to the sliver of light coming through the window. I climb into bed next to him. "I'm glad you're here," I say, and consider playing the birthday card, but I already hate myself enough without manipulating him, too.

"I want to make sure you don't start vomiting or have a seizure in the middle of the night," he says as he rolls toward me.

Forgetting about my cut, I roll over, too, and prop my head up on my hand. I yelp in pain and sit up to protect my head.

"I think we should go to the ER," he says.

"I know you do, but it's just a flesh wound, I'm sure. Do you have any idea what a Saturday night in a Manhattan ER is like? This isn't Salem County," I murmur, returning my head to my pillow. We lie on our backs—not touching, not talking. "Noble, do you hate me?"

"Not yet," he says. He's probably getting the hint that if this ever gets started, it can only end badly.

"Thank you," I say.

He doesn't speak another word the rest of the night.

~ 13 ~

Let Us Give Thanks

I'm not in the mood to deal with Butch today, especially to talk about Thanksgiving, but I prefer it to dealing with Jason on Thanksgiving. I use my new key to enter Butch's house. It's good he's not the type to sit around in his underwear. The aroma of garlic and peppers penetrates the door before I get the last lock opened.

"It smells amazing in here," I say as I inhale deeply.

"Marie," Butch says, motioning toward a Crock-Pot on the counter.

"Wow! On a Sunday? She's good to you."

"She's coming over for dinner," Butch says nonchalantly.

"Really?" I say, not letting him off that easy.

Butch rolls his eyes at me. He really is mellowing.

"Are you and Marie going to hang out on Thanksgiving?" I ask, thankful for the opening.

"We might," he says gruffly, tiring of this conversation already.

"Do you think anyone else might be joining you for dinner?"

Butch looks as if his patience is completely gone, but when I give him a timid smile, he relents.

"Yes, I might have some family coming to town for the holiday."

I take a deep breath, thankful for his understanding.

"I see."

"They're coming in on Wednesday and supposed to stay until Sunday morning."

They're. Does that mean two people are coming?

"Good information. Thanks, and enjoy your dinner," I say, and leave without another word.

* * *

I'm thankful to have Violet's house to hide at for Thanksgiving. Her parents' magnificent home is decorated floor to ceiling with handsome furnishings and designer holiday decorations. No one seemed to notice I arrived Wednesday afternoon for her Saturday-night engagement party. I, myself, am one more decoration. I knew Jason was home and I wasn't interested in giving thanks anywhere near him. He has much more to be thankful for than I do.

Looking at myself in the mirror, in my dress that's hanging off me, I wish I had bought something new when Violet and I went shopping yesterday. The dress she finally settled on for tonight's festivities is a deep red, floor-length sheath that she's pairing with sky-high patent leather peep toes. She's going to be gorgeous, especially after today's day of beauty. All the bridesmaids are meeting for a full day at the salon.

My dress is a black and white geometric print dress. I wore it to my office holiday party last year. It hugged every curve on me and was slightly low cut but still perfect for a work party. Today it's like I borrowed it from my pudgy older sister. No matter how I stand, it can't seem to capture the *va-va-voom*. The last eight pounds I've yet to gain back from this summer still elude me, even though I've been trying to eat more. It seems crazy to try to gain weight, but I'm tired of people looking at me like I might be contagious.

I switch back into jeans just as I hear the doorbell ring.

"Charlotte, Julia's here," Violet calls from downstairs.

I still can't believe Violet's getting married. I walk downstairs and Julia hugs me hello but lets me slide on the kissing. She's holding a dress bag covering some appropriate frock and I am again pissed I didn't try on my dress ahead of time and buy something new. In my defense, I didn't realize this was going to be such an extravagant affair until the tent company pulled up this morning and started assembling the heated tent, including a dance floor that faces the lake behind her parents' house. Maybe I can run out today.

"We have mani-pedis in an hour and makeup and blow-outs after lunch," I hear Violet explaining to Julia, and I'm pretty sure Violet will kill me if I mention I have to run to the mall. Although there's a chance she'll kill me when she sees my dress, too. It's quite a conundrum.

"Julia, let me see your dress," I say, hoping to find an ill-fitting, nun-worthy frock.

"It's actually the dress I wore to my cousin Lorraine's wedding in Vermont last year."

I start to frown as she lifts the bag on an awesome mocha-colored jersey dress that's going to be beautiful on her. "I thought it would be perfect once Violet described her vision for the engagement party," she adds, and I start to think Julia secretly hates me.

"When did she describe her vision? Was there some sort of e-mail newsletter I missed?" I ask sourly. "Or maybe a flyer?"

"What? You have something other than jeans, right?" Julia asks with fear in her eyes.

Violet turns from watching the construction through the window and refocuses on our conversation.

"Julia, that's gorgeous!"

I scrunch up my top lip behind Violet and Julia again looks scared.

"Do you know what Sydney's wearing?" I ask.

"I think she's wearing black pants," Julia offers.

"What?" Violet yelps. "Sydney's wearing pants to my engagement party?"

"I think she's pairing them with a sparkly sweater of some kind. You know Sydney. It'll be over the top." Violet seems soothed. I feel sick.

"Violet, is Noble coming?"

Violet's face flashes her patented enormous grin.

"Yes, he is—why? Are you thinking about him?" she asks in a teasing tone.

I can't roll my eyes far enough back in my head. Over the last two weeks I've avoided Noble, not able to address kissing him on my birthday. I'm going to stick with avoiding. It's my new modus operandi. I mentally go through each dress in my closet. There's never been a dress in any closet that can keep up with Violet's red one. The only slim possibility I can remember is the dress I bought for the spring formal my junior year. Jason couldn't come up, so I didn't go. It still has the tags on it.

"Violet, do you have boob tape?" I ask.

"Of course. What are you wearing?" she says, smiling. "Or do you just want to tape something to your boob?" Julia and Violet both laugh.

"Do you remember the dress I bought for my junior formal?"

"You didn't go to the spring formal," Julia says disapprovingly, still pissed at Jason for causing me to miss it, or more likely still pissed at me for missing it.

"I know, but I bought that long black dress. Remember the one with the dramatically plunging neckline," I say, adding air quotes.

"Oh yeah, that would be great," Julia offers.

"Not too much?" I ask.

"No. It's long, and simple except for the neckline. It'll be perfect."

The dress is a plain black jersey wrap dress. I'm sure I can make it fit. The wrap forms a V-neck that comes almost to my belly button. The only hitch is it requires perfect posture the entire night.

I dread texting Noble. I've been successfully avoiding him since my birthday, and asking for a favor is going to put me in a vulnerable position.

**Hey. R u coming to Violet
and Blake's engagement party?**

ARE YOU ASKING ME TO BE YOUR DATE?

I sigh. I knew this wasn't going to be easy.

**Actually I'm asking you for
a favor. Can you stop at my
house and pick up something for me?**

It feels like ten minutes pass before he responds.

SURE

Thank you! It's in my closet.
It's a dress. Hanging on a
hanger with a pink plastic bag
over it. It should be a black
floor length dress.

HOW DO I GET IN?

Use the key under the turtle
rock by the back door. What
time are you coming to the party?

IT STARTS AT 7, RIGHT?

Yeah. I kind of need you here
before then…

I'LL SEE WHAT I CAN DO.

That definitely could have been worse.

The day flies by, filled with beauty treatments and nonstop talking. No wonder the guys always leave us; we never really shut up. Julia and I head to the bar after opting out of the blow-outs. Violet and Sydney happily stay behind to finish their beautifications.

Violet gives us both a stern look as she warns, "Do not get drunk before the party."

"Yes, Mother. We wouldn't dare," we promise as we both kiss her cheeks simultaneously.

"You're lucky my makeup isn't done yet," she says, and Julia pulls her hair.

* * *

Julia and I settle onto our barstools and order our first martini as I hear my text ding.

WHERE ARE YOU?
PJ's Pub
ON RT 38?
Yes
OK. I'LL BE THERE IN 5.
ORDER ME A BEER. YOU OWE ME.

I'll gladly pay up with a beer. I smile because I always smile when it has to do with Noble. "Noble will be here in a few minutes."

"What?" Julia says.

"He's bringing me the dress."

Julia and I sip our drinks in silence, watching the TVs above us and savoring the last few minutes of peace we'll have today.

"You know he searched through your underwear drawer while he was at your house."

"No, he didn't," I say, shaking my head and signaling the bartender that we need another round and to add Noble's beer to the order.

"I would have," Julia says.

"If you want to rummage through my underwear you can. Just ask," I say, and Julia starts laughing so hard her drink comes out her nose, which makes us laugh even harder.

"Hey, you two crack-ups! This is a serious day," Noble says as he walks in with my dress. Apparently he received the informational e-mail from Violet because he's wearing an impeccably tailored suit. Julia waves to him as she runs off to the bathroom with a napkin covering her nose. Noble sits down just as the bartender sets a beer down in front of him.

"Impressive," he says, smiling at the beer, the bartender, and me.

"Thank you. I owe you one," I say, and inspect the dress.

"Is it the right one?"

"It is. Violet would have my hide if I wore the dress I brought with me. This engagement party is Mac Daddy."

"I gathered that when the invitation was nicer than any wedding invitation I've ever seen."

I stare into my drink, trying to remember if I ever received an invitation. Did Violet just tell me about the party, or did I never open the invitation? Noble's watch catches my eye and I follow it right up to his shoulder. He's wearing a charcoal suit with a deep blue tie and his shoulders look amazing in it. Every inch of him looks amazing.

"You—"

"Sorry about that. Hi, Nick," Julia interrupts me, complimenting Noble as she hugs him a proper hello.

"Hey, Julia."

Noble gives her an easy hug and I realize after four years of hanging out, Julia and Noble have become friends.

They proceed to catch up, switching easily from work, to the weather, to pop culture, and eventually settle on my birthday. We missed the debrief since Noble was still pissed at me for the night before and neither of us felt like eating breakfast. At the time I knew they all thought we hooked up and I couldn't face them, especially with Noble.

I look up and Julia and Noble are both staring at me, concerned. I brighten to a practiced smile. "What? I'm fine. Just wondering how many people are coming tonight."

"Two hundred and seventy," Julia answers, and both Noble and I drop our mouths open.

"What?" is all I can muster. Thank God Noble brought me this dress.

Noble checks his watch and finishes his beer. "Well, my gorgeous lady friends, as much as I could, and would, sit here with you all night, I have to meet some guys up the road for some pre-party partying."

I'm jealous as Noble stands up and bear-hugs Julia. I could use a pre-party before this formal engagement party with Violet and Blake, and 270 of their closest friends and family. I shake my head, still unable to fully consider the number.

"Thanks again," I say as Noble gives me a much gentler hug.

"It was my pleasure. It gave me a chance to rummage through your drawers," Noble says with his signature naughty smile. I punch him in the arm rather than say you're welcome. "And I love the idea of you owing me one."

I watch Noble walk out of the restaurant and across the parking lot.

"Stop staring at Nick's ass," Julia says. I just keep looking, though. "Seriously, why don't you just go out with him, or have sex with him, or something?"

"I'm trying to protect him. I need him to still like me and if we have sex he'll end up hating me," I admit as I request the check from the bartender.

"Are you that bad in bed?" Julia asks, and we both lose it.

* * *

Julia and I sneak down to Violet's patio, which offers a view into the tent, and, unbelievably, 270 people have gathered in Moorestown on the Saturday of Thanksgiving weekend to congratulate Violet and Blake on their engagement. *Wow.*

Julia pulls my elbow and I follow her up the back stairs to Violet's room. We're due downstairs in ten minutes for some introductions with the groomsmen. We know Danny well, Blake's roommate at Rutgers. There's also his brother Carson and some guy named Trey who was Blake's best friend in high school. I'm hoping Trey is tall. Julia, Sydney, and Violet all hover at or below five-five, and Blake, his brother, and Danny all hit at about five-ten. I could use a six-footer or I'm going to be the giraffe in front of 270 people.

Violet's day of beauty paid off. "You look so pretty, Violet," I say, and give her an air hug, careful not to dent her in any way.

"Thanks, Charlotte. And thank you for being here." Her words are filled with sympathy.

"I wouldn't miss it for the world."

Violet leads us down to the formal living room where Blake says all the right things about Violet's stunning look, and we're all properly introduced. There's a strange feeling of camaraderie, as if we're about to experience something that'll be difficult to explain to anyone outside of this small circle.

"Charlotte O'Brien, this is Trey Taylor, Blake's very best friend from high school," Violet says as she introduces me to the only guy I don't know in the room. "You guys'll be walking together tonight and in the wedding," she adds, and I couldn't be more pleased.

Trey is a whopping six-one or six-two, with black hair and dark eyes. He's quite handsome and surprisingly appealing. Unfortunately, I no longer have the will to explore. Lucky for him.

"Blake told me he had a present for me, but he was unusually secretive. Now I see why. This is my lucky day," Trey says as he shamelessly appraises me.

I blush and try to think of something in response. Suddenly

the deep plunging neckline is a little too revealing, even if the rest of the dress is long and boring.

"Where do you live, Trey?" I ask.

"I'm in the city. You?"

"I'm in the country," I say. Salem County is definitely the country. "Julia lives in the city."

"Really? You should come up and we can all get together." Trey leans into me, letting Violet's mother pass to his right. When she clears us, he's still touching my side.

"I actually work for a company at Fifty-Sixth and Madison."

"That's crazy. I'm at Fifty-Eighth and Madison. Do you come to the city often?" he asks excitedly.

"Recently, I've been coming up about once a week, but I'm technically a virtual employee."

"Nice!" he says, impressed with my setup.

Julia comes over and I introduce her to Trey just as Violet's mom tells us to line up for our announcements. *Announcements?* For the first time I'm actually glad Violet is going to mandate our dresses for the wedding. At least I won't screw it up. Trey and I dutifully line up and I actually appreciate him looping my arm around his and covering the top of my hand with his own. If he's not completely full of shit, it seems as if he's going to make sure we skate through this. Julia and Danny go first, and the crowd applauds their entrance as if they're celebrities.

Trey squeezes my hand. "All you have to do is smile."

"Right. Smile…no problem." I flash my best smile as the lead singer of the eight-piece band announces us and we step into the spotlight. Trey is a pro and leads me gracefully past the crowd to our spot next to Julia. It's very dark in the tent, providing a dramatic backdrop for the spotlight on the bridal party. Sydney and Carson come in and, finally, the happy couple. We take our spots on the dance floor for the first dance. Trey is a great dancer, and so far the perfect groomsman.

"Have you ever been to an engagement party of this magnitude?" I ask him.

"Has there ever been one of this magnitude? I'm going to ask Blake if we can have a joint bachelor/bachelorette party on an island somewhere," Trey says, and spins me unexpectedly.

"Wouldn't that ruin some of the fun?"

"Not at all. I'd love to go away with you," he says with an air of total confidence.

I get the feeling that Trey usually gets whichever girl he fancies. I wonder if Blake has told him I'm a psychopath. Surely he has; Blake is half girl when it comes to communication.

The song ends and Trey leads me to our table, his hand on the small of my back. It feels all wrong. Jason would rip his arm off for touching me there, for touching me at all. It's the first time I've thought of him all day. Although it would be difficult to navigate Trey with Jason here, I still miss him. Does he even know Violet's getting married?

The food, the lights, and the music all begin to pull me in and I'm actually enjoying myself. After dinner I stop by Noble's table. Sitting with him are three couples and three single girls I know from our sorority. I'm sure he's in his glory. From what I can see, he's having his usual impact on the girls.

Trey pulls me onto the dance floor for one more dance, but I'm not interested in tangoing with him. As soon as a fast song comes on, I make an excuse to get some air. The tent has French doors that lead onto the back patio, which has been decorated with portable trees ensconced in thousands of white lights. There are heaters every few feet and the side closest to the tent has become a smoking section.

I make my way through the cloud and move toward the back wall. Has this all been constructed for the party or is this a permanent wall? Did the workers put it up with the tent? I try to move it with my hands. Violet's engagement party's beginning to hamper my identification of reality. I lean on the wall and envision it toppling over, sending all 270 guests outside to see who ruined the elaborate props.

I inhale, the cool air finding my nostrils despite the heaters. It smells like snow. I tilt my head toward the sky, but the patio is so well lit I can barely make out a star. I miss the endless sky of Oklahoma.

"Are you hiding out here?" Noble's voice is soft and mischievous from behind me.

"Apparently not very well," I say without turning around.

Noble comes and leans on the wall next to me. He gazes up in the same direction I am.

"Are you enjoying yourself?" he asks, still quiet.

"I am." I turn and study Noble's enamoring profile. His jaw is square and strong and anchors his face, which would seem large except it's sitting on top of his incredible shoulders. "How about you? Have you selected a ZTA yet?" Noble quiets as if he has a secret he's about to divulge. "I wanted to tell you earlier that you—"

"Charlotte, there you are," Trey interrupts as he walks up to Noble and me.

I turn toward him, forgetting I was about to tell Noble how handsome he looks tonight.

"Hi, Trey," I say. "This is Nick Sinclair; he went to Rutgers with us." I turn toward Noble, who has a smug grin on his face.

"Noble, this is Trey. He's Blake's friend from high school."

"I thought you said his name was Nick?" Trey warmly shakes Noble's hand.

"It is Nick. Charlotte calls me Noble." He doesn't bother to explain further.

"Well, nice to meet you either way," Trey says. "Charlotte, a few of us were about to take a walk on the side yard if you want to get some air." Trey makes the sign for a joint.

"You know what…I'm good. Thanks for thinking of me, though."

"No problem. I haven't been able to stop thinking of you." Trey admires me as if Noble isn't with us. "Well…don't take too long." He walks away and yells over his shoulder to Noble, "Again, nice meeting you."

I turn back to the wall and close my eyes as I take in the snow-heavy air. It's peaceful out here. *Aah…peace.* I remember I wanted to compliment Noble and turn to tell him, but he's watching me.

"What?" I ask.

"Why is it you have no problem wrapping Trey around your little finger, but you won't let me in at all?" Noble's face turns serious.

"Come on, Noble," I say, trying to make light of it.

"No, I need to know," Noble says, threatening our delicate peace. "Two weeks ago YOU kissed ME, and you've avoided me every day since. What the hell, Charlotte?"

Oh, Noble. Why tonight? Why now? It's so nice out here. As if in argument, I shiver unexpectedly.

"Come here," Noble says as he opens his arms wide and beckons me into his jacket with him. I accept, hoping it will change the subject…and because he looks so good.

"You know, the reason you're cold is because you're missing the front piece of your dress," he says, and I laugh as I put my arms around his back and rest my face on his solid chest. He surrenders and puts his arms around me, which automatically causes me to close my eyes. He smells of beer and soap, and I find myself tilting my head toward his neck as if some magnet is forcing me to nuzzle there.

"I'm still waiting for an answer, Charlotte. I don't understand. Do I not appeal to you?" *Not with all this talking.*

After a long sigh, I lean back and look Noble in the eye. "With Trey, or people like Trey, I'm instituting a 'swim at your own risk' approach. If someone finds my wretched self attractive"—I put both hands to my chest, forgetting it's bare in the middle—"and they've been made aware of the dangers, it's their responsibility to make their own decisions." I pause and Noble's even more annoyed than he was before I started the ocean reference. "You, though, my beautiful friend, are far too precious to swim without a lifeguard. I would never be reckless with you."

Noble pulls me close and kisses me. I freeze for a brief moment and give in to the warmth spreading through me. I cross my wrists behind Noble's neck and lean into him, enjoying his lips for the second time. It's becoming less and less possible to deny him, especially if he's going to look this good. Over the band, I hear tires squeal and I expect the crash sound effect to play, befitting the situation. Noble's lips graze my neck and my ear. His breath steals my doubts and he whispers, "I'm a big boy, you know." *Oh, I know.* "You can let your guard down."

I return my head to Noble's wonderful shoulder. This is crazy. I'm not starting a relationship with Noble Sinclair!

"Noble."

"Yes?"

"I want to be your friend."

"You are my friend." The snowflakes come down in a mass flurry from the start, a thousand with the first one.

"No, I want to be your incredibly dear friend. I want to date someone I don't like half as much as you."

Noble pulls back so he can see my face and I try to remain as serious as possible.

"I am thankful to have you in my life. Never more so than the past few months. I need you in a hundred different ways, but I can't keep sneaking kisses from you. It's a waste of time for both of us."

Snowflakes continue to fall on us and Noble continues to study me, probably trying to figure out why he's out here in the first place. Then, just as surprisingly as before, he kisses me. And again, I kiss him back. He's not throwing it out there or testing the waters. Noble claims me with his lips, denying every rationale I've clung to. I should be his forever.

I really do hate myself.

"You're not listening," I say, returning my face to its home right between his neck and shoulder.

"Perceptive," he says, nodding.

"Sorry to interrupt you guys," Julia says, sounding like someone just died. "Jason was just here."

~ 14 ~

Lost Dog

My stomach clenches and I bend over slightly, in pain. *Jason was just here.* I grab my stomach, hoping to thwart the vomit. Tears fill my eyes in preparation for an all-out emotional and physical breakdown. Noble's arms around me are a cage I can't escape. I have to get out of here.

"Jesus, Charlotte, are you okay?"

"This is why you should stay away," I manage, before running into the house and up the stairs to Violet's room. I thank God for the timing as I throw up at the exact moment I lean over her toilet. Julia is holding my hair back before I know she's there.

When I finish, I rinse out my mouth with water and glare at myself in the mirror. Bloodshot eyes and a blotchy face streaked with black slithers of makeup running down remind me of the last two weeks in August. Julia watches me begin the repairs as she silently sits on the edge of the bathtub.

"Tell me," I demand, my words barely audible. I see the pity on her face in the mirror and it doesn't move me.

"Security found him watching through the side of the tent. He was sitting on the lawn smoking a cigarette when they approached him." I keep working, unable to face her. "He said he wanted to see you, but they told him no one gets in without an invitation. They argued and Blake went out there. Jason demanded to know who was touching you. Blake wasn't about to give Trey up. They argued and Jason was escorted out."

"Does Violet know?" I ask, scared I've ruined her night.

"No." Julia's quiet for a moment. "Blake said Jason was drunk."

"Good. Maybe he'll die in a car accident," I say flatly. "But it's never the drunk who dies," I add, disappointed.

Julia stares at me, horrified. *Oh, did I not introduce you to the new Charlotte? She's sweet.*

I take a deep breath and try to think of something to say that will make Julia stop looking at me that way. "I've become too secure at home. I'm sure he's been in town, and he knows I'm there, but he hasn't come to my house. It never occurred to me he would come up here. Damn Facebook," I say, and start to cry again. "Do you think it's okay if I just go to bed?"

"Definitely," she says too quickly, probably relieved I'm not going back to the party. I'm sure the Charlotte she's consorting with in the bathroom doesn't belong at an engagement party. "I'll tell Violet you aren't feeling well."

I change my clothes and climb onto the air mattress I've been camping on for the last few nights.

My phone dings with a text from Noble:

I NEED TO KNOW YOU'RE OK

I'm ok

BTW, I meant to tell you...

you looked really good tonight.

I don't know why but this makes me cry. I turn off my phone and roll over, sobbing alone in the dark.

* * *

"Charlotte... Charlotte..."

Why is Julia waking me up? Why is she shaking my arm?

"What?" I say without opening my eyes.

"Your brother's on my cell phone for you."

"Sean?"

"Yes, Sean. Now wake up. I'm assuming it's important since he never calls me," Julia says as she pokes me with her phone.

"Hello?" I say.

"Hey, it's your brother. I just wanted to make sure you weren't home. Mrs. Heitter just called me. Someone broke into the house."

I sit straight up in bed.

"Mom and Dad's house?" *My house?*

"Yes. I'm driving there now. I guess she could see the front door was broken when she drove by."

"I'm on my way," I say as I get up and search for my bag. I've been here so long my things are all over the place.

"Don't rush home. I just wanted to make sure you're okay. I'll handle things down here. Oh, and I need some of your friends' phone numbers. I had to wake up Nick Sinclair to get Julia's."

"Did you tell Noble about the break-in?"

"Yes. Are you still keeping things from Sinclair?"

"No, no, not at all. I'll be home in forty-five minutes."

"All right."

* * *

I pull out of Violet's driveway and turn on my cell phone. As expected, it blows up with text and voice messages. All of them are from either Noble or Sean. I begin to listen to them, but they start with last night and I'm too selfish to think about how Noble felt when the mere proximity of Jason made me ill.

By the time I pull off the turnpike at Exit 2, I'm convinced it was Jason who was in the house. He must have been hoping I'd come back there or had assumed I would after I heard he'd been at the party.

Maybe I'm being stupid. Maybe it was just a burglar.

I pull into the driveway and Sean's truck is behind Noble's, both of which are blocked in by a state trooper's cruiser. As I approach the house, I see the trooper is fingerprinting the front door. There are two windowpanes broken out of the door and the side jamb is ripped clear off the wall inside, the chain lock still attached to it. Sean and Noble are lost in a deep conversation.

"Hi," I say for lack of knowing what to say.

"Charlotte." Noble walks over and hugs me tightly. I can't concentrate on Noble, though. The sight of the front door lures me. I leave Noble standing in the driveway and walk toward the house. The carnage left by the intruder is powerful, and angry, and reeks of Jason Leer. The trooper stops brushing the door and introduces himself as Trooper Hite.

"Would you mind taking a look around and letting me know if anything's missing?" he asks.

"No, I don't mind." I inspect the door, easily envisioning Jason kicking it in.

It's comforting to think it was Jason here. Why would he

break in, though? I walk around the back of the house and look in the rear flower bed. The rocks are all overturned, including the turtle rock with no key taped to it. It must have been hellishly frustrating to be here and not be able to get in.

I walk back around to the front of the house and slide past Trooper Hite. The house is exactly the way I left it. The living room's untouched. In fact, untouched since my mom died. I should update it. I move to the kitchen. I can't be sure, but I think some things have been moved at the desk. I rummage through the "important drawer" and my checkbook, passport, birth certificate, and car title are all there. Something's different, though.

I check the bathroom, laundry room, and family room. All are exactly the same as they were before the holiday. I touch the back of the recliner in the family room. *Did you sit here? You used to love to.* I can almost see him. I rub the back of the chair.

"Charlotte, are you all right?" Sean asks. He and Noble are both studying me.

"Yes, I'm fine." I nod to try to reassure them. Oddly, I feel better than fine. I feel exhilarated.

I make my way to my bedroom with both of them in tow. There's a piece of paper tacked to the wall where my headboard used to be. I realize now what was different in the kitchen. The tablet and pen I keep by the phone are missing. I walk over and untack the paper. **Nice bed** is written in handwriting that leaps off the page and chokes me. I turn it over quickly, hoping for more, but that's all it says.

"What's that?" Sean asks.

I fold the paper slowly, trying to seem nonchalant. "Just a note Jenn left when she was here," I say.

"I never noticed it before," Sean says, but lets it go. Noble, though, is still focused on me, not letting anything go. I open my jewelry box and it appears to be exactly how I left it. My emergency cash is still in my favorite purse in my closet.

"I don't think anything's missing," I say, and look at the spot where the note was left. "I mean, I don't think anything's been taken."

"It's possible the perpetrator was spooked by a passing car," the trooper offers. "I'm going to write this up, but there's not much to go on. The door has too many prints; it's impossible to determine a set specific to last night."

I nod, trying to listen but still surveying the room. *I know you were in here.* I go back to the closet and let my hand touch each hanging garment. *Did you do this last night? Did you remember any of the clothes?*

"Here's my card." Trooper Hite breaks my concentration.

I blush and hope no one notices. "Thanks."

Sean walks him out and I'm left with Noble regarding me sorrowfully. He knows it was Jason. He realized the note wasn't there the night before.

"It seems like a week ago we were on Violet's back patio," I say.

Noble's silence, the voice of abandonment, replaces my energy with guilt.

"Here's your key. I didn't have tape to replace it." Noble places the key in my hand and I just look at it. What would have happened if Noble had never come to the house, if the key had been under the turtle where it was supposed to be? Would Jason be lying in my bed right now? "Do you want to come to my house for a while?"

"No. I have some calls to make," I say as Sean returns.

"Noble, do you know anything about replacing doorjambs and windowpanes?" Sean asks.

"I was actually going to see if Clint can do it," I say as I walk to the kitchen to find his card.

"Clint East?" Sean asks.

"Yes, he has a construction business. If he can't, I'll have to employ you two," I say, and look back at Noble.

"No problem. I've got some things to take care of. If you can't get hold of Clint, or if he can't do it, call me," Noble says as he grabs his hat and keys.

Sean follows Noble out and I'm able to reach Clint. He promises to be over within the hour and thinks he can fix it. It's 11:30 a.m. on Sunday morning. Butch will be at church. I reach in my pocket for the note Jason left me. All these messages, literally hundreds of them, begging for my forgiveness, and he writes *nice bed*. He must have been completely crocked. Now that I'm alone, I can properly search through everything. In the first few weeks after we broke up, I destroyed every scrap of evidence that Jason existed. I'm sure seeing my room minus all mementos of him was unpleasant.

Good.

* * *

Twelve straight days of wondering what Jason did while he was in here and what I would have done to him if I'd found him have depleted my confidence. I sit on the floor folding towels, lost in the mindless chore. *What are we doing?* What am I doing, and why can't I just forgive him? I hang my head, and the familiar ache of missing him seeps into my bones.

My heart races before the idea of calling him is fully formed in my subconscious.

What would he say? What would I say?

What difference would it make?

I dial Margo's number instead.

"What's up, sista?" she answers.

"I'm dangerously close to making some unquestionably bad decisions." Margo is silent. "I'm folding towels, and all I want to do is call Jason."

"You know, you can call him." Margo's voice is gentle. She's always gentle with me.

"I should have called Jenn," I say.

"What happens if you forgive him?"

"Forgive him? I can barely hear his voice without vomiting. Let alone forgive him or trust him. In fact, I absolutely hate him…" My voice trails off and I begin to cry.

"Char, don't cry." This makes me cry harder. "Please don't cry. I know this hurts worse than the bee sting from a soda can." The reference to Jenn getting stung in fifth grade rescues me from the horror. "I don't know how this works…It's like cosmic energy or witchcraft."

What…the hell…is she talking about?

"But time is going to go by, and you're going to move on, and it's all going to get better." I take a deep breath to slow the tears. "Your life, your version of home and everyone in it, will begin a reconstruction phase, even though you're not in on the plans. You just have to trust it because I know it seems impossible right now."

"Right. It's cosmic," I say.

"It's divine," Margo says. I close my eyes and bow my head. "You'll be better soon, I promise."

I hang up with Margo as the back door opens. As soon as it unlatches, a dog comes barreling into the room. He jumps on me, spins around in the towels, and runs into the hallway. He's in and out of every bedroom before Sean has a chance to say, "Hey, it's your brother and some crazy-ass dog."

The dog comes back to say hello again and jumps up on me, paws on my shoulders. He's a beagle, at least for the most part, with large black spots covering his brown coat. His face is an adorable mix of brown, black, and white and his eyes are the sweetest things I've ever seen.

"Well hello there, little friend. What's your name?" I say as I start scratching his chest. The dog lifts his head to the sky in delight.

"Do you want a dog?" Sean asks, and I am in shock. "I was having breakfast with Johnny Half this morning and he said the dog just showed up at his back door. He'd heard someone hunting earlier. The Biegen twins stopped by and said he's their dog, but he's scared of gunshots. He runs off every time they shoot. Said he's useless to them."

"Useless, huh?" I say to the dog, and start to massage behind his ears. He leans into me with affection. "A hunting dog that hates guns. I can imagine you're not very popular." I give him a kiss on the head. "Especially when out looking for rabbits."

"He's been housed outside, so he's going to need some training."

"Are you poorly behaved?" I ask, now speaking in some crazy baby dog talk, and the dog tilts his head from one side to the other, listening. I look up at Sean, who's smiling at me and my new best friend. "He can stay." The dog jumps up on me again for a big hug. He's obviously intelligent.

"What shall we call you?" I ask my new little dog with the

kindest eyes I've ever seen. "Would you like to meet Butch?"

The dog wags his tail, excited to do anything but hunt I suppose. I dig through a drawer full of tape, ribbons, and bows and find a red-and-green-plaid ribbon to adorn his collar. "We definitely have to pick out a name for you." I tie the ribbon in a bow and take a picture of him. I text it to Margo and Jenn with the caption "My love."

* * *

I can barely keep the dog on the leash as I unlock the multiple dead bolts on Butch's doors. He's pulling, trying to get loose to chase all the smells around the farm. Seriously, what is so freaking valuable in here? By the time I get the last lock opened, the dog's weakened my arm and pulls the leash out of my hand, barreling past me into the house.

"What the—" is all I hear and I assume the two of them have met. "Why is this goddamned animal in my house?" Butch is yelling and sounds even crabbier than usual. "Annie!"

That one hurt. He rarely says my name, but the sound of Jason's voice yelling it wounds me. I grab the wall with one hand to steady myself. The dog runs out to me, unsure of his surroundings.

"Are you making sure I'm still here? I wouldn't leave you." I rub behind his ears and he looks at me full of love. "Let's go meet Butch. He's not as bad as he sounds."

I walk into the family room and Butch is sitting in his recliner with his feet up.

"Is your knee okay?" I ask, wondering why he doesn't sit up like he usually does.

"Knee ain't worth a damn," he grumbles. The dog stays by

my side. He's such a smart little guy. "Why did you bring that damn dog in here?"

"He's my dog," I say flatly.

"What the hell did you get a dog for?"

"Sean brought him over. He needs a good home...and I fell in love with him." The dog walks over to Butch, who glares at him. "I thought you might like to have him over once in a while. He's good company."

"Hell no! I don't want any damn dog hanging around."

"We'll see," I say.

"We'll see nothing. You leave him here and I'm going to call him shithead."

"That's so funny. I was going to name him BJ, for Butch Junior. Isn't it crazy how we're on the same page?" I say, making the eye-to-eye symbol with my hand.

"You're an imbecile," Butch growls.

"Come on, BJ, we need to go call Dr. Grubb and see if we can get Butch Senior an appointment." A pillow whizzes by my head. I pick it up and throw it back at him.

"You're a crazy old man!"

Both Butch and I laugh and BJ jumps up and down, joining the fun.

~ 15 ~

Company

The halls have been decked, God help me. Another Christmas without my parents. This will be my third without them and my first without Jason. I push the memories of last Christmas from my mind and cut the wrapping paper to the wrong size for the box in front of me. I cut a new piece, a do-over... I have five days to find some Christmas spirit. I'm hoping it's hidden in a bottle of wine. Noble knocks on the back door at the same time he opens it.

"Hello?"

"Come in," I yell, surprised at how excited I am to see him. Noble's dressed in navy overalls that cover several other layers that puff him up like the Michelin Man. He's like a child ready to go make snow angels in the drifts.

"I'm not interrupting, am I?"

I look around at the empty room. "No."

"I saw Clint's truck outside and..." His voice trails off as his eyes fall to the floor.

"And you thought we were in here making passionate love by the fireplace?" I can barely finish the sentence before bursting into laughter.

Clint comes into the room carrying two-by-fours, a pencil behind his ear, and a tape measure hooked to his belt. He gives Noble a big grin and shakes his hand excitedly. "Hey, Nick, how's it going?"

"Good, great. Yourself?"

"Pretty good. Keeping busy. I just started Charlotte's renovations, so that'll keep me working for a few weeks."

"A few weeks, huh?" *Is that jealousy?* "That's great."

Clint moves toward the door. "I'll see you tomorrow, Charlita. Later, Sinclair."

As Clint closes the door behind himself, Noble echoes, "Charlita?"

"Did you stop by for a reason or are you monitoring building permits in your spare time?"

"Just making sure you weren't being killed."

"Clint's harmless," I say, turning and walking toward the living room.

"…or seduced," he adds.

"I should be so lucky!" I yell as I disappear out of sight and return carrying Noble's Christmas present.

"What's this?" He's surprised, even a bit uncomfortable staring at the shirt box wrapped in silver metallic paper with a large red bow on it.

"It's nothing," I say, hoping to downplay any hint of a big gesture. "Just something I picked up on Fifty-Fourth Street."

He slowly opens the box and unfolds the tissue paper. Noble admires the picture inside for a long time. I move closer to him to see it as well. I bought it from a street vendor when I was in

New York City last month. It's a hand-drawn picture of Wollman Rink in Central Park decorated with traces of metallic
paint. It's an enchanting scene of a moment in time that will
always remind me of Noble.

"Do you remember the date night you went ice-skating
with my sorority?" I ask, watching him from only a few inches
away.

"Yes," he says, still gazing at the picture.

"I fixed you up with my pledge sister, Raquel."

"And you went alone because Jason couldn't make it." Noble
watches me silently, still holding the picture. I know he's remembering the one time he convinced Raquel to pity me
enough to let him skate with me. It was the highlight of my
night. We were skating when our high school graduation song
came on. He grabbed my hand and started belting it out.

I was embarrassed. We almost fell twice. Finally, Noble
picked me up and threw me over his shoulder, still singing.
I looked up to see Raquel's face just before we fell and went
sliding full speed toward the wall. Noble hit first, and I
slid right into him as if in slow motion. By that time I had
completely forgotten about Raquel and the other few hundred people at Wollman Rink. I just lay on top of him and
laughed.

Noble pulled it together long enough to sing the last few
lyrics in my ear. I can't hear the song without thinking of it,
and that's what the picture reminds me of—happy times. I
can't think of a time with Noble that wasn't happy.

He scoops me up into his arms and hugs me. I'm not pre-
pared. He'd been looking at the picture so thoughtfully. He
holds me at arm's length and says, "I love it. I do. Thank you."

He's going to kiss me.

I want him to kiss me.
I can't let him kiss me.

I look down as I whisper, "You're welcome," and move out of his grasp.

* * *

Last year Jason and I spent Christmas here. Butch and Sean and Michelle came over and we ate and exchanged gifts like a real family. I gave him a picture of me hugging him, his back to the camera. Someone was taking the picture of another person when I just happened to be hugging Jason in the background. My face depicted pure joy, my infatuation with him spilling over from my heart through my eyes and my enormous smile. I was so in love with him. I cropped us out, framed a copy for Jason, and kept another in my wallet—until I burned it in August.

I reach up and touch the rowel necklace around my neck. It's the only reminder of our first Christmas together, of a time when we were too broken to properly celebrate. Jason had it custom made with a turquoise stone in the center and garnet spikes. It is gorgeous, and a one-of-a-kind, and I still get compliments on it all the time.

Why do I still wear it?
Why didn't I burn it?

* * *

I have a couple of options for tonight, none of which appeal to me. I can spend Christmas Eve with my brother at Michelle's mother's house. Or I can leave town completely and spend the holiday imposing on someone else's family. Or I can go to my aunt Diane's. They'd all love to shelter me on Christmas Eve. Integrating me into their celebrations seems rather woeful to me. In hindsight I should have evacuated to Margo's or Jenn's as soon as they said they weren't coming home. An exotic location may have helped ease the complete emptiness I feel right now.

Probably not.

I shower and blow my hair dry, still unsure of where I'm headed. If I go with Sean, at least he won't worry about me all night. Or maybe he'll worry more. As I sort through my closet, dress by dress, I find the dress I wore the last Christmas Eve my parents were alive. My mom helped me pick it out. Without intention, I slip it over my head. It has these crazy lapels that turn into a tie that wraps around your waist. I remember coming out of the dressing room laughing because I had the straps all over the place, and my mother telling me deadpan, "That looks correct." I cross the straps at my belly, wrap them around my back and tie them in the front. My mother loved its deep teal color against my complexion. I study myself in the mirror and pick up my purse and coat.

* * *

I sit on the end of my pew, closest to the center aisle. The sanctuary is empty except for the organist and someone helping with a primitive sound check. I close my eyes and take a deep breath. It fills me with peace. I eye the candles flickering on the windowsills, the wreaths above the altar, and the hundreds of poinsettias dotting the room—their cards dedicating them to the living who are loved and the dead who we've lost. Somewhere in this sea of red are poinsettias with the names of my grandmother and both my parents.

Thank you, God, for Sean. Please don't let anything happen to him.

Pastor Johnson would be happy to know I began my prayer by thanking God for something before launching into my requests. I have a lot to be thankful for.

Thank you, too, for my health, my sanity—although it's been questionable the last few months—and BJ. For Butch, too, I guess.

This internal dialogue feels righteous and I have a sense of pride at my improvement in preparing my heart for worship. Surely this is closer to the objective.

Thank you, Lord, for the collection of incredible friends you have provided me.

I'm almost giddy with the ease of my praise. I flip open the pew Bible and read:

> *The Lord hath appeared of old unto me, saying,*
> *Yea, I have loved thee with an everlasting love:*
> *therefore with loving kindness have I drawn thee.*
> *Again I will build thee, and thou shalt be built,*
> (KJV 31.3–4)

If only it were that simple. But I guess that's precisely what the Bible's saying. It is that simple. God is, and always has been, right here with me, reconstructing my life when I could barely live it. For the first time since my parents' deaths, I realize I'm not alone. I continue my praise.

For Margo, and Jenn, and—

"Are you by yourself?" Noble asks, and I look up at him,

surprised. He's to my left, having entered my pew from the far side. I feel at peace...and joyful, and the complete opposite of alone.

"No, but no one's sitting here."

Noble sits down immediately to my left.

"You'll wish you were in a few minutes," he says, and his impish grin warms me.

And thank you for Noble.

"Charlotte O'Brien, look at you! You're as pretty as ever." Mrs. Sinclair barrels into my pew and hugs me before I can answer. She holds me at arm's length. "How have you been? How's that brother of yours, and Michelle?"

I begin to answer, but she continues. "Where are you going after church?"

"Now, Larissa, give the girl a chance to speak. Merry Christmas, Charlotte," Mr. Sinclair says as he also moves into my pew.

"Merry Christmas," I say. "Noble mentioned you guys were coming home. How long are you here for?"

"Oh, I'll bet he mentioned it, Charlotte," Noble's sister Jackie pipes in, and we all move farther down the pew, allowing room for her and her family to join us. "Are you guys dating?" She gives us the once-over. "You're pretty good together."

"Jackie!" Noble barks. "It's Christmas; give us a break."

"Nick and Charlotte. They *are* good together." Enter his other sister, Tracy. Both their husbands look at me sympathetically as they try to keep their broods from climbing over the pews. In all, we fill two rows in the church. My pew is hosting eight people and I'm squeezed between Noble and his dad.

No. Definitely not alone. Thank you, Jesus, for this cast of characters, too.

Mr. Sinclair leans over and whispers in my ear, "You should come by later. I went to visit my old buddies down at the crick. Picked up some moonshine. Real smooth." He closes his eyes as he says it, conjuring up the taste. I look at Noble and he's barely containing his laughter.

The church is now bursting with neighbors and Pastor Johnson begins his announcements. Noble labors to raise his arm over my head and rests it on my shoulder. Someone gasps one pew back.

"Let's start some rumors," he says, leaning toward me and rubbing my shoulder with his outstretched hand, thoroughly enjoying himself. I lean in so only he can hear me whisper.

"I think I've had a lifetime of scandal already."

"Lily-liver," he says, and I shake my head and lay it on his shoulder. The woman behind me clears her throat and Mr. Sinclair rolls his eyes at me. *Is he drunk?* Either way, he's adorable. I think you probably have to drink to enjoy this wildly animated and most endearing family he's created.

I go home alone but happy and peaceful for the first holiday since my parents passed. My answering machine is blinking, but I don't press play. Not tonight. I want to savor this feeling for as long as possible.

~ 16 ~

Auld Lang Syne

12:01 a.m.

Annie, you have to believe that we're going to make this work."

There's a long pause on the line and I wait for the familiar, overused words of apology to come floating from the answering machine. Instead he hangs up and I roll over.

"New year, new you, Charlotte," I say as BJ jumps on the bed and snuggles in next to me. I think he's beginning to recognize Jason's voice on the answering machine and its devastating effect on me. He's probably thankful I'm not throwing it across the room.

I fall back to sleep.

~ 17 ~

Snow Angel

I pull into my driveway as the first flakes begin to fall on January 10. The wind's beginning to whip and all of the blackbirds have sought cover. The town's buzzing with the news of our first big snowstorm. As is always the case, the meteorologists have been vague with the forecast until about two hours ago, when they started declaring "blizzard conditions, including near whiteout visibility, downed trees, power outages, and several feet of snow." What's not to love?

The grocery store—as in *the only* grocery store in town—was mobbed with people buying batteries, milk, eggs, bread, and water. I got BJ some dog treats and a new toy; a sleeve of premade cookie dough; the last gallon of milk, which I promptly gave to the frazzled woman carting her three kids through the chaos who was only moments too late to grab it for herself; and the new *Vanity Fair*.

I begin to explain to BJ what the storm means and to look for my dad's snow shovel. It's hanging on the wall at the end of a series of shovels organized by use and size within each classification. "I miss you, Dad. You and your freakish OCD ways in your garage." Right below the shovel is a crate with bags of salt stacked in it. I love this man. There's a milk crate on a shelf with ice scrapers and work gloves. I take one of each and hear my phone ring.

It rings again, but I can't find it. I grab it just as it rings the fourth time and slide the bar to answer.

"Hey," he says as if we talk every day.

"Hey, Noble. Excited about the storm?"

"Very much so," he says with an air of mischief. "I'm coming to get you around six. Bring BJ, too."

"You're coming to get me?" I ask, enunciating every word in disbelief.

"That's right. Six o'clock. We're having a sleepover. We'll cook some dinner, watch TV until the power goes out, and you'll spend the night." Sensing the hesitation in my silence, he adds, "In the guest room. You'll sleep in the guest room. No hanky-panky, I promise." There's silence on the other end of the phone as I digest the invitation. "If we get as much snow as they're calling for, it's going to be a long few days," he says, the jovial tone missing, his concern intact.

Without thinking, I answer, "Okay," and with that I put away the cookie dough. It's not like we've never slept together before. Noble used to crash at my house at Rutgers all the time. Sometimes he'd sleep on the couch, sometimes…before Jason…in my bed. And I don't want to be alone. I want to be with Noble. I try to figure out what I should take to my first sleepover on Noble's farm.

The phone rings again.

"Hello."

"Hey, it's your brother. You need anything for tonight?"

"No. BJ and I are actually going to stay at Noble's tonight."

Without missing a beat, Sean says, "Right. Of course you are. I'm sure there's an appropriate response or piece of advice that I should say, but I'm glad you're not going to be alone. I'll be over after the storm to do the driveway."

"Sounds good. Keep in touch. Oh, and don't worry about the advice. I'm too screwed up to date. I wouldn't inflict myself on someone as nice as Noble."

"Whatever you say."

*　*　*

Noble's truck pulls into the driveway at exactly six. He's punctual. I'm on my second trip to the garage with things BJ and I need for a sleepover. By the time I get to his truck with the first load, the windshield is already icing up.

"Man, it's getting bad," I say, and deposit my overnight duffel bag between us on the front seat. I start to make another trip inside and Noble jumps out of the truck.

"I didn't realize you have more stuff," he says, embarrassed, always a gentleman.

"Oh, I don't. It's BJ's." I hand him a large boat bag containing BJ's bed and blanket, some toys, his water and food bowls, a large Ziploc of food, and his leash. It's billowing out of the top and awkward to carry because the bag is too small to hold everything. BJ hops in the truck and perches himself right between us on top of my duffel.

"Too much?" I ask, feeling like a burden.

"Not at all." Noble flashes a sincere grin that only slightly hides a little chuckle. He has a way of laughing at me that, rather than offending me, always makes me smile, too.

On the way to his house we pass two cars that have skidded off the road. We slow almost to a stop and confirm they don't need any help. Both of them have tows on the way and we see large farm equipment to the rescue about a half-mile down. It's becoming difficult to judge the side of the road without power lines, and if it weren't for Noble's mailbox, his driveway would be completely indiscernible. We slowly pass Butch's house and BJ gives out a bark and wags his tail furiously.

"I know. We'll go check on Butch," I assure him as I scratch behind his ears.

We literally slide into the last open spot in the L-shed. The four-mile drive took forty-five minutes.

"I'm going to take BJ next door."

"Okay. I'll grab your copious amount of gear and meet you inside."

My eyes linger on Noble as he hauls our bags out of the truck. When he notices, I step in the direction of Butch's, following BJ, who's run ahead.

Butch's small house is cooking from the woodstove heat. He's sitting at the kitchen table and shows not one ounce of surprise, irritation, or joy at the sight of me.

"Out for a ride?" he asks nonchalantly.

"Kind of. BJ and I are staying at Noble's tonight." I start to talk faster. "It's not a real sleepover; I'll be in the guest room." Rambling actually. "Although that's where guests usually sleep. He just thought since we might be locked in-doors for a while it would be more fun with company." *My God, can I make this sound worse?* "It sounded like a good idea since we'll probably lose power and…what I mean is he was worried about—"

Butch's hand darts up and demands I shut up as his eyes close slightly and he shakes his head. I appreciate the gesture, even though it's rude. BJ's wagging his tail at Butch's feet and Butch gives him some love in spite of himself.

"Do you need anything? Milk, food, flashlight?"

"I'll be fine. It's not the apocalypse, for Christ's sake. Everyone's so damn worked up about a little snowstorm."

"Clearly you don't watch the weather. This is the big one," I say with my arms stretched out in exaggeration. Butch watches me like I'm some wacky kid. "All right, then. BJ and I'll be back in the morning to check on you."

BJ starts crying and nuzzles in closer to Butch.

"Traitor!" I harshly denounce him with a phony sneer.

"Just leave him here," Butch says.

"Really?"

"Yeah. Just leave him." BJ's tail starts wagging. I don't get the appeal, but whatever. BJ is the great equalizer. No matter how much Butch and I have lost, this dog reminds us we can love again.

"Do you have enough food?" I get up to check his bin.

"Yes," he says, his impatience returning. It's time to go.

* * *

The fifty yards to Noble's is harsh and numbing. The snow's coming down sideways and the bottoms of my jeans are saturated and stick to my legs. Even with my hood up my head's freezing from the wind. We're definitely going to lose power tonight.

Noble's standing at the back door and opens it for me when I get close. I bang the snow off my boots and swat as much off my parka as I can before stepping inside.

"Where's BJ?" he asks as I remove some layers by the door. My hoodie hooks on my shirt and as I pull it up, my shirt comes up, too. I don't notice at first but the left side of my bra is showing. I redden with embarrassment and haul it back down. Noble has his usual shit-eating grin splattered across his face.

"I'm glad I amuse you so. Butch is going to keep him. I think it's good; now no one will be alone tonight."

I don't look up to meet his stare.

"Aaah, it's warm in here." I rub my hands up and down my biceps and consider walking over and pressing myself against the front of him. *Get hold of yourself, Charlotte. You act like you've never been cold before.*

"I just stoked the fire and brought in some extra wood," he says, and I take a deep breath, inhaling the warm air.

My bags are on top of the large kitchen table. BJ's large boat bag dwarfs my duffel.

Noble walks over to the table and dramatically gestures toward my bag. "This I find interesting," he says. I don't get the joke. Noting my confusion, he motions toward my baggage. "May I?"

I shrug. Noble takes out BJ's bed and blanket and puts them on the floor. He inventories the rest. "Three balls, food, treats, a leash, a chewed-up stuffed bear with his face missing..." He opens my duffel, a deflated balloon in comparison, and I understand. I start to laugh before he does. To his credit he's able to keep going. "Let's see. A flashlight, a bottle of whiskey"—he raises both eyebrows—"a toothbrush, much appreciated, and about four small items of clothing. All the essentials," he adds mockingly. "Do you realize you take better care of your dog than yourself?"

"If you're not going to spoil them, why have one?"

* * *

We make dinner in tandem. After cooking alone for months, I've forgotten what camaraderie feels like. I'm smiling so much I forget to be sad. We chop celery, carrots, potatoes, green peppers, and garlic for venison stew. I hand Noble the butcher knife to cut the meat. "Did you shoot this?"

"No," he answers with a hint of deception. I eye him knowingly and he gives in. "Bow."

"Impressive, Noble." And not all that surprising. "I can see you running around the woods with a bow. Like Cupid." The statement makes me giggle, but the image in my head has no humor. It's Noble, still and powerful, aiming a bow in the middle of the cold woods.

I finish cutting the tomatoes as Noble browns the meat in a skillet. I add whiskey when I think Noble isn't looking and add another splash for good measure. The meat's been frozen, but it will still taste delicious. I'll have to take some to Butch tomorrow.

We eat by candlelight at the large table in Noble's kitchen. We sit at either end and I can barely see his face the light's so dim. Noble has the radio set to the Philadelphia classic rock station and the music serenades us.

"The stew's delicious," I say.

"It is."

"You, and your bow, are a great provider." There's a peace in the room, as if the snow has formed a giant pillow around the house, absorbing anything unpleasant.

We finish our meal and clean up together, joking the entire time. Dinner with Noble is the adult equivalent of children catching snowflakes and making snow angels. It's innocence and love and family. It's home.

* * *

"Do you want some wine or are you drunk from your recipe for venison stew?" he asks.

"If I didn't know better, I'd think you were making fun of my Irish heritage. Everything tastes better with whiskey."

"You know, I find myself saying the exact same thing all the time—breakfast cereal, pudding, spaghetti sauce," he says as he hands me a glass of Cabernet. He sits on the end of the couch I'm comfortably sprawled out on. "I'm glad you're here." His gaze turns serious.

"I am, too," I quietly admit. I shiver. I think from a chill, but it may have something to do with his stare.

Noble leaps up and pokes the fire. Embers float through the air but stay safely enclosed beyond the hearth. He adds three more logs and the sparks fly up the chimney. The crackling of the fire warms my insides as the flames warm the rest of me. My father would have a fire burning on a night like this.

"You're family," I blurt out, and he turns to look at me.

"Please tell me not like a brother."

"No, not a brother, but safe, very safe. Being with you reminds me of my childhood."

He returns to poking the fire with his back to me.

"Did you know?" I ask. Noble stops moving and doesn't

turn around. He knows what I'm talking about. "When I saw you at the fair last August, did you know that he'd gotten her pregnant?" I wince as I say it. It's the first time I've ever brought it up to anyone. I take a gulp of wine to dull the pain.

Noble takes a deep breath.

"I'll never lie to you, Charlotte," he says, turning to face me. His brow wrinkles as his eyes break contact with mine. He's tortured by guilt. "If you promise not to lie to me."

Noble pauses and I nod in agreement.

"Did you know it was Jason who broke into your house?"

I sigh, already regretting the pledge of honesty. "When Sean called me, I suspected it was Jason. When I saw the note above my bed, I knew it was him. He looked for the key under the turtle, but you had it."

Noble looks down at the mention of the key, hiding his face from me.

"Why didn't you tell the police?"

"Tell them what? That my ex-boyfriend had too much to drink and was desperate to talk to me so he broke into my house?"

"Yes, some version of that," Noble says without any humor.

"He shouldn't have been at my house that night, or at Violet's party, but I've done some things during this separation I'm not proud of," I say, remembering my hate-filled rants. "He didn't deserve to be arrested for being in my house." *I'm no longer sure what he deserves.*

"Did you know?" I ask again, not relenting. "At the fair, you hugged me and it felt…unlike anything I'd ever felt with you before. I remember thinking there was something behind it, but I couldn't figure out what." Looking back now, it was sorrow I felt when Noble hugged me. An emotion completely foreign to our relationship.

"You knew, didn't you?"

Noble's eyes bore into me and I know I don't want to hear the answer.

"Yes," he says, both angry and guilty at the same time.

The outrage is searing my insides. I knew it. I knew all along, but I couldn't accept he knew. The idea that he knew for one second and didn't—

"I didn't know what to do. I didn't want you to go to Oklahoma, but I couldn't be the one to tell you." He pauses and stares into the fire.

"How could you have let me go down there?" I aim my disgust of the entire situation squarely at Noble.

"How could I say those words to you?" Noble counters, and I know he would never have to. Not Noble. "When you were missing after he told you, I looked all over for you. I went to your house, but you never answered the door. Your brother, Margo, Julia—none of them would tell me where you were. By the third week, Julia took pity on me and at least said you were in horrible shape but better than the first two weeks." Noble's eyes plead with me to understand, but I'm lost in the horror of the summer.

"It got easier after the first few weeks," I say. "He stopped trying to contact me, and I could function from hour to hour. I also had to go back to work, which helped. But I'm glad you couldn't find me."

"Why?" he asks, the hurt evident on his face.

"Because the people who were with me the first two weeks still don't look at me the same way they did before." I lower my eyes, too ashamed to face him. "I think I scared them beyond their ability to trust me again. Sean's called or texted me every single day since I came home."

"I can only imagine, because when I first saw you in Butch's yard, you looked like hell." His eyes are kind as he breaks into a small, sympathetic smile. The memory of how everyone looked at me when I first came home still haunts me.

"Can we talk about something else?" I ask, still miffed he didn't stop me.

He breaks out his patented all-purpose smile. "How are your renovations going?"

"That's right; you haven't been there in a few weeks. Clint's doing a great job."

"I'm sure he is," Noble says with an air of sarcasm.

"What? He does beautiful work." He does. I don't get the attitude. "When he's done with the bathroom, I'm going to ask him to start working on the bedrooms."

"I'd give him a few weeks off in between. He could use the break, I'm sure." His words bruise me and I wonder if Clint's told him he's tired of being at my house. Maybe I'm there too much. He never seems annoyed, though.

"Does Clint not like working at my house?"

"He likes working there plenty." He looks at me, trying to figure out if I'm teasing him or not. "Do you really not know that Clint's hot for you?"

My head snaps up and my smile vanishes.

"What, Charlotte? Seriously...this is news to you?" Noble lifts my legs up and sits underneath them on the couch.

I dismiss Noble and the idea. "He doesn't like me."

"The hell he doesn't. He's just trying to figure out how to make his move. While we're on the subject, Rob's texted me twice for your number. Apparently you put some kind of spell on him, too."

My muscles clench as I sit up straight. The very thought of a guy calling me is beyond my comprehension. I've only just started showering regularly.

"You didn't give him my number, did you?"

He is indignant.

"After it took me a month to get it myself? Do you think I'm going to help those two yahoos?"

I relax some and take a sip of my wine. Rob's not a shock, but Clint...

"You should all stay away from me. I wouldn't want any of you to get hurt."

"You're right. They should stay away." His eyes darken. "But why don't you let me worry about me?" He's rubbing my legs with his fingertips and tracing something, a word, possibly. Now seems like a good time to exit.

* * *

My room is directly across the hall from Noble's. It's a large square with a window on one wall surrounded by bookshelves on both sides and a storage bench beneath it. A radiator with chipped white paint is to the left and a closet door is to the right. To my delight, the old doors all have glass knobs and the window curtains are homemade.

There are three pictures on the dresser: Noble's Rutgers graduation picture and wedding portraits of each of his two older sisters. Mrs. Sinclair has beautiful children. To the left of the door is a double bed that has a lavender and beige quilt on it and about six pillows at the head. I feel at home in this old farmhouse. I've spent so much time the past few months in Julia's and my ultra-modern apartment I've become accustomed to the cold, shiny surfaces. This room is warm. As if hearing my thoughts, the radiator begins to tick and Noble comes around the corner with towels in his arms.

"I brought you some towels."

He puts the stack of at least five towels on the chair next to my bed. "I see that."

"You know, in case you want to wash your car or something," he says, and we both laugh. "I'm not used to having house guests."

I tilt my head, knowing this is a lie.

"At least not ones that arrive before one a.m."

"I'm going to take a shower."

"Would you like me to help? You are my guest, after all." His eyebrows rise, his devious intentions masked by his sweet eyes and innocent grin.

"I think I can manage alone. Do you mind if I use your stuff?"

"Stuff?" he asks.

"Shampoo, soap, razor—whatever you have in there I can make work."

"My products are your products. Seriously, if you need anything I'm right across the hall." With that, he lightly kisses me on the cheek and whispers, "Good night."

Oh, Noble, so gentle. What would it be like in your bed?

I pass his room on the way to the shower and hear music coming from under the door. The bathroom reminds me of my mother's except it's twice as big. The toilet, sink, and shower are all a light teal and the shower curtain incorporates the same teal with pink and brown. There are rooster-shaped soaps in a henhouse dish, which make me laugh. Mrs. Sinclair is funny, like Noble. I shower, taking my time because I have plenty of it and the hot water is incredible.

When I'm done, I wrap myself in the robe hanging on the back of the door, assuming it's Noble's. It's blue and the same material as a sweatshirt and has a hood, which I put up after I finish brushing my hair. I brought my own toothbrush but use Noble's toothpaste.

While I brush, I look out the window. The bathroom faces south across fields and eventually Pointary Road. For as far as I can see, there's only snow, like the horizon at the end of the ocean. To the left, there's a light post and Butch's house beyond that. *Good night, BJ.* I smile at the thought of him. I'm blessed to have him. In the glow of the light post the storm's full fury is visible. The snow is now coming straight down, inconceivably fast. At this rate we may never get out of here. I spit and rinse and place my toothbrush in the cup alongside Noble's. I hang up my wet towel before hitting the light switch and opening the door.

Noble's leaning against the side of his bedroom door. "Nice robe."

I touch the soft fabric on the arms. "Do you mind?" I ask.

He's my sweetest friend, standing here. "No. You're a funny girl, Charlotte."

"Are you waiting for me?" I ask.

"I didn't know that was an option." I tilt my head to the side and he adds, "I have to go to the bathroom."

"Oh, Noble, I'm sorry. I took the longest shower because the water felt so good."

"Can we talk about the water in a minute?" he asks as he moves by me.

I call, "Good night," and escape to my room.

~ 18 ~

The Beginning of the End, Or...

The radiator bangs as if someone's hitting it with a wrench. It doesn't keep me up because I'm not sleeping anyway. I just lie in my bed and stare at the ceiling. A crack of light seeps under the door and creates a gray glow in the room. What would Jason say about me staying here? He and Noble are friends. Noble and I are friends. Jason and I were so unexpected I think it took us all by surprise. I tried to keep my close relationship with Noble, but Jason didn't make it easy. He thought every guy who spent any time with me wanted to have sex with me or, worse, was in love with me. Noble was no exception. By my senior year, I stopped telling him when Noble came to my house at Rutgers. I assume Noble instinctively kept it to himself, although I never would have conspired with him to keep something from Jason. It's the only thing I did keep from him. In my head I justified it because I'd given up so much that was available at Rutgers to be with him. Giving up Noble was too much to ask.

I hate you, Jason. You ruin everything.

I can think of a few sorority sisters who probably wouldn't be thrilled I'm here either. I can see why they want him. Noble's one of those rare individuals who appeals to both men and women. He's a guy's guy and women adore him. I think it's because, besides being hot, he's also hilarious. I've laughed so hard with Noble I've forgotten how handsome he is.

I wonder what he sleeps in…

Not his robe. At least not tonight. I roll over on my stomach and try to quiet my brain. The sheets are cold on my bare legs. I was so worried about forgetting something BJ might need that I completely forgot anything to wear to bed. If I'm still here tomorrow night, I can borrow a T-shirt from Noble.

I wish I'd taken Noble to my spring formal. I wish I'd taken him and had sex with him until he couldn't remember his name. A sob catches in my throat. I won't cry over Jason Leer. Not here, not in Noble's house.

Fuck you, Jason Leer.

I get out of bed and look into the small round mirror on top of the dresser. I'm starting to look more like myself. Eating helps. My hand swipes away a stray eyelash from my cheek and moves down my face and rests on the rowel necklace Jason gave me our first Christmas together. It hasn't left my neck since.

"Why didn't I take this off?" I ask my reflection. *Great, now I'm starting to talk to myself.* I take it off and throw it in the side pocket of my overnight bag. I rub my neck, disturbed by its absence.

I stand frozen by my reflection in the mirror. If I look like myself, when am I going to start feeling like myself? There's nothing left to wait for. Unsure of what I'm doing, I cross the hall and knock on Noble's door. I hear music coming from inside and swing the door open without waiting for a response. Noble's sitting up with his glasses on, filling out some forms in bed. He's shirtless, and his shoulders arrest my sight. He takes off his glasses and starts to gather up the papers when he sees me.

"Charlotte, what's wrong?"

I slowly shake my head but say nothing. He's bewildered and I know if I don't leave now, I won't until morning. Oh, I should stay away from him. My breath quickens and I slowly walk over to him, confusion letting go to hope on his face. I straddle him and the robe opens, exposing my collarbone to the tips of my shoulders. My hair, still damp, hangs down my back, cold and wet.

His stare morphs to complete desire, and I can feel him responding on my thigh. I kiss him, gently at first, but I succumb to months of loneliness. It quickly gets away from me and I'm pressing my lips on him hard, excited by his immediate response. His flexed arms, his generous lips, everything responds to me with an unleashed hunger.

I stop, breathless, and try to regain some control. Noble's face is inches from mine and he reminds me of an animal being stalked as prey. No sudden movements.

"Noble, promise me you won't hate me in the morning," I say, knowing he should stop this, not sure if I can go back to my room if he asks me to.

"Why would I hate you?" His voice is quiet and his words are slow.

"Because tomorrow I'll call this a huge mistake. I'll say it's too soon and I'm not ready. That it cannot happen again."

Noble bends me backward and lays me flat on top of the

covers. His boxer shorts hang low on his waist and my eyes pause there. My gaze saunters past his defined stomach and lingers at his shoulders, his incomparable shoulders, before passing his expressionless lips and settling on his stare. Noble waits for a breath and kisses me with an urgency that pushes every thought from my mind. He sits up and unties my robe, unveiling me to the night air. My best friend's eyes behold me, naked in his grasp. Nothing will ever be the same again. I shiver and he kisses me again, my body warming under his touch. Noble kisses my neck, pauses, and looks at it as he runs his hand over where my necklace used to rest. He moves to my ear and kisses behind it and plays with my lobe with his tongue, finishing by grabbing it with his teeth and yanking a little.

My breath catches.

"A huge mistake, huh?" His head hovers inches above me as his eyes bore holes into mine. They are dark and mischievous, and I want him inside me immediately.

I reach up and grab his hair. He kisses me as he takes each of my hands and gently places them above my head. "Then let's make sure it's indelible." He moves down, sliding his body against mine and begins playing at my nipple with his tongue, his amazing tongue. My knees rise and he lowers them, maximizing my exposure and my excitement. I may come just from this, and I start rocking my hips forward and backward slowly. He leaves my nipples to face me again. "Not yet, Charlotte. Hang on."

Easy for you to say.

He lands on the other nipple and quickens his pace, taking it in his mouth and sucking it hard, blowing on it gently until my control is gone. He releases it and gives me a second to steady my breathing. Always thinking of me. I concentrate on the music to hold on. The beat quickens as my heart rate comes down from arrest levels.

Noble moves down my stomach, kissing my navel, letting his lips drag on my skin as his hand finds my nipple. He searches for what I want, what I need, as he kisses each thigh and he spreads my legs. I can't seem to get enough air in me and my breathing mimics my pelvis, thrusting forward slowly to the rhythm of my wanting. He's moving slowly, calculated, and I hate him and love him for it at the same time. He…is…driving…me…crazy…ER.

He keeps his hands on my hips and touches only the tip of his tongue to me and I moan. I stop moving my hips. Frozen. Noble pauses, too, and when I look down at him, he's smiling up at me with a glint in his eye. He pays the same attention there as he did to each nipple and I'm lost. I cover my eyes with my hands and try to slow the tempest but can't manage it. I come and he places one hand flat on my stomach as I writhe beneath him. It rocks my entire body and I can't catch my breath. I could cry—such a sweet release. Noble lies on top of me and warms me as he kisses my neck.

"I promised you wouldn't forget it."

"I won't," I vow breathlessly.

"We're not done yet." Noble climbs on top of me and I try my best to focus, still dizzy and electrified from my orgasm. He enters me and my body convulses again, the perfect fit of Noble causing my body to engage again. He rocks gently at first and takes his time. How does he manage such control?

I can't take much more and whisper, "I'm going to come again."

He says, "Be my guest," and pounds into me harder. I wrap

my legs around his waist and cross my ankles behind his back. My hands clutch his biceps as they flex, supporting most of him. Noble speeds up and I close my eyes, arch my back, and surrender to my beautiful friend. I cry out and he comes at the same time. He rests on top of me. The full weight of him makes it difficult to breathe—or maybe I'll never breathe normally again.

* * *

It's 3:37 a.m. when the thunder wakes me. We've lost power and Noble's iPod must have finally drained its battery because the room is silent except for the storm. I watch Noble sleep. He's so big. Long and broad. Light brown hair that's playfully long, big blue eyes, and a smile from ear to ear; everything about him is wonderfully large—and I'm going to ruin his life.

When I'm done with you, you won't have the same smile. People will look at you the way they look at me.

I withdraw from Noble's bed and go to the window as the thunder cracks again. I consider waking him to hear it. Snow thunder is rare in Salem County, but he's so peaceful I can't disturb him. The radiators are kicking into gear now and the room's hot. The warm air is soft against my bare skin. Noble's kicked off most of his covers and his arms and chest are completely exposed. The violent sky fills the black room with flashes of light, warning of the coming thunder, and Noble reaches out. I watch as he opens his eyes and rolls over, searching for me.

"I'm sorry if I woke you," I say, and admire his beautiful face. I can't look away.

"I'm not. What are you doing?"

"Thinking about you." My face becomes sad as I think of how our friendship will be in ruins. "And how incredibly powerful, unpredictable, and magnificent the weather is. Just like you. It's gorgeous out there...and in here." I choke on the final word and turn toward the window to keep from crying.

"Come back to bed," he says. The thunder booms and shakes the walls of his bedroom. And this time Noble doesn't take his time.

* * *

I wake up the second time with Noble spooning me. His one arm is under my pillow and the other is wrapped around me, cupping my breast. How we slept like this I don't know. I slide out and Noble rolls over on his other side without opening an eye. I tiptoe around the bed and out the bedroom door.

I turn on the light, thankful the power's returned, and once the bathroom door is closed, I look in the mirror. There's not a bruise, bite, pinch, or scratch on me. Not one sign of rough sex. Apparently a person can have an orgasm without Jason's version of mixed martial arts. I lower my head and chastise myself for comparing the two.

Let it go, Charlotte.

"Charlotte!" Noble bellows from the bedroom in a funny, barbaric way, as if he's going to find me and drag me back to bed by my hair. I go and stand in his doorway, still brushing my teeth, completely naked.

"Yes?"

Noble watches me, grinning.

"Come back to bed," he says, his sweet voice having been restored.

I smile and point out the toothbrush. I hold up one finger in answer.

When I return, Noble lifts the covers so I can slide in next to him, and I'm again reminded of why he's popular with the ladies. My friend Noble is beautiful.

"Do you always walk around naked so much?"

I pull my head up and meet his eyes to try to gauge the question. "Do I offend you?" I ask, wanting to laugh but not wanting to offend him further.

"No, no, of course not. I love it. I've just never seen another girl walk around naked like you. Everyone else seems to prefer to be covered up the majority of the time."

Since I don't spend a lot of time naked with my friends, I've never noticed. I sit up and get cross-legged, and he laughs.

"What?" I ask, becoming frustrated.

He gestures toward my legs. "I know for a fact no girl has ever sat in my bed crisscross applesauce, naked." I look down at my spread-eagle bird. Noble reaches out and touches my mermaid's tail. "Charlotte, is this a monogram?"

I'm delighted. "Yes, the tail wraps around to form a C, the fins make the A, and the hole in between is the O. I'm impressed you figured it out," I say shyly.

"Do all the other guys you walk around naked in front of have trouble with it?" Noble asks with his eyebrows raised.

Ignoring his question, I ask, "Have you had sex with many swimmers?"

Noble's smile lights up his eyes.

"I'm being serious. In swimming we had to be completely naked before and after every practice or meet. It wasn't like basketball where you just change your shorts and shoes. And once practice started, we were pretty much just swimming around half naked the whole time, girls and boys together."

"I should have given the swim team more consideration in high school."

I roll my eyes dramatically. "Perhaps if you'd stopped bedding so many girls, my oddities wouldn't be this obvious. Did you ever consider that?"

"Are you hungry?" he asks.

"Are you changing the subject?"

Noble lunges forward and has me on my back, arms locked by my sides as he kisses me right below my navel, and at the side of my breast, and on my collarbone, and my neck. A short breath escapes my lips and I feel a tingling spread just below the surface of my skin.

"All my past experiences were just practice for being with you," he says in my ear, right before he kisses my lobe and gently bites the tip. I feel like the center of Noble's world and his is better than my own. I close my eyes and turn my head, letting my brain stop functioning and just feeling him on me. He runs one finger down the center of my chest as he kisses me, the desire in his tongue searching again and again. He spreads my legs with his knee and climbs between, siting up.

When I open my eyes, he's staring at me with the same look I've seen before. Desire, urgency, fear, love...I don't know.

"Charlotte, you belong here." Rising to his knees, he lifts my pelvis and legs up and I instinctively wrap them around his waist.

My shoulders are still on the bed, but every part of me beneath them is suspended in air, connected to Noble. He plunges into me with a force I hadn't anticipated. "Oh...Noble," escapes me. He pulls out slowly, letting his tip rest at my entrance. I open my eyes just before he plunges into me again, and I grab the sheets with both hands to steady myself. I look into Noble's eyes with a greedy smile on my face. I lower my stare to his bare chest and let my eyes feed on his divine shoulders. They devour his biceps and traps, all flexed holding me up as he—"Mmmm..."—plunges into me again.

He's tilted at the perfect angle, and I close my eyes. I squeeze the sheets in my hands and try to hold on to something, unwilling to let go of everything. He begins a rhythm that launches me into orbit at the same time as he comes. He's still supporting the lower half of me when he pulls out for the last time, and an aftershock convulses my body. He lies next to me and we each try to steady our breathing.

"Practice does make perfect," I say, and again focus on my breathing.

"Do you like French toast?"

"It's my favorite," I say, still a little out of breath and hungry for food.

"I'm going downstairs to start making it. Would you mind wearing some clothes to breakfast? It's incredibly distracting." He stands and puts his pajama pants back on. He smiles at me as he moves. "And I believe you wanted to talk to me about your readiness for this type of relationship," he adds, and his smile disappears. "I must admit, though, I've been impressed with your readiness thus far." Noble turns and leaves the room.

* * *

I dawdle, not wanting to face this discussion. I've been playing house with Noble in a blizzard and the sun will come out soon, melting away our safe hold.

I pull on yoga pants and my favorite tee, a Mardi Gras shirt with all the parade names and dates from two years ago. Jason was furious that I went, but I'm still thankful Jenn convinced me to go. I wouldn't dare wear this shirt around him, but like most other things, it's easier with Noble.

Stop comparing them. You're a stupid idiot.

I'm pulling my hair into a ponytail as I enter the kitchen and see the snowdrift on the panes of the back door. The snow is stacked against the door at least two feet high. I measure it against my leg and it's halfway between my knee and my thigh. The snow continues to fall without any sign of slowing.

"How long can this go on?" I ask, staring out the window.

"The snow or us?" Noble asks as I turn around and see him placing two breakfast plates on the table. "Milk?"

"I'll get it," I offer as I make my way to the refrigerator. I pour two glasses and replace the gallon. "I see you planned ahead for the storm."

"I knew I'd be entertaining."

"You knew I'd say yes?"

"I hoped."

I hand him his milk and take my seat at the other end of the table in front of a plate full of French toast. The smell of the cinnamon warms me and I inhale deeply. There are two pats of butter melting in a pool on top, and two country links of sausage next to it.

"I have a proposition," he says, interrupting my salivating. "We'll talk this through, and no matter what the conclusion is, let's promise to enjoy the rest of the storm the same way we did last night." He smiles a naughty smile.

"What if you hate me when we're done speaking?" I ask.

"I could never hate you enough to not repeat last night."

He lowers his eyes to his plate and my heart aches for him.

He has no idea how screwed up I am. He can't possibly want what he thinks he wants.

"The only thing I ask is that you tell me the complete truth, even if you believe it's going to hurt me. I'd rather hear everything now."

I nod, understanding. I take a bite of my French toast and it melts in my mouth.

The next thirty seconds drag like hours as we eat in silence.

"What are your feelings for me?" Noble asks.

That's an easy one.

"I love you," I reply, never breaking eye contact with him. "I've always loved you. In high school and at Rutgers I loved being with you. Everything is just better when you're around." I mentally dwell upon a decade of fond memories. "Noble Sinclair, you're one of the few guaranteed good times in life. I might have wanted to hug you or hold your hand then." I move my French toast around in the syrup. "Now I feel exactly the same way except, instead of hugging you, I want to take off my clothes when you're around." I meet his gaze again and the joy on his face mirrors my own.

"That's good." He's more comfortable than he was when I first came downstairs.

"What are your current feelings for him?" He kindly omits his name. I take a deep breath and search for the answer—the one least painful for Noble to hear and yet still close to the truth. "Please be honest," he says, reading my thoughts.

I start out slow. "I hate him for being with her. I believe I could actually kill him for having sex with her and getting her pregnant." I drop my fork on the edge of my plate. "I despise him for making me wish such evil things on him, her, and the baby." The latter is barely a whisper and I look down, consumed with shame. "But I long for him every day." I realize yesterday was different and revise. "Almost every day.

"I'm scared that I'm ruining both of our lives by being unable to forgive him, and I question my ability to fairly judge the situation. Am I just being stubborn? Sometimes I think it was my fault." I take a deep breath. "Mostly, I'm terrified of him. I'm afraid to see him again." I sigh, signaling that's the whole story.

Noble's face turns crimson as the blood rushes to the surface. "Charlotte, has he ever hurt you?" His jaw is clenched and I note his hands are in tight fists still resting on the table.

"Not with his hands." I remember all the bruises and marks from our times together and amend, "Not out of anger." I blush as my eyes again survey my plate.

When I look up, Noble has his head in his hands, hiding his face from me. This is why I didn't think we should have sex. *My God, am I hurting him?*

"Why are you afraid of him?" he asks as he moves to sit in the chair next to me. It's as if I might try to lie and closing the distance between us will force me to render the truth. I reach up and thread my fingers through his hair, my forearms resting on his shoulders as I look into his beautiful blue eyes.

He pulls my hands down and holds them firmly in his own. "Please tell me, Charlotte. It can't be any worse than what I'm imagining."

"Did Jason ever tell you about the last day we were together?" I ask, trying to remain stable as I say his name.

"Only that he told you about the baby and you left. He said he didn't know where you were and it was killing him."

I take a deep breath and push aside the sorrow I feel for Jason.

"I thought it was going to be our last weekend together before I moved there. Finally the travel and weeks apart—and separate lives—were coming to an end." I look down at my hands in Noble's and continue. "Jason seemed strange from the second he picked me up at the airport. He was despondent, one minute cagey, the next angry. I couldn't discern what was going on. I even asked him if he was on something."

Noble sits motionless, not letting his face betray his feelings. His silence beckons me to continue.

"I haven't discussed this with anyone, not even Sean," I say as I wipe away a rogue tear running down my cheek. Noble reaches out but returns his hand to his side without touching me.

"The ride to his house was long and terrifying. When we finally got inside he told me that he cheated on me. That he had sex with someone else. To say I was stunned doesn't communicate what happened inside my mind. Pieces of my brain dislodged and started bouncing off the sides of my skull. A dull ache became a debilitating banging. I just couldn't comprehend that he was telling me he made love to someone else. Not Jason, not to me. I didn't cry. I didn't take my eyes off him, and I didn't feel any empathy for how truly tortured he looked."

I remember the sight of him, sitting on his bed, the fear of desertion crippling him.

"I asked him, 'Who?' Just like that, one word, and he told me Stephanie Harding. It stung as I pictured them together, the same way I've imagined them every day since. It made sense, though. She always seemed exceedingly happy to see Jason and rather disappointed by my presence.

"I asked him, 'When?' and he said the night before my

spring formal. I'd called him that night and he didn't answer. I looked around his loft and I could hear my message as I imagined her on top of him. I don't know how I kept from getting sick, my head still pounding.

"I asked him, 'Why?' and he told me he didn't know—which I thought would make my head explode. How could he have done it and not tell me why?

"And finally, I asked him, 'Why are you telling me now?' It was August. I remember thinking, 'you bastard, why did you wait three months,' and then it hit me. I knew she was pregnant. I got up to leave and he tried to hold me there. I promised him if he'd just let me leave, I'd come back and talk to him. He let me go and I checked into a hotel. Three days later I called Sean and he flew down to pick me up. He got the rest of my stuff from Jason's and I've only spoken to him once since."

Noble blurts out, "When? When did you talk to him?"

I begin again, remembering the sound of his voice when I finally answered the phone. "After I moved home, he was relentless. Calling my cell phone, my friends, and my work trying to find out where I was. I finally answered the phone and begged him to stop calling." I stand up and walk to the sink with my plate. Without turning toward Noble, I add, "I told him if he didn't stop calling me I was going to kill myself." I pause, remembering the silence on the other end of the line as Jason digested my statement. "And I meant it."

I rinse my dishes and turn toward Noble. Judging from his face, he's repulsed by me, or at least disturbed by me. "Most days are easier than the one before. I can't use you to get over him, and I know I'm going to see him again. Butch knows if he tells him anything about me, I'll cut him off." I see a glimmer of something in Noble's eyes. "But it's a small town. As long as I stay in Salem County, I'll see him again."

"Is that why you're here? Why you didn't go to New York?"

"No—at least I don't think that's why."

I walk over and kneel down in front of Noble. "I can't be with you because if he walks through that door right now, even after last night, I can't guarantee I won't leave with him." Noble looks like he might throw up. "Nothing feels finished."

"Okay, that's enough truth for right now."

Noble gets up and carries his plate to the sink. "I'm going to go plow and make a dent in the first round." I try to think of what to say to repair us. "I want you to be here when I get back," he says, and kisses me on the cheek.

I nod and silently wipe away a few more tears.

~ 19 ~

The End of the Beginning

I clean up breakfast and dress in the layers I took off last night to walk over and check on Butch and BJ. The snow has slowed almost to a stop, but the forecasters say the storm is circling around and coming back in, accumulating another foot. It will begin snowing again by sunset. I hear the plows out, making the main roads passable. Noble may decide it's best I leave tonight. I grab the container with Butch's stew and walk out the back door into a drift almost as high as my waist. I look over to see Noble watching me from atop a tractor. He's too far to see, but I sense he's laughing at me. I make my way to Butch's, taking exaggerated steps that leave my thighs burning before I reach the door. Once inside the shed, I peel off my top two layers to avoid tracking water onto Butch's floor and knock before letting myself in.

Butch is asleep on his La-Z-Boy with BJ on his lap. When the dog sees me, he starts wagging his tail and jumps off. Butch doesn't wake up and, for a minute, fear grips me as I wonder if he's alive. He answers with a snore and repositions himself on the chair. I put the stew in the fridge and leave a note on the table about it. I also take out a loaf of crusty bread from the freezer I'd left a few weeks ago.

"Do you want to go out and play in the snow?" I ask as I kneel down to hug BJ. He wags his tail and jumps up on me with both paws on my shoulders. He's such a lover!

Once outside, BJ runs in circles like a crazed lunatic. He obviously loves the snow. He dives in and throws it up in the air with his snout. He also stops four times to mark places, his scent having been covered by the thick blanket. Finally, he has his fill and I take him back inside. I use the towel we keep in the shed to dry him off as best I can, but I can already hear Butch grumbling about "this goddamned wet dog" in his house. I fill BJ's bowl with food, freshen up his water, and pack myself back into my layers and parka.

Noble's driving his enormous green tractor toward me, and with the chains on the wheels it's even more impressive. When he gets within a few feet, he cuts the engine and leans out of the cab. I have to shield my eyes to see him. The sun's taken back the sky for now and it's glaring off the snow.

"Paul Hackl just called. There are two ambulances stuck in a drift at Eldridges Hill. They were transporting when they slid off the road. We're going to take a couple of tractors up to see if we can help."

"Do you want me to come with you—" I ask hopefully, but he begins shaking his head no before I can even finish.

"Nah. You stay here where it's warm. I'll be home in a few hours."

"Okay," I say weakly.

"Call me if you need anything," he adds as he starts up the engine again. It roars close to me and I instinctively move back.

* * *

The house feels strange without him. Without anyone. If I wasn't here, he'd be all alone, or with some other girl. I realize Noble's young to be running this farm on his own. *How many acres did he say?* I think two thousand. His parents retired from farming and now winter in Florida and travel in an RV throughout the summer. That'd be a fun way to live with Noble.

Since I'm not sure how long we're going to be here, and more importantly how long we're going to have power, I throw in a load of laundry. The layers of snow clothes alone fill the washer. I bring in some firewood and light another fire. I jump at the sound of the ringing phone and run to the kitchen to find my cell. I'm disappointed to see it's Sean calling and not Noble. He should be back by now.

"Hey. It's your brother."

"Hi. Isn't this crazy?" I ask.

"Completely. We measured eighteen inches already," Sean says.

"Noble went up to Eldridges Hill to help with some ambulances."

"He went? I heard it's bad. They were transporting a husband and wife that were in an accident just south of there. They brought a fire truck to pull them out and it got stuck. This snow is slick; it's hard to get any traction. It's heavy, too. Be careful shoveling it." Sean continues to tell me all the county news: power losses, accidents, roof collapses, and any other snow-related incidents he's heard.

I wish Noble would come home.

The sun goes down and the snow unleashes again. The lights flicker and I decide it's time to shower before it's not an option. I didn't bring any body wash or cleanser, so I make do with the Irish Spring soap and Pantene that Noble has in the shower. Since most of my clothes are in the dryer, I find Noble's shirt drawer and select a dark green T-shirt that says GARDENERS DO IT WITH HOES on it. I smell it before I put it over my head and the fragrance reminds me of Noble, and last night. It hangs low enough that I don't need anything else, although my tolerance for nudity is apparently high.

With nothing left to do, I turn on the TV. The local news has been covering nothing but the storm for the past twenty-four hours. They report in from the Jersey shore; Delaware; Center City, Philadelphia; and Allentown. There are massive accumulations, but it appears we're getting the worst of it. I wish my mom were here. She would tell me what to do about Noble—and Jason. Of course, if she were here, I'd probably never have been with Jason.

The lights flicker and the TV turns off and I'm completely in the dark. Literally and figuratively. I lie down, afraid to move because I might break my toe or something else. The last thing I hear is the howling of the wind being echoed by a whistling in the chimney.

* * *

I'm startled awake by Noble on top of me. He has one leg between my legs, the other on the floor, and both hands on either side of my head on the couch. He's supporting most of his weight but touching me the length of my body.

"I'm glad you're home," I murmur. The light from the fire flickers across his face and I think I make out a smile, but it's dim and I'm half asleep. He's still on top of me and hasn't said a word. Thoughts of what he could say are running through my head.

I hate you. You shouldn't be here. You're an idiot.
Get out.

I start to breathe faster just from his stare and I feel him on my leg. I still don't move, completely unsure of what he's thinking. He smells of smoke and gasoline and snow, except for his breath, which has the sweet smell of mint as it flashes across me with each exhale. The crackling of the fire drowns out my breathing and I think I feel the same heat from his eyes that I hear from the fire. He kisses me gently.

We kiss like this for a while, slowly, without touching each other, just lips and tongues exploring. My mind's racing with need and want and then it's empty of any real thought except his body on mine. The anticipation's driving me crazy and I say it with my lips, kissing him harder, willing him to lower himself onto me.

"What do you want, Charlotte?" he asks, his mouth hovering over mine. He's teasing me and it's working, his hard-on thrusting onto my leg with a slight gyration. My hips respond and I'm raising my body, chasing his above me. I try to slow down but my longing escapes and takes me hostage. I wrap one leg around his back and flip us both over. Now I'm on top. He inhales sharply at the shock of being on the bottom.

"You." I look in his eyes and kiss him hard. I can't help myself. I need his clothes off him. I have to feel his skin on mine.

I pull my shirt over my head and unbutton his jeans. I move down to use both hands to pull them off and throw them on the floor. I begin to move back up his body, dragging my hands gently on his thighs, letting my fingertips linger as they move up. I cup his balls in my hand as I gently roll them and place the tip of him in my mouth. He moans softly and I feel the fervor start between my legs. I roll my tongue around and around the tip and let my teeth rest on it as I gently roll his balls again. I let my lips trail down his entire shaft, taking the whole thing in my mouth, and lick my way up.

Again, and again, and again until he says, "Char...lotte...oh, Charlotte." He pulls me on top of him and guides my hips to take him in. I rise and fall, with Noble matching each of my descents. I arch my back and throw my head back and he uses his hands to play with my nipples. I moan and begin to move faster and faster until I rise up one last time and can't figure out how to come back down. He holds me steady as he comes, too, and lets me collapse onto his chest. His heartbeat races on the side of my face, and I never want to leave this moment.

"You're amazing," he says, kissing my head, and I feel pretty amazing. I lie naked in his arms until I regain my faculties. I start to sit up and he grabs both arms and holds me just far enough away to make eye contact.

"Promise me you'll never talk about—or think about—hurting yourself again," he demands as his stare bores into me.

I lower my eyes, too filled with self-loathing to let him see. "I promise."

God help you, Noble.

I wake up in Noble's bed, feeling like I've been asleep for a week. I reach out to find Noble's side of the bed empty. My watch says it's 9:30, but that seems impossible. How could I have slept so long? I grab my cell phone and text him:

Where are you?

IN THE KITCHEN

I miss you...

I KNOW WHAT YOU MEAN

What the hell does that mean? He definitely doesn't seem like my happy Noble. If he's not up here in three minutes, I'll know something's wrong. Maybe he finally got the message that this whole thing is a horrible idea.

After three excruciatingly long minutes, I lose hope. I throw on one of his shirts and head downstairs. He's sitting at the kitchen table drinking a cup of coffee. As I sit down, I hear the plow dragging down the street.

"Have you been out?" I ask meekly, unsure of what's going on.

"Yes." He finally looks up at me.

"How are the roads?" I have to resist the urge to go and sit on his lap. Something tells me that's no longer acceptable.

"This road is clear; I doubt they've gotten to the secondary roads yet. Probably by this afternoon we can get you home."

I look down at my hands on the table and the sadness washes over me. I feel the tears welling up in my eyes and I will myself not to cry. As I concentrate on not crying, the tears fight free and I manage to say, "Good," just before standing and walking upstairs a little too fast.

I go back to my original room and let the tears spill over. I stay as still as possible. I don't want Noble to hear me. I start gathering my things and placing them on the bed. I sling my bag down and the rowel necklace falls out. I pick it up and hold it to my forehead as I completely lose control.

You fucking idiot, Jason Leer. Have you ruined me for all future relationships? Now Noble and I won't even be friends. I. Hate. You. I hope you live every day in utter misery and die in a car crash on a country road where vultures peck out your eyeballs.

I lie down on my back and cover my eyes with my hand, still holding my necklace.

"What are you thinking about?" His voice is soft and incredibly kind. It barely breaks into my hatred-filled thoughts.

"Nothing, just packing," I answer, but don't bother to look at him.

"Please don't lie to me, not now." Noble moves onto the bed and moves my hand away from my face. The necklace partially falls out.

"What will become of us." That's the truth, minus a murderous rant.

"What do you want to happen?"

I turn my head and his eyes convey the emotion I can't put my finger on. Need, mixed with fear, love, or something I can no longer identify.

"I want us to be friends the way we were at Rutgers." I take a deep breath. "I want to not care about Oklahoma any longer." Oklahoma will always be between us. "And I want to never be a source of pain for you." Noble's look changes to one of sad understanding. "And I want the last two nights to go on for the rest of my life."

I am so selfish! I am. I'm not supposed to think about hurting myself, but I should jump off the Delaware Memorial Bridge.

"I've been thinking…a lot," he begins. "I've screwed this up a bit, too. I underestimated what was a possibility in one snowstorm. My feelings for you have changed and I can't go back to the way things were at Rutgers. I don't think I'll ever be able to."

I start to cry. Why did I come here? I'm going to have to move to New York.

"I want to tell you to just stay here, that I'm not afraid of anyone from your past, and that I know better than you do what you need." Noble wipes the tears from my cheeks. His eyes are filled with sympathy. "But you've made it clear I don't know what's going on in your head and your heart. You and Jason getting back together is not an option I can consider. I can't move forward, constantly afraid of the next time you see him."

He's right. He's right about everything.

"Charlotte, you thought you were going to spend the rest of your life with him. I'm sure it was quite a shock to find out you're not going to be. It hasn't even been six months, and you're totally different than you were in September. You're moving on whether you realize it or not."

I consider the truth of what he's saying, but functioning compared to near death is not exactly a success story. "I'm going to try to keep my hands off of you until you realize what you want is right here in front of you."

"You don't hate me?" Is that possible?

"Quite the opposite."

I roll over and hug him. He wraps his arm around my shoulders and my smile alone could warm us both.

Abruptly he gets out of the bed and asks, "Do you want to come help me shovel?"

"No, but I do want to see BJ, and Butch certainly can't shovel, so I will."

* * *

Noble gets BJ and me home safely. He helps me carry all of BJ's stuff into the house. It's cold in here, and I already miss the warmth of Noble's. We just stare at each other, my kitchen table a barrier between us. I fight every urge to run across the room and throw myself at him. His stare starts the heat and I want him. He was right; something changed during that snowstorm.

"Well, I'd better go. You guys going to be okay here?"

"Yeah. It looks like Sean made it over to plow the driveway and shovel the walk. We should be fine."

He walks toward me and I put my hands in my pockets and pretend they're handcuffs. He kisses me on the cheek and it burns. He pulls away. I know he felt that, too.

"I'll give you a call tomorrow and check on you."

"Okay," I croak out, having apparently traded my voice for desire. My whole body is a traitor.

As I walk Noble out, I notice BJ's watching us with a WTF look on his face. *I don't know what the hell's going on either, buddy.*

~ 20 ~

Dirt on the Casket

I unpack the groceries and toss the coffee cake on the table for Butch. BJ is perched by his feet. I suspect he gets to sample most of Butch's food. As I wash off an apple to slice for them, the calendar to the left of the sink catches my eye. It's a different NJ scene for each month. January is an aerial view of Mountain Creek ski resort in North Jersey. I nailed the calendar up and suggested Butch write down any visitors he's expecting so Marie and I can make sure we have everything he needs for company, *especially* company that might be staying overnight. After our awkward conversation before Thanksgiving, this is the system I came up with.

I take the calendar off the nail and turn it to February. The picture is Main Street, Lambertville, in the snow. How can it be February 1? January flew by. Since the blizzard, I've thrown myself into work and spent at least two nights a week in New York. Thank goodness BJ and Butch love each other or else I'm not sure what I'd do with him.

I've tried to keep my Christmas Eve revelation alive. I'm incredibly blessed. I've been making weekly donations and volunteering at the county food pantry. Watching the line of neighbors, children in tow, waiting for food is a powerful reminder of my blessings. I find myself replacing my internal hateful rants at Jason with thanks to God more often and it feels like some sort of recovery. Other than one night out in New York City and two platonic lunches with Noble, my new routine is work, BJ, church, and the food pantry.

Butch's phone rings and I jump a little; I don't know if I've ever heard it ring. It's a bright yellow wall phone next to the door with a long cord hanging over the top of it. I imagine Mrs. Leer standing at the sink while talking on the phone, the cord stretching the length of the room. I pick up the receiver and hand it to Butch without saying hello. He's annoyed as usual. How dare someone call him and interrupt his time doing nothing at all?

"Hello." He's as sweet on the phone as in person and I catch myself smiling. "You okay?" I turn toward Butch and he's looking at me with fear in his eyes. I know this call has something to do with Jason. Is he hurt? "Oh. I see. Okay, well, thanks for calling, and congratulations."

I'm frozen in position as my breathing stops and the cadence of my heartbeat shakes my chest. He said congratulations. Stephanie had the baby and people will now be congratulating her. Butch tries to hang up the phone and I take it from him and put it on the hook. Dizziness sets in and I grab the wall for support. I'm hot and sweating and darkness is closing my vision.

I need...to get...some air.

"I'll be right back." I run out the door to the side of the barn. Just as I turn the corner, I throw up everything I had for lunch. Violent heaves originating deep in my stomach keep coming long after there's nothing left in me. My God, she had the baby. That dumbass baby they created the night Jason fucked Stephanie. I hate them all. Why wouldn't he just agree to come to the formal in the first place?

I stumble into the barn and sit on two stacked bags of water softener salt and unleash the torrent of tears the vomiting delayed. I'm sobbing and moaning, and I might be sick again. My mother's voice gently sings in my head, saying, *"Calm down or you'll make yourself sick."* I take a deep breath and rest my face in my hands. I stay like this, completely void and only focusing on breathing for over an hour.

* * *

"Charlotte?" I squeeze my eyes shut, hating myself for crying.

It's Noble and I don't want to see him. I hold deathly still and stop crying, hoping not to be detected. I see his shoes in front of me, but I still don't release my face from my arms.

"Charlotte, are you okay?"

No.

"Butch called me and said he was worried about you. He said he got some news that might have upset you." Noble's voice is incredibly humane and it makes my stomach lurch.

"Please just go away," I say without looking up. No one's going to say anything that will console me, unless they've completed a paternity test and it's not Jason's baby.

Would that even make me feel better?

He sits next to me and puts his arm around me. "Look, I know you're upset."

"You don't know a thing, Noble," I spew at him as I get up, out of his reach. "Please just leave."

Noble's wounded and I don't care.

"Be a bitch to me if you want, Charlotte. When are you going to realize these people are not worth your time? They never were."

"Please just stop talking. And leave," I say, disgusted by the sound of his voice. "The best thing you can do is stay far away from me."

"Why? So you can sit around and cry over something that's over?" he provokes. "You're better than this. How long are you going to mourn it? If it was so great, why was he with her in the first place?"

I run to the trash and throw up again. He's right; it must have been terrible the whole time. I can barely show my face. I'm hysterical and ashamed and I want to be alone, but he's clearly not leaving.

"You don't understand. You can't understand," I scream, pointing my finger at him.

"Then make me understand!" Noble stands, frustrated, and runs his hand through his hair.

I stay silent; there's nothing to say that will make either of us feel better. He walks out and I think he's finally had enough of the new Charlotte.

* * *

Three long days later, I pull myself together. I shower and start collecting some vegetables to make a salad. I won't sink into the darkness again. It's time to put one foot in front of the other. At least that's been Sean's mantra for months. There's a knock at the door, which starts BJ barking.

Noble's truck is in the driveway and I smile without realizing it and skip to the back door. He appears worried as he quietly asks, "Can I come in?"

I'm paralyzed with fear, remembering the way he walked out of the barn. He must be here to tell me he's completely done with me. What I want to do is hug him, but my arms won't rise and my feet won't move.

"Can I get you something to drink?" I ask, because the silence is suffocating me.

He finally looks at me and I can't help myself, I smile even though the sight of him could make me cry. I keep smiling, willing it to touch him.

"I just wanted to make sure you're okay. I stayed away as long as I could. Butch said he hasn't seen you or BJ and…I just wanted to make sure…"

I get it now. He thinks I could kill myself. My God, he is a masochist to want me. He should be more worried about himself.

"I'm never going to be okay. I'm an orphan who found out her life could actually get worse." I move closer to him and his stare never falters. "I'm totally screwed up, beyond redemption."

"Then get better. Pull your shit together. Get over him. I'm right here waiting, Charlotte."

"Yeah, well, as your friend, I have to tell you to run as fast as you can in the opposite direction. You can have any girl you want and I guarantee all of them are a better choice." I move to stand right before him and take both of his hands in mine. I bring them to my mouth and kiss them. He remains silent and gives nothing away. "I don't want you to, though."

I want you to stay with me and endure whatever pain I dish out. I want you to not ask me hard questions, not require any real commitment, and have an endless supply of patience. Can't you see how wretched I am? I'm free falling and reaching to take you down with me.

"Don't fabricate a version of me that offers you what you want. You'll only be disappointed."

Noble looks down at our hands. He moves them to his mouth and grazes his lips with my fingers.

Eventually he says, "You're a complete asshole, you know?"

Finally we agree about something.

"I'm not some guy who knows nothing about you or your past. I know who you were when your parents were here, and I know you're the same person now. Can you not see that you survived it? That you're strong? Charlotte, you continue to make people feel love, and humor, and respect every day."

He drops my hands and goes into the kitchen to grab a beer out of the refrigerator. I follow him in and lean against the kitchen counter.

"I do deserve better than you're offering right now, but you can give it to me. I can't help it, Charlotte. I want you. As much as you tell me to stay away, I can't. Believe me I've tried."

He moves near and leans against me, pressing me harder against the counter. Something inside me moans and I'm surprised by how much I want him, his hips touching me as he rests his forehead on mine. I could easily reach up and run my hand through his hair, but I don't. "You want me, too. You may not admit it, but I know. I haven't figured out if you're truly saving me or saving yourself for someone else."

Oh, I want you.

He begins to softly kiss my neck and slowly moves up to kiss right behind my ear. I arch my back and extend my neck, answering him.

"You must really enjoy being tortured," I force out with labored breathing. It's hard to concentrate.

He brings his left hand up my jawline, grabs the hair behind my ear, and says, "I've never considered it, but I'd try it with you. I'd try anything with you."

I can feel him hardening on my leg and I stop trying to form a sentence or complete a thought.

He kisses my neck again and says, "You're making this more difficult than it needs to be." Noble kisses me gently and my resolve completely disappears. "I'm right here, Charlotte, and I'm not going anywhere. All you have to do is let go and let me love you."

I look down at the floor because if I look at him, he'll start to make sense. He caresses the side of my face with his thumb and I rest my head in his hand, wanting him.

"I know you love me, Charlotte."

I stay silent. Too frightened by what I might say. Noble steps away from me and I will myself to face him.

"You insist on hanging on to memories of a failed relationship that was nothing but a strain. It's memorialized as perfection in your head, but it was never meant to last." Noble takes a sip of his beer. "For now, I'm willing to wait until you come to your senses."

"Until I come to my senses?"

He takes the last sip of his beer and carries the empty bottle to the sink. His bright blue eyes sparkle as a smile finally lights them.

"Yes, I'll wait for you to realize who you still are and what you want." With that he heads for the door. "But don't make me wait too long, Charlotte. We're missing out on a lot of fun."

* * *

I stand between them in the woods. Each a straight line about twenty-five feet from me. The birds are everywhere, sailing, swooping, and soaring around us. Their chirps meld together, forming a few harsh sounds and adding to the chaos. My eyes ignore the birds and their violent song and race between the two of them. The two men who will surely hate me if something doesn't change.

And then it all becomes clear.

I raise the bow and hold it at a ninety-degree angle to my feet. I pull the string back to my cheek, my sight unfaltering from his heart. I've tried to find another solution but the three of us can no longer exist on Earth. I release the arrow and watch Jason fall to the ground.

I can no longer hear the beating of his heart and no longer smell the kiwi. The sun streams through the trees and washes over him and I turn and walk toward Noble, who's waiting to take my hand in his as the birds continue with their performance.

Time will keep moving on … It's cosmic.

It's divine.

I wake up to the sound of crying and realize it's me.

I need to go to church today. God forgive me.

~ 21 ~

The Most Stupid Day of the Year

I roll over and cover my head. Valentine's Day. The world will be full of lovers today. Lovers and losers, and I fall in with the latter. It's so bad for us losers that we can't even comfort each other. We just try to ignore the date but it's impossible, having had it burned into our brains since cutting out construction paper hearts in kindergarten. Thankfully today is Sunday and my whole weekend wasn't ruined with this nonsense. *Screw you, people who are in love.* I wonder what Jason's doing today, if he's running out to get Stephanie a card.

I should call him and ask, just out of the blue. A call to wish him a happy holiday and catch up. The absurdity of the thought makes me chuckle a little, just enough to get me out of bed even though I feel as if I haven't slept. I'm tired. Thankfully I have plenty of work to do to keep my mind off this day.

I take the longest, hottest shower I can tolerate. My skin is red when I get out and I know I'll be punished with itchy, dry skin the rest of the day. Sexy. I'm spending Valentine's Day alone, just walking around yawning and scratching my itchy ass. I wrap my hair in a towel and myself in my big, comfy robe. I'll only lie down for a second. Just a few minutes before I really get the day started.

The sight of the box halts me. It was definitely not there a few minutes ago. Light blue with a white satin ribbon...just resting on my pillow. I scan the room and pull the sides of my robe up around my neck. Someone's been in here. I check for cars in the driveway and confirm the doors are locked. *Are you still in here?* I remember the back door key under the turtle rock: everyone I know knows about it—including Jason.

My heart is racing, throbbing in my neck. I run back to my room, and even though I am sure I'm alone, I still check all of the closets and under all the beds. I slowly approach it. I sit on my bed and guardedly undo the bow of my first ever present from Tiffany's. No, it's not a present. It's a gift, as in "gift from God" or "love is the greatest gift." When it comes in the light blue box, it's most definitely a gift.

My heart slows and I feel strange that I'm alone, but then again, who should I have here? I lift the lid to discover the most exquisite diamond letter C on a chain. I pull it out of the box and dangle it in the air. The winter sun, shining through the window, sparkles off it, shooting light beams onto my wall and I gasp. It is unbelievable. Under the necklace there's a card and I don't know what to hope for. Before I reach for it, I put the necklace on and look at my reflection in the mirror. I can't help smiling. It's perfect, and I'm already in love with it. Maybe it's from Sean and I'll be able to keep it.

The card. The card, Charlotte!

A little something to remind you of who you are.
Don't make me wait too long.
Love,
Noble

I gasp at the sight of his name. He's lost his mind. He can't buy me a diamond necklace. He can't buy me, period! If I didn't love it so much, I'd take this gift over there and throw it at him. This has to go back. Things are complicated enough without this type of gift. If my mother were here, she would make me give it back. Actually, that's not true. She would love it, too. My father would try to make me give the necklace back. Noble's insane. Welcome aboard the crazy train. Maybe I'm causing him to go mad. Perhaps I literally make men crazy. I shake my head and try to focus. What am I going to do about this?

* * *

I check my neck twice in the rearview mirror on the drive to his house. The necklace is stunning. The light beams off it hanging in the most perfect position at the base of my neck, right below the biggest smile I've seen on my face in six months.

Well played, Noble Sinclair. Fortunately for you, I care more about your emotional health than you do.

He's climbing down from a tractor as I reach the drive. I have to wait for the train to pass, but I can see him between each car. Noble doesn't even notice, a lifetime of watching a train pass through his driveway having immunized him to the novelty. I still can't get used to it.

The train passes and I make my way down the long dirt drive. I pull up to the house just as he's about to open the side door. He stops and waits for me to get out of the Volvo. A few steps closer to him and his expression changes to pure delight. He's seen the necklace around my neck.

See? Even he thought I should return it, again possessing a higher opinion of me than I deserve. He has no regard for himself! I should tackle him and rip off his clothes, but that's not in his best interest either—only my own. This is why people recommend a rebound relationship. I should be able to bang Noble without any regard for his feelings, but noooo, I have to get involved with one of the greatest people I know. I should be "dating" some dirtbag from another state.

"Happy Valentine's Day," he says, still smiling, but doesn't make a move toward me.

I shrug and tilt my head to the side. "Oh, is it Valentine's Day? I hadn't noticed. Just like any other day." His joy registers on his face. He's so playful all the time. "You know, wake up, shower, open diamond necklace, go to church. Typical Sunday." I walk toward him slowly. Let him keep smiling and wonder what I'm going to do.

"You don't say. A diamond necklace? You must be deeply admired," he says, still not breaking his gaze.

"You know I should return it."

He raises his eyebrows questioning me. He thought it was a possibility.

"You thought I might? Once again you have misjudged me. I have no parents to assist with my moral compass. I'm a ship adrift, without the benefit of guidance, a spoiled child who takes what she wants without regard to the ramifications," I dramatically proclaim.

His smile broadens. "Oh, you're wrong. If you were what you claim to be, you'd have undressed me already. But you don't, and instead you torture yourself. You have to keep the necklace."

"Why is that?"

This ought to be good.

"It would be too embarrassing to return it, and I've recently broken up with Christine, Carly, and Claire."

"Pity for them." I close the space between us with three long strides. I wrap my arms around his waist and rest my head on his chest. His arms encircle my back and I'm contemplating never moving. This would be so easy. Being with Noble every day would be so easy. I lift my head to see him, and he's looking down at me.

With as matter-of-fact a tone as I can muster in his arms, I proclaim, "I'm keeping the necklace. It has nothing to do with being in love with you; it's just too beautiful to give up."

A small laugh escapes him. "I know the feeling well." He hugs me a little tighter. "Be careful, though. It'll quickly evolve into love and then you'll never be able to give it up."

"Thank you," I whisper as I pull myself out of his arms and walk away. Why does he have to be freaking perfect? If I'd been with him all this time instead of Jason, would he be the father of someone else's child?

I really do hate myself for comparing them.

~ 22 ~

A Generous Harvest

Hey, Clint, do you want a beer?"

"Ah, yeah, Charlotte. I'll be done in about five minutes."

"Meet me on the deck," I yell as I grab the bottle opener. For the past few weeks Clint's been working on Sean's room, turning it into a library/office with built-in bookshelves on three walls. It's nice having him here. Most days we have lunch together and he fills me in on the current gossip. Clint must go out a lot because he seems to know everything that's going on. Between him and Margo it's almost as if I have a social life.

I cut a sub in half and split it onto two plates. Clint comes out and flops into the chair next to me. "Oh man. Thanks, Charlotte. You don't have to keep feeding me." He takes a big bite of the sub and smiles broadly. "I like it, though."

We eat in silence as we absently observe the unplowed fields in front of us. It's a gorgeous evening. Blue sky with brush-stroked clouds highlighting the sun. The birds have started to return and two are singing on the fence.

"Crazy March, huh?" I ask, referring to the current seventy degrees in comparison to the three feet of snow in January.

"Totally crazy." Clint pulls out a joint, lights and inhales, and hands it to me. I gratefully accept. "Hey, Charlotte, are you going to the Harvest Dance with Nick?"

I stop smoking and ask, "What are you talking about?"

"What? Are you going to the dance with Sinclair?"

"Does everyone go to the Harvest Dance?" I ask, taking a deep drag of the joint. All of a sudden, the whole idea is hilarious.

"Yes, everyone goes," Clint explains. "I was wondering if you're going. I saw Sinclair the other day and he said he didn't have a date yet." Clint continues a little shyly. "I know you guys aren't together, but you're more together than you are apart."

I lean back and study the sky. What a charming way to describe us—more together than we are apart. Clint's leaning back, too, and the evening sun is hitting his face, forcing him to close his eyes. "Do you think I should ask him?"

Clint looks at me. "Him or me. I'd choose me, but you two seem to have something going on that I don't want to get in the way of."

"Right. Like you said, we're more together than we are apart." I lie back and cover my eyes. I focus on the clouds and watch the birds fly in and out of my view. "Do I have to dress up?"

Clint laughs. "Yes. You've never been to the dance before?"

"No, I've never been. I moved away by the time I was finally old enough to go. Is it fun?"

Clint inhales the joint deeply. "It's fun because the whole town goes. Afterward we all go out to the bars and keep partying." He exhales. "You have to dress up. It's almost like the prom."

I moan.

"Okay, not as bad as the prom, but dress, hair, and whatever else girls do."

"When is this Harvest Dance?"

Clint laughs again. "Charlotte, seriously, it's like you're submerged. Besides me, do you talk to anyone? It's Saturday."

"I guess I better ask Noble." I take a deep breath and then a big bite of my sandwich. "What do guys wear?"

"Suits. Think of it like a wedding."

"Okay. It's just been a while since I tried to look nice." I can't imagine going to a formal.

"I'm sure it comes easy to you," Clint says as we hear a truck pull in.

"Charlotte!" Noble yells as he walks around the side of the house. Clint starts collecting his stuff.

"I think I'd better get out of here. You two need to talk."

Noble turns the corner and walks toward me, void of his signature smile. Did he hear us?

"Here, take this to go," I say as I wrap up Clint's half of the sub and hand it to him. He thanks me on his way out.

"See you guys!" he yells over his shoulder.

Noble and I stand silent and watch Clint's truck pull away.

Noble walks to the picnic table and runs his hand along the edge as he surveys the ashes and beers.

I walk closer to him. "I'm glad you're here."

"Really?" His tone is dripping with contempt. Icy.

"Really. I wanted to talk to you about something."

"Something you talked to Clint about first?"

He's jealous of Clint? Still? Of all the reasons he should run from me, Clint is what he has a problem with?

"Yes, I was first discussing it with Clint. He remi—"

Noble's hand shoots up to silence me before I can finish. "Are you seeing Clint?" His face is stricken.

Without thinking, I walk over to him and wrap my arms around him. "No, I'm not seeing Clint."

He calms and returns my embrace.

I grab his face in both my hands. "If you would let me finish…Clint reminded me Saturday is the Harvest Dance and I wanted to see if you would escort me."

Noble is uncharacteristically shocked. His smile slowly comes back. "You're asking me to take you to the Harvest Dance?"

"That's right. If you don't already have a date. Why are you looking at me like that?"

"I just—in a million years—didn't think you'd want to go to the dance."

"Why? Clint says it's fun."

"Well, if Clint says it's fun…" He starts to laugh at himself.

"Great!" I give him a big hug and take two steps back, providing the distance I need to think straight around him.

* * *

I'm searching the top drawer of my desk when Clint arrives in the morning. Papers are strewn on the floor and stacked on the top of the desk. How the hell did all this stuff fit in this drawer?

"Looking for something?" he asks, jovial as always.

I sigh, about to give up. "A business card for Nadine's

salon. I think I need some maintenance before Saturday night."

"It's 0440," Clint offers, still watching me tear apart my parents' drawer that I've inherited. I pick up another stack of papers and they cascade to the ground. They scatter across the floor, happy to finally escape. Clint kneels down to help me corral them and hands me a picture that almost got away.

"Look at this."

He hands the picture to me. It was from the junior prom I went to with Brian Matlin.

"I remember this prom, Charlotte. You were hot."

We were hot, both of us.

"Why did you and Matlin break up?"

I've been asked that question at least a dozen times. On paper, Brian and I were the perfect couple. Had we stayed together, we'd probably be expecting a perfect little baby by now, but it just didn't work out.

"Brian is a great guy, but…don't tell anyone this"—Clint nods silently, not wanting to interrupt—"but he just didn't hold my interest."

"That's the big secret? I thought you were going to tell me he has six nipples or something."

"No. He does not have six nipples." Clint and I laugh at the same time. "I don't know why, but it just wasn't that exciting. No one wanted it to work out more than me. Well, maybe my mother; she liked Brian. We tried to get back together the summer before my parents died, but we broke up after only two weeks. After the funeral, things were completely awkward."

"Because of all the extra nipples?"

I ignore Clint and look at the picture. I was tan, sporting a manicure, pedicure, makeup, a new dress, and jewelry. God, I need some maintenance.

I dial Nadine's salon. I only need the last four digits because there's still only one exchange in Salem County. "Salon Nadine," a woman answers.

"Hi, is Nadine there?"

"Is this Charlotte O'Brien? I was going to call you if I didn't hear from you today. I hear you're going to the Harvest Dance."

I'm stupefied. "How in the world—"

Nadine interrupts me. "Oh please. News travels fast in this county and there hasn't been much to talk about lately. Now, what are you thinking? Hair, of course. What about fingers, toes, waxing, airbrush, lashes?"

"I don't know," I answer slowly, quite overwhelmed.

"Can you come in tomorrow? Say around three? We'll start with the hair."

"I can do three," I say.

"Awesome. I'll see you then. I can't wait to catch up."

I hang up and take a deep breath. Reluctantly, I press redial and squeeze my eyes shut as I place the phone to my ear. "Salon Nadine."

"Nadine, it's me again."

"I know." I can hear a giant smile in her voice.

"What am I supposed to wear to this thing?"

"Oh, girl, you'll see a little bit of everything Saturday night. The doctors and lawyers will bring the class, the cowgirls will have the sparkle, and the farmers, well…they've got their own look going, too. We call the collection 'farmhand fabulous' here in the salon. Seriously, you can wear whatever you want. There'll be recycled prom dresses, jeans, and sequins hobnobbing with Nicole Miller and Missoni."

I try to digest it all. "Oh."

"Last year I was talking to Rebecca Hopkins in the bathroom. She had on this slinky white dress. I told her I liked it and she said it was left over from her mother's third wedding. I told her I was surprised her mother let her wear white to her wedding, and she said she didn't... it was her mom's dress." Nadine breaks into a raucous laugh and I join in. "Good luck. I can't wait to see what you come up with."

I call Bruce and ask to take one of my flex days tomorrow. After assuring him I'm fine, he allows the time off. On a whim, I tell him I need today, too. Again, I have to promise him things are fine. Is there not one person who knows me who doesn't believe I might jump off a bridge? Apparently not, because Renee e-mails me to ask if I'm "fucking suicidal or something itchy-twat worse?" It's difficult to respond.

I wish my mother were here. I've never shopped for a formal dress without her. For the few events I attended after her death, I just borrowed something from a roommate or ordered something online. The last dress I bought was the blue sequined dress I wore to my spring formal, and then I just grabbed the first one I tried on during a group shopping trip. It just wasn't the same without my mother's opinion and patience. I could call my aunt Diane or Michelle, but I want to leave now and it seems unfair to give them no notice, especially knowing they'll both drop everything.

My cell rings, interrupting my melancholy thoughts. I perk up when I see it's Noble.

"Good morning," I say.

"Hey. How'd you sleep?"

His voice sounds sexy. I have to calm myself down a little.

"Good, you?"

"Not good. It's lonely in my bed. I just lie there awake and pray for a blizzard."

"Did you call for a reason?" I ignore his former statement as usual. I no longer engage in the discussion of us. Unlike Noble, I don't think it's getting us anywhere.

"Yes." He sighs, frustrated as usual. "I need to know what you're wearing so I can get you the correct color flowers."

"Flowers?" I say, stressing the plural.

"Yes, I was thinking three dozen roses. One for each time you attacked me during the snowstorm."

I can feel his smug smile through the phone.

"I'm beginning to think you escorting me to this dance is a huge mistake. Please tell me you're not getting the wrong idea about my intentions."

"Oh, Charlotte. I find your intentions very easy to read. I'm just patiently waiting for you to catch up," he says, unhurt.

Again I ignore him completely. "I don't have a dress yet."

There's silence on the other end of the line.

"I have to go get one. Do you have a color preference I should consider?" I ask, businesslike.

"Why don't you wear the blue dress from your spring formal last year? You looked incredible in it." He pauses before adding with a raspy voice, "Good enough to eat."

"Something happened to that dress and I don't have it anymore," I answer sadly.

Something like, since I was wearing it when Jason tried to confess he fucked Stephanie until she was pregnant, I set it on fire out back. You know, something like that.

Noble puts it all together and doesn't bring the dress up again. "Whatever you wear will be beautiful. Personally, I'd go with something small, perhaps invisible. I know how you like to be one with your surroundings."

"I'm leaving in a few minutes to go shopping. Can I call you when, if, I find something?"

"I look forward to hearing from you."

I hang up and text Margo and Jenn:

Any chance you guys will come home and go to the Harvest Dance with me on Saturday?

Clint walks by on his way to his truck, and I surprise myself when I ask, "Clint, do you want to go for a ride with me? I'll buy you lunch."

"Sure. Where are we going?"

"I need to get a dress."

Clint's expression changes as he thinks the offer over.

"This will be a new one for me."

"You'll be fine. I just need an extra opinion. Bring a magazine or something to read because it might involve some waiting."

We take the Volvo and head across the river to the King of Prussia Mall. It's a forty-five-minute drive to the mall. Even leaving at 9:30 it's guaranteed to take through lunch. Clint lights a joint and offers it to me.

"Rain check. I don't want to come home with a rainbow-colored dress that doesn't fit but we both think is outstandingly hilarious."

Clint nods in agreement as he laughs. He's a good choice. Not at all like my mother.

We pull into Nordstrom's lot and my phone dings with a text from Margo:

OH, I WISH I COULD. I HEARD IT IS

SO MUCH FUN! I THINK SAM, BOB,
AND TRICIA ARE GOING. TELL ME
EVERYTHING! OH, AND I THINK BRIAN
MIGHT BE THERE (JUST AN FYI)
How does she know all this in Colorado?

I'm pretty sure Clint's never been to Nordstrom before. We walk into the shoe department and Clint looks around wide-eyed, at least as wide-eyed as he can be, as high as he is.

"Fancy," he says, and I lead him up the escalator to the Special Occasion department.

"Can I help you find something special today?" a woman in her late twenties, dressed ridiculously stylishly, asks as she coyly looks over the rims of her glasses. I decide the easiest way to get through this is to just throw myself at her mercy.

"Yes, Clint here has been gracious enough to agree to help me select a dress for our county's Harvest Dance." Clint grins proudly, having been placed at the center of her attention. "It's a large formal dance with"—I pause, trying to come up with the right wording—"an eclectic mix of socioeconomic levels and their respective styles."

Clint's eyes glaze over. I've lost him to the woman's long legs, which are partially covered by over-the-knee boots.

"Okay," the woman says, drawing out the word as she considers the information. "And what style of dress are you interested in wearing?"

I don't freakin' know.

* * *

I didn't know what I wanted, but the saleswoman at Nordstrom apparently did. That's probably why she works at Nordstrom and I'm a statistician. Dress, shoes, earrings—it is a bit like the prom. Except I didn't bring Clint prom gown shopping with me. I'm glad he's here now, though.

We eat at the cafe on the third floor. Clint selects a big booth right by the window. I push all my new items in first and then slide in, making sure the dress is hanging nicely so it doesn't wrinkle.

"Who are you taking to the Harvest Dance?" I ask as I stir the sugar in my tea.

"Jocelyn Marks."

"Sounds familiar. Do I know her?"

"She was three years behind us. Works at Salon Nadine."

"Oh," I say, registering the information leak in my head.

We eat in comfortable silence, both starving from the long morning. When the server clears our plates, Clint orders two chocolate chip cookies for us. He's such a sweet guy.

"Do you think it's too soon for me to start dating someone?" I blurt out.

"It doesn't matter what I think. What do you think?" Clint cautiously asks.

"Most of the time I think it's too soon, but then again I've had no indication the time will ever come when it feels right. There are times when I no longer care and just want to do whatever I want in that moment. Even though I hate Jason, I feel like I'm betraying him. I don't know what's right and I'm just scared to death I'm going to hurt Noble," I say, sending every thought in my head scattering out of my mouth.

Clint takes a bite of his cookie. "Charlotte, very few people in the world have what you and Jason did. I don't know how long you'll be apart but I do know I've never seen anything like the two of you together." I might start to cry. "But Nick's a smart guy, always has been. He understands as much as any of us does what you and Jason were. He knows exactly the risk he's taking by being with you—and it's worth it."

I force myself to take a bite of my cookie, too.

"Let Nick worry about himself. You deserve to be happy and I think he'll take good care of you. No more dra-maa," Clint adds, and I think he sounds like the smartest person I've ever known.

"Thanks for coming with me, Clint."

He smiles as he takes another bite of his giant cookie.

"My pleasure. I had no idea dress shopping was this fun." He leans in a little. "Sinclair's going to lose his shit when he sees you in that dress." Clint's eyes motion toward the dress, hidden behind the Nordstrom bag.

"You don't think it's too tight?"

"Oh no, Charlotte—don't start fidgeting already. The only way you're going to pull it off is to wear the hell out of it. I know you can do it."

I grab my necklace and nervously bite my lip.

"Come on, it's just a dress."

Clint's right. I could have gone way shorter with a cutout back or something.

My phone dings with a text from Jenn, always six hours behind:

YEHA! SORRY I CAN'T MAKE IT,
BUT LOVING YOU GOING. SAY
HOWDY FOR ME AND HAVE TOO
MUCH TO DRINK!

* * *

After Clint hauls in all my bags and leaves, I take the dress out and hang it on the back of my closet door, placing the shoes on the floor beneath it. I get a text from Noble:

FLOWERS?

Don't need any.

YOU WON'T LIKE WHAT I COME UP WITH ON MY OWN. DID YOU GET A DRESS?

Yes.

WILL I LIKE IT?

That's the intention.

WHAT COLOR?

Off white. Get a SINGLE, bright colored flower for my wrist if you can. Ruby, purple, blue, any deep color, but only one flower.

WHY ONLY ONE?

Dress speaks for itself.

WHAT DOES IT SAY?

Get your hands off me, mostly :)

I really do hate those little smiley faces. I throw my phone on the bed happily. Tomorrow's Friday. Now that I have a dress, I'm excited for the dance. I spend some time on Sephora's website researching makeup. I say natural, but I think most other people would call my look plain. I order some brown eyeliner and mascara, a multipack of shadow, some bronzer, sparkly lip gloss, brushes, and a liquid blush product called Orgasm Illuminator because really, how could I resist? I check out, and Sephora promises to have it to me by tomorrow.

Sean lets himself in the back door, yelling my name to make sure I'm dressed.

"I'm in my room."

"Are you decent?" he asks as he walks right in. I'm lying on my bed with my laptop. He whistles when he sees the dress and shoes.

"Harvest Dance?" he asks, not quite able to believe it.

"Yes. Are you and Michelle going?"

"No, she's not feeling well."

I'm overwhelmed with how much Sean loves me. "Are you ever going to tell me she's pregnant?"

"You caught that, huh?" He's sheepish. "It just never seems like a good time."

I place my hand on his shoulder. "When's she due?"

"May. Are you going to the dance with Nick Sinclair?"

"Yes," I say, nodding.

"For what it's worth, I think he's a good guy."

"That's worth a lot, Sean." My sweet brother, who's kept his firstborn a secret to not upset me or hurt my feelings, thinks Noble's a good guy.

"You know, sometimes you seem more comfortable with him than I've seen you since we were kids. He's good for you."

"I get it."

I should be with Noble because Jason and I getting back to-gether scares the shit out of you.

~ 23 ~

A Complete Overhaul

Nadine combs out my hair and glares at it with contempt. "What took you so long to call?" she asks, looking at my face in her mirror.

"I don't know. I just haven't been properly focused on my appearance." This conversation would be ridiculous anywhere but in here.

"Well, you're here now. What are we doing with this color?"

I scrutinize my hair and have no idea. I should have looked at some magazines before I came.

"Whatever you want, Nadine. You're the expert."

She beams, giddy with the freedom, and says something that sounds like, "Serena, can you mix me up some PN-thirty-two, a little XJ-seventy, and some forty-seven for around her face?" Serena hurries off to concoct whatever it is Nadine just requested. "What about your feet?"

I slide them out of my UGGs and Nadine's eyes widen to the point of popping. "Jocelyn, bring over the soaking tub, please. Jesus, Charlotte, have you been under some kind of a rock?"

"Yes," I say, shaking my head and silently promising to make some serious changes.

Nadine works diligently, sectioning my hair and painting it with alternating colors. Sometimes she separates the hair twice until she deems the section perfect. I soak my feet until Serena comes over and starts working on my pedicure.

"What kind of shoes are you wearing tomorrow?" Serena asks.

"The most gorgeous blue suede crocheted sandals I've ever seen," I gush.

"You need to shave your toes."

What?!

She holds my foot up and Nadine agrees.

"Yeah, you need to get rid of that." Seeing that I am feeling like the hairy-toed sloth, she adds, "Everybody's got it. Serena, before you paint her, wax her toes."

If I had any pride left, this would be a humiliating day.

After two and a half hours I'm finally having my hair dried by Nadine. She's taken about three inches of dead ends off and it's still long. The color's magnificent. Amazingly bright and blond with some other color I can't even describe mixed in. Around my face is a honey-blond color applied sparingly to soften it. As she blows me out, she asks what I'm going to do with my hair tomorrow.

"I don't know. I haven't even thought about it."

"What's your dress like? It must be something to go with blue suede sandals." Nadine doesn't forget the details.

"It's off-white and lace with a high-low hem." I try to describe it the same way the Nordstrom's saleswoman did, but

Nadine looks a cross between perplexed and repulsed. I try again. "It looks like a simple off-white slip with a lace dress over top, but it's actually all one dress. The slip ends mid-thigh and the lace falls to my ankles in the back, but hits just below my knee in the front. The neckline's wider and lower than a traditional tank dress, and the stitching pushes my breasts up, but I swear somehow it's subtle." That's the best I've got.

Nadine nods. "I'm going to give you the benefit of the doubt because I know you've still got some hotness in there." She pulls the top section of my hair up and into a clip. "How about I just blow it out straight and you can pull it back—or not—tomorrow."

"That sounds good."

I'm admiring my toes when Nadine says, "Jason's not coming—in case you were wondering."

"I wasn't." Dumbfounded, I look at the floor, too afraid I'll cry if I look up.

"I'm sorry. I didn't mean to upset you." Nadine tries to catch things before they spiral out of control.

"It's okay. I'm just not used to talking about him."

"Do you guys ever speak?"

"Not since August twenty-seventh." I'm ashamed of having divulged the exact date.

Nadine looks at me sympathetically as she grasps the depth of my psychosis. "I'm sorry, Charlotte."

"It's okay. Actually it's good practice. I'm sure his name's going to come up tomorrow night. I think it's progress it never occurred to me that he might be there," I lie. And Nadine knows it. I'll add *lying sack of shit* to my list of things I hate about myself. Oh wait: *inept* lying sack of shit.

* * *

"You look beautiful, Charlotte," Nadine's mom says as she checks me out of the salon. Highlights and a cut, pedicure, toe wax—God help me, clear manicure, eyebrow wax, and a blow-out.

"Thanks, but if I didn't look good after all this, it would be pretty sad, don't you think?"

"We see it all in here," she says, and we both start to laugh.

* * *

I let myself into Butch's and the smell of the lasagna I dropped off earlier makes my mouth water before I get the key out of the door. Butch is sitting at the kitchen table and BJ is, as usual, at his feet. Butch studies me. I strut around the table showing off my new look.

"What do you think?"

"What did you go and do?" he asks gruffly.

I don't let it bruise my new confidence. "What *didn't* I do is a better question. Too much?" I ask, twirling around. When was the last time a girl twirled in here?

"I think you're nuttier than a bat, that's what I think." Even Butch starts laughing at the tail end of his statement.

I take the lasagna out of the oven and soon we begin to eat in silence.

"Can I ask you something, Butch?"

"Have I ever had a choice with all the damn questions?" he replies.

"Why do they call it the Harvest Dance if it's at the beginning of the planting season?" The question keeps popping into my head, but I always forget to ask.

"Damn idiots that are in charge," he answers, and takes a large bite of lasagna. It's his favorite of my limited cooking repertoire.

"Huh?"

He finishes chewing and rolls his eyes. "Originally it took place in the fall, after the harvest, to celebrate the end of the season, but the fall got so damn busy they decided to move it to the end of the farmer's summer, March. They billed it as a "good luck to the harvest" festival, or some dumb shit. I have no idea." He takes another bite. "Do you have a date?"

"Don't I have to have a date?" I ask.

"How the hell should I know?" he barks.

"Did you have a bad experience at this dance? You seem a bit agitated."

We eat the rest of the meal in silence.

"Can BJ spend the night tomorrow night?" I ask as I clear the dishes, expecting some nasty comment about not coming home after the dance.

"Of course he can."

I turn to see him scratching BJ under the neck and practically cooing at him. I think Butch might be bipolar.

* * *

I take a long shower in an empty house. No parents, no roommates, no friends. At Rutgers I had to wait in line for the shower. I stay busy to keep from getting depressed. I can hear my mother saying, *"So what if you're alone. A lot of people have it worse.*" She always had a knack for making me feel better by guilting me.

Once out of the shower, I start with lotion and apply it all over my body. If yesterday's visit to Nadine's taught me one thing, it's that I need to pay a great deal more attention to my body. I carefully brush and floss. I find a sample of moisturizer in my makeup bag and apply it liberally. Starting Over by Origins. My God, who would want to start this over? I'm barely surviving as it is. It feels good on my face, though.

I try to use the eyelash curler, but my lashes are long and unruly. I end up making my eyes bloodshot. Deep breath. I will not get frustrated. *Eyedrops, that's all, now calm down. What are you nervous about?*

My eyes move toward the dress and I know what I'm nervous about.

Clint's words echo in my head: *Wear the hell out of it!*

I find a few samples of perfume Sephora was kind enough to include in my package and spray each one out the open window. I settle on one that's more citrus than floral and wonder if Noble has a preference. Unsure of how much to apply, and scared of smelling like a French whore—or an American one—I spray it into the air and run into it. I'm an idiot. Am I supposed to put some of this on my inner thighs? Neck, wrists, ankles, thighs, right? I'm sure if I asked my mother she'd tell me no one's nose should be down there.

I pull a small section of hair from each side and twist them toward the back. I bought a simple pearlized barrette at the drugstore that I use to secure both pieces behind my head. It's flower child meets socialite. At least it is in my head. I use all my new Sephora finds and put on my earrings and bangles.

I grab the silver metallic purse I found in my mother's

things and feel a little like she's going with me. I stuff it with my driver's license, credit card, insurance card, AAA card, phone, lip gloss, and some cash—it's like I'm a real grown-up. I look up and catch my reflection in the mirror, and even without the dress on yet, I am a grown-up.

I wish Jason could see me like this. If only it were possible without having to see him at the same time.

I slip out of my robe and take the dress off the hanger. I try three different styles of underwear and none of them work. It's not see-through, just spectacularly tight, and even a thong leaves a small indention. I can already hear Noble's commentary on my lack of underwear to our county's biggest social event. If I thought he could behave himself, I'd tell him.

I step into the dress and pull it up over my shoulders. I try to zip it, but I can't get the zipper up more than a couple of inches. Man! I want to look perfect when Noble comes. If he has to zip me up, we'll never get out of here. Why am I completely alone?

As if sent by God, I hear the back door open. "It's your brother."

"And Michelle," she pipes in.

"Oh, I'm glad you guys are here." I slowly blink to keep from crying and ruining my makeup. "Michelle, can you come in here a second?"

She comes through the doorway and stops moving as she sees me. I stop, too, awaiting the first Salem County female reaction, although since she married my brother she's not exactly impartial.

"Charlotte, you're…stunning." I let out my breath. "Sean's going to be ecstatic to see you like this. Really, you're gorgeous."

"Can you zip me?"

Michelle walks behind me in her obvious maternity shirt.

"Thank you. I was worried it was too much. I—"

She interrupts me. "It's definitely not too much. I love it. And, man, I love your shoes!"

"I wanted to tell you congratulations, and thank you. Thank you for keeping it quiet for so long. You and Sean are too good to me."

"We love you." Michelle hugs me, being careful not to touch more than the bare minimum necessary. As we embrace, we hear the back door opening one more time and Sean and Noble greeting each other. Michelle looks at me with excited anticipation. "You ready?"

"I doubt it."

Michelle lets me lead the way out to the family room. Noble and Sean are sitting in chairs, both facing the doorway that I enter through. Sean actually blinks his eyes as if he's hallucinating. I'm embarrassed. I've overdone everything.

Michelle steps to the side of me and tries to alleviate the shock. "Boys, I'd like to introduce Charlotte O'Brien." She curtsies in my direction and moves to stand next to them. She slaps Sean on the shoulder and he briefly moves his head. "Sean, I think you know her as your sister." She smiles at me encouragingly. "And, Noble, I believe you know her as your date for the evening."

Nice job, Michelle. I'm not sure I'd have known exactly what to call me.

Noble stands up and crosses over to me, staring into my eyes. Surprising myself, I don't look away.

"Charlotte, you're the prettiest girl I've ever seen."

My smile is so big it hurts my face a little. I tip up on my toes and kiss him on the lips.

"I have something for you." He returns to his seat and pulls out a small plastic box. His suit is navy blue and the jacket stretches from one shoulder to the other, fitted perfectly. He has a crisp white shirt and a navy blue tie with flowers swirling through it in all types of deep colors. I see blue, ruby, and purple. He pulls out a single gerbera daisy on a wrist strap. It matches the floral pattern of the lace on my dress, and I wonder if Clint's provided him an overview, but for now I'm willing to give him all the credit. It's a deep raspberry color. Our eyes meet again as he places it on my wrist.

"It's perfect," I say.

"No. *It's* not perfect." He kisses my hand. "I see what you mean about the dress speaking for itself."

"Let's get a picture," Sean says, and for the first time since I kissed Noble, I remember we're not alone.

Noble congratulates Michelle as we walk to the car.

"Why did you guys come here tonight?" I ask Sean.

"To get a picture, of course. You can't take one of yourselves." He stops walking and turns to me. "You look great, Charlotte. Listen, no matter what happens tonight, enjoy it. Nights like this only come around a few times in your life."

"I will. I promise."

Noble opens the door to the Volvo and boosts me into it. I catch him staring at my breasts and he shakes his head as he closes the door. He climbs into the driver's side and I hand him the keys. I wave as Sean and Michelle pull out of the driveway. I can smell the citrus perfume and I hope Noble likes it.

"Charlotte, I'm not going to ask you to talk about us tonight. I want us to just enjoy each other the way we usually do. No heavy topics."

I should say something, but I don't think he's done.

"I'll tell you this, though: If your brother hadn't been in there, you wouldn't be wearing that dress right now. As it is, I'm having an extremely difficult time controlling myself."

I feel my entire body flush and I squeeze my upper thighs together in response and try to control my breathing.

His eyes turn dark. "Please forgive me if I'm a little possessive tonight. I didn't think it was possible to feel about another person the way I feel about you...in that dress."

I nod, not knowing what to say, and he turns the key in the ignition. I grab his hand and hold it between both of mine, and it seems to take the edge off. His face softens, but not the look in his eyes.

We head toward the Reed farm without a word. The sun is setting and the sky, in its final minutes of light, is streaked with red and pink lines.

"Red sky at night, sailors' delight," I say.

"It's a great sunset."

"It'll be dark by the time we get to the dance," I say, suggesting something, but I'm not sure what I'm willing to give. I do know I'm thankful for the gearshift between us. I let go of his hand and take my phone out of my mother's purse. He watches me, dejected. I want to get a picture of the sunset, but it's always behind us.

"Noble, will you do me a favor?"

"Anything," he answers with anticipation.

"Can you pull over?" He raises his eyebrows the tiniest bit. "I want to take a picture of the sunset."

They always slip away; even the memory of the amazing ones fade, disappear without my consent. I want a picture of this sunset. It's magnificent. Noble pulls the car over without regard for traffic since there are no other cars on the road.

"Thanks. Hurry up, it's almost down." Impossibly the sky is blazing deeper crimson than before. Noble stays seated and I grab his hand. "Come on, I want you in it." *You're magnificent, too.*

He jumps out of the car and I meet him behind it and position him with his back to the most incredible sunset I've ever seen. I take a few full-length shots, which he tires of quickly. I take a few close-ups of his face, angled to include the maximum amount of red. As I snap the last one, the colors fade and the sun dips low. Two cars go by following each other. They beep and yell something out the window.

"Sam," he says, waving to his closest friend. "We should get going." He takes my hand and, for the second time tonight, he helps me into the car. When I sit back in the seat, he pulls the seat belt out and wraps it around me, his lips practically touching my breast as he leans over to find the buckle.

My nipple hardens at his closeness. My God, without even touching me he's driving me wild. My breath quickens. We're not going to make it through tonight. Noble pauses at the sight of my nipple, still leaning over me slightly.

"We'd better go," I utter while having some difficulty breathing. As Noble walks around the car, I watch the sun disappear behind us. When he puts the car in gear, I take his hand and hold it tight in my lap, not willing to lose him, too.

~ 24 ~

Change of Heart

On a normal night you wouldn't know this tree-lined lane leads to the Reed farm. Tonight, though, each tree is decorated with hundreds of white lights. There's a glow coming from the other side of the hill, and when we get to the top, the house and tent come into view, lit up like a stadium. This is no ordinary farm; it's an estate by any measure. The main house is a massive two-story brick colonial with pillars lining the front porch. There are thirty-seven windows on the front of the house, each with a candle adorning the sill. A group of teenagers is dressed in valet uniforms, and Noble hands them the keys to the Volvo as one opens my door to help me out of the car. I take his hand and before my feet hit the ground, Noble is holding my elbow and dismissing the valet.

"I'll take it from here," he says, not very politely.

We follow the other guests through the house and onto the back patio, which opens onto the largest tent I've ever seen. It's decorated with tree branches and glass-globe candleholders hanging from the ceiling over the tables. A rod is extended the length of the dance floor with iron lanterns suspended from it every few feet and candles gently lighting the area. The tables have glass mason jars with a few daisies popping out next to miniature iron lanterns with candles. The gentleness and innocence of the flowers next to the cold lanterns reminds me of Noble and myself. I admire the sight as I slip my arm through Noble's and he grabs my hand, holding it firmly in place.

There are already at least two hundred people here, talking over the music, clinking glasses, and laughing at anecdotes. I'm a little overwhelmed. Noble squeezes my arm in his, sensing my apprehension. "I'm going to be right here the entire night." The warmth from his hand gives me a little shiver. "Are you cold?"

"No, just the opposite," I say with a suggestive smile.

"Holy hell, Charlotte. I love the dress, but I'm completely obsessed with the shoes. Where did you get them?" Nadine interrupts us and gives me a big hug.

"Nordstrom," Jocelyn says, and I see Noble register something, but he lets it go.

"Sinclair." Clint shakes Noble's hand as they move to the side, discussing something quietly.

"You two look gorgeous!" I exclaim. They really do. Nadine has an electric blue dress that's both short and tight, but she can totally pull it off, and Jocelyn is wearing floor-length black with no back. It just skims the top of her backside. She turns around, showing me the back, and shakes her bottom at me.

We stand shoulder to shoulder and drink in the sights of the tent. "Didn't I say you'd see a little bit of everything?" Nadine reiterates.

She's right. There are ball gowns, prom gowns, cocktail

dresses, some women in black work pants, a few velvet blazers, and even one or two in jeans—not even dark denim. If only the Rutgers girls could see this. Everyone is intermingled, making the dress choices seem like a patterned quilt ready to be auctioned off at a fund-raiser.

Nadine's boyfriend, Derrick, and a few of his friends come over and we exchange hellos without any kisses. Kissing hello is definitely a North Jersey thing. My old swimming buddy, Chris Black, is with them and pulls me into a bear hug.

"Ooh, hottie!" he says a little too loudly. As he spins me around, I see Noble on his way over. I wiggle free and maintain a smile so it's not awkward. Noble is by my side as Chris tells me about the open-water swimming he's competing in now. He offers to train with me if I want to enter a race. Noble's face is unmistakably dismissing the entire idea.

Dr. and Mrs. Garrisch stop by to greet us and I give them each a hug. He has known me my entire life. Dr. Garrisch makes small talk with Noble, and I admire Mrs. Garrisch's pearl necklace. It is a strand of large pearls, but the outstanding part is halfway up one side: a daisy made out of large yellow and white diamonds. She tells me it was a gift from Dr. Garrisch for their twenty-fifth wedding anniversary.

Wow. Twenty-five years. Jason and I couldn't make it three.

"It's nice to see you again, Charlotte. You kids have fun tonight," Dr. Garrisch says as he escorts Mrs. Garrisch away.

I can't believe I know this many people. I get phone numbers for Amy Johnson and Dina Lowry and promise to call so we can do Happy Hour. I catch up on swim team news with my ex-teammates and I even get a big hug from Coach Edwards. The way he looks at me makes it clear he's all too familiar with my recent breakup. Was it recent? I count on my fingers: September, October, November, December, January, February, March…seven months. How is that possible? I see Noble talking with some farmers across the dance floor and I realize *he* is how it's possible. If it weren't for him, I would still be walking around like the undead. As if he can feel me thinking about him, he looks up and gazes at me. His face turns to concern as Darla and Darlene walk over to give me fake hugs.

"I love your dress, Charlotte," Darla says, and smiles, but it doesn't touch her eyes. It barely touches her lips.

"Thanks, you guys look great, too," I say, having no idea why they're even talking to me. We weren't close in high school, and I'm pretty sure Darlene was chasing Jason when we unexpectedly got together. She's been icy ever since.

"I was surprised to see you here, especially with Nick."

"Why's that?" I ask, not understanding what she's getting at. I see Noble hurrying across the dance floor.

"Well, we figured you'd be avoiding large, public events," Darlene says, exaggerating "large" and "public."

"We just thought you'd be afraid Jason would be here."

Oh, that's how this is going to go.

"With Stephanie…and Jason Junior."

I close my eyes for a second and swallow hard.

Noble's at my side, supporting my arm as I say, "It's a shame they couldn't make it," and smile like a crazy person.

"Sorry, ladies, I need to steal my beautiful date," Noble says, guiding me away to the dance floor. His arms around me are a life jacket, and I leave it to him to sway us back and forth in some version of dancing as I restore myself. Even though I've stopped wishing horrible things on the baby, I'm still not ready to think of "him" as a person. Hearing his rather obvious name off the sour lips of Darla wounds me more than I should let it.

"What did they say to you?" Noble demands.

I lay my head on his shoulder and inhale deeply. His scent takes me back to him placing the daisy on my wrist and I am soothed.

I will not ruin tonight, so help me God. Noble will not see me cry over a baby in Oklahoma again.

"Charlotte, please say something before I go over there and choke Darla."

I almost achieve a smile. "It was nothing really. They were just filling me in on some county gossip."

"Do you ever get tired of taking the high road with people?"

"I deserve what I get."

He holds me away from him, ready to admonish me.

But I continue with a genuine smile. "This dress, Noble Sinclair as my date—I should have known every girl here was going to hate me."

Noble pulls me close to him and we legitimately dance to the music.

"Darla did invite me to the dance first."

"What?" I gasp, and pull back to see Noble's face. "Why didn't you tell me?"

"Because I'd already told her no. I wasn't coming here without you. I would have spent the entire night thinking about you and she'd be twice as mad as she is right now."

I look over at Darla's sneer as Darlene spews something in her ear.

I don't think Darla could be twice as mad as she is right now.

The band starts playing the next song as the singer entices more people onto the dance floor. The song is hauntingly familiar: My mother used to play it on Sunday afternoons. "What song is this?" I ask.

Noble nods. "I don't know, but you're beautiful."

He slowly twirls me around and returns me to him. I'm safe in his arms. Just like that, easy and uncomplicated. I pull back to see him. He has that same look I've seen for months and it finally dawns on me what it is. I wish my father could be here to see Noble look at me this way.

In my life I've been desired, and wanted, and needed, and loved, but when Noble Sinclair looks at me, I'm cherished.

My father deserved to know his daughter was with someone like Noble and that Noble loves me as much as he did. I'm safe, even if he's not here to make sure of it. We continue to move to the music as I pull his face down to kiss him gently on the lips. I return my head to his shoulder, completely at peace.

Brian Matlin is dancing with Lauren Melson. I wonder if they're a couple now. Brian's as classically handsome as he was five years ago: tall with dark brown hair and kind hazel eyes. He kind of reminds me of BJ. I'll have to remember *not* to tell him. When we broke up, girls told me I was crazy. Lauren's a sweet girl, much more his style. If there was anything sweet about me, it's long been obliterated. Maybe Noble should be with a sweet girl.

As I consider it, he moves one hand down to my lower back. It's still for a few seconds before moving slowly back and forth, up and down, searching for something. He pulls me to him and I feel his hard-on jabbing into my hip.

"Charlotte," he begins in an authoritative way, "has your complete disregard for proper attire allowed you to come to the Harvest Dance sans underpants?" His voice is low and his breath hot on my neck.

I want him right now.

I stand on my toes and challenge in his ear, "Prove it," and raise my eyebrows as I rock back a little. He watches me, considering his options, and I bite my lower lip and lick it. The pulsing between my legs starts and I know it's just a matter of time. He grabs my hand, walking briskly out the door. Hopefully everyone will think we're having a fight.

"Where are you guys going?" Sam asks as we rush by.

"We'll be right back. I want to show Charlotte the ring around the moon."

"There isn't going to be a ring around the moon," I explain as Noble grabs our keys from the wall of hooks and we traverse the adjacent field searching for the Volvo. "Red sky at night, sailors' delight. No rain tomorrow."

"Charlotte." His voice is strained. "I'm having trouble thinking because I have a giant throbbing rod in my pants." He labors over each word.

We find the car and he opens the back door and throws me in just before diving in on top of me. He's grabbing, and pulling, and touching me everywhere at once.

"Slow down," I beg.

He stops, his breathing loud and heavy. I sit him up and straddle him. I ease off his jacket and bring his face close as I kiss him gently, trying to provide some control. I'm so wet and my breasts are pawing their way out of my dress.

"Unzip my dress," I demand as I lean over for him to reach it. My lips find his neck and kiss it gently. He follows my instructions, dependent. I pull both arms from the dress and sit up, letting it fall to my waist. Noble reaches out and plays with my nipple as I watch. He pauses and looks at me voraciously. I take his face in my hands and kiss him. Noble's tongue communicates his need as it blocks my thoughts and steals my breath. My face is hot like the rest of my body and I need him in me now. I reach for his pants' zipper and he stops my hand, laying it flat on his pants. I feel him, huge and throbbing through the material. I try to move my hand up it, but he holds it still as my heart pounds in my chest.

"Be careful, it can only take so much of you," he says, and looks at me, pleasure personified.

"Take off your pants," I demand, and as soon as I see his giant hard-on fall back against his dress shirt, I pull up my skirt and pounce on him. I'm straddling him as we kiss frantically, and he lifts me up, plunging himself into me on the way down.

"Oh, Noble..." I try to breathe as he lifts me up, and again he fills me.

I can't think straight—or crooked, or frontward, or backward. I arch my back just enough for an intense wave of pleasure to gush from every descent. I ride him with my face pointed toward the stars and my hands resting on his beautiful shoulders. Seconds, minutes, hours—time itself is one of the many concepts I can no longer grasp. Noble grabs my head with both hands and moves my face within an inch of his own.

"Oh, Charlotte, what you do to me," he whispers, and kisses me with the full suppressed desire of the past three months.

I return to my frenzied rhythm, unable to stop. I throw my head back and completely disintegrate around him. It goes on and on, and as I rest my head on his shoulder, I still shudder some. I again just try to breathe.

"Did you come?" I ask, embarrassed I don't know but not wanting to neglect him. His head is turned away from me and his heart beats against my cheek.

"Noble?"

"What? Sorry..." He turns toward me. "I can't understand the question. I think you literally fucked my brains out."

I study him triumphantly and kiss his neck.

He grabs my hand. "I never thought I'd say this, but please stop. My body can't take any more."

But it could. And it did.

* * *

I'm lying on top of Noble in the backseat of the car when we hear voices of guests leaving the dance. I feel invisible as I rest on his chest. *Boom, boom, boom.*

"Yo, Sinclair, you two had better be at the Barnyard in thirty minutes or I'm bringing everyone I know to your house and we'll drink all your beer." It's Sam.

"Would you stop? How do you even know they're in there?" I hear his girlfriend, Kim, ask.

"Oh, they're in there. Sinclair told me he almost attacked her when he picked her up and he's been ogling at her, lovesick, all night." Sam is drunk. "And don't think you can hide at O'Brien's. I'll find you there, too."

"Sam, would you shut up? Come on, you're being an idiot." When the voices quiet, I see them pulling away with Sam driving.

I look closely at Noble's handsome face. "You do look a little lovesick."

"Believe me, I'm not well." He kisses the top of my head. "Let's go change before we go to the Barnyard, or else I'm going to imagine that dress pulled up around your waist all night."

Something stirs in me, but I agree to the plan.

Noble drops me off at my house and takes my car to go change. I hop in the shower for a quick rinse and reapply the lotion and citrus perfume, again spraying it in the air and running through it like an imbecile as it falls. It seemed to work fine earlier; why screw with a good thing? I put on my favorite jeans and a teal V-neck shirt. Noble will be happy I'm wearing a bra. I let my hair down on both sides. I feel better without all the makeup and opt to only replace the lip gloss.

My phone rings and I pick it up. The number is familiar, but not in my new contacts. "Hello," I answer.

"Charlotte? It's Brian." I can hear noise behind him and I assume he's at the Barnyard Saloon already. "Charlotte? Can you hear me?"

"Yes, I can hear you." I'm screaming into the phone, battling the background noise although my house is completely silent.

"Are you coming to the Barnyard tonight?"

"Yes, Noble's bringing me out," I answer instinctively.

Brian's quiet and I wonder if he heard me or if he passed out.

"Oh, well, I need to talk to you." I start thinking of ways to blow him off as Noble opens my back door and walks toward me. His smile fades as he sees I'm on the phone. "It's important." Brian's voice is desperate and pulls on my heartstrings. I've never wished anything but the best for him, a stark 180 degrees from what I wish on Jason every day.

"Okay. Noble and I'll be there soon." I purposely say his name. This time for Noble's benefit rather than Brian's.

"Thanks," he says, and hangs up.

"Who was that?" Noble asks, not hiding his irritation.

I take a deep breath. "Brian Matlin. He wants to talk to me at the Barnyard." I end the sentence lightly. This isn't a big deal.

"Well, he can't." Noble dismisses the subject and turns around, grabbing a beer from the fridge.

"What?"

"He can't," he reiterates.

"Who says?"

"I just did. Twice. I'm not going to stand around while Brian Matlin professes his love to you because he finally got drunk enough to do it. No way."

I turn around, searching for something on my back.

"What are you doing?" he asks, watching me.

"I'm looking for the sold sign on my back. Or perhaps you have some shipping slip from when you mail-ordered me from Russia."

He grabs my hand. "Oh, if it were only that easy with you."

"Look, to avoid ruining our night with a long drawn-out conversation about my need for freedom and your lack of trust, I'll tell you this. I broke up with Brian because even though he's a great guy, he bored me. He bored me in the car, he bored me in the restaurant, he bored me on the phone, and God help me for saying this, he bored me in the bedroom." Noble watches me, giving nothing away. "And if you think, after spending an hour in the backseat of my car with you tonight, that there are words that exist in this world"—I stress the next part—"that could draw me to Brian Matlin, then you are an idiot."

Noble laughs.

"Oh, it's funny. You *can't* talk to him. You're a barbarian." I stress each syllable. "Now take me to the Barnyard, where I can speak to whomever I wish." I walk to the back door.

"I always wondered why you were with Matlin," he says, and opens the door for me. "He is kind of boring. Poor guy."

* * *

Noble and I park about an acre from the bar. The entire town must be here. I'm shocked at the hundreds of cars.

"A lot of people who don't go to the dance still come out and party afterward," Noble explains.

"I can see that." I look around for Jason's truck.

Please, God, don't let Jason be here… not tonight.

As we approach the bar, I see two guys hauling Brian Matlin out. His head is down and he can barely walk. They prop him up against a truck's wheel and try to communicate with him.

"Looks like that's not going to be an issue," Noble says, smiling.

I smile back, relieved to not have to deal with any big conversations.

The bar's absolutely packed. Noble opens the door for me and we can barely squeeze into the room. A bouncer leans down from his milk crate and says something in Noble's ear. He nods and takes my hand, leading me toward the back door. We maneuver through the Barnyard's back door and out to a pasture that's been transformed into an extension of the bar. There's a large dance floor and a fenced-in area with a mechanical bull. There's room to move, but it's still crowded. The mechanical bull is going and revelers line the fence surrounding it, cheering on the riders. To the right are the DJ and the dance floor, with about eighty people line-dancing. I've been spending so much time in New York that this scene reminds me a little too much of Oklahoma.

Out of nowhere, Sam comes running over and jumps on Noble, and we're quickly engulfed by a dozen people we graduated with. There's a lot of catching up to do. Everyone graciously avoids the subject of Jason and I feel myself relaxing.

I leave Noble to steady Sam and start to cross the dance

floor to Nadine. I want to thank her again for all her hard work. I'm just about to the other side when Jason's favorite song comes on and almost drops me to my knees. I turn around and see Noble watching me, only half paying attention to what Sam's telling him. I blow him a kiss to keep him from worrying. I've got to find a way to get over this. I can't have them both and Noble deserves better. Jason deserves nothing.

As I turn back around to complete my journey to Nadine, I run straight into Jack Reynolds.

"Sorry, I wasn't paying attention," I say.

Jack grabs my arms and pulls me toward him. "You're just who I was looking for, Charlotte." His sneer is sinister and my fight-or-flight instinct is screaming at me to get the hell away from him. I've known of him for years but only hung out with him twice when he was in Oklahoma visiting Stephanie. Jack is three or four years older than Stephanie and always seemed to be an unlikely choice for her boyfriend, but they were together for at least two years.

I yank one arm loose and he tightens his grip on my other. "What? Don't be like that. I just want to talk." Jack is tall and solid, and his grip is hurting my arm. "We have something in common."

"No, we don't. Now get the hell off of me," I say as I try to pry his hand loose.

"We need some privacy," he says, and starts to pull me out of the bar. We're lost in the crowd and I can't break his grip. I dig in my heels as I try to yank his hand off me. Neither is working. He's dragging me through the crowd by my bicep.

"Wait!" I scream at him. "What do you want?"

Jack stops and turns toward me. He bends over and brushes

close to my face. His breath smells of tequila and his brow is covered in sweat. He moves his lips to my ear.

"An eye for an eye," he says, backing up and staring at me with hatred filling his gaze. He tightens his grip on my arm and turns to pull me forward.

"Get your hands off her," Noble says, just loud enough for the crowd immediately around us to hear. His eyes are savage and I cower away from him. I've only seen Noble angry once—after I found out about Stephanie's baby—and it didn't come close to the look in his eyes now.

"What do you care, Sinclair? It's none of your business. Leer's got Stephanie and the baby now."

Noble steps closer to Jack, who's still killing my arm, and the crowd starts to form a circle around us.

"This is the last time I'm going to tell you to let her go before I rip your fucking head off."

Jack should let go. It's pretty obvious Noble is going to kill him.

He releases my arm and takes a swing at Noble. Noble blocks it and lands a haymaker to the right side of Jack's face. He dives on top of him and they both fall to the floor. Noble's on top of Jack, punching him over and over again. I don't even move, too stunned by what's happening. Two guys pull Noble off and swing him around to the waiting punch of Jack's brother, Jim. Clint and Sam are now involved and the scene quickly escalates to a complete brawl. I dodge two bodies and Noble grabs my hand and pulls me through the crowd. We pass the bouncers running toward the fight as we exit the bar.

"Charlotte, are you okay? Did he hurt you?"

I shake my head because I still can't speak. I can hear the

mayhem continuing inside as we walk away from the building. Noble leads me to the car and puts me in the passenger seat. We pull out of the Barnyard Saloon as the state troopers pull in.

* * *

We drive in silence as I hold Noble's hand in my lap. "You know you can't go around punching everyone who says something mean to me," I say.

"You're wrong," he says as he squeezes my hand. "I plan on punching every single person who's ever mean to you." I move his hand to my lips and kiss it. "For the record, though, I think Jack was about to do more than speak meanly to you." His words make me shiver. "I'd have killed him first." Noble's eyes are murderous again and I squeeze his hand to bring back my happy Noble.

Noble pulls the car directly into the garage and comes to my side to help me out. When he opens the door, the light shines on his cut and already bruising forehead.

"Noble, your head. Does it hurt?" I ask as I inspect the cut that's beginning to swell above his eye.

"Yes. But it was worth it."

I don't like the look of his eye. "Come inside."

"It's not a big deal. A friend told me once that heads bleed a lot," he says.

"You hang out with a bunch of fools, though."

We make our way into the house. I turn on the lights and motion for him to sit on the stool next to the island. I pour us each a glass of whiskey, add some ice, and begin the search for the first-aid kit. I find it under the sink and vow to clean out the entire cabinet. It's crammed with stuff my mother put in there a lifetime ago.

I turn to Noble and he's smiling, his old self again. I begin by using the wound cleaner with a gauze pad, gently wiping the cut. "You know, you scared me at the bar," I quietly admit, standing between his legs as I work.

"Why?" He touches my hand and stops my work. "You shouldn't ever be afraid of me, Charlotte. I'll never hurt you."

"It wasn't me I was afraid you were going to hurt," I say, and look down. "I've never seen you like that before."

With a finger to my chin, Noble raises my eyes to his. "I've never wanted to kill someone more than I wanted to kill Jack Reynolds tonight. I saw him come up behind you on the dance floor, but I couldn't get through the crowd. I saw the look on his face and I knew he was drunk. By the time I got to you, I was ready to annihilate something."

I hold Noble's face in my hands and kiss him tenderly. I pull away and finish bandaging his head. "There. Good as new," I say as I lean back, admiring my bandage. Noble pulls me close and kisses me again. He's greedy and rough, and I feel my body responding as I wrap my arms around his neck. "Spend the night," I beckon in his ear.

He pulls back and looks deeply into my eyes. "At the risk of saying something that will cause us to still have our clothes on in ten minutes," Noble sighs, "I just don't want a repeat of the last time we spent the night together."

Aah, the blizzard. Noble's tortured face reminds me that for some inconceivable reason he loves me.

"Funny, because a repeat is exactly what I'm looking for." I flash him a greedy smile. It's impossible to comprehend why Noble's willing to ignore his better judgment and take a chance on me. It's a stupid gamble, but I'm happy with him, and I need him. I need him in every way I can imagine. I'll trade his love to keep me alive in return for the promise I'll never let Jason Leer come between us—that is, if he's not already firmly perched there.

"Hey. What are you thinking about? You're so serious. I lost you for a minute," he says, his brow furrowed.

"Noble, I want you. I want you tonight and every night thereafter." I lean into him. "I love you." Then more playfully I say, "I want to be your girlfriend."

Noble's face registers complete exaltation as he picks me up and carries me to my bedroom.

* * *

I'm not sure if it was the heels, the fight, or spending the night with Noble, but I'm sore this morning. I pull my knees to my chest and try to stretch out in bed. Noble is asleep next to me, and besides the bandage above his left eye, he is perfect. I want to wake him up just to see him smile. Instead I opt for a hot shower.

In the bathroom I notice the bruise on my upper arm. I can make out four purple and gray fingers. What an ass. I hope that was all caused by alcohol. Did Jack really think that would piss off Stephanie? Of course, I barely know Stephanie and have no idea what would piss her off. I'm pretty sure it would incense Jason, and maybe that was his intention. I should take a picture of my arm and text it to him, letting him know that a full seven months later I'm still being abused for his mistake. Maybe he doesn't see it as a mistake. Maybe Jason's happy with Stephanie and the baby.

"Maybe you should stop thinking about assholes," I say to myself in the mirror.

* * *

The hot water engulfs me. It heals the majority of my aches. Once I'm dry, I climb back into bed next to Noble and snuggle in beside him. He wraps his arm around me without opening his eyes. It can be like this for the rest of my life if I just keep it together. My phone dings and I reach over Noble to grab it off the nightstand on his side.

WTF HAPPENED LAST NIGHT? JACK REYNOLDS IS SUCH AN ASSHOLE. HEARD NOBLE BEAT THE SHIT OUT OF HIM.

"Apparently the morning edition has hit Colorado."

Noble opens his eyes. "Really?"

"Margo's exceptional at knowing what's going on," I explain as Noble's phone dings. I lie back down on his chest.

"Let's see who else is in the loop." He picks up his phone for both of us to read. The text is from Jason Leer.

HEARD WHAT YOU DID LAST NIGHT.

THANKS FOR LOOKING OUT FOR HER.

I close my eyes. Of course Jason would be here with us. Noble and I will never escape him, not in Salem County. Probably not anywhere.

"Charlotte, I'm sorry," Noble laments. I start to sit up and he pulls me back down.

"It's okay," I lie. "Really, it's not a big deal. I'm thankful you're looking out for me, too." I lay my head on his chest. Noble seems cautious but satisfied I'm not going to have some type of breakdown. Loving me must be a special form of torture. "Now, do you want to go out for breakfast or lie low and make something here?"

"I don't ever want to leave this house," he says without a hint of humor.

"I'll go warm up the griddle." I kiss him with all the heart I can muster after seeing a text Jason sent through the universe moments before.

"I'm going to grab a shower." He gets out of bed and walks into the bathroom completely naked. I sigh at the sight of him. How did I not attack him at Rutgers?

I put on yoga pants, a T-shirt, and the hoodie Noble gave me for my birthday. It's ten o'clock but feels like the afternoon. I pull out some eggs, cinnamon bread, and bacon. I start the bacon first and turn on some music.

The back door opens as Sean walks in. How does he move so fast?

"How's it going?" Sean says, his version of *What's up?*

"It's going," I say, and get back to work.

Sean takes out a plate and arranges a half-dozen donuts on it. They remind me of my mother, placed so daintily.

"How's Sinclair's right arm? I heard he was swinging it like a hammer last night."

I shake my head. "I'll never get over how fast word travels around here."

"It's the day after the biggest event of the year. The whole town is out talking about it. How did you guys get out of there without getting arrested?"

"Noble," I say.

As if on cue, Noble comes into the kitchen wearing just a towel and drying his hair with another.

"Man, that felt great," he says as he puts the towel around

his neck. The sight of Sean stops him from speaking and moving. Sean and I both laugh at him.

"Hey, Sean," Noble says, and holds out his hand.

Sean shakes it with a warm smile. "Did you guys have fun last night? At the dance?" Sean asks Noble, totally screwing with him.

Noble grins. "It was lovely. I'm going to go put some clothes on."

"Not necessary. I'm just here for the food," Sean says.

"I'm fine with what you're wearing." I give Noble an appraising glance and Sean and I laugh again. Noble leaves us alone, cracking each other up. He returns properly dressed and seems ready to start the morning over.

* * *

Noble goes home and I pick up BJ before I head back to bed. I haven't had a nap in weeks and it's been almost a year since I took one contented and not completely depressed. I wake up to BJ jumping on my bed and licking my face. I usually don't let him in my bed, but I'm in such a good mood I let him disappear under the covers. He burrows in next to my ankles and I close my eyes, at peace. *Thank you, God, for peace.*

After a solid two hours, I get out of bed as BJ crawls on top of the covers and looks at me sadly.

"What? I can't lie in bed all day. Even though you'd love that," I say, rubbing his ears. "Maybe for your birthday that's what we'll do." BJ tilts his head back and forth, listening. "What do you think of Noble Sinclair?" BJ's tail starts banging the quilt. "Yeah, yeah. He's a crowd pleaser."

~ 25 ~

Perfect

I keep looking in my closet. I go through each hanger one by one. There must be something in here I can take to Key West with me. The plane departs at 7:50 a.m. tomorrow, which leaves me today to assemble a suitable island wardrobe to celebrate Violet's last few days as a bachelorette. I still don't know how Trey convinced Violet's dad to pay for all of us to go, or even more unbelievable, how he convinced Blake to agree to a joint bachelor/bachelorette party.

"Good morning, Naked Girl," Noble says groggily, staring at me from my bed. He's rolled onto his back and is lying with one arm behind his head. He's yummy. I walk over and kiss him, rubbing my fingertips over the inside of his bicep. "What are you busy doing without your clothes on?"

"I'm trying to find something to wear in Key West," I say as I get back up and remember my bottom drawer is full of bathing suits. "This trip's kind of snuck up on me."

"I wish you weren't going. I'm going to miss you." Noble

pauses and breaks into a wide smile. "Plus, I think that guy Trey is going to spend the whole trip trying to fuck you."

"Noble, is that any way to speak to a lady?" I ask dramatically.

"Well, it's true. I can't blame him. It took me years, literally, to get this far." He laughs, but I don't think Noble's version of our "courtship" is all that funny.

"Based on your predictions, it doesn't sound like you're the right person to take shopping for some resort attire. Maybe Clint's free."

"Oh no. I've seen what you and Clint come up with."

I sit down on the bed next to Noble and lie across his stomach on my side. "Noble, do you trust me?" I'm smiling, but the question is serious.

"Sometimes it seems as if you don't trust yourself, Charlotte," he says as he runs his fingers through my hair.

"What do you mean?"

He grazes my face with the backs of his fingers. I lean into his hand and stare into his eyes.

He stops and asks, "Do we have to talk about this today? I want our last day together to be memorable in a good way."

"A good way like you're going to have sex with me until I can't sit down on the plane tomorrow?" I ask.

Noble pulls me down and under him. He kisses my neck and brushes across it with his lips. "Do you have any idea how crazy you make me?" His words are a hot whisper in my ear.

"It's the last thing I mean to do," I say.

He again kisses my neck and I fight for a deep breath. "I'm sorry," I add weakly, already finding it difficult to complete a thought.

"You should be. You're forcing me into uncharted territory."

I lean into his kisses, his breath and tongue tickling me.

"What's that?" I ask, not hiding my arousal.

"You're the first girl I'm terrified of losing." With that statement, his lips land on my mouth and crush any response my brain might have concocted.

I want my clothes off me, but I don't want him to stop kissing me. His hunger is conveyed by his tongue in the most enticing way. As if sensing my need, Noble pulls back and lifts my dress over my head. My exposed breasts stand at attention for their master and he rewards them by taking each one in his mouth until I moan.

He pulls me to the edge of the bed and sinks to his knees. Noble's tongue has its way with me, and just before I think I'll lose my mind completely, he stops.

"Not yet, Charlotte."

"Please, don't stop," I beg.

"I want to be in you when you come."

Noble stands up and delicately enters me. He feels twice as big as I've ever known him. He's gentle and teasing me and depleting my self-control. When he pauses, I take my middle finger into my mouth and slowly remove it. I begin to play with myself and hold Noble's stare as long as I can, but when he begins to thrust into me again, the look in his eyes is too much. I arch my back and see my ceiling fan spinning above my head just before losing my entire grasp on reality; my orgasm surrounds Noble as he comes, too, my hand still in place, touching myself.

Noble pulls out and lies down beside me. I'm lost in myself and cover my eyes with my forearm, enjoying my stupidity.

"I want you to touch yourself every day in Key West and think of me while you do it."

"It will be my pleasure" is all I can muster.

* * *

I open my eyes and realize it's still light out. Noble lies behind me and my head's resting on his scrumptious bicep. I gently kiss it because I love it, and him, so very much. He stirs from the affection and rolls toward me, spooning me. I'm torn about whether to get up and make us dinner or lie here until tomorrow morning. Being in bed with Noble makes me wish I wasn't going to Key West. Things are perfect right now, exactly the way they are.

"How did we fall asleep?" Noble asks with his eyes still closed.

"Good sex will put you right out," I say, and roll over to face him. I want to revisit his comment about being terrified of losing me. I want to tell him it'll never happen, that he can trust me, that there's nothing in this world that could tear us apart, but all I'm able to say for sure is, "I love you, Noble." He kisses the top of my head, not realizing my inability to make a guarantee. "Are you hungry?"

"I'm completely satisfied." He grins. "But since it's your last night in town, let's go out to dinner. You can wear your new jeans."

So thoughtful.

"Your ass looks amazing in them."

So Noble.

"I'm hopping in the shower." I extricate myself from his heavy arms and make my way to the bathroom. I turn on the shower to give the water time to warm and head back to Noble. I sit down next to him on the bed and bounce up and down a few times.

"You know, I'm still able to comfortably sit down. Would you like to join me in the shower?"

Beneath the sheets, I see Noble's answer before he speaks as his growing hard-on bulges. "That sounds like a challenge." He pulls me down to the bed, kissing me as he pins me under him. My groin aches with anticipation, its memory short. Noble stands and pulls me up and over his shoulder. I yelp in surprise and laugh as he places me down right under the showerhead. I laugh right up until the minute he steps into the shower, and suddenly the humor is sucked from the room.

"Bend over," he says, hungry and rough. I oblige and bend over, my back to him as he runs his fingers up and down me, one trailing the next, until he slides one, then two, into me. He continues in and out until I'm as wet as the shower. Noble pulls out his fingers and slaps my bottom just hard enough. I yelp with pleasure and turn around to look into the eyes of the man who's about to fuck me.

"You may have to stand on your tiptoes."

I do and Noble guides himself into me. I hold on to the ledge in the back of the shower and balance on my toes.

"Is it okay?" he asks.

"It's perfect," I say without turning around. With that he begins an absolute onslaught, ramming himself into me until I forget the shower water is even falling on us. His rhythm quickens as he pulls me to him each time by my hips. It is rough, and carnal, and dirty, and I almost forget it's Noble behind me as he pounds me again and again and again. I cry out as I come and Noble wraps his arm around my waist to keep me on my toes as he finishes. His mission accomplished, a delicious rawness endures as he pulls out for the last time.

I stand up and already feel sore. I stretch and Noble kisses me, his gentle kisses that I love. He takes shampoo and lathers my hair, being careful not to let soap fall into my eyes. I return the favor and wash his hair and his whole body with the bubbles from the shampoo. His arms, his wonderful arms. I would linger there except I can't wait to get to his shoulders.

"You have incredible shoulders," I say absently. I hear him chuckling at me as usual. I rinse my hair as Noble finishes and steps out of the shower, leaving me to condition my hair, shave, and body-wash the rest of me.

I can't screw this up—not the shower but Noble.

~ 26 ~

A Mural Belongs on a Wall

Our flight lands in Tampa and we all head to the nearest bar. We have a two-hour, forty-minute layover, and this group is ready to put the party in bridal party. I still can't believe Trey convinced Blake to agree to it. I text Noble that I've made it to Florida; he was unusually quiet when I left for the airport.

"Charlotte, what'll you have?" Trey asks. He's been quite attentive on the trip thus far. We were seated next to each other on the plane since Trey suggested mixing up the group to break the ice before our weekend together, and Violet's father agreed it was a great idea.

"Umm, I'll take a vodka and grapefruit juice," I answer, unsure of what I feel like drinking. We've missed lunch, but no one mentions hunger—only thirst. Trey hands me the glass and I miss Noble, or maybe I just feel guilty being here without him. His words from yesterday still ring in my head: *It seems as if you don't trust yourself.* "Thank you. I'll get the next one."

"Charlotte, I haven't seen you all day!" Violet says as she closes in between Trey and me.

"I know! These crazy seat assignments," I say, and Violet knows exactly what I'm thinking. "I'm hoping we don't use the same logic with the sleeping arrangements."

"You're going to love where we're staying," Violet says, and Julia moves in for the information. "It's an island off the coast of Key West with cottages on it. We'll take a boat from the Westin."

I have so many questions. "How many cottages?" is where I start. "I mean, how many bedrooms?"

"I think there's one cottage for the guys and one for us." I relax slightly. "Of course, we're going to have to shift things around a little because I'm probably going to sleep with Blake every night."

"Of course" is all I can respond.

Julia shoots me a look like, "What the hell?" and we both take a big gulp of our drinks. Sydney joins the three of us at the bar, and it strikes me that we're the group that should be traveling today—without guys. Finally together, the four of us fall into our usual party rhythm and laugh our way through three more rounds.

"By the way, I ran into Renee on Tuesday," Julia says, and lowers her voice. "She said to tell you to party like you've got a thumb up your ass." I almost choke on my vodka and grapefruit. "There's seriously something wrong with her," she proclaims.

I finish my drink and ask Julia to watch my bag as I go to the bathroom. I'm practically skipping back to the bar when I stop, frozen by the sight ahead. At a magazine kiosk about ten feet away is Harlan Wilder, Jason's best friend in Oklahoma, possibly in the entire world. My brain screams at me to run, instinctively avoiding all things Jason, but I don't run. I look in every direction around him expecting to see Jason not far away. Harlan finishes flipping through the magazine and turns toward me. Seconds become minutes that I stand facing Harlan. He cracks a smile, small at first, but when I don't throw anything at him, it turns into his signature enormous grin. Without a nod, a smile, or a wave, I turn around and begin to walk away.

"Oh no you don't, Jersey," Harlan says as he runs to stand in front of me. "You're not gettin' away that easy."

"Believe me, nothing is easy," I say, and consider my options with Harlan barricading my escape route. I'm deathly still, staring at him, my petrified heart unclear of its reaction.

Harlan's tall and broad. He has sandy blond hair and green eyes, a black suede hat, and a giant silver belt buckle to match. His face is as sweet as the last time I saw him, but it doesn't move me. Harlan, and the memories of him, are all mixed in with my feelings for Jason. He absolutely had to know about Stephanie. Harlan knows everything about Jason.

"Charlotte, it's like you died. I've been worried sick about you."

"You should have been. I almost died," I admit, still unwilling to feel any emotion. "It's been as close to hell as I ever want to be."

Harlan grabs my hand and starts to walk toward the chairs lining the concourse. I pull it away and stop walking.

"Please, darlin'. Don't be like that. I just wanna talk." Harlan could always make me laugh. "I didn't do anything." His plea weakens me ever so slightly and I relax the scowl on my face. Harlan moves to the side and holds out his hand, directing me to lead the way. As we sit down, I notice a large group of cowboys at the gate facing us. Some of them I recognize from Oklahoma.

My chest tightens and I swallow hard. "Harlan, is he here?"

"No, and he's gonna rip the head off a bull when he finds out he missed you. He came in yesterday." Harlan's prediction unearths a smile. I can't help myself. Harlan was the one guy Jason almost trusted me with. He treated me like a little sister, always looking out for me when we traveled to rodeos.

"What are you doing here?" I ask.

"The Pro Rodeo's at the Florida State Fairgrounds this weekend. We're waitin' for the second flight to land. A bunch of us made the trip." *A bunch of us as in Stephanie and the baby, too?* I feel sick at the thought of them being anywhere near me. If Jason had never been with Stephanie, I'd be at the rodeo with them this weekend.

"What're you doing here? You goin' to the rodeo?"

"No. I don't go to the rodeo anymore," I say. "I'm on a bachelor/bachelorette weekend. It's in Key West, but we have some time before our connection." I look down at my hands resting in my lap and realize as much as I've moved on, I still want Jason. God I wish none of this ever happened.

"When are you coming back to Oklahoma?" Harlan asks as if I've been away on a vacation. "Don't you miss me?" He's as ridiculous as he always was. "Don't you miss him?"

"There's no time to miss him. I'm too busy hating him." My voice is too loud, trapped in a half-laugh, and I'm on the verge of hysteria. Harlan joins in and I can't stop myself. "I mean it! I know it doesn't seem like it, but I hate him more than anything in this world! I want to kill him. I'm exhausted from hating him so much." Harlan and I keep it up and I'm beaming in the wake of it. To an observer, we probably appear like we're talking about something hilarious, rather than my desire to kill his best friend. "And don't think because I'm laughing that I don't hate you, too." Harlan roughly hugs me, still horsing around.

I quiet down and try to collect the courage to ask him the question that's haunted me since August.

"Harlan?"

"Yes, darlin'."

"Why did he do it?" I swallow hard and squeeze my eyes shut, unsuccessfully fighting tears stronger than my will.

"Oh, Charlotte," he says, and pulls me to him, "I don't even know if he knows. I do know this, though—he loves you more than the earth loves the sun, and not seein' you is killin' him. That boy's in misery."

I take a deep breath and close my eyes. If only it was last year again. Being with this cowboy reminds me of what it was like to be with the other, and I feel alive. It's my soul. I know it. I left it in Oklahoma.

I lean on Harlan's shoulder for what feels like a few seconds, but it must have been much longer because Sydney walks up to us and says, "Uhhhh, Charlotte? You okay? They're getting ready to board our flight."

"Sydney, this is Harlan, my friend from Oklahoma that I haven't seen or talked to in months," I explain.

"Pleased to meet ya," Harlan says as he tips his hat to Sydney.

"Likewise." Sydney is uncharacteristically lost for words. "Okay, are you coming?"

"Maybe you can catch a later flight?" Harlan suggests.

"Maybe I should get Julia," Sydney says, and starts looking behind her for reinforcements. "Oookay, I'm sure you'd like to catch up, but if you aren't on that flight, Violet's going to pitch a fit."

She's right, of course.

"How long are you in Key West?" Harlan asks.

"We fly home Sunday afternoon," Sydney answers quickly.

I stay resting on Harlan, not focusing on what I should be doing.

"If you can stay a little while, I'll call Jason and he'll meet us. In fact, someone's probably already talked to him. I'll bet he's on his way here now," Harlan says as he motions at the group of cowboys near the gate. The majority of them are still staring at us.

On his way...here...now. His words reverberate in my head, and a familiar pounding returns. I stand up next to Sydney.

"I should go."

"Don't go, Charlotte. He's dyin' to see you—and I'm dyin' to see you. Please don't go." Harlan grabs my hand again as we hear the announcement for my flight to Key West.

"Harlan, I can't see him." My resolve returns. "It's taken me this long to start living. Seeing him will dismantle me." Harlan's defeated. I take back my hand and move a few steps back.

"I'll see you around, Harlan."

"Will you?" he asks hopefully.

"Not a chance." I shake my head and smile warmly at Harlan. He's hard to hate. I turn and walk away. Sydney and I join our party waiting in line to board. I ignore the cowboys staring at me, and my friends who are staring at me and the cowboys, and I walk onto the Jetway without looking back.

* * *

In the cab along with me are Violet, Blake, and Trey, and I'm reminded again that this whole bachelor/bachelorette concept isn't going to be easy to navigate and that it's stupid. Who throws eight more-or-less strangers on vacation together when the theme is debauchery? This isn't MTV. I notice Trey looking at me and turn my gaze out the window. I'm going to have to shut him down soon. Seeing Harlan stole more of my energy than I thought and I need every reserve to make sure Violet has the time of her life.

We're dropped off at the Westin and a bellhop takes our luggage. Blake and Violet disappear into the hotel lobby and I survey the grounds, but I don't see any cottages. They return with a waitress holding a tray of drinks. I take one and gulp it down; it's definitely something with rum. I turn my attention to the water view beyond the lobby area. The crystal-blue water meets the cloudless blue sky and soothes me instantly.

The waitress motions for us to follow her and leads us past the hotel lobby and the pool to a dock. There we all board a boat. The captain welcomes us, asking if this is our first time to Sunset Key and I mentally correct him, thinking Key West, but when we take off, I realize we're heading to a separate island and everything Violet told us in the airport starts to make sense. Very impressive.

There's an element of safety because we're not staying in Key West proper, although even for Jason a trip to Key West would be extreme. He knows where I live, after all. From the boat, we climb onto golf carts that take us to our cottages. They're next to each other, both oceanfront. Sydney, Julia, and I run into ours, giddy to see what a Sunset Key cottage is like. From the doorway we can see there are two bedrooms in each cottage with two king-size beds and a full bath. A staircase to the second floor leads to the kitchen and family room, opening onto a large balcony that faces the Gulf of Mexico. It's absolutely magical. "So, to go out in Key West we take a boat to the mainland first?" I ask, stating the obvious.

I hang up my clothes, totally wrinkled from the suitcase, and jump in the shower. I select the least damaged maxidress. It's red and white striped with spaghetti straps, a deep neck, and crossed straps in the back. This will have to do. I leave my hair down. It's long and Nadine just lightened the color, so it's a sun-kissed blond. Not an easy feat in New Jersey in April. That and a spray tan and I'm ready for a night out in the Keys. I go upstairs to make a cocktail while the other girls get ready. I find Danny and Trey sitting in my living room as if they're anxiously awaiting their prom dates' entrance. Violet's plan of a group dinner and happy hour must have been agreeable to the groomsmen as well.

"Well hello, gentlemen. Don't you guys look handsome," I say, appraising both of them in their cargo shorts and "tight in all the right places" shirts.

Trey is instantly on me. "Hello yourself. You look great."

"Do you want a drink?" I ask, ignoring him. Danny and Trey say yes at exactly the same time. "Vodka?"

"Why not?" says Trey, and Danny nods in agreement.

We finish our first drink and start on our second as the rest of the group arrives. I make another round for everyone but hold off myself. I'm still starving.

* * *

We arrive at the Hog's Breath Saloon and secure a table for eight. I'll never get used to the idea of being on an island off the coast of an island.

When the bartender suggests the clothing-optional bar, the Garden of Eden, to the girls, it seems like a fun idea, a great story to tell. Our naïveté makes the final decision and we're on our way to our first ever naked night out.

I couldn't care less. I'll stand around nude if they want. We all agree we won't tell the boys. We're downright giddy on our way upstairs to the entrance.

I'm the first of us to walk into the bar and the bartender has the biggest breasts I've ever seen, hanging down to her waist. "What're you having?" she asks, and all I can think of is milk.

"Four vodka and grapefruits, please," I say, and suddenly feel very thankful for my small breasts. I don't ever want anything on my body to hang down that far. Dealer's choice, I guess.

Violet's the first one to spot the body painter and suggests we all get painted.

"Why don't we get a scene that when you put the four of us next to each other it makes a picture?" I ask.

"Yeah! Like a daytime scene on the front and a sunset when you turn us all around," Julia adds, now in on the brainstorming. The painter seems excited to try something different and luckily there isn't a line of any kind. He plots things out in his head and starts on Violet. The rest of us keep drinking and try to not gawk; we wouldn't want to give her a complex.

He does a fantastic job. Each of us has an incredible paint job, but when you put us together it's a work of art. He asks if he can take a picture for his portfolio; he waves his hand at a bulletin board full of pictures.

"Only if you take one for us, too," I say.

Julia bites her lip, probably afraid of her naked, painted body being splashed all over the Internet.

"It's up to you guys," I say. "I have no parents to embarrass." In the end, one photo is taken and it goes into my purse because mine is the largest. I'm not sure if it's everyone else's nudity or the body paint, but we all just forget we're naked. We dance, drink, and talk to everyone we meet as if we're all dressed. Our paint job brings notoriety—that and the fact that the clientele is generally about ten years older than us.

Violet selects a rather yummy bar-back to spend her night flirting with. I thought she was just looking for attention, but when she starts to dance with him, I find myself checking the door to make sure the groomsmen don't also find the Garden an intriguing option.

As if the situation were attached to a timer, it detonates just as Julia walks over to me. "What the hell is she doing?" she asks.

I look up and see Violet French-kissing her bar-back on the dance floor. My mouth falls open.

"Wow."

"Charlotte, this is ridiculous!" Julia appears to be getting even angrier. Sydney must have felt the shrapnel on the other side of the bar because on her way back from the bathroom she pulls Violet free and leads her to us.

"Hi, girls," Violet says with a huge grin on her face. She's licking her lips.

"Violet! What are you doing?" Julia asks with spit flying out of her mouth, having said good-bye to sober hours ago herself. "You're getting married in a month."

"Oh, Jule Jules," Violet mocks as Sydney and I exchange a look of terror. "Loosen up!"

"Loosen up? Loosen up?!" I can actually see the blood rising in Julia's neck and turning her ears a deep ruby color. "You have no respect for the sanctity of marriage!" she erupts, pointing a finger in Violet's face.

It's a poignant scene, watching two sections of a mural fighting.

As if on cue, Violet's new friend comes over and wraps his arms around Violet's waist from the back and buries his face in her neck. Sydney and I stand paralyzed as Julia pulls back and throws her drink on both of them.

* * *

Sydney and I manage to get everyone back into their clothes and out of the bar ahead of being thrown out. It doesn't appear the staff wants to deal with us at all. I can't blame them because I don't want to deal with us either. Violet and her friend stumble down the street arm in arm as Julia continues her verbal assault. She manages to reiterate her concerns about the sanctity of marriage as Violet gives her the finger over her head.

"Which one do you want?" Sydney asks, and I can't decide which is worse: trying to calm Julia down or trying to keep Violet's pants on.

"Do something, you idiots!" Julia rails at us both.

"I'll take the bride," I say, and follow the happy couple down Duval Street.

I'm trying to pay attention to where we're walking as I catch up to Violet and this dude. We go five blocks down Duval and make a right on Petronia. The Bourbon Bar is on the corner and I almost give up on Violet's virtue and head in by myself.

Maybe our destination will have a glass of Jack for the walk home. I count the blocks, passing several restaurants as I get to the sixth block and see we're at the end. We make a right and head up the front steps of a cottage with a small porch facing the street. I think the ocean must be across the street, but I can't see a thing beyond the streetlights.

"Dave!" the dude calls up the stairs, and a short, athletic-looking guy comes bounding down. "This is who I was telling you about on the phone," he says, and dramatically presents Violet to Dave as he scoops her up and kisses her. Rather than being as repulsed as I should be, I feel completely detached from the whole situation. It's just so silly.

"She is my soul mate, Dave! I've found her!"

At this I feel my eyes rolling up into my head.

"Who's this?" Dave asks as he moves to stand right in front of me, my eyes slightly higher than his.

"I'm the witness to the moment when your friend found his soul mate, drunk and naked in a bar on Duval Street," I answer, the sarcasm stinging even my own throat.

Dave leans up and mutters into my ear, "I think he has multiple souls."

"I think we should leave," I whisper back.

"Want a drink?" Dave offers as he heads into the kitchen.

Violet's now cuddled on this dude's lap, making out old school. I curl my lip in disgust.

"Do you have any whiskey?" I ask as I follow him into the kitchen.

I need to get Violet out of here. It's already after one and we have a long walk back to our boat launch. I'm sure it'll take twice as long since Violet probably can't navigate a straight line.

"Violet, can I talk to you for a minute?" I direct my voice toward the living room without actually looking in, petrified of what I might see. God forbid the dude has made it past first base. "It will only take a minute, I promise." I smile at Dave.

"Yeeesss?" Violet says as she enters the kitchen with pure joy covering her face.

"Can I talk to you out back for a minute?" I ask. We walk through the screen door and sit on the railing of a tiny porch right outside the door.

"What the hell are you doing?"

"Charlotte, I'm fine."

"Fine? Violet, you are not fine. You're about to ruin your life," I say as I grab her by the arms. "We need to go back to our island."

Okay, that statement is absurd.

"Charlotte, seriously, I've never been happier," she says again with a straight face. "This is exactly what a bachelorette party's for."

"No, it's not! Really, it's not! Especially not the one you're on with your future husband."

I'm feeling a little delirious. I wonder if I can lift Violet and just carry her a few blocks to get her out of here.

"What would you do if Blake was doing the same thing you are right now?" I lob out.

"I couldn't care less. I'm going to spend the rest of my life with Blake, every day of it. Tonight I'm going to put myself first," she insists. "And there's nothing you can do to stop me." She straightens her back, signaling the end of the conversation.

"Do you really think you can cover this wager?"

"Tonight's not about thinking, Charlotte."

The words ring in my ears. In one sentence, Violet's finally answered my most haunting question about Jason and Stephanie. What was he thinking? She's right. It's not about thinking.

"Let's get a drink," she says as she holds the door open for me. I pause, still contemplating her words, then down the Jack in my glass and walk through the door.

Dave, thank God, turns out to not be a total creep and lets me borrow a towel to shower. Watching the body paint disintegrate and run down the drain is poetic. I put my dress back on and join Dave on the couch.

"You're a good friend," he says gently.

"I'm not hooking up with you," I return sourly.

"Blunt, too," he says.

"Look, it's late. I don't want to waste your time. I'm totally in love with my boyfriend," I say, and add "and my exboyfriend." Neither of us speaks as we let my last confession marinate. My God, I am still in love with Jason. I know it and now Dave knows it.

"How does that happen?" Dave asks, and I can hear Violet giggling in the bedroom.

"Well, Dave, you have to be a giant fuck-up."

Dave considers this for a few minutes. "I'll bet you're awesome in bed," he says, but it doesn't seem like a compliment. "Crazy chicks are always great in bed."

I ignore him and pass out.

* * *

"Hey, Cuckoo, your alarm's going off." Dave is shaking my shoulders.

"Huh?" I say as I try to recall where I am. I open my eyes

and recognize Dave. My head begins to throb as I remember Violet's night. "Where's Violet?"

"She's still asleep. Can you please turn off your alarm?" he pleads as he tosses my phone onto my chest. I slide the bar and stop the alarm from sounding. The phone says it is 10:00 a.m. We're all supposed to meet at Hog's Breath for lunch at eleven.

"God help me."

I get up and take an extra minute to steady myself. Knocking on the bedroom door, I speak too loudly for my head trauma. "Violet, get up." I repeat it ten more times before she finally comes to the door. "Wow, you look horrible."

Violet's face is completely blank, as if she has no understanding of our situation. "You need to get in the shower"—still blank—"right now!"

I lead Violet toward the small bathroom and start the shower running.

"Charlotte," she says on the verge of tears.

"Just get a shower, okay?" I say, and leave her in the bathroom.

I don't want to do it, but we need some help. I call Julia.

"Yes?" she answers, salty. I'm guessing she waited up to yell at us and fell asleep unsatisfied.

"Hey, I need your help." I purposely choose *I* over *we* since I figure she's not going to lift a finger for Violet.

"No."

"Look, I know you're pissed, but we can sort this all out lat—"

"I can't believe you're *not* pissed," Julia interrupts me. "After everything you've been through because Jason cheated on you, how can you defend her?"

I take a deep breath, unsure of the answer.

"I'm not defending anyone. I just don't think this morning is the time for everyone to find out about last night."

"When is, Charlotte? In three months when she's pregnant?"

It's a low blow. Julia's angry at Violet and she'll say anything at this point for company in her fury.

"Can I please speak with Sydney?"

There's silence on the other end.

"Charlotte?" Sydney says.

"Hey, we need your help," I say, desperate because we're running out of time.

"How's Violet?"

"I'm not sure."

"What do you need me to do?" Sydney asks, and I feel a milligram of relief.

"I need you to bring us both dresses and flip-flops to the Hog's Breath right now. I need you to leave before the guys and meet us there so we can change. Just pick something out of our closets. It doesn't matter what it is," I say as I hear Violet turn off the shower. "Bring our sunglasses, too—and eyedrops if you can find them." My eyes feel like someone poured gravel in them.

"All right," Sydney agrees.

"Leave right now. If you're on the same launch as them, we're sunk."

"Okay, okay. I'm on my way."

I hang up and rush Violet out of the shower. She gives the dude a kiss and hug good-bye and I wave to Dave on our way out. I retrace our route from last night and easily find Duval. We're halfway to the Hog's Breath when Violet starts crying.

I take a deep breath. What have I done to deserve this?

"Listen." I stop walking and face Violet, trying to keep my voice level but feeling like I could burst into tears myself. "We have the rest of our lives to figure this out but only the next few hours to completely screw it up," I start, and it kind of makes sense. "Admit nothing—nothing to Blake and nothing to yourself."

We start walking again.

"Charlotte, how can you be like this?" Violet asks.

"I know a little something about being unable to move past things," I answer.

We walk the rest of the way in silence.

I leave Violet on a curb around the corner on Fitzpatrick and go into the Hog's Breath Saloon. I buy three T-shirts and ask them for a large bag. Sydney comes in just as I'm thanking the woman at the register. She's rushing through the door, obviously worried.

"It's going to be fine," I tell her, but don't believe a word of it.

We collect Violet and go back into the restaurant to change in their bathroom. We both look like hell, but at least we have new clothes on and sunglasses to hide the guilt. I put our clothes from last night into the bag, bury them beneath my T-shirts, and pour eyedrops into my eyes until they overflow onto my dress. Sydney brought our toothbrushes, which is a nice addition.

"Let's go get settled at a table," I suggest.

We anchor the table for eight and it surprises me it's not tilting up on the other side, our guilt weighing so heavily on us. I am again reminded how stupid a joint bachelor/bachelorette party is. I almost tell Violet for her next wedding we're not doing this, but catch myself in time. Instead I grab her hand as I hear the guys and Julia approaching.

"There's my gorgeous bride!" Blake says as he kisses Violet. "Sorry we're late; we just missed a launch and had to wait for the boat to return."

Sydney and I exchange a knowing glance. That must have been her.

"How long have you guys been here?"

"Not long," I say. "We came in early to do a little shopping."

Julia looks at me with ice in her eyes, but she isn't going to tell. She would have done so already.

"Are you guys hungry?" I ask to keep the conversation going.

Sydney thankfully picks up my end of the conversation and I focus on my Bloody Mary. I can't wait to go to bed. My phone dings with two texts from Noble.

NOTHING IS THE SAME WITHOUT YOU.

I NEED YOU TO COME HOME.

I've been so focused on keeping Violet out of trouble that I haven't let myself obsess over the fact that I'm still in love with Jason and what that means for Noble and me. I see the tortured look on Violet's face and I'm thankful I'm not her. Although not behaving like Violet is not exactly the upside to my situation.

Somehow we all make it through breakfast without breaking down, crying, or confessing Violet's sins. The boys are more than happy to tell us about their night—an edited version, I'm sure.

We'll show you edited.

We tell them about the Garden of Eden, minus the barback, and everyone agrees to let Violet and Blake have a nice, quiet, romantic dinner tonight. After a long nap, I suggest, since we've all had too little sleep.

On the boat ride back to our island, I stew over my response to Noble's text. It's overdue. I can't seem to collect the right words to assuage him.

Just a few more hours.
I'll see you tomorrow night.
WILL I SEE YOU TOMORROW NIGHT?
Yes. My plane gets in late,
but I'll come over if you'd like.
LIKE OR LOVE?
I'll see you tomorrow :)
I absolutely hate those fucking smiley faces.

~ 27 ~

Vulnerable Proximity

I'm tired and thirsty, but I have to get out of here. The cab pulls into the airport and I pray I can get a flight home this morning. Violet won't be happy, but at most I'm missing the last breakfast. Maybe lunch, too, but our original flight was supposed to leave at 2:30 p.m. It's not like we're going to be doing much today. The seven of them have got to be hungover. The last few rounds I stuck to water, but they just kept drinking, progressing to shots by the end of the night. The girls at least had good reason. We were trying to repair the damage we inflicted on each other the night before. Friday night was awful.

The lady at the United counter hooks me up with an 8:10 a.m. departure to Tampa. I was hoping to avoid Tampa completely, but I'm still thankful. I've spent the entire weekend thinking of Jason and trying to appear as if I was having the best time at Violet's bachelorette party. My justified fear of calling Jason or Noble in a drunken stupor kept my consumption in check last night. What exactly would I tell them? *I love you*, I guess. Tragic that it would work for both. At least I still hate Jason.

As I walk toward security, a young man in a suit too large for him hands me a card. I absently smile and continue walking. On the front there's a picture of a sunbeam shining through a cloud, and on the back is a Bible verse:

> *And be ye kind one to another, tenderhearted, forgiving one another, even as God for Christ's sake hath forgiven you.*
> Ephesians: 4:32

* * *

I settle into my seat only twenty minutes after the cab dropped me off. The plane is practically empty. I text Julia that I've left. I'm sure they're all still asleep, but if the plane goes down, it'll be nice for someone to know I'm on it.

Julia's rant of "You have no respect for the sanctity of marriage" still rings in my head. I've never seen her so mad. We have three weeks until the wedding to get all this worked out. If working this out is even possible. I've abandoned the need to understand what happened. Every theory I come up with leads me back to trying to figure out Jason and Stephanie.

Tonight is not about thinking.

* * *

My meander down the concourse is filled with familiarity. The bar we stopped at for drinks is on my right. It feels like three weeks ago we were in here. Usually that's a sign of a great trip.

This one was more like a painful medical procedure. I see the bathroom and the chairs I sat in with Harlan. The sadness starts to creep up on me and my pace slows. My eyes linger on the chairs.

I look up and in an instant the whole world stops. My breath catches in my throat and my knees buckle slightly under me. I blink several times, not trusting my eyes. It can't be him. It is, though. I'd be able to spot him a hundred yards away and covered by a blanket. Jason is sitting in an empty gate area. He's slouched down with his arms crossed at his stomach and his hat pulled down over his eyes. I move to the wall of the concourse but never take my eyes off him. He doesn't move. He's asleep. My mouth is unbearably dry and I remind myself to breathe. It's not possible, but I think I can smell his shampoo from here.

I discreetly move closer, hugging the wall as long as I can. I'm interrupted by bathrooms, closets, and kiosks of magazines, pretzels, and sodas. He still doesn't move. When I'm less than fifteen feet from him, I stand and wait. I count in my head: *September, October, November, December, January, February, March, April*—eight months. Now that he's sitting here in front of me, alone, it seems like eight seconds ago. I take a deep breath and my chest rises to my chin.

The seats in every row around Jason are empty. Three rows back, overflowing from a neighboring gate, are a woman with a stroller and an older gentleman reading the newspaper, but other than that it's just Jason and me. Just as it always is...was.

I tiptoe the last fifteen feet and sit in the seat directly across from him. Our feet, both touching the ground, are separated by a mere twelve inches. His boots are the ones I bought him, his Old Gringo Mad Dogs. I remember having trouble finding a pair I thought did him justice. It seemed as if no boot was as beautiful as Jason.

His legs are crossed at the ankles and one pant leg is up slightly. His jeans are a deep, dull blue, that dark color that looks like it's seen some dirt in its day. His thighs are enormous. His jeans tighten just above the knee and I remember exactly why: the muscles in his legs used to support his enormous chest. My eyes continue up his thigh and I rest my admiration at his zipper. I swallow hard and can feel my heart beating. The rest of my body kicks into gear and I shift in my seat. Jason moves slightly, too, as if sensing my need. His head tilts back a little and his arms loosen.

In his new position, I can see the belt buckle I gave him. It's large and silver with a steer engraved on the front. At the sight of it, I bite my lower lip and try to fight back the tears. On the back I had JL + AO engraved the same way he carved it in a tree once. I remember taking a picture of the carving to the jeweler. The engraver said he'd never seen such attention to detail. I told him he'd never seen Jason Leer.

He loves me. He still loves me. All these months I've been telling myself he hasn't wanted me, but he's loved me every minute. Why didn't I believe him when he said it?

His shirt is a red-and-black plaid button-down. His chest is every inch as broad as I remember. I smile sadly and put my fingers to my mouth, recalling how I used to tease him that lying on his chest was like lying on a sofa cushion.

"Get used to it—it's all you'll ever have," he would tell me. It's as hard as a concrete block. There's a small patch of black hair right in the middle of his chest and the memory of it turns my sadness into something hot and wet. His arms are protruding from his shirt's rolled-up sleeves. Enormous and heavy, they're crossed now with one twisted slightly toward the ceiling, the muscle in his forearm sticking up. Most men don't even know they have a muscle there and Jason's is flexed in his sleep. I can still feel the weight of his arms wrapped around me.

I'm startled by the announcement of the impending boarding of my flight. We're not alone here, but we could be.

Jason's hat hangs low, hiding most of his face. His juicy red lips peek out from the bottom and I can taste them in my mouth. I sit on my hands to keep from crossing the few feet between us and touching him. I wish I could see his eyes. If he wakes and opens his eyes, I'll stay here with him. I'll get a room, or get on a plane with him, and I'll run my lips over every inch of him. I'll drink him down until he can no longer stand. I'll not say a word to him about what he's done; in fact, I won't say a word about anything. If he wakes up…

"We will now begin our preboarding of Flight Six Thirty-Eight to Philadelphia. We welcome aboard our first-class and elite club members, as well as families flying with small children."

I stare at his black felt hat and see the turquoise bead I added to the strap and realize he's still my Jason, no matter what he did with Stephanie or anyone else.

Wake up.

If you just wake up, I'll do the unthinkable. I'll call Noble and ruin his life, I'll leave BJ with Butch, and I'll somehow face my brother after everything I've put him through. I'll do all of it if you just wake up right now and touch me.

Touch me anywhere.

Place your rough palm on the side of my face. Wrap your massive arms around me. Pull my hair and press your lips on mine.

Take me by the hand and pull me to the nearest hotel room, or car, or bathroom. I don't care, just wake up.

"We are now boarding rows twenty-five through forty-five on United Flight Six Thirty-Eight to Philadelphia. Rows twenty-five through forty-five, please board at this time."

I sit silently, only looking away to see my gate and the passengers filing in. My eyes can't release him for long and return to devouring the sight of him. His lips curl up the tiniest bit on each side. He's smiling and I smile, too. I'm going to cry, or scream, or something far worse.

Jason, wake up, and take me…away.

I watch him silently, his breathing mirroring my own.

"We are now boarding all remaining rows on Flight Six Thirty-Eight to Philadelphia. Once again, all rows please board Flight Six Thirty-Eight to Philadelphia at gate seventeen."

The line's dwindling. There are only minutes remaining and Jason still sleeps across from me. I can taste his lips. I will him to wake up.

Defeated, I rummage through my wallet. I find the folded paper I've been carrying around for months. Twice I've almost thrown it away. I know if Noble finds it, it will only hurt him, but I just couldn't relinquish it. I open it one last time.

nice bed

I refold it and rise to my feet. My legs are shaky and I confirm I'm steady before moving closer to him. I leave the note between his arm and chest, and my skin's electrified without actually touching him. My stomach flips and I might throw up all over him. I turn and walk away. Each step takes sheer will and I still listen without breathing for him to wake and say my name.

"I saw you were sitting with our cowboy," the lady who checks my boarding pass says. I silently look back at him again. Still sleeping. "He's been here for three days."

"Seriously?" I ask, horror covering my face.

"He said the only girl he's ever loved would be here this weekend and he didn't want to miss her. Apparently, she won't talk to him and he wants her back."

"Three days?" I ask again, unable to believe her.

"He had to buy a ticket to get through security on Friday. We've taken pity on him and let him shower in the club lounge." The lady scans my boarding pass. "He's gorgeous. I hope she comes before I get off today." She absently adds, "Enjoy your flight," as she looks past me at Jason.

"When my flight takes off, you can tell him he missed her," I say, and swallow hard to avoid crying.

"It's you," she says after a few seconds of staring at me. "Oh, honey, you've got to wake him up. That boy's in love with you!" She gently holds my elbow as I hold on to my grasp of reason.

"No. Imagine the tragedy that's led us here." I shake my head and start to cry. "It wasn't meant to be. Not today...not ever."

She lets go and looks at me sympathetically, sensing the two sides to this story are wretched. I walk past her and board my plane home. Through the window, I can see the black clouds barreling toward me. They shut the cabin door and we pull away from the gate. My chest relaxes as we turn onto the runway. I think I can hear thunder as I begin to cry and the plane shakes and moans into our ascent, away from here and away from Jason Leer.

~ 28 ~

Plowing On

I consider the flight a success since I was able to sleep the second half of it—that is, after I cried for the first half. Perhaps I should check myself into a facility of some kind. I must be losing my mind. I can't still be in love with Jason. Not eight months after we broke up. Not after his son was born. And God help me, not after Noble Sinclair's fallen in love with me.

My life with Jason is over. And until I saw him today, I was happy with Noble. I'm going to find a way to be with Noble if it kills me. He deserves for this to work out. And I deserve for this to work out. The light on my answering machine is blinking, and I know I should just unplug it and throw it away. But I can't.

"While you were sitting there, I was dreaming about you. I could feel you near me. We'll be that close again, Annie," he quietly says. "Why didn't you wake me?" There's a long pause. I stop brushing my hair and turn toward the machine. "The Annie I love would have woken me up. She wouldn't give up on us, no matter what. I need you."

I hit the erase button. My answering machine escapes being heaved against the wall. Its casing is taped from previous messages even though it's the second one I've had in eight months.

I'm too exhausted to react. Defeated, I lie in my bed and let sleep heal me. At least enough to see Noble. I know I'll never be well again.

* * *

My eyes open and I feel as sad as I did when I went to sleep. I'm less exhausted, though, no longer feeling as if I might burst into tears at any point. I shower and wander around my room, assessing the changes Clint's made. New windows, new crown molding, a built-in entertainment unit, and new doors all make the room seem totally different from what it was a year ago. Totally different...

I pause at the pictures of Noble and me from the Harvest Dance. My happiness is real. I was, and am, happy with Noble. A familiar knot in my stomach returns as I remember how close I came to throwing him away. I pull the last clean items—a black skirt and white tank top—out of my suitcase and throw them on, forgoing underwear. I leave my hair wet and grab my sunglasses before heading out the door.

* * *

The big green monster is in a field several acres away from the farmhouse. I pull off the road onto a dirt access lane. The dust rolls up and over my car as the Volvo plunges into every hole and dip. I pop toward the ceiling on a particularly large bump and slow down to avoid breaking my neck. Noble makes a turn in the tractor and is now heading toward me. I drive within fifty feet of him, get out of my car, and wait, leaning on the driver's door. The tractor's towing an enormous plow and looks like a large green beetle with a clear bubble on the front of it.

It comes to a halt thirty feet in front of me. I see Noble pick up his phone and I grab my own out of the car. He's looking at me as my phone starts ringing. Without breaking my stare, I answer.

"Hello."

"You're early. Do you want a ride?" His voice is naughty and scrumptious, and I'm particularly thankful Noble is the same as he was when I left, because I am not.

"I'll be right up. If I can figure out how to get up there," I say, and Noble laughs at me.

The inside of the tractor is luxurious and unexpectedly high-tech. There's a touch screen within reach of the seat and an armful of buttons to the right of the steering column. I climb into the cab and directly onto Noble's lap, straddling and facing him.

"What happened to your head?" I frantically ask after noticing the purple bruise with seven or eight stitches running through the middle of it.

"Let's not talk about that right now." Noble pulls me to him and kisses me. I close my eyes, trying to push out any thoughts that don't belong to Noble—equitable distribution of my thoughts and emotions. Noble's smiling when I lean back and he tangles both hands in my hair.

"This is quite impressive," I say, and notice Noble's hard-on beneath my thigh.

"Exactly what part?" He kisses my neck.

"I've never been in a tractor this large."

"Aah, the size of it. I get that a lot," he whispers in my ear.

I look over my shoulder and see the field before us with not a soul moving in it. Above my head is a radio.

"All the comforts of home." I turn up the volume on the radio and stare back at the field. I glance down and see my senior picture taped to the dash. I pull it off and come face-to-face with my old self, before the demons took over.

"I look so innocent in this picture."

"You look exactly the same now, Charlotte, just slightly prettier."

I look at Noble and he's admiring me. He loves me and this morning I was going to call him and tell him he may never see me again. If he's lucky. I turn the picture over and read my message on the back from five years ago.

Noble,

You will always be Noble to me. You're the greatest and I'm SO glad we're going to Rutgers together. There's no one I'd rather make the trip with.

Love,
Charlotte

I close my eyes and digest my own words.

"Hey, what are you doing? Are you crying?" Noble wipes a lone tear from my cheek. "What's wrong?" He silently pleads with me to deny his fears. "Did something happen this weekend?"

"No…no, nothing happened. I just realized this weekend how significant you are."

It's not a lie. The answer is just not significant enough. Noble smiles again and kisses with lips that readily convey three long days away. I make every effort to focus on him, and the tractor, and his farm. Maintaining my position here on Earth is my only focus. I look at my high school picture again. Even then I knew what a wonderful guy Noble is, and always will be. At least until I'm done with him.

"Tell me what happened to your gorgeous face," I demand as I caress his forehead.

"I had the chance to speak with Jack Reynolds again about my expectations regarding him not coming anywhere near you. It's kind of a gentleman's restraining order."

"What exactly happened?" I quietly ask as I kiss his forehead.

"Nothing really," he continues. "I approached Jack to talk about it and he broke a bottle over my head. Then we discussed it some more." Noble reaches above us and turns down the radio. "I think he's pretty clear on the parameters of the order now."

"Oh, Noble." I run my hands down his bare arms. I move them back to his neck and let my eyes linger on his shoulders.

"What do the other instruments in here do?"

"Farming is more interesting than you thought, huh?" Noble responds, playful again.

"Oh yeah, you should speak at career day at the high school." I undo the button on his jeans and unzip them. I have to maneuver to release him because he's so hard. I wrap my hand around him and begin stroking up and down. I move closer, and the stroking now touches us both and I'm pleased with my clever positioning. I arch my back and begin moving up and down to match the rhythm of my hand. Noble pulls my top down and a hard nipple pops out. He begins to play with it with his tongue and I slow my movements. Around and around he goes, stroking my nipple with the tip of his tongue. A little moan escapes me and he moves to my other breast.

Noble lifts me up and puts me down with him inside me, and we begin to move together. *Always together.* Me using the floor as much as I can and Noble moving me up and down with his hands supporting my bottom. He is my home. I arch my back, feeling nothing but Noble inside of me. He runs his hand down the center of my chest and lands between my legs. His finger on me is too much. I'm panting and sweating, on the verge of crying, and desperate to love Noble the way he deserves. I concentrate on his finger as I throw my head back and continue my heady rhythm, holding off a complete frenzy. Up, down, and all around, I can take no more and come as I feel Noble give in beneath me. I'm drained. Willing to let him be everything because there's nothing else left.

"Welcome home, Charlotte," Noble whispers into my neck, and the exhaustion again sets in.

* * *

"You need to be careful with perfect. It's brilliant at hiding its flaws," Jason says as he pushes me away. "How could you do this?" he asks. "We're supposed to be together. No one else, remember?"

"I didn't do it on purpose," I plead with him. "Please, you have to forgive me." I start to cry.

"*And with Nick Sinclair. For God's sake, Annie, we grew up together. When did you become that much of a bitch?*"

"*Jason, please, don't say that. I love you!*" I walk over to him and wrap my arms around his neck. He pushes me back.

"*I can't do it, Annie. You went too far. It's over for good.*"

"*No, it's not. It doesn't have to be,*" I insist, but he walks away. "*Come back! Jason, come back!*" I sob, and I can no longer breathe.

I wake up, grabbing at my throat and crying. I'm alone, thank God. Noble can't ever see me like this. I lie flat on my back and stare at the ceiling, trying to make sense of why in my dreams I'm begging for Jason's forgiveness.

It's 11:30 at night. Noble slept at his house because of a late grange meeting. I text him:

Hi

I don't really have anything to say. I just want to feel his presence somehow.

WHAT R U STILL DOING UP?

Bad dream

I'LL BE RIGHT OVER.

I don't deserve Noble. I have a bad dream about Jason and Noble comes over to comfort me.

I lie awake waiting for Noble to come and not wanting to fall back asleep. There's a strange noise outside, but I can't see what's making it from my window. For a minute I think Noble's somehow behind it. It's a cracking noise that comes again and again. Almost like wood hitting wood in a sword fight. I stare out into the dark night, the new moon hiding the source of the noise from my view. I hear it again and sense it's violent. I rest my chin on the windowsill and stake out the darkness. All of a sudden, two bucks come into view.

They're pushing each other, and after one pulls back, they run toward each other, antlers first. I've only seen a buck fight once before, when I was little. My dad explained there can only be one male per herd; the second must try to fight his way in. The strongest will win the battle and the does. I feel sorry for the loser. What will become of him? I leave the window without seeing who wins.

~ 29 ~

7,059,000,001 People on Earth, Most of Them Crazy

I start my walk down the aisle with a smile plastered on my face the same way Trey instructed me to at the engagement party. The dresses Violet bought for us are exceedingly high drama. It's a Pamella Roland long-sleeved, metallic-sequined dress. At the top the sequins are silver and navy mixed, and they fade into all navy. It reminds me of a starry night, and on the deck of the tall ship *Moshulu*, it's glistening in the moonlight. As if the sequins aren't enough, the dress has a wide V-neck and a short hem. Only Violet.

I hear gasps from the elderly as I approach their rows and they're able to see the scant length. Violet paired the dress with one long-stem calla lily...more drama. The bridesmaids, though, are nothing compared to the thirty-seven layers of tulle and I don't know what else ballooning from the bottom of Violet's strapless gown. The enormity of it is balanced by her gigantic smile.

Now that we're all up here in front of hundreds of people,

I'm even more self-conscious of the dress length. Despite that, it's a magnificent dress, and I feel incredible in it. I'm pretty sure most brides don't let their attendants rock it like Violet has. I scan the congregation with me on the Delaware River and find Noble about sixteen rows back. I love the sight of him. Julia taps my elbow and I lean over to provide access to my ear.

"What the fuck?" she asks through a clenched jaw.

I request more information with a lunatic's smile and raised eyebrows.

"Fourth row back, groom's side," she says. "She is un-fucking-believable."

I count the rows and go down person by person. The fifth person in, smirking as he stares at the blushing bride, is Violet's soul mate from Key West. She is unbelievable. I look to Noble, who's watching Julia and me, and glancing to his right to decipher the problem. I keep my smile plastered on my face. This is a wedding even if the bride has invited her boyfriend.

"Into this holy union Blake and Violet now come to be joined. If any of you can show just cause why they may not lawfully be married, speak now or forever hold your peace," the priest intones.

I hold my breath.

"If I could get off this godforsaken ship with these heels on, I'd walk out right now," Julia whispers rather loudly to me. I keep smiling like Trey told me to, but the rest of the wedding party and the priest, as well as the entire congregation I'm sure, are now looking at us. "The bride is a whore without any respect for the sanctity of marriage," she adds.

I hope I'm shielding everyone from deciphering her rant. I find Noble's face as he shakes his head and lowers his forehead into his hand. We're probably going to ruin this wedding.

I lean toward the priest and say, "She's fine. Just a little sea-sick." He clears his throat but can't erase the baffled look from his face. Probably because the *Moshulu* is permanently docked at Penn's Landing, thus making it impossible to become sea-sick aboard the ship. If someone has a better plan, I'd love for them to interject it.

I'm not sure if it's just in my head or not, but the priest seems to speed through the remainder of the ceremony. Blake hops off the altar and helps Violet down, followed by each groomsman taking the hand of his assigned bridesmaid. Julia storms right off the boat, and the rest of the bridal party, in-cluding Violet's father, are left looking at me for answers.

"What? I think she's really sick." I give Violet a look that conveys to her I've seen her special guest and I'm not im-pressed. Trey says he's going to check on Julia and I tell him to check the hotel bar. We could all use a drink after this cer-emony. I'm ready to find Noble, but first I have to take some photographs with the happy couple.

Violet's a pro. If I hadn't seen it with my own eyes, I'd never believe her actions in Key West, and I definitely wouldn't be-lieve this dude is here. What could she possibly hope to get out of it? We're all lined up in different configurations with the city, the aquarium, the Ben Franklin Bridge, and the river be-hind us. In between shots I wonder how Jason and I couldn't survive when these two yahoos will probably be married for sixty years. Although if Violet keeps it up, I give them sixty minutes.

I search the sky for stars. The lights are too bright to see any, so I close my eyes and imagine them. Hawaii and Colorado…and Oklahoma. I keep my eyes closed as I throw my head back and take a deep breath. One more and the photographer yells, "Hey! Are you going to pass out back there?"

"What the hell is going on?" Blake demands, and everyone turns to stare at me. "Is it something you guys ate?" he barks, completely having lost his patience with Violet's maids.

"I'm fine. Really…just drinking in the sea air."

"Over the river?" Blake angrily asks.

"It's a beautiful night."

"Okay, we're done here," the photographer says as he checks the shots on his camera screen.

"Let's party," Blake says, and we all head for the walkway to the bow of the ship and the cocktail hour.

I'm anxious to find Noble. I have this sense that I've left him alone too long. As I exit the restaurant on the other side of the ship, I see him in the corner of the deck. He's standing with Violet's dad and his business partners. They're talking, periodically raising their glasses and drinking. Noble's smile is easy. He's completely at home. His Rutgers dual degree in agriculture and finance gives him the ability to speak with just about anyone. I realize it's not him I was anxious about leaving. If Jason were here, he'd be standing alone waiting for me, patiently waiting but impatient to see me.

I rest against the railing and watch Noble. He's lovely, strong, and kind, and I drink him in. As if he can hear my thoughts, he turns and looks straight at me, a smile settling across his face. There's a soloist playing an acoustical set. He and his guitar are on a platform between us and it's as if he's singing exclusively for the two of us.

Noble excuses himself from his conversation and makes his way to me. It's impossible to believe it's only been seven weeks since the Harvest Dance. I guess that's what happens when you tell your best friend that you love him. Things change instantly.

I watch him maneuver through the crowd, women of all ages stopping to regard him. A few he says something to, enchanting them further.

"I love you, Noble Sinclair," I say when he reaches me.

Just probably not enough.

"I know." Noble sighs. "The way you chase me is embarrassing." He rewards me with a sly grin.

"I'm sorry. Embarrassing you is not my intention."

He puts his arm around my waist and pulls me toward him.

"What is your intention, Charlotte?" Noble kisses me. "Are you going to force me to marry you someday?"

"When you say 'force,' do you mean finally accept your barrage of gifts and proposals of marriage?"

"I am getting tired of sleeping alone. And I wouldn't mind having a dog," he says, and pulls me back, examining my appearance. "And it appears you'll make gorgeous babies."

I push back the thoughts of Jason's son.

"You know us Salem County girls. Good stock," I say, and kiss him lightly on the lips. "Although I have to admit, I'm not really feeling marriage lately." I lean into him and lay my head on his chest. Solid, as usual.

"Does it have anything to do with Violet's friend from Key West?" he asks, and I freeze, still hidden in his chest.

"Friend?" I ask, because I'm not sure what else to say.

"Yes. I got to talk to him while you were taking pictures. He seemed to know you, too. He said he's seen you naked."

"Hmm, interesting. You'd think I'd remember him," I say, still not looking up.

"One would think, although with you it's not a given. You were on the swim team and all," Noble says, and I can tell he's not mad.

"Hey, can you guys go check on Julia? They want to start announcements soon and we're still missing her and Trey," Blake asks as he downs his drink.

"Where's Violet?" I ask, afraid of the answer.

"I'm not sure. She said she needed a minute, that she had something special to take care of." Blake shrugs. "I actually thought she was with you."

"Maybe she's with Julia. We'll go check on them," Noble offers. So very Noble.

The walk to the hotel is not a long one, but these are four-inch peep toes. Noble gives me a piggyback ride the last fifty yards. The Ben Franklin Bridge looms above us, connecting Philadelphia and New Jersey. Noble puts me down as the hotel doors slide open automatically. We head to the bar and aren't surprised to find Julia downing a cocktail. I think she and I look completely absurd together. These are the least "bridesmaidy" dresses I've ever seen. It appears we just wanted to wear the same dress. Backup singers, perhaps.

"Have you seen Violet? Did you kill her?" I'm actually serious.

"It would take a cannon to get through that ridiculous dress," Julia growls, and takes another gulp. I see Trey speaking with someone at the front desk. He turns and walks toward us with his signature smile intact.

"Did you tell Trey about Key West?" I ask.

"Well, well, well. Charlotte, you've been holding out on me. Apparently there was a lot to gossip about in Key West." Trey seems happy. I'm still not sure if Julia told him everything. "I can't believe Blake married such a whore." Now I'm sure. "Hey, Nick, how's it going, man?"

Trey shakes Noble's hand, and I wonder if he was ever hitting on me or is just overly attentive to everyone. Noble's mentally fitting all the pieces together.

"Are you going to tell Blake?" I ask.

"Hell no. You always hate the person who delivers that news."

I remember Noble saying he couldn't tell me about the baby before I went to Oklahoma.

"I'm going to make that whore he married tell him, though. I'm just waiting for her to come down. She went up to her room shortly after we got here," Trey adds as something catches his eye in the lobby. "I'll be right back."

"Do you guys think Violet has a brain tumor?" I ask. That would explain why she's gone crazy.

"Maybe she's scared to get married?" Noble offers. Maybe Jason was afraid. How much does Noble know about why Jason did what he did?

"In Key West she said she was going to spend the rest of her life with Blake," I offer.

"Was that before or after she fucked this guy?" Julia asks.

"Both."

"Why the hell would she invite him here, then?" Noble asks.

I don't recognize the voice at first because the tone is so nasty. As people start to stand up from their barstools and move toward the doorway to the lobby, I realize that it's Trey. His usual smooth demeanor has been replaced with a dark and hateful tone as he yells at Violet. She's out of my line of sight but I can see billows of the dress.

"You are a complete whore and you're going back there right now to tell him everything," Trey spews at her.

I look at Julia, who seems equally alarmed.

"I'm not going anywhere with you."

I stand up and start to move toward the door.

"Where are you going?" Noble asks as he grabs my hand.

"To help Violet." I wait for Julia to get up, too.

"What are you going to do?" Julia wants to know.

"I don't know. We're bridesmaids. We're supposed to tend to her, aren't we?" I have no idea what I'm doing, but she's about to be killed, and in that dress. "We don't know the whole story either. Maybe he's a crazed stalker and she didn't invite him."

Julia rolls her eyes but follows me to the doorway.

Sydney enters the lobby from the elevator bank at the same time Blake comes in the front door.

"Tell him," Trey says, his brow covered in sweat, his eyes icily fixed on Violet and her thirty-seven layers of tulle.

"Tell him what?" Blake asks, and the fear sets in. It's hard to watch and I turn away and slowly walk back into the bar. Noble and Julia follow me. We all sit on barstools and Julia orders a round of tequila shots.

"Why did she do this?" I ask no one in particular.

"What do you think Blake's going to do?" Julia adds.

"I can tell you what I'd do: I'd kill that guy from Key West." Noble's face is grim and a chill runs down my back. He smiles to soften the comment, but it hardened in midair.

Julia and I exchange a look and she downs her shot and goes to find Sydney.

"I love you," I say.

"I know you do" is all Noble offers in return. He's still lost in horror as he walks to the bathroom.

As if the night isn't emotional enough, my phone dings with a text from Sean.

LILY CHARLOTTE O'BRIEN
8LBS. 2OZ.
EVERYONE IS WONDERFUL.

I start to cry a little for Michelle and Sean. They're going to be amazing parents—that is, if I haven't worn them down completely with my convalescence. I dial Sean.

"Hey!" Sean says, brimming with joy.

"Congratulations!" I can barely get out before I start to cry.

"Oh, Charlotte, she's crazy beautiful. Wait until you see her—she looks just like Mom."

With this statement, I completely lose myself. Noble walks to me and wraps me in his arms. He doesn't even ask who I'm on the phone with. I don't think Noble cares what's wrong; he's just going to fix it no matter what.

"I'm so happy for you guys. She's a lucky little girl," I tell Sean, and Noble gazes down at me, knowing who I'm talking to now. "I'll be there first thing tomorrow morning. Do you guys need anything?"

"There's not another thing in this world I need," Sean says, and we hang up.

And so it goes on, this life, my life, without my parents. I bury my face in Noble's chest, unwilling to think about how this all works.

Welcome to the world, Lily Charlotte.

~ 30 ~

Coming to Terms

I'm working in the kitchen since Clint's been hammering away at the other end of the house most of the day while I'm stuck on a conference call. He went to pick up lunch and some more fresh strawberries. We finished my quarts this morning. The Jersey strawberries are delicious this year. They're only around for a few weeks, so the entire county's been gorging themselves since early May.

The door opens and without looking up I assume it's Clint. Noble kisses me on the cheek and the surprise makes me jump.

I beam at him. "Hey."

"How's it going?" he asks as he plops the mail on the table beside me. I continue to listen to my conference call as Bruce wraps up the meeting. The mail's mostly catalogs with a few envelopes on top. I absently flip through them until I get to one that stops my breathing. I swallow hard. It's Jason's handwriting. I haven't received a letter from him in about a month and I thought they'd stopped forever. But here's another one.

I feel the center of the envelope and can tell it's lengthy, whatever it is. It doesn't matter. It's going to be thrown away, unopened, like all the others. I look up and Noble's watching me sadly. He knows who the letter is from.

Bruce ends the conference call and I hang up, finally free of the phone attached to my ear.

"Aren't you going to open it?" Noble asks.

"No," I say, and go over to the refrigerator. "Do you want something to drink?" I pour myself a glass of water.

"No. What I want is for you to open the letter," he says, seeming angry. "Actually, what I want is for him to stop sending them or for you to be able to open them."

Neither of those things is going to happen.

"It's just a letter," I say weakly. "It says whatever it says and doesn't change a thing."

"You really don't get it, do you?" Noble picks up the letter and starts pumping it in the air. "This letter is a dark cloud hanging over us. You two never actually settled anything, so now I get to live my life with letters arriving, you running out of town when he's here, and being worried sick about someone mentioning him to you."

I want to say *I told you from the beginning that's how it was going to be*, but even to me that seems unfair. "Nothing in that letter changes a thing. Nothing. Why waste my time reading it?"

"What you're doing is no different than Violet inviting that guy to the wedding."

"What? How can you say that?" I'm hurt and offended.

I would never do what Violet did and the suggestion disgusts me.

"You let him in. He's everywhere. You can't get rid of him, so he's right here between us every single day we're together.

Violet was just more public about it." Noble and I haven't talked about Violet since the night of the wedding. She and Blake fought in Philadelphia and then boarded a plane for Fiji. Somehow, they came home still married.

"That's not fair."

"What are you afraid of?"

That everything you are saying is true.

Defeat creeps across his face. "I went through a horrific breakup," I say, stating the obvious. "And the way I survived it was to avoid my ex. Now you're asking me to start communicating with him again. If I read the letter, it will be for you to feel some security rather than for my benefit."

"Then do it for me"—Noble walks over and puts his arms around me—"because you avoiding his letters is starting to piss me off."

"What about it pisses you off?"

"The fact that you think something written in them will make you want him again."

I put my head on his chest and try to figure out what to do. I don't want to read his letter, but if I'm going to have a future with Noble, I need to make it so he doesn't have to worry about Jason Leer every day.

"Okay, I'll read it. But only because I love you."

* * *

I have about two hours before Noble picks me up for dinner. The letter stares at me every time I walk past the kitchen counter. As I sit drinking a cup of tea, it's almost taunting me. This is stupid. I don't want to read it because I don't want to read it. What does it matter to Noble?

I slowly open the envelope and unfold the papers.

Annie,

Please end this. Come back and this will all be over. I'm not surviving without you. I'm dead.

Good.

I know you wanted to wake me at the airport. I could never have been that close to you and not touched you. You're still your strong, bullheaded self.
    It's time to give in, Annie.

Give in or give up?

Look up at the sky tonight—

I feel the dark sadness blanket me and I put my head in my hands and start to cry. *My God, Jason, I've missed you.* I find a lighter in the desk drawer and set the corners of the pages on fire. There are five or six pages, all written on by Jason. Watching them burn brings me some comfort and I relax knowing they aren't in the house anymore. As the flames reach my fingertips, I drop the letter into the sink and watch it completely disintegrate like our relationship. Gone in a trice.

* * *

Noble arrives for dinner and asks if I mind going to Delaware and eating outside. He seems hesitant around me. How can one stamped envelope cause so much angst? As usual, he opens the truck door for me and closes it after I'm in. I'm lost in thought, staring out the window at the darkening sky, and I don't notice the delay at first. Rather than starting the truck right away, Noble leans forward on the steering wheel, staring at me silently.

"Yes?" I say when I realize he's waiting for something.

Noble stares out the windshield. "Did you read Jason's letter, Charlotte?" The mention of his name in the same sentence as my own stings a little.

"What are you, the mail police?" I immaturely ask, trying to change the subject.

Noble's face sours and his eyes harden.

I stare forward out the window. "You know what? I don't feel like eating anymore," I say as I get out of the truck and enter the garage door code without turning back. Once inside the door, I push the button and the door lowers on the sight of Noble.

I walk into my room and lie flat on my bed as I listen to the sound of Noble's truck pull out of the driveway. I don't care if he ever comes back. How dare he think he can tell me what to read and when to read it? I pick up the phone to call him and my anger dials the number for me.

"Hello?" It's a voice I don't recognize.

"Oh, I think I have the wrong number," I say, completely confused.

"This is 405-555-8822. Who you lookin' for?"

Oh. My. God.

"Is Jason there?" I say, although I have no idea what I'm doing.

"Jason, oh no. He done moved out a few weeks ago," the

voice answers with a country twang. "He's over at Stephanie's now."

"Oh, right. Sure," I say. "Of course."

"Hey, do you want me to tell him you called?" the voice asks.

"No, uh, no thanks." I hang up the phone.

What am I holding on to here? He doesn't live in the loft anymore. Our loft. Some other guy's sleeping there. He lives with her. They're one big happy family...

I grab my keys off the counter on my way out the door. It starts to rain as soon as I pull out of my driveway. The rain pours down hard and my wipers can barely keep up. I park next to Noble's truck and realize he's still sitting in it. The mere sight of him makes me feel better. I walk to his side of the truck and knock on his window. The rain hasn't slowed. I'm getting soaked and a cool, drenched area is quickly spreading toward my lower back. My sopping hair lies on my head and shoulders like a wet blanket as large drops fall from my eyelashes. The whole time Noble sits in his truck, his head resting on his arms across the steering wheel.

"I don't know what to do, Noble," I yell at the closed window. "I don't know how to fix it. How to fix me." I bang on the window with my open hand. "Tell me what to do."

I lower my head and gently cry. The rain comes harder and the sound of it is lovely. It falls on the leaves of the tree next to us and the roof of the L-shed in the distance. Noble gets out of the truck and wraps his arms around me. For the eight hundredth time his warmth engulfs me. I look up at his tortured face and kiss him because I still don't know what else to do. Noble kisses me back but there's something missing. His usual hunger is gone, replaced by reticence.

"Charlotte, I'll fight for you. I'll beat down the locals and Rob, but I can't fight something that isn't there. He's invisible, locked in your head...or your heart."

I've never seen the Noble standing before me. He's detached. I move even closer to him, willing him to return to me. He refuses and stares toward the house as the rain washes over us in sheets. With my hand, I move his face until he's staring down at me. By the look in his eyes he's starting to hate me.

"I want this to work more than anything, but you're scaring the shit out of me," he says as he removes my hand from his face.

"How am I scaring you?"

"Because no matter how much time passes, you still see yourself with him."

I stop and put my hands on my chest, shaking my head.

"No...no, I don't." I search his eyes for understanding. He has to believe me. "Can we please go inside?" I ask, grabbing his hand. Noble nods and we walk into his house, a river of questions running off us. I stop just inside the door and take off my flip-flops.

"Why can't you let it go?" he asks as we go through the kitchen door.

"I don't know why I can't let it go, but I'm not buying time until we're together again." I force him to look at me "Noble, you aren't some fill-in until we work it out. I love you." He doesn't believe me. I take a deep breath. I know the next few sentences that come out of my mouth are going to end something.

"Jason and I were"—I search for the word—"different." I take a deep breath and move back so I can gauge his reaction as I continue. "We moved hastily into a serious relationship in the middle of a tragedy. We didn't put a lot of thought into things during a time when the last thing I wanted to do was think." I pause, remembering the first few weeks we were together and how little conversation there was.

Noble is listening, patient again.

"I don't want to talk to him or read his letters because it's over. I've come to terms with the fact that I'll never understand why it ended, why it didn't work." I stand motionless. "Quite frankly it never made sense how it worked in the first place. We were probably careening toward a fiery ending for months."

I remember the fights toward the end about me being at Rutgers. Jason refusing to come up for my spring formal was the worst of it. He had assumed I'd relent and spend the weekend with him in Oklahoma, but I surprised us both by choosing to go alone rather than miss it.

He showed me…

"Charlotte, I just don't want you to regret anything. And I don't want to end up in jail for killing someone." Noble's face is unrecognizable, dark.

"I've stopped questioning if I'm making the wrong decision. If I should forgive him. I don't believe it's a possibility anymore." Noble softens. "He lives with Stephanie and his son now." I omit the baby's name.

"How do you know that?"

"I called him," I answer, trying to sound unaffected. "I didn't talk to him—some guy told me—but I didn't have some major breakdown. I'm still standing." I throw my hands out, displaying the evidence, ignoring that I'm soaking wet and have been crying in Noble's driveway in a monsoon.

"Wait here," he says. He walks upstairs and I hear the shower turn on.

"Here," he says, handing me a towel as he returns to the kitchen. I take it and bury my face in it. "The shower's warming up," he says, the heat back in his eyes.

~ 31 ~

We Meet Again

I'm still a coward. When Butch "mentioned" Jason was coming to town for the weekend, I immediately decided to head out. I braced myself for Noble's reaction. But instead of forcing me to face Jason, to face what we lost, Noble accompanied me to New York. It's a significant compromise, or maybe a sad acceptance.

The weekend away was nice, but I miss BJ. I want to drive right there and pick him up, but first I have to check with Butch. Again, I'm a coward. Noble drops me off and I linger in the Jeep, delaying my departure from him, enjoying his kisses for the hundredth time in three days. I felt bad for Julia—we weren't much in the mood to go out or see other people. We spent almost the entire weekend in my bed.

"What are you up to now?" I ask.

"I have to go back to work. I have about a week's worth of plowing to do."

"Will I see you tonight?" I ask, hopeful.

"If you do, it'll be late. The tractor has headlights."

"Headlights, huh?" I tease him.

"Apparently I didn't have time to go away this weekend."

"Why did you? You never come with me to New York."

Noble stares out the Jeep's windshield for too long. "Something about this weekend…I just had to be with you."

My mind quickly recalls the intense sex we've been having since last Friday in the barn. It reminds me of Jason and I immediately push that from my mind. I look down, ensuring Noble can't read my thoughts.

"I felt that." I kiss him on the cheek. "I'll see you tomorrow, okay? I'll make you dinner."

"Perfect," he says, and looks at me full of love.

No messages on the machine. Why do I even have a house phone? It's so 1990. It's because my parents would still have one. It seems like one last link to their presence in this world: It still has their phone number. I pick up the phone and call Butch, ready to hang up if Jason answers. So juvenile.

"Yeah," Butch answers, as sweet as ever.

"Hey. Did your company leave?"

"Stormed out of here Saturday. I don't know what the hell happened. I thought you had something to do with it."

"Me? You know I stay out of the drama. Have you eaten yet?" I ask as I look through my own refrigerator.

"No, it's only four o'clock." Butch leaves off the "you damn idiot" but I can hear it in his voice.

"I'll come over and make us lasagna." I find all the ingredients for a salad in my fridge and take out some Italian bread from the freezer.

"Good. You can take this damn annoying dog home, too."

I hang up without saying good-bye. If his voice wasn't close to Jason's, I wouldn't even let him speak. Such an absolute crab.

* * *

BJ is happy to see me. It's worth making Butch dinner. "How dare he call you annoying?" I say as I get down on my knees and let BJ put his paws on my shoulders to hug and kiss me. He's the sweetest dog. "Where is the old cuss?"

"Butch, you in here?" I yell as I stick my head into the family room. It's empty and the TV is off, a clear indication Butch isn't in the house.

I empty my grocery bags and get to work. I wash the peppers and tomatoes first and begin chopping them on a cutting board straddling the sink. This weekend has put me in an excellent mood; not even Butch will be able to drown it out. I sing, adding air drums as I swing my knife around. I stop when I hear the screen door. No need to hear Butch's thoughts on my singing.

"I hope you're hungry."

"Starving."

An immediate chill goes through me from head to toe. It's an ice-blue electrical current with waves reaching every corner of my body and settling in my breasts. I struggle to remain standing, to breathe.

I can't.

I try to connect Jason's voice to its rightful owner—and then he's upon me. So close behind me that a glimmer of light couldn't squeeze between us. He wraps one arm around me and places it on the counter in front of me. With the other he moves my hair to the side and kisses my neck right behind my ear. He brushes my neck with his lips and whispers, "Finally, Annie."

The chill is burning the tops of my thighs as it rises up the rest of my body. I'm sinking and can't save myself. I can't open my eyes. I can't hear anything. I again buckle under his breath on my neck.

I am completely his.

In this moment I don't care. I don't care that he was with another, that he's a father and it's not my baby, that he broke me into a million pieces.

I drop the knife and he laughs. "Probably a good idea to put down the knife." His laugh is big, but whispered against my neck.

I just need a minute to pull myself together, but every inch of the back of me is touching him and I can barely stand. I open my eyes and through the window I see Noble's tractor parked by his house.

My mouth is dry and my voice is weak. "We need to talk."

"Oh, I'm not leaving until we talk." He leans into me, his weight crushing me against the counter. "I'm not leaving without you." He kisses my neck again and I start to sweat. "You can bring the dog."

Jason takes a step back and I turn my head and see BJ staring at us. He's completely confused.

What, little guy, wondering where Noble is?

I look out the window at the tractor again before I turn around and face Jason. He's even more beautiful than I give him credit for in my dreams. I inhale deeply and let my eyes feast on him. His stare never leaves me. He's smiling slightly, but I can tell he doesn't mean it by the look in his eyes. He's angry and doesn't want me to know it. Yet. I walk past him, hugging the wall to avoid touching him, and go through the back door. His footsteps crunching on the gravel echo my own.

I open the door to the barn and silently pray, *Please God*, but I have no idea what I'm praying for. I walk in and past the workbench, hoping to use it as a barricade. Jason moves toward me, a hunter with his prey.

"Stay right where you are," I command.

He stops and the expression on his face attests to some victory he's won in his head. "What are you afraid of, Annie?"

"Doing something stupid that I'll regret for the rest of my life," I sneer. "Have any experience with that?"

"It's not going to be for the rest of my life—or yours. We're going to be together."

I throw my hand up to halt his tired plea. "We'll never be together again." My voice is quiet, filled with the hatred I've been carrying around for almost a year.

Jason's eyes are searing me, and I look away for protection.

"Where's your necklace?"

"I took it off with my pride when I left Oklahoma," I lie. I can feel him staring at me, taking everything that's his.

"I wake up every morning and think of you. I suffer through my miserable days hoping this is going to end, Annie. I've spent almost an entire year waiting for you to come back and trying to figure out how to make this right."

"It'll never be right. You should move on." My voice and my body are void of emotion. If I let myself feel anything but the familiar anger, I'll launch myself into his arms.

"Like you did?"

Jason's angrily grasping the workbench directly opposite me. "You ran home and started fucking Nick Sinclair. You're taking the easy way out. You should be fighting for us."

The taste in my mouth is bitter and I hunt for a weapon. There's wood piled all around the bench and I hurl a two-by-four at him and scream, "Fuck you, Jason Leer!"

He raises his arms just in time for his left hand to be hit by the board. He shakes it in pain and I smile, having inflicted the blow. He's bleeding and grabs a towel to wrap around it. He looks at me again, this time his eyes on fire.

"What about this has been the easy way?" I whisper, and regain my strength. "Was having my heart ripped out by you easy? Was moving home to Salem County, where everyone knows exactly how you left me, easy?" My voice grows louder. "Was hearing about the birth of your son easy?" I hurl another board at him, which he dodges.

I will not cry.

"You've been spending time with Butch," he says, and I feel caught in a lie. "Does being with him, in my house, remind you of me?"

"Your father needed help."

"What about Sinclair? Did he need your help, too?"

I shake my head and lower my eyes. "It's none of your business."

"I had you first!" he roars.

"And then you destroyed me!" I scream.

"You have to forgive me."

"No!" I yell defiantly with a stare that can leave no question of my hatred.

"This thing with Sinclair is never going to last, Annie." His words are defined but restrained. "He's never going to make you feel the way I do. He'll never love you the way I do. It won't last."

"Last? Like the way we lasted? The way we were so happy

together?" Each word fires sarcastic daggers from my tongue. "You were *so* happy you knocked up Stephanie Harding." At the mention of her name I begin to crumble. "How could you? I deserve better than this." My anger reignites as I imagine them lying together in bed. "You were so fucking scared you couldn't spend one fucking weekend alone? Or was it more than one weekend?"

"Annie, calm down. It was *one* mistake. One horrible mistake." He puts his hands up, pleading for my restraint. "Maybe you just need to clear your head." His voice is soothing now. Reminding me of how an orgasm would always clear our heads. He grins. "I can help you with that."

"It's already clear," I answer with a wicked smirk.

"Why are you being such an ass?" he asks, which infuriates me further.

"I'm an ass? *I'm* an ass?" I howl. I find another board and heave it toward his head. He ducks. "I'm an ass because I fucking hate you." I throw another. "I'm an ass because I ever loved you." Another. "I'm an ass for letting you ever touch me in the first place." I throw another and this one hits him square in the shoulder, not moving the ox at all. "I should have been with Noble instead of you."

"Don't even try it, Annie. He doesn't compare and you know it," Jason calmly replies.

"Actually he compared just fine while we were at Rutgers."

Jason's face hardens and I know I've landed a direct hit. "I love him."

"I don't believe you." He begins to walk around the workbench, having completely lost his composure.

"I don't care anymore." I throw another board at him and pick up the last one.

Jason catches it and throws it toward the wall, yelling, "Stop throwing the fucking boards at me!" at the exact time I launch the last one. The boards meet midair, and just like Jason and me, explosively collide. They splinter and change trajectory, one careening straight for my head.

The pain is intolerable and then there's nothing.

~ 32 ~

Apologies

So much for the high road.

I think I actually felt the ground shift as my father rolled over in his grave. Oh yes, he'd be very proud of the decisions that have brought me to this place.

We are a disaster.

"Oh my God, Annie." Jason's talking to me, but I can't sit up. The cold concrete of the barn floor feels too good on my face. There's a throbbing pain in my head, as if the blood's gushing out of it, and I can't see out of my right eye. I hear a choking sob and realize it's coming from me.

What's happening?

"Annie, Annie, get up." Jason puts one arm around my shoulders and lifts me from the comfort of the floor.

Sitting up, I can see him with my left eye.

"Oh my God, Annie. We have to get you to the hospital." His face is stricken and scaring me in a way I've never felt with him before. He's frightened.

"What happened?" I ask, still dazed, and lift my hand to my face, which is wet. I edge my hand toward my left eye and see it's covered in blood. "Jason...Jason!" I cry, and he lifts me into his arms. He takes the towel from his hand and rests it on my face.

"Hold this here. It's going to be okay. You're going to be okay."

He's speaking but I don't believe a word of it. Jason carries me to my car and gently puts me in the passenger seat. He buckles my seat belt and runs inside the house to get my keys. Detached, I stare through the car window at Noble's back door. It's as if I've never been in the house. Nothing is familiar or safe anymore.

Jason runs out of the house and practically rips the car door off as he gets in and fumbles with getting the key in the ignition. I reach out and touch his hand. "I'm okay."

Jason looks at me again, terror in his eyes.

"I'm starting to feel better." I force a painful smile.

He starts the car and tears off toward the lane, kicking dust up as we go.

When we get to Route 40, I feel a little better. The throbbing has slowed to a dull pound and I'm able to form complete thoughts. "I shouldn't have said what I said." I grab his hand and hold it on my lap. I thread my fingers through his, and even through the pain in my head I feel the twisting and aching in my lower abdomen. Even in this, the ugliest moment we've ever shared, my body craves him. I watch my hand caress his, both covered in blood.

"Which part?"

I look at Jason, unsure of what he's talking about since I've become lost in his touch. "Which part shouldn't you have said? Do you not love him?"

"I do love him. Of course I love him. He's the most decent and kind person I've ever met, and neither of us deserve to have him in our lives." I should feel guilty about the way I feel with Jason right now, but I don't. "He was never anything but a loyal friend to both of us at Rutgers."

"Yeah, that's what I call him—loyal friend."

I rest my head on the headrest and admire Jason. How did we end up here?

"It's different with him. It's easy, and safe, and calm, and peaceful."

Jason stares at me silently for a few minutes.

"You know, even a girl who worships the sun loves a storm once in a while," he says, and squeezes my hand.

I can't take my eyes off Jason's profile as I contemplate his prediction of my future boredom. He's such a beautiful storm. I begin to cough and the tin taste fills my mouth. I take the towel off my head and spit blood from my mouth into it.

"We're almost there," he says, looking like he might throw up. I close my eyes because the sight of fear on Jason's face is unbearable to witness without holding him.

* * *

Jason is waiting at the entrance to the ER with my car as the nurse wheels me through the door. He takes my hand, my arm, and finally picks me up and gently places me in the car. I have twenty-two stitches above my eye and fourteen across my cheek. The bruising is coming and I can tell it's going to be a rough-looking few weeks.

"That doctor thought I hit you," he says, and closes my

door, stomping to the driver's side. "I wanted to deck him." He climbs behind the wheel.

"That definitely would have put his mind at ease about you hitting me," I say, and laugh at the thought of it.

"Annie, me or anyone else hitting you isn't something to laugh at. I'll kill the person who hurts you."

"No one could hit me hard enough to hurt me more than you did last year."

I said it.

Jason's eyes fall to the keys in his hands and I know he finally understands.

"This is nothing compared to last August."

I start to cry a little, remembering my heartache. Jason starts the car and pulls away from the hospital.

"Annie, please let me fix this. Let me make it up to you. I love you." He takes my hand in his and steers with his battered one. "I don't want to have a life without you in it. I can't just forget what it was like between us. I want it back. I need it back. You have to forgive me."

"I forgave you a long time ago. I didn't realize until Florida, but I forgave you," I say, admitting it to myself for the first time. "Look at me."

Jason turns from the road and stares at me. "The last two times we've been together have been disastrous. It's not going to get better. Too much has happened."

Jason starts shaking his head in protest.

"If this were anyone else but you, you'd make sure I never saw the person again."

Jason looks at me, utter sadness in his eyes.

"Go back to Oklahoma and make a life," I say, and Jason stares out the windshield, someplace far away. I'm not even sure he's still listening. "Love Stephanie even if you never marry her, love her as the mother of your son." I swallow hard at my last words.

"She'll never be you, Annie. She doesn't even compare."

"Then stop comparing."

"Is that how you get through it?"

He knows it's exactly how I get through it. Nothing, and no one, will ever compare to him or to what I am when I'm with him. And now that he's next to me, I know it's not gone. It was never gone; I just left it with him when I walked out.

I look at the bright blue sky with barely a cloud in it and wonder if the sun will ever shine the same again. The way it used to before my parents died, before I knew what it was like to walk around with my heart having been ripped out of my chest. That's the way Noble walks. He's the blue sky and the calm breeze.

"You know what they say: if you can't get out of it, get into it," I say with little else to offer.

"Nobody fucking says that."

"Oh, I think it's catching on," I say, and start to laugh. Jason barely smiles. So much time has passed and the only thing I know of the passage of time is that people are lost within it. Nothing will stay with you forever.

"Just be a good father," I blurt out, finally acknowledging there's someone else with us. Someone who will always be a part of Jason and Charlotte even though he'll never belong with me. "If we're not going to be together, make it count. You're the only dad he's ever going to have. Tell him every day how much you love him and how proud you are of him. Don't wait to make it right. Get it right the first time."

I try to breathe. Even if I mean every word, it's choking me. "Butch is incredibly proud of you," I eek out.

We drive the rest of the way in silence, both coming to terms with our future situation. I take a deep breath but can barely smell Jason under the antiseptic, bandages, and God knows what else they put on me. Jason turns into my driveway, opens the garage door, and pulls right in. He comes around to my side of the car, opens the door, and lifts me out. He kicks the door closed with his Old Gringo boot and walks into the house.

Jason puts me down in the kitchen and I lean into him. I lay the good side of my face on his shoulder and inhale him, soothed by his scent. If only it were one year ago. His arms around me are my foundation and I don't want him to ever leave. Jason kisses the top of my head and my body responds even to this innocent gesture. I close my eyes and a hundred days we were together run roughshod through my mind: the first time when he drove life back into me, every rest stop between here and Oklahoma, his shower, the counter we're leaning on, the night my bed broke.

I turn my head and stare into Jason's eyes. Gray pools of need stare back at me, and I don't release his stare as I move my lips toward his. I kiss him, just a simple kiss, and I feel my nipples harden. I pull back to drink it in and my breathing quickens. Jason tightens his arms around me and gently kisses me again, his need restrained because of my injury. His tongue in my mouth is euphoric and I wrap my arms around his neck and thread my fingers through his hair as a chill runs down me.

I pull back, looking at Jason for answers, but his eyes are crazed. I swallow hard and he kisses me again. He's never touched me so gently. His lips bear down on me and his greedy tongue searches for answers. He leans my head to the side and kisses my neck and I welcome the intoxication. He reaches up and pulls my hair to move my head and I squeal in pain.

"Oh my God, Annie. Are you all right?"

I open my mouth but can only manage, "I'm perfect," and I start to cry.

"No, you were perfect before me. Now you're broken. I broke you." Jason's hands hang at his sides, unwilling to trust himself touching me.

I gently rest my forehead on his chest. "You didn't break me. You saved me three years ago."

"What are you going to do now? Will you marry Sinclair?" he softly inquires.

"I don't know…I don't want to talk about this," I murmur, drained by twelve months of hatred mixed with need.

Jason holds my face in his hands, barely touching the right side, and leans down to kiss my left cheek. He tilts my face toward his and his lips gently touch mine. My stomach clenches and my heart aches. I know this kiss will be forever. The last one and I can't accept it. I focus on the roundness of his lips, the playfulness of his tongue, and the taste of him. It will have to sustain me for a lifetime. I stop thinking and let my body have him, for he's what it's longed for the last year.

With one hand on each of his wrists, I pull down his hands and move closer to him. I ignore the pain in my head and force myself toward him, kissing him with the hunger I've been unable to satisfy for twelve months. I won't waste this last moment on pain; enough time has been wasted on it already. My heart races and my groin throbs with anticipation. His hard-on gropes my thigh and I close my eyes and try to breathe. I feel my knee rise and my leg wrap around the back of him, and I know I've gone too far.

I take one step back and stare at him with ravenous eyes. My breathing, still heavy, breaks the silence of the room and I think Jason might cry. "My God, what have we done to each other?" I ask, not expecting an answer.

"I have to go," Jason says.

But I can't let him go like this. There's no way I can ever let him go.

"You know, you're right." He caresses my swollen face. "Whoever had been with you when this happened, I'd never let them near you again." He kisses me above my eye and I wince at the sting. "Just remember, Annie, I'm always thinking of you. No matter what becomes of me, it's always you that matters. If I win the NFR, if I have ten kids, if I marry someone else, every minute of it I'll be thinking of you. No matter where I am or who I'm with, it will always be you." He moves my head so I can see him. "Do you understand?"

I understand all too well.

"Jason, when we were together, it was everything," I say, and I know he knows what I mean. "I still love you."

He gently kisses me once more.

"I'm goin'," Jason says, staring at me with empty eyes.

"I'll drive you."

"It's okay. I'm in no rush to be anywhere." With that, he lets go of my hands and walks out the door without looking back.

I walk to the front window and watch him walk for about an acre and a half—until he reaches the top of the overpass and I can no longer see him.

Epilogue

Noble and I carry our boat as we wade into the calm sea. The water is flat with barely a break at the edge. It's more like a lake today than an ocean, and I welcome the peacefulness. Noble's birthday seems fitting to take *Mindless* out for a sail, I think as I pull myself over the side of the boat. We drove down after dinner, avoiding the crowds, and it couldn't be more perfect. Noble and I lie head to feet, rocking over the gentle waves in our boat as Noble sings "Happy Birthday" to himself, and the cloudless blue sky, and the sun hanging low to hear him better. His voice is soft and gentle and floats along the tamed surf.

The sun warms my skin and I throw some water on both of us from over the side.

"Hey! Do you mind? I'm trying to enjoy a relaxing evening on my boat."

"This bathing suit is made to get wet, isn't it?" I ask as I rub the hem of his board shorts. I mentally compare Noble's bathing suit to Jason's cutoff jeans and it reminds me of Jason's accusation that I'm taking the easy way out. Maybe I am only in love with Noble because it's easy. We've always been more together than we are apart. Does that make it wrong, or just comfortable? I rub the scar on my cheek. Noble applied the SPF 75 he bought for it—twice. Right before he put my hat on my head.

"What are you thinking about?" he asks, interrupting my ridiculous thoughts.

"How much I love you," I answer, forgoing the lack of a conclusion.

Noble rocks the boat as he sits up, but I keep my face toward the sun. "That's perfect," he says, "because I want to know if you'll marry me."

"Again with the begging, Noble?" I smile at our joke and look up at him. His face is void of amusement and on the end of his pinky finger sits a ring. "Noble?" I am breathless.

Jason jumps into my head, and what accepting this ring will do to him, and I silently chastise myself for letting him into *Mindless*. His invasions are still constant, even after the finality of our last meeting. It's not fair to marry Noble and care what someone else will think. He absolutely deserves better.

"Charlotte," Noble says, and I force myself to focus on him. His hair is wet and shaken off his face. His blue eyes are deeper than the ocean yet shallow enough to reach. The sun's warmth is centered on him, only shining on me because I'm near him. He is glorious. "You are the most stubborn, frustrating girl I've ever known. The months between the snowstorm and the Harvest Dance were the longest of my entire life."

I remember the look on his face when I told him I loved him that night.

"I believe you could literally drive me insane," Noble continues confidently. His expression is the one he always has when he laughs at me. "You have a tendency to collect things in need, specifically misbehaving hound dogs and crotchety old men—and you insist on spoiling them both rotten. And to my chagrin, you lack a basic understanding of the purpose of undergarments in everyday attire." He raises his eyebrows, tilting his head in the most adorable way. "Your impact on the opposite sex is an enormous burden to manage, and I'll spend the rest of my life fighting men off you."

I listen to him, speechless.

"Your use of whiskey in recipes is questionable, and your driving—harrowing."

"Does this pick up?" I finally ask. The joking question is out of habit; the uncertainty in my voice is born of consternation.

"Yes, I'm getting there," he says, grinning. "For months, I've watched in awe as you painstakingly reconstructed your life, and unbeknownst to me, each day I fell more in love with you. Charlotte, I always knew I wanted to farm my land. I never thought much further than that"—Noble looks down at the ring and back at me—"until the snowstorm in January."

He smiles his wonderful, carefree smile and my heart warms.

"I don't know what made you come into my room that night, but that one step through my doorway rearranged every element of my life forever. Since then, I see myself cooking Sunday dinners, and playing cards by the fire, and taking road trips and boat rides, and God help me, going to church."

Noble laughs and I can't take my eyes off him.

"And hauling in Christmas trees, and hiding Easter eggs, and reading bedtime stories." His voice softens. "And, Charlotte, all of it I see with you."

My eyes move from Noble's to the ring around his finger. It's a round diamond surrounded by emeralds, each a half-moon shape. It's like a flower and I've never seen anything like it, and like the man holding it, it's perfect.

With a finger to my chin, Noble tilts my face and my eyes meet his again. "I want to spend every day of my life like this." I look at the ocean around us. It is vast and calm and meets the quiet sky at an unbroken horizon. "With you."

Noble should be giving this ring to someone who loves him, forsaking all others. "You are extraordinary, Charlotte, and you deserve an extraordinary life."

What I deserve is to fall off this boat and drown.

"I love you, and no one's ever going to take better care of you." Noble takes my face in his hand and runs his thumb across the fresh scar on my cheek.

I close my eyes and lean into his hand. A heaviness washes over me and threatens to pull our entire boat to the bottom of the ocean. Why didn't I see this coming? What did I think was going to happen? I know exactly what this will do to Jason because I've lived through it, every day imagining his life with someone else. I can't inflict that kind of pain on him.

And yet, out here on the water, I belong with Noble.

If it weren't for Noble, I wouldn't be here in this boat, maybe not here at all. As inconceivable as my parents' deaths are in relation to a grand plan for my life, Noble seems to fit it perfectly. He's the only thing that really makes sense. But I learned long ago life isn't about making sense; it's about survival. Noble kisses me; his lips pressing against mine force the guilt from my mind and remind me that I deserve to live this life.

"If in your heart...you know...this is how you should

spend the rest of your life, then say yes and we'll figure the rest out later. Trust in me, Charlotte."

I open my eyes and see on Noble's face what took me months to comprehend.

My lovely Noble cherishes me.

"Yes," I say, and silently pray for Noble, and me... and Jason.

Dear God, thank you for this beautiful day,
And this beautiful man in front of me.
Please watch over all three of us,
And protect us from ourselves and each other,
As we embark on a thousand tomorrows.

Bonus Scene

NOBLE SINCLAIR

My cell phone rings as I pull the tractor into the L-shed. I fumble trying to get it out of my pocket and turn off the engine as I see the number. I was hoping for Charlotte, but it's Jason. I don't want to talk to Jason right now, or really ever again, but I know that's not a possibility.

"Hello," I say, hoping my voice isn't filled with the dread I feel.

"Sinclair, what's up?" Jason says, and I can't help feeling guilty.

"Nada. How's it going in Oklahoma?" I ask, hoping there's an obvious opening to tell him I'm in love with Charlotte. I'm sure I'll be able to slip it right in. I roll my eyes.

"Shitty, as usual. How's Annie? I haven't heard from you in months," Jason says.

"I've been meaning to call you, but I was hoping to talk to you in person." I pause, still not knowing exactly how to continue. "I won't talk to you about Charlotte anymore."

"Why's that?" he asks, showing no understanding of why.

"I'm in love with her. I'm sorry, man. Really sorry to tell you over the phone. Like I said, I was hoping to talk to you in person."

"Dude, it's okay. I've always known you love her," Jason says kindly, almost smugly, then pauses. "What's different now?"

Silence.

"Oh, the difference is now you're making a run for her? You think you have a chance?"

"Jason, I'm really sorry," I get out right before he hangs up.

I walk into the house and take a beer out of the refrigerator. I sit down at the table, open it, and stare out the back window. The beer bubbles and hisses but doesn't spill over. Jason's pissed and that's a problem. He'll come home. Home to get her. He's not stupid, just impulsive. He's a hothead. He reacts faster than most people can comprehend the situation. Probably an instinct honed from wrestling animals.

A storm's coming and I have to make the necessary preparations. Instead of bringing in the patio furniture and moving the grill, the only real preparation is finding Charlotte. Now would be the perfect time for her to go away for a few weeks. I always knew this day would come. The day when she and Jason would be together in the same room, when they'd finally talk about everything that happened. For months I've been telling both of us there's nothing to avoid, nothing Jason can say or do that could bring her back to him, but now I think I've been lying to us both.

The irony stings my throat as I take a large gulp of the beer. Charlotte and I have fought over her running out of town to avoid him and now I'd throw her in the Jeep and drive her away myself if I could. Maybe I should just tell her the truth. If

I tell her, she'll probably leave on her own. If I only knew that she sincerely hates him.

No matter how secure I feel with her, I can't get the memories out of my head of the way the two of them were together. I keep questioning whether she hates him or is afraid to let herself feel anything else, especially since she went to Key West. I don't know if I'll ever know exactly what happened down there, but something's been different about Charlotte since she returned.

Jason and Charlotte came out of nowhere. I remember watching from her parents' front door as he lifted her into his truck. It was bizarre and completely unexpected. We all knew each other. Knew everything about each other, just like every other person raised in this town, but Jason and Charlotte had never been "together" before. Margo didn't even know what was going on.

From that moment on it was uncomfortable to be around them, their connection palpable. They would speak eerily little, as if they were already aware of each other's thoughts and feelings. Actually, it was as if they had no thoughts or feelings outside of each other. They were always touching. Holding hands and hugging, and whenever they sat, it was next to, in front of, or on top of each other. I've known both of them my entire life and I'd never seen them act that way before. I've never seen anyone act that way before. When they looked at each other, I felt like I should leave the room, and I literally did. After the first few months, I stopped visiting Charlotte and her roommates when Jason was in town.

I down the beer, crush the can, and throw it across the room into the sink. Jason writing her letters pisses me off, but him coming home terrifies me. When he calls her Annie, it enrages me. I can't stand that he has any piece of her, even a stupid nickname from preschool. I hate that she still dreams about him, even speaking his name in a whimper some nights.

But what I hate most of all is that he thinks she's still in love with him and she'll forgive him. No. Actually, what I hate is that I think that, too.

She can't go back to him.

At Homecoming I was surprised by how much I wanted her, during the blizzard I fell in love with her without considering it a possibility, and at the Harvest Dance I became completely obsessed with her. Losing her is out of the question. I have no idea how Jason let her go, but I'm not going to let it happen.

I see the Volvo pull up to the barn, and Charlotte unloads groceries. I don't know what I'm going to do, but I need to be near her. When I open the side door to the barn, she's balancing a bag of ice over her raised knee as she rearranges items in the freezer. She has on a strapless green dress that goes all the way to her ankles and silver flip-flops. It's one of my favorites on her. Her blond hair hangs freely down her back, and just seeing her in this ridiculous position gives me a hard-on.

I walk over and remove the ice from her leg. She looks up at me. Her green eyes dance as her perfect smile spreads across her face.

"Hello, lover," she greets me playfully. I can't lose her...ever. Since the blizzard, she's become the center of my world. Charlotte reassembles the contents of the freezer and replaces the ice.

"Are you okay?" she asks as she raises both hands to my head.

I close my eyes, trying to remember every millisecond of her touch. "Do you have any idea how much I love you?" I ask, knowing she can't possibly. It's difficult for me to understand.

"Show me," she says with an inviting tone as she gently kisses me. I lift her up, kissing her the entire time, my hunger out of hand. She responds without any hesitation and wraps her legs around my waist. I carry her to the workbench and set her down on it. I hold her head in my hands and kiss her, savoring the taste of Charlotte. Her back arches and I know she wants more. More from me. As I kiss her neck, I pull down one side of her dress and play with her nipple. Her breasts are full and soft, and without even seeing them I throb in my pants. The trouble with Charlotte is I can never get enough, and at the same time she's entirely too much.

Her legs are spread and I'm standing between them as Charlotte reaches down and unbuckles my belt. She is staring at me and I want to invade her. I want to enter her and never pull out. Her dazzling green eyes tell me every sweet word a girl can say while her deft little hands unzip my pants and release me, the dichotomy of Charlotte unraveling me.

I bend her back onto the table and spread her legs wide. She has no underpants on and the sight of her naked almost makes me come. I run my hand up her inner thigh, imagining me inside of her, and she shivers. I look up at her angelic face as I slip one finger into her. Charlotte closes her eyes and moans, a small smile resting on her lips. She is always so ready. My Charlotte. I enter her slowly and take a deep breath, trying to control myself. She opens her eyes and looks at me as if she can see straight through to my soul. If anyone can, it's her.

"I'm yours, Noble," she says. *Please say this to me every day for the rest of our lives.* I begin as slowly as possible, but when she takes her own hand to herself, I can no longer control myself. I pound away at her, over and over again, trying to leave a mark on every inch of her. *He...will...not...have...you.* I come, watching Charlotte crumble beneath me.

I bend over and rest my head on her shoulder. Charlotte wraps her legs tightly around my waist and her arms around my neck. "I love you, Noble," she says, and I want to crush her into a million pieces, never to be found.

"I know." *I just don't know if I'm the only one.*

"I'm going to New York tonight," she says hesitantly, as if I'll protest.

"Maybe I'll go with you."

Bonus Scene

JASON LEER

I hurl the phone against the wall without hanging it up.

"Lying sack of shit," I growl as I open my closet door and start searching the floor. Under Stephanie's eighty-seven pairs of shoes I find my black duffel bag and throw it on the bed. I grab some underwear, a handful of socks, and a few undershirts and shove them into the bag, my anger not dissipating.

"Where are you going?" Stephanie interrupts my internal rant with her annoying question asked in her annoying voice. "I said, where are you going?"

"I heard what you said," I answer, turning all my anger toward her. She is, after all, the reason I'm in this mess. "I'm going home for a few days."

"We'll go with you," she says as she watches me pack all of my toiletries in one swoop.

"No, you won't."

"Why not?" she asks, annoying again.

"Because I don't want you to. I have some things to take care of."

"It's her, isn't it? You're going to see your precious Annie?" Stephanie spews her name as if it's curdled in her stomach.

"It's always been her. You knew when you climbed on top of my semiconscious body that it was her, and it still is." I turn my back on her and keep packing. Something about Stephanie's increasing fury is calming to me.

"She doesn't want you anymore," she spits. "She's with Nick Sinclair now, and has been for months. You two are DONE. And by the way, you seemed pretty happy the night I climbed on top of you."

"I'll say when we're done." I grab my bag and walk out, letting the screen door slam shut behind me.

Unbelievable. All these months I've been trying to give her time and she's been dating. And Sinclair, no less. I'm going to kill him. I am NOT going to call her. She's not getting any notice. Somehow I keep missing her, but not this time. She will talk to me.

Why didn't you wake me in the Tampa airport?

At the first traffic light, I flip through the pictures on my phone and find the one Earl sent me of Annie hugging Harlan. I almost ripped his arms off for it. This is what I am reduced to: pining over a picture of one friend touching her while she's out dating another one. As I turn onto the I-44 on-ramp, it occurs to me they might be having sex. I accelerate to seventy. Seventy-five would be much faster, but this old truck can only go so fast. Maybe I should have flown.

You can't be fucking Nick Sinclair.

Focus—I've got to focus. I have a twenty-four-hour drive and I can't spend every minute of it imagining her with Sinclair. I'll crash this truck. As soon as I get home, I'm crashing it right through his front door.

It's been nine long months. I should never have let her leave my apartment that day. I believed she'd come back. She promised she'd come back. She'd never lied to me before.

* * *

The sign says sixteen miles to St. Louis. During the six hours I've been driving, I've gone over every letter I've written and every message I've left at least twice. Why won't she forgive me? There's got to be something I can do, something I can say. I wonder if Butch has seen her at Sinclair's. I dial my old number and after the phone's answered, there's a pause before he says hello.

"Pops!"

"You okay?" he always asks.

"Yeah, and I'm heading home for a few days."

"How come? It's not a holiday, is it?" He sounds suspicious.

"Can't a guy come home for a few days?" This is weird, about to get weirder. "Hey, Pops, do you ever see Sinclair? Nick Sinclair, the son."

"I know who he is. And no, I never see him. Why do you want to know?"

"No reason. I'm going to crash tonight at a friend's in St. Louis and stop tomorrow in Morgantown. I'll see you Friday."

"No rodeo this weekend?" Butch asks, and it's the first time I've thought about it. Of course there's a rodeo this weekend. I'm not going to be there, though—not without Annie.

"No. I'll be home until Sunday. I'll see you in a couple of days."

* * *

"How long do you have to drive today?" Ollie asks as he walks me out to my truck.

"Probably about nine or ten hours," I answer. "That is if I don't drive into a ravine because I'm picturing Annie with him the whole way."

"Well, now, you know what she's been going through for months," Ollie says.

I stop walking and consider punching him in the face. Just because he let me crash on his couch does not mean he gets to discuss Annie's feelings with me.

"Sorry, man," he says, sensing his impending beating. "Look, I know you want her—and she's great and all—but a lot's happened. Maybe too much."

"Shut up." I throw my bag across the truck seat and get in behind it. "Thanks for the place to crash." I slam the truck door and roll down the window. "I'll be back on Monday night, hopefully with Annie."

"Good luck, man." Ollie looks like I don't have a chance in hell. It makes me think he's heard about Annie dating Sinclair before last night.

I take the on-ramp for I-64 toward Louisville and settle in for the next few hours. I can't lose her. She can't really be happy right now. She scared me after she found out. She's always so strong, but when she said she'd kill herself, I could hear in her voice a revolting determination. I've never even seen her afraid of anything. The thought of her hurting herself was the only thing that kept me from driving home as soon as I found out she was there.

She's strong. What other person could go back to Rutgers

and finish with a 4.0 after losing both her parents? There's no way this is unsalvageable. That girl can survive anything.

* * *

Louisville comes and goes and I cross into West Virginia. If Annie was here, she'd be following us on the map and have at least one hand between my legs. She's smart and is, without a doubt, the reason I passed calculus. The weekends she came down, we had naked math class, with her having sex with me first to "clear my head," then going over all the concepts. Nothing clears the mind like an orgasm.

When I left Oklahoma, I was angry enough to kill someone; now I'm depressed enough to kill someone. I wish I could get my hands on Sinclair, or maybe Jack Reynolds. When I heard that asshole had touched her, I was on my way home. Ralph Tighe called and said it wasn't necessary, that Sinclair had taken care of it. Fucking Sinclair. I ALWAYS knew he wanted her. A blind idiot would have known it. Annie told me I was crazy. She refused to see one bad thing about him. Friends, my ass.

As I pull into Lee's driveway, I see Lee and two other guys drinking on the side patio. I put the truck in park and rest my head on the steering wheel.

I'll never let her go, and she'll never be able to replace me with Sinclair. It's not possible.

I pull out my phone and start to dial her number.

"Boy, how many hours did you drive today? GooodNESS!" Lee opens my door and stalls my call.

"Too many, way too many. How you been?" I grab my bag and put my phone in my pocket as I jump out of the truck.

"Been the same." Lee hands me a beer. "How you holding up?"

I narrow my eyes.

"Stephanie called bitching about you going home to get Charlotte and told me she's with Sinclair now," Lee admits. "I figured this was probably a long ride for ya."

"Yeah, it's been a long ride." I take a big gulp of my beer and it burns my throat on the way down. "Stephanie is so fucking annoying."

"Yes, she is." Lee holds his can up as he tips his head in agreement.

"It's been a long month," I say, realizing I've been living with Stephanie for five weeks and I can't bring myself to even look at her. What I thought was going to be a money-saving solution is turning into an exercise in anger mismanagement.

* * *

Five and a half hours left. Lee had people in and out of his house all night, which took my mind off Annie and that ass Sinclair. It didn't help me get much sleep, though. Three hours to Frederick, then two and a half from there. Annie and I can spend Happy Hour in bed today.

How the hell did things get so screwed up? I worried about her every minute she was away. New Brunswick and Rutgers seemed like the most unsafe place to leave her. I wish her father were still alive. I'd ask him how he could stand to drop her off up there. When she started working in Manhattan, I thought I would completely lose my mind. Every day on the train, walking through the streets… The nights she worked late were the worst. She was too beautiful to be traveling back to New Jersey on her own. The only peace I've had the last year is knowing she's in Salem County and not Manhattan.

Why didn't she just come to Oklahoma that weekend?

What was the big deal about that dance? I went to a few and they weren't that great. I could usually persuade her, but not that time. Up until she called me the day before I thought she was going to surprise me and come down. The surprise was she wasn't coming. I still remember the sting of her words. Not only was she not coming to Oklahoma, but she was also going to the dance without me. She was choosing New Brunswick over me.

No matter how many times she swore she didn't mind giving it all up, I knew how much she loved it. I hung up on her and spent the next hour imagining all those Rutgers assholes thinking tonight was finally their chance to make a move. None of them were worthy of her. My mind punished me every minute she was away. The only reprieve was touching her and having her all to myself. Her visits filled me with confidence that shrunk with each passing day she was away. Her boss in New York, Sinclair, and all the rest of them were obviously just waiting for the right time. When she told me she was staying in New Jersey, all I could think of was the turkey buzzards descending. It literally drove me to drink.

Apparently Rutgers isn't the only place with vultures because Stephanie didn't waste any time descending on me either.

* * *

Three days of driving and I'm waiting for the freaking train to pass so I can pull into my driveway. I lean over in my seat.

My back's hurting worse than if I'd ridden bareback broncs last night. The train finally passes and I turn onto the farm lane. The sadness I used to feel driving down this lane, missing my mother every inch of the ride, is replaced by a hatred for Sinclair. I notice I'm clenching my teeth, and I rub my jaw as I consciously relax it. I've got to get hold of myself or someone's going to get hurt.

I pull the truck to the side of Butch's and hop out. There are posies or pansies or some other crazy shit lining the short walk to the front door. Mums in the fall, now tiny little purple and pink flowers. This chick Marie is definitely good for the place. By the looks of Butch, she's good for him, too. This year he's slightly less crusty than he has been. Since Mom died, he's been miserable, but the last few months have been different. I actually think he smiled the last time I was home.

The flowers remind me of Annie. She was always buying me stuff: a pillow for my bed, a new shower curtain. Crap I couldn't care less about, but it reminded me of her when she wasn't there. They're treasures now. In the move, Stephanie accidentally broke a mosaic candleholder that was a present from Annie, and I couldn't decide whether to scream at her or bend down and cry. I ended up storming out, leaving her to finish unpacking. Moving in with her was a mistake. It's saved us a lot of money—and I do get to see Jason Jr.—but Stephanie and I are never going to make it as a couple. I can barely stand the sight of her.

The kitchen mimics the front walk with new curtains over the sink and a bunch of shiny surfaces everywhere. The little dog comes running out and starts wagging his tail at the sight of me.

"You still here?" I ask him as I scratch behind each ear.

There are meatballs bubbling in a Crock-Pot on the counter and a spoon resting on a sunshine spoon holder I've never seen before. The contrast between the sun's animated face and Butch's joyless scowl is not lost on me. I like this Marie's sense of humor. I'll bet Annie will like her, too. The smell is intoxicating. It's been days since I've had anything hot to eat.

"How was the ride?" Butch startles me.

I have the lid of the Crock-Pot in my hand, my nose inhaling the steam. "Long." I replace the lid and find a glass in the cupboard. There's a filtering water pitcher in the fridge. Butch is being well taken care of and I like it.

"Why the sudden visit?" Butch asks as he limps over to the table and sits in the chair farthest from me.

"I came to see Annie," I say, and pour myself a glass of water, no ice. I put it on the table and search the other cupboards. "You got any rolls?"

"In the bread drawer."

I look at him, disoriented. He hasn't actually used the bread drawer for bread in five years. "And there's fresh provolone in the fridge."

I can barely hide my complete fascination.

"When are you going to let this thing with Annie go?"

"This thing is my life and I'm never going to let it go," I say, and fill my roll with too many meatballs. I add a slice of provolone and my mouth begins to water.

"It seems to me that it's time to move on," he says as he glances back at the doorway.

"Why's that?" I take a huge bite of the sandwich and it doesn't disappoint.

"Maybe because you have a kid with someone else!" he barks.

Aah, there is the short temper I'm used to. I was beginning
to think Butch was getting soft on me. I can't help smiling as
I look up at him. Even the sunshine spoon holder can't completely fix Butch.

"Look, I love Jason Junior, but that doesn't mean I have to
love his mother, and I never will. Annie and I belong together.
I just need to"—*What do I need to do?*—"explain it to her."

"She's a lot like your mother, as proud as she is stubborn. It's
time to let it go."

I take the last bite of my sandwich and put my plate in the
sink.

"I'm never letting it go." I grab my truck keys and head for
the door.

"You'll break before you break her. Don't make it worse
than it already is."

Could it possibly be worse?

"Besides, it might be too late," Butch adds.

I stop listening.

* * *

There are no signs of life at the farmhouse. Its owner and the
work have halted. I should have halted him a long time ago. I'll
deal with Nick later, or perhaps he is at Annie's and I can deal
with him now. God, I want to kill him.

No truck in the driveway means Nick will have to wait. I
ring the doorbell and even that pisses me off. Knocking on the
door like a stranger. I practically lived here. There is no answer,
so I go around back. Annie's replaced the key under the turtle
rock. It's there, just waiting for me to come home. I open the
back door and let myself in.

"Annie!" I yell. The last thing I want is for her to shoot me. "Oh, Annie." No one's home. I'm going to wait right here until she comes back. Back to this house and back to me. The police are going to have to remove me. I lock the back door behind me and make my way to the kitchen that's exactly the same as when her parents were alive. I still remember walking up to her at the luncheon after her parents' funeral. She was leaning against the kitchen counter. It was an endless wait for her to finally be alone, finished with trite, meaningless conversations. I wasn't sure what I was going to say, but when she looked at me with her empty green eyes, I just knew I had to get her out of here. She didn't belong here. I survey the room and see a dog's water and food bowls. Were they here before? I was so drunk the last time I was in here I can't remember. "What kind of dog did you get, Annie?"

I stop at the sight of the answering machine recuperating on the desk, bandaged with packaging tape. God, I love this girl. Apparently she does not like my messages. What I need is a shower. I walk through the house and grab a towel from the linen closet. The bathroom's completely different. It's navy with white wainscoting and those weird sinks that rise above the countertop. She has flowers in a vase by each sink and a brightly patterned towel hanging on the bar. The new tub is big enough for two with a ledge behind it and jets. *Oh, Annie, I wish you were here.* I turn on the water and remember how long it takes to heat up. While it runs, I borrow her toothbrush. If there is anyone alive who doesn't mind, it's Annie. I use her body wash, shampoo, and conditioner. I never knew the name but searched all over Oklahoma for a bottle that looked like it. I figured it was some fancy shampoo she got in New York. I just wanted to smell her. I adjust the showerhead to massage and rest against the back wall, letting it pound my back. She has to take me back. She has to...

I dry off and make my way to her new room. It's like a different house in here. Paint, carpeting, a built-in shelving unit, crown molding; everything new except the bed. That has to mean something. She didn't get rid of the bed for a reason. It's still tilted down on the one corner. I mentally beat back a budding hard-on. I crawl naked into her bed and nuzzle my face into her pillow. It's heaven compared to the hell that is Stephanie's couch. I can't wait until Annie comes home.

* * *

"What the hell?"

The noise is deafening. I roll over and hide my head under the pillow. The assault gets closer. Goddamn crop duster. I forgot how close they get to the ground. What the hell time is it? I uncover my head and find the clock on the side of her bed. 6:45 a.m. I slept over twelve hours. The ride must have taken its toll. Why do these freaking farmers have to get up so early?

And where the hell is Annie?

It occurs to me the dog isn't here for a reason. She's away, probably gone with that jackass Nick. How do I always miss her? Butch is probably thinking she murdered me. I hate to leave her bed, but I'm starving. Even though it's not even 8:00 a.m., those meatballs sound good. I peel myself from Annie's bed and put my clothes back on.

You can't stay away forever, and I plan on being right here when you get back.

I go out the back door and lock it up and put the key back under the turtle rock. Who exactly does she think she's keeping out? Why even lock the door? Everyone who knows her knows where the key is, and I think I demonstrated in November that anyone who doesn't know about the key can get in pretty easily.

I pull out of her driveway and the sadness creeps up on me again. Her bed washed away the anger and left me melancholy. The ride home takes about five minutes and I'm no longer surprised to see the farmhouse empty.

I let myself in and rummage through the refrigerator until I find the meatballs from yesterday. I open the bread drawer and take out two rolls. I put seven meatballs in a bowl and cover them with a paper towel, and turn on the microwave for two minutes. As it spins, the calendar nailed to the wall catches my eye. It has my name with a line across this entire weekend. I look back over the past six months and every time I've come home has been written on the calendar. How did I not notice this before? There's barely anything else on it: my visits, a few church meetings, the VFW pancake breakfast, and a few doctors' appointments.

Then, on February 18, as clear as a piece of glass, is a doctor's appointment for 1:00 p.m.—in Annie's handwriting.

Please see the next page for an excerpt from
the first book in the Lost Souls series

Forgive Me

Available now!

~ 1 ~

"My soul is forgotten, veiled by a boring complication"

My foot will bleed soon. Judging by the familiar curve in the road, I'm still at least two miles from home. Of course I end up walking home the night I'm wearing great shoes. The pain shoots through my heel as the clouds flash with lightning in the dark sky.

Maybe I'm bleeding already. I mentally review the last few hours. Anything to distract me from the agony of each step. The texts, the endless stream of drunken texts, run through my mind.

We're soul mates. I roll my eyes. Brian deserves a nicer girlfriend, someone sweet like him. Someone who doesn't roll their eyes at this statement.

We belong together. Bleh.

What does it say about my relationship when the only thing I ever tell people about my boyfriend is, "He's a really nice guy"? And how, after two years of being apart, did I ever take him back? The last three weeks have felt like years, years I was asleep.

We're perfect together. My mother thought we were perfect. Hell, this whole town thought it.

No one is ever going to know you the way I do. He was watching me as I read this one and I had to work hard to keep a straight face. At the time I wasn't sure why, but here on this deserted road, in the middle of a thunderstorm Brian would never walk through, I know it's because he never knew me at all. Or my soul. It's not his fault. I'd nearly forgotten it myself.

I stop to adjust the strap on my sandals and two sets of eyes peer out from the ditch next to the road. They're low to the ground, watching me. I've always hated nocturnal animals.

"Anyone else come out to play in the storm?" I say to the other hidden nightlife. I move to the edge of the shoulder, facing the nonexistent traffic, and give my new friends some room. I wince as I step forward and watch as a set of headlights shines on the road in front of me and the scene around me turns mystical. The steam rises off the pavement at least five feet high before disappearing into the blue-tinted night. The rain lasted only twenty spectacular minutes, not long enough to cool the scorched earth.

I'm lost in it as the truck pulls up beside me, now driving on the wrong side of the road, and Jason Leer rolls down his window. I glance at him and turn to stare straight ahead, trying not to let the excruciating torture of each step show on my face.

"Hi, Annie," he says, and immediately pisses me off. I might look sweet in my new rose-colored shorts romper, but these wedges have me ready to commit murder.

"My name is Charlotte," I say without looking at him, and

keep walking. The strap is an ax cutting my heel from my foot. *Why won't he call me Charlotte?* Of course the cowboy would show up. What this night needs is a steer wrestler to confound me further. The same two desires he always evokes in me surface now. Wanting to punch him and wanting to climb on top of him.

"What the hell are you doing out here? Alone—" A guttural moan of thunder interrupts him, and I tilt my head to determine the origin, but it surrounds us. The clouds circle, blanketing us with darkness, but when the moon is visible it's bright enough to see in this blue-gray night. We're in the eye of the storm and there will never be a night like this again. *God I love a storm.* The crunching of the truck's tires on the road reminds me of my cohort.

"I'm not alone. You're here, irritating me as usual." I will not look at him. I can feel his smartass grin without even seeing him, the same way I can feel a chill slip across my skin. It's hot as hell out and Jason Leer is giving me the chills.

Lightning strikes, reaching the ground in the field just to our left, and I stop walking to watch it. Every minute of today brought me here. The mind-numbing dinner date with Brian Matlin, the conversation on the way to Michelle's party about how we should see other people, the repeated and *annoying* texts declaring his love, and the eleven beers and four shots I watched Brian pour down his throat, all brought me here.

"If you're trying to kill yourself by being struck by lightning, I could just hit you with my truck. It'll be faster," he says, stealing my eyes from the field. His arm rests out his truck window and it's enormous. He tilts his body toward the door and the width of his chest holds my gaze for a moment too long.

"Annie!"

I shake my head, freeing myself from him. "What? What do you want? I'm not afraid of a storm." I am, however, exhausted by this conversation.

I finally allow myself to look him in the eyes. They are dark tonight, like the slick, steamy road before me, and I shouldn't have looked.

"I want you." His voice is tranquil, as if he's talking a suicide jumper off a bridge. "I want you to get in the truck and I'll drive you home." Thunder growls in the distance and the lightning strikes to the left and right of the road at the same time. The storm surrounds us, but the rain was gone too soon, leaving us with the suffocating heat that set the road on fire.

I close my eyes as my sandal cuts deeper into my foot, and Jason finally pulls away. My grandmother always said the heat brings out the crazy in people. It was ninety-seven degrees at 7:00 p.m. The humidity was unbearable. Too hot to eat. Too hot to laugh. The only thing you could do was talk about how miserably hot it was outside. By the time Brian and I arrived, most of the party had already been in the lake at some point. Even that didn't look refreshing. The sky unleashed, and Michelle kicked everyone out rather than let them destroy her house.

I stop walking and shift my foot in the shoe. The strap is now sticking; I've probably already shed blood. Jason drives onto the right side of the road and stops the truck on the tiny shoulder. He turns on his hazard lights and gets out of the truck. *He's a hazard.* I plaster a smile on my face and begin walking again. As soon as he leaves, I'm taking off these shoes and throwing them in the pepper field next to me.

Before I endure two steps, he's in front of me. He's as fast as I remember. Like lightning: always picked first for kickball in elementary school. His hair is the same thick, jet-black as back then, too. The moonlight shines off it and I wonder where his cowboy hat is. He's too beautiful to piss me off as much as he does. He blocks my path, a concrete wall, and I stop just inches from him.

"I'm going to ask you one more time to get in the truck." A lightning strike hits the road near his truck and without flinching he looks back at me, waiting for my answer.

"Or what?" I challenge him with my words and an "I dare you" look on my face. He hoists me over his shoulder and walks back to the truck as if I'm a sweatshirt he grabbed as an afterthought before walking out the door.

"Put me down! I'm not some steer you can toss around!" I yell as I fist my hands and pound on his back. He's laughing and pissing me off even more. I pull his shirt up and start to reach for his underwear and Jason runs the last few steps to the truck.

"Do you ever behave?" he asks, and swings the truck door open. He drops me on the seat and leans in the truck between my legs. I push my hair out of my face, my chest still heaving with anger. "Why the hell are you walking alone on a country road, in a goddamned storm, this late at night?"

My stomach knots at his closeness and this angers me, too. Why can't Jason Leer bore me the way Brian Matlin does? Jason raises his eyebrows and tilts his head at the perfect angle to send a chill down my spine.

"Brian and I broke up tonight."

"And he made you walk home?" Shock is written all over his face. Brian would never make me walk home. He is the nicest of guys. Not great at holding his liquor, but nice.

"No." I roll my eyes, calling him an idiot, and he somehow

leans in closer, making my stomach flip. "He proceeded to get drunk at Michelle Farrell's party and I drove him home so he wouldn't die." I think back to all the parties of the last six years, since Jason and I entered high school. Besides graduation, we were rarely in the same place. I've barely hung out with Jason Leer since eighth grade. At the start of high school everyone broke into groups, and this cowboy wasn't in mine.

"Why didn't you call someone for a ride?" He breaks my reverie.

"Because apparently when Brian gets drunk, he texts a lot. My battery died after the fiftieth message professing his love for me."

"Poor guy."

"Poor guy? What about me? I'm the one who had to delete them and drive him home. I thought he'd never pass out." I'm still mourning the time I lost with Brian's drunken mess.

"Why didn't you just take his car?"

"Because I left him passed out in it in his parents' driveway. I got him home safe, but I'm not going to carry him to bed."

At this Jason lowers his head and laughs. My irritation with him twists into annoyance at myself for telling him anything. For telling him everything. I want to punch him in his laughing mouth. His lips are perfect, though.

"It's not easy to love you, Annie."

"Yeah, well, I've got fifty texts that claim otherwise. Judging from the fact that you can't even get my name right, everything's probably hard for you." Jason leans on the dash and his jeans scrape against my maimed foot, causing my face to twist in pain. Before I can regain my composure, his eyes are on me. He moves back and holds my foot up near his face. He slips the strap off my heel and runs his thumb across the now broken and purple blister. I close my eyes, the sight of the wound amplifying the pain.

"My God, you are stubborn," he says, his eyes still on my foot. Thunder groans behind us and he straightens my leg, examining it in the glimmer of moonlight. I'm not angry anymore. One urge has silenced another and has awakened me in the process. He pulls my foot to him and kisses the inside of my ankle, and a chill runs from my leg to both breasts and settles in the back of my throat, stealing my breath.

I swallow hard. "Are all your first kisses on the inside of the ankle?" I ask. His hands grip my ankle harshly, but he's careful with my heel.

His eyes find mine as he drags his lips up my calf and kisses the inside of my knee. I shut up and shudder from a chill. There are no words. Only the beginning of a thought. *What if* arises in my mind against the sound of the clicking of the hazard lights.

The lightning strikes again and unveils the darkness in his eyes. He lowers my leg and backs up, but I'm not ready to let him go. I grab his belt buckle and pull him toward me. Jason doesn't budge. He is an ox. His eyes bore into me and for a moment I think he hates me. He's holding a raging river behind a dam, and I'm recklessly breaching it.

With a hand gripping each shoulder, he forces me back to the seat and hovers over me. Even in the darkness I can see the emptiness in his eyes and I can't leave it alone. He kisses me. He kisses me as if he's done it a hundred times before, and when his lips touch mine, some animalistic need growls inside of me. He's like nothing I've ever known, and my body craves a hundred things all at once, every one of them him. With his tongue in my mouth, I tighten my arms around his thick neck and pull him closer, wanting to climb inside of him.

Jason pulls away, devastating me, until I realize there are flashing lights behind us. His eyes fixed on mine, he takes my hands from behind his head and pulls me upright before the state trooper steps out of his car and walks to our side of the truck.

* * *

"Charlotte, honey, are you going to get up? I heard you come in late last night."

I roll over and put my head under the pillow. I don't want to get up. I don't want to tell my mom that I broke up with Brian…again.

"Is everything okay?" She's worried.

I take a deep breath and sit up in bed. The sheet rubs against my heel and the pain reminds me of Jason Leer.

"I broke up with Brian last night."

"Oh no. I have to see his mother at book club on Wednesday."

"I can't marry him just because you can't face his mother at book club."

"I'm not suggesting you marry him, just that you stop dating him if you're going to keep breaking his heart." My mom leaves my room. Her face is plagued with frustration mixed with disappointment.

I climb out of bed and lumber to the bathroom. My green eyes sparkle in the mirror, hinting at our indelicate secret from last night. I wink at myself as if something exciting is about to happen. My long blond hair barely looks slept on. I think breaking up with Brian was good for me.

* * *

"Jack, she broke up with Brian again," I catch as I enter the kitchen.

"Through with him, huh?" My father never seems to have an opinion on who I date as long as they treat me well. Brian certainly did that.

"Dad, he just didn't do it for me." Jason's eyes pierce my thoughts again, haunting me. The trooper sent us home and I left him in his truck without a word. There wasn't one to say.

"Do what? What did you expect him to do for you?" my mother spouts. She's not taking the news well.

"When he looks at me a certain way, I want to get chills," I start, surprised by how easily my needs are verbalized. "When he leans into me, I want my stomach to flip, and when he walks away I want to care if he comes back." My parents both watch me silently as if I'm reciting a poem at the second-grade music program. They are pondering me.

"What? Don't your stomachs flip when you're together? Ever?"

"Does your stomach flip when you look at me, Jack?" she asks.

"Only if I eat chili the same day," my dad says, and they both start laughing.

"Charlotte, I remember what it was like to be young. And your father did make my stomach flip, but I think you're too hard on Brian. He's a nice boy."

"Yeah yeah. He's nice." I butter my toast and move to sit next to my father at the table. *He is nice.* For some reason Brian's kindness frustrates me. He's a boring complication. "I ran into Jason Leer last night." *And he kissed the inside of my leg.* I smile ruefully.

My mother's eyebrows rise and I fear I've divulged too much. My father never looks up from the newspaper.

"Butch and Joanie's son?"

"That's the one." I try to sound nonchalant as a tiny chill runs down my neck.

"I haven't seen him since Joanie's funeral. Poor boy. She was lovely. Do you remember her?"

I nod and take a bite of the toast. "From Sunday school."

"Jack, do you remember Joanie Leer? Died of cancer about a year ago."

"I remember," my dad says, and appears to be ignoring us, but I know he's not. He always hears everything.

"If you don't want to be with Brian, that's fine, but please not a rodeo cowboy," my mother pleads, not missing a thing.

"I only said I saw him. What's wrong with a rodeo cowboy?"

"Nothing. For someone else's daughter. I really want you to marry someone with a job. Someone who can take care of you."

"Can't a cowboy do that?" *From what I've seen, he can take very good care of me.*

"Charlotte, please tell me you're not serious. They're always on the road. Their income's not steady. It's a very difficult life." My mother's stern warning is delivered while she fills the dishwasher, as if we're discussing a fairy tale, a situation so absurd it barely warrants a discussion. She's still beautiful, even when she's lecturing me. "I know safe choices aren't attractive to the young, but believe me you do not belong in that world and he'd wither up and die in yours. Do not underestimate the power of safety in this crazy life."

"How do you know so much about rodeo cowboys?" I ask.

"Yeah, how do you know so much?" my dad asks. He stares at her over the newspaper.

"Is your stomach flipping?" she asks, and gives him her beautiful smile she's flashed to quell him my entire life.

"Yes," he says, and winks at her.

Please see the next page for a preview of
the next book in the Lost Souls series

Save Me

Available Winter 2015

~ 1 ~

A Second Proposal

I pull my robe tight around my neck and sit at the head of the table. Right in front of the most glorious breakfast I've ever seen...or smelled. I am spoiled. I inhale the warm, sweet syrup's aroma that conjures every perfect memory still left in me, and study Noble Sinclair. He might be the human equivalent of syrup—warm, sweet, and perfect.

"So what do you have to get done today?" I ask as he pours himself a cup of coffee. He slides the glass pitcher back in the coffeemaker and takes a sip from the steaming cup. He looks so young, shirtless and in his pajama pants, incapable of running this farm on his own. But he does. Noble can do anything. My eyes linger on his shoulders and I wish he never wore a shirt; it covers my favorite part of him.

"Plowing something? Planting something?" There's an endless list of things to do now.

Noble keeps his back to me as he lingers at the counter. He rubs a ribbon between his fingers and looks out the window at the fields on the side of the house. The ribbon is blue with silver wired edges and is wrapped around five bridal magazines my friend Violet gave me when Noble proposed, almost a year ago. The fabric facing out is dusty and faded now.

Why didn't I ever open them?

"I want you to go to the shore with me." Noble breaks my contemplation. I'm surprised. He's barely had time to sleep lately, let alone take the day off. We've both been busy.

"I would love to." My eyes traipse across Noble's chest. He and the shore are two of my favorite things. "Will you promise to keep your shirt off the whole day?"

"If you do the same," he says, always so naughty.

Noble sits on the table near the Belgian waffle he made me. He sips his coffee as I cut through the Jersey strawberries and let the syrup waterfall throughout the waffle. It's as close to heaven as possible on a plate. Giving Noble a waffle maker last year for Christmas was a stroke of genius.

He notices the whipped cream and exchanges his coffee for the canister. Noble tilts the whipped cream can at my waffle and raises his eyebrows to me.

"Let me have it."

He forms a perfect whipped cream heart and places the canister down next to my plate. My heart rate spikes as I grab his hand and hold his whip-cream-covered finger in front of my smiling face. I lick the tip and take his finger in my mouth. His whole finger. I slide my teeth down the side before sucking the tip as I run my tongue over it. Noble never takes his eyes off his hand and my mouth.

When I release his finger from my teeth, Noble stands and drops his pajama pants to the floor. He takes the whipped cream and sprays some on his now-hard penis with the naughtiest look ever.

"You missed a little," he says.

I take my tongue to the cream and raise my eyes to Noble as I lick the tip and then my lips. I take him in my mouth completely, and he closes his eyes and raises his face to the ceiling. The sight of him pleasured spreads the heat through my body and I shift in my seat, wanting him in me.

I hold Noble's balls in one hand as I stroke him with the other. My mouth finds him again and with only a few minutes of attention, I finish my lovely off.

"Aaah. You have no idea how good that feels."

"Oh, I think I do," I say, trying to ignore the throbbing between my legs.

In one swoop, Noble lifts me to my feet and pulls my shirt over my head. He shamelessly caresses my breasts with his eyes. They rise under his stare, wanting his familiar touch. "Yes, that's exactly how you should ride to the shore with me."

"We'll get arrested."

"It'll be worth it. I'll spend my days rotting in the cell, imagining you topless."

Noble kisses me, gently at first. He's in control, as usual. I, however, am not. I wrap my leg around his waist and grind against the front of him. I pull myself up him and want him inside of me. Immediately.

"What am I going to do with you, Charlotte? You're insatiable," he whispers in my ear as if it's our little secret. I cannot get enough of Noble Sinclair.

He bends slightly and hoists me over his shoulder. He practically runs up the stairs, jolting me with each step, my arms holding on to the back of him. Noble carries me to the bedroom we've been sharing most nights of the week and throws me onto the bed. The devotion in his stare, always filled with the same promise—my home is with him—sends heat to every fraction of my body and I acknowledge the depth to which I need him. It's still profound. I rise up to my knees and wrap my arms around his neck and pull him closer to me. I grab him and try to quiet the throbbing between my legs with him in my hand. I kiss him, my tongue telling him I won't wait any longer, and when I'm sure he's gotten the message, I lean back and pull him down with me. I want him on top of me. I need the weight of his love to settle me, now and forever.

He wraps each arm under my shoulders as he pulls me toward him. Noble finds me more than ready as he buries his lips on my neck and slowly enters me. He lowers his naked chest to mine and we are one. He is touching me everywhere. He rocks back and forth, never leaving the top of me, always connected. Again, and again, and again I take Noble, wanting more of him every time. He is controlled, deliberately driving me to my breaking point. It's his rhythm that is his gift. I take in air and acknowledge Noble has many gifts.

I tilt my pelvis and let him stroke me as he comes into me and I remember to breathe. I thread my fingers through his hair and bury my face in his shoulder and release every thought from my mind except the touch of Noble Sinclair. My notched breathing conveys my diminishing hold and I can feel him smiling on my neck.

"Come for me, Charlotte," he whispers, and I oblige, crumbling around him. He doesn't stop, though; he's in me again and I close my eyes as he gives himself away and I again pull him to me.

He anchors me. I hold Noble close, not a chance of something getting between us. Sometimes it feels as if he'll never be close enough.

About the Author

Eliza Freed graduated from Rutgers University and returned to her hometown in rural South Jersey. Her mother encouraged her to take some time and find herself. After three months of searching, she began to bounce checks and her neighbors began to talk; her mother told her to find a job.

She settled into Corporate America, learning systems and practices and the bureaucracy that slows them. Eliza quickly discovered her creativity and gift for storytelling as a corporate trainer and spent years perfecting her presentation skills and studying diversity. It was during this time that she became an avid observer of the characters we meet and the heartaches we endure. Her years of study have taught her laughter is the key to survival, even when it's completely inappropriate.

She currently lives in New Jersey with her family and a misbehaving beagle named Odin. An avid swimmer, if Eliza is not with her family and friends, she'd rather be underwater. While she enjoys many genres, she has always been a sucker for a love story...the more screwed up the better.

Learn more at:
ElizaFreed.com
Twitter, @ElizabFreed
Facebook.com/ElizabFreed